THE CRIMINALS

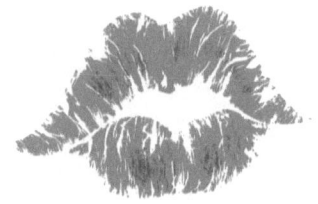

EVERNIGHT PUBLISHING ®

www.evernightpublishing.com

Copyright© 2019

Erin M. Leaf

Editor: Karyn White

Cover Art: Jay Aheer

ISBN: 978-0-3695-0019-9

THE CRIMINALS

THE NULLIFIER

The Criminals, 1

Erin M. Leaf

Copyright © 2017

Chapter One

"I'm too old for this shit," Felix Zamaro muttered, setting down his binoculars. He rubbed his eyes, wishing he'd managed more than four hours of sleep last night. He peered through the open window tiredly. His target loitered at an outdoor café across the street drinking his sixth cup of coffee, two floors below the apartment building in which Felix currently sat. How the hell could one guy drink so much caffeine? Felix didn't get it. If he did that, he'd be fucking pissing every half hour.

He picked up his binoculars and resumed staring at the man currently on the top of his to-off list. He hated this part of the job—the constant surveillance really fucked with his mood these days. Didn't matter if it was sunny or rainy or fucking three below. The boredom really got to him. It hadn't always been this bad. He wasn't a man given to strong emotions, but he remembered enjoying the chase just a bit more when he'd first gotten into this business. *That* sense of satisfaction had long worn off. Now it was just a job, and a tedious one, at that.

The guy finally waved down a waiter for his check, and Felix breathed out a sigh of relief. "Fucking finally." He had no idea why the contract stipulated the man had to be taken out at this particular café, and he didn't much care as long as the money went into his account in a timely fashion. He squinted down at the mark. The guy's hair had fluffed up in the slight breeze. He'd have to take the wind into consideration when shooting, but that was nothing new.

He exchanged his binoculars for his Ruger M77. He'd been using this type of rifle for so long, he didn't even have to think about what to do with his hands. It slid into position on his shoulder almost automatically, and when he squeezed the trigger, his target went down in a fraction of a second. Felix stood up and stepped back from the peeling windowsill, already shoving the rifle into its soft case. He scanned the room for any stray speck of evidence, then grunted in satisfaction. As per his usual, the place held no sign of his presence. The occupants of this grimy apartment would never even know he'd been here.

At least not until the police come knocking on their door, looking for a killer, he thought, resetting their deadbolt with his lockpicks. He walked down the hall of the apartment building at a normal pace. He felt no guilt over what they'd go through. There was enough drug paraphernalia in their nasty little place to choke a horse *and* his rider. The people that lived there deserved everything that would happen to them. He looked at the elevator, then decided to take the stairs. He needed the physical exertion after all the sitting around. He pushed open the door, then peeled off his gloves and shoved them into his pockets. When he reached the ground floor, he opened the outer door with his hip, careful not to touch anything with his bare hands.

"And that's three frigging days of my life I'll never get back," he said under his breath, readjusting his bag on his shoulder. He spared a glance for the commotion across the street, ducking his head so the security camera on the corner wouldn't get a good bead on him. The bullet they'd find in the guy's head would be completely unremarkable: it was one of the most common rounds used worldwide. His rifle wasn't expensive, either, and could be easily replaced, and therefore not easily traced. In fact, he'd replaced it several times over the past twenty years. He didn't get attached to his equipment, not like some people did. No sense in it.

Two and a half hours later, after traveling out of the city and dropping off his gear at his storage unit, he entered the small mini mart near his latest house rental, looking for something quick and easy to eat for dinner. They had decent sandwiches and coffee. He'd only lived here six months, and he'd be moving on soon, but even so, he recognized the cashier. She smiled at him, and he nodded, friendly and unassuming. It wouldn't do to get pegged as a loner creep. Two shoppers on their way out, an old lady and her husband, took no note of him as he walked through the store, which was just how he liked it. He decided to fill up the tank on his pickup while he was there, and headed toward the rear refrigerators to get his dinner first. The rattle of the bell over the door told him some new people had entered, and he automatically checked the exits at the rear of the store. It wouldn't do to get lazy. When he turned around, hands full of turkey salad on rye, he cursed under his breath. A stupid young punk had a gun pointed at the forehead of the girl behind the counter.

"Empty the drawer and no one gets hurt." The guy looked around nervously, hoodie falling half off his head. He shoved it back up impatiently, red shot eyes bright with adrenaline and some other illegal substance.

Felix put his sandwich down on the shelf holding bright rows of chip bags. He didn't have any weapons on him except his pocketknife. He didn't like to carry when he wasn't working because men with guns had a tendency to use them, and he didn't need the temptation or the hassle. He eased forward. The idiot with the pistol couldn't see him from this angle. Just as he reached the end of the row of snack foods, he noticed another guy with a shotgun. Felix's stomach growled, and he pressed his lips together. He wanted his dinner. He wanted to fill up his damn gas tank. He did *not* want to be dicking around with two loser punks in a mini mart. *What a clusterfuck*, he thought, irritated.

"Hurry up," the one with the shotgun growled, swinging it around. "We don't got all night."

Felix narrowed his eyes. Mr. Shotgun didn't have a fucking clue what he was doing with his equipment. Didn't even have the safety off. He wasn't sure if he felt more annoyed at the lack of professionalism, or at the amount of time it was going to take to deal with this bullshit. He edged forward, eyes on the robber with the shotgun. The moment he rounded the end cap, the guy would see him, so he'd have to act fast. Sobs from the cashier told him that she wasn't too happy at the way her night was going, either. He paused and centered himself, pushing away the fatigue of a long, boring day. Just as he was about to crouch down and take out shotgun guy, the front door opened.

"Fuck." His options suddenly narrowed, Felix rushed forward, grabbing the shotgun and wrestling it out of the man's grip. He reversed it, then clubbed the asshole over the head. The guy staggered, but didn't go down. "Stupid ox." He tossed the shotgun down the aisle, and it skittered under the rear refrigerators as he blocked a wild throw to his face. From the corner of his eye, he saw the man who'd opened the front door freeze, eyes wide. "Gonna be collateral fucking damage if he doesn't move," Felix muttered, grunting when Mr. Shotgun managed to land a punch on his hip. "Stupid." Twisting, he swung cupped hands at the man's head, and Mr. Shotgun screamed as his eardrums burst. He went down, writhing in pain.

A shot rang out and glass shattered, but Felix was already moving. He grabbed the guy with the smoking handgun in one swift move. Two seconds later the robber had a fractured wrist, and Felix was breaking down the gun into pieces. He put them on the counter in front of the sobbing cashier. Mr. Handgun slumped to the floor, holding his wrist and moaning.

"Jesus. Shut the fuck up. You're not dead," Felix said, shoving at the punk's thigh with the tip of his boot. "It's just a simple fracture."

The guy blinked, but he shut his mouth once he got a good look at the annoyance on Felix's face.

"Oh my God," the cashier said, trembling and staring at man on the floor. "Oh my God." She gripped the counter as if that was the only thing holding her upright.

And maybe it is, Felix thought, exasperated. "You're all right. It's all over," he told her, tossing the magazine of the robber's weapon onto the counter. "Call nine-one-one," he told the girl, and then he turned to the front door. The man coming in hadn't moved. Felix let his eyes catalogue the guy: jeans, a soft pullover sweater, keys in hand. No weapons. Shaggy blond hair falling across his forehead, blue eyes. Broken glass all around him. Good looking. Not a threat.

Felix turned back to the cashier. "Did you call the cops?"

She hiccupped, shaking her head. "What?" Mascara ran down her face in thick black streaks.

Felix inhaled deeply, then let it out again slowly. He couldn't afford to lose his cool. Not now. Not ever. "Call nine-one-one," he said again, more gently this time. The girl picked up the phone near the register with shaky hands.

"All I wanted was some damned coffee," the blond guy near the door said, staring at the carnage. He held his right hand over his left shoulder. Blood dripped down through his fingers. "Shit." He grimaced.

Felix sighed and strode over. He was really fucking hungry, but he knew he wouldn't be eating anytime soon. "Let me see."

The blond frowned at him.

Felix impatiently pulled the man's hand away and inspected the wound. "Grazed you. Might need stitches." He craned his head, then nodded in satisfaction when he saw the round stuck in the column just outside the door. "It's a clean in and out. You'll live."

The guy blinked. "I never thought I wouldn't."

Felix put the man's hand back over the wound. "Steady pressure." He paused, more than a little surprised by how irritated he was that the bullet had hurt an innocent bystander. The guy didn't deserve it, but it wasn't like Felix gave a shit. He didn't dwell on random bullshit much. "Sorry. I had to deal with the shotgun first, or we would've had a bigger mess in here," he offered, not sure why he was talking to the man.

The blond guy stared at him. "I'm not angry with you."

Felix stepped back, inexplicably distracted. The blue sweater the guy wore was a perfect match for his eyes. "Good." He turned as the punk with the broken wrist tried to struggle to his feet. "Stay down, dumbass." Felix walked over and loomed over him. The other robber was still on the floor, hands over his ears. Felix knew how much burst eardrums hurt, so he wasn't surprised that guy wasn't trying to get up.

"Fuck you," the guy at Felix's feet said, glaring.

Felix sighed, then put his boot on the man's thigh. "I can break your knee, too."

The man's eyes went wide with rage, but he went still. "Asshole," he muttered.

Felix shrugged. "Yeah. Yeah, I am. So, don't push me. I'm already in a bad fucking mood." He looked towards the door as the sound of sirens in the distance grew louder. "You doing okay?" He asked the guy with the arm injury. "Not feeling dizzy?"

The blond shrugged, then winced. He'd slumped against the doorjamb, and looked tired. "I'm fine."

Felix glanced at the cashier. She nodded at him, phone still against her ear. He looked back down at the jerk at his feet, tempted to break the man's knee just because. He really just wanted a fucking sandwich. And then he wanted to go home and crack open a cold beer while he checked to make sure all the money he was owed went into the proper accounts.

"We're going to be here a while, aren't we?" the blond guy asked.

Felix stepped back from the man on the floor, taking himself away from temptation. The cops were already going to be all over him for breaking the guy's wrist. "Yeah," he said, resigned to going hungry for at least a few hours. "We are."

****

THE CRIMINALS

Nick Banner's left arm throbbed, even after the shot of anesthetic the EMT had given him before she'd sewn him up. He hadn't wanted to go to the hospital, so she'd stitched him up and told him to get himself to his doctor for antibiotics. Now, he sat on the curb outside the mini mart, waiting for the cop grilling his hero to stop being an asshole.

"I told you, I saw the guy with the pistol first. When the guy with the shotgun tackled me, I grabbed it and hit him over the head with it. He kept coming. My training kicked in. End of story," the man was explaining. Again.

Nick watched the expression on the guy's face grow increasingly colder as the idiot cop repeated the same questions for the fifth time, as if that would get him a different answer. Nick needed his caffeine fix. And he desperately wanted to be the hell away from here, preferably with tall, dark, and handsome joining him. The guy was just his type: thick, dark hair a man could grab onto, and a beard that highlighted the dude's excellent jaw line. Piercing hazel eyes held a multitude of secrets. Nick shook his head. He had to stop staring, or the guy would catch on to how badly he wanted in his pants, and he was almost one hundred percent sure the man was straight. And if Nick had one rule it was this one: don't fuck straight guys. That was a good way to get your heart broken.

And very possibly my face, too, he thought, remembering that one time in college and the black eye it'd taken weeks to heal. He wasn't likely to lose a fight these days, but he still preferred to avoid confrontations if he could. He was more of a silent but deadly type than a showman.

"Look, I'm done here. You have my info." The guy walked away in the middle of the cop's question.

Damn. Guy's got balls to spare, Nick thought, amused. When the man neared him, he struggled to his feet, trying to ignore the pain in his bicep. "Hey," he said. His voice cracked. The guy stood at least four inches taller than he did. He cleared his throat. "Thanks for saving my life." He held out his right hand.

The guy frowned at him. "I didn't save your life."

Nick persisted. "Okay, but you probably saved the cashier's life. That guy looked seriously tweaked out on something." He kept his hand extended. He wanted to see what the man did. Nick was an excellent judge of character, especially when he had the opportunity to interact with a person. "I'm Nick. Nice to meet you."

Slowly, the man reached out and shook his hand. "Felix."

Nick smiled. Felix's hand was warm and slightly calloused, as if the guy did a fair amount of work with some sort of tool. *Golf? Weights? A shovel?* he wondered, making sure to not clasp the guy's hand for too long. *Nope. Probably military something or other, with those moves he pulled on the robbers.* He resisted the urge to ask the man out for dinner. He hadn't moved back to his hometown to start dating. He was here to help his sister for a few months, and then he'd be gone again, long before the homophobic gossips could start anything. "Anyway, thanks, man." Before Felix could respond, the cop that had been questioning him interrupted.

"Mr. Cooper, we aren't done speaking with you yet." The policeman grabbed Felix's arm and hauled him around.

Nick could barely believe the fat policeman had the strength to budge the guy. He glanced at the cop's partner slowly stepping closer. *She* had the sense to look nervous in the face of so much muscular testosterone. She took a deep breath and marched over determinedly.

"Arnold," she said, clearly working to keep her tone calm. The cop ignored her. She glanced at Nick.

He shrugged, then immediately wished he hadn't when the wound in his arm throbbed, even with the numbing medicine.

"You didn't answer all of my questions," Fat Cop said to Felix, as if his partner wasn't even there. He thrust his chin out belligerently.

Nick watched anger flash across Felix's face, but almost immediately, his expression smoothed into a perfectly controlled mask. *Interesting. That's some impressive self-control there.*

"I told you I was done answering questions," Felix said, shrugging off the cop's grip.

The fat cop's face reddened. "Now, see here—"

"Is he under arrest?" Nick asked, opening his mouth to insert his foot. *What the hell am I doing? No drama, remember? That's your motto,* he told himself, even as he continued talking. "I mean, this guy saved us from those losers." He gestured to the cop car where the two robbers sat handcuffed in the back. *Total amateurs,* he thought, disgusted. They were due to head to the hospital, but since neither man's injuries was life-threatening, the police had opted to question the witnesses before driving the men to the emergency room. "You're questioning the wrong guy. You should be asking them why they thought robbing a mini mart and terrorizing the poor girl who works here was a good idea."

"I don't need any advice on how to do my job." The cop turned to Nick, scowling. "We already have your statement."

Nick blinked at this example of utter stupidity. "Yes. I know. Are you going to answer my question?"

The female officer intervened again, this time

putting a hand on her partner's arm. "I think we're done here, right, Arnold? If Mr. Cooper or Mr. Banner—" She nodded at Nick. "—have any more information, they'll call us. Right?"

Not even if all the pigs in New Jersey learn to fly, Nick thought, but he nodded, eager to not be involved in some random clusterfuck with the cops. "Of course." He stepped back before Fat Cop could get any ideas about his involvement in the situation.

Felix didn't nod. He didn't retreat. He just stared steely eyed and controlled right at Fat Cop's face until the moron backed up, readjusting his utility belt as if that gave him some sort of authority. His face had turned red with anger or embarrassment, or possibly some unsavory combination of the two emotions. Nick didn't much care. He was busy enjoying the way Felix loomed.

Fat Cop doesn't have a chance. Nick bit back a smile.

"Don't leave town," Fat Cop warned, then pivoted and stalked away, handcuffs jingling from his belt.

His partner sighed. "Thanks for your patience," she said, and then she followed her partner back to the patrol car.

Nick rolled his eyes, amused. "I didn't know I was going to end up as a sidekick in a bad cop movie when I woke up this morning."

To his surprise, Felix laughed. "You never know when a situation is going to go sideways."

Nick blinked. The smile had transformed Felix's face from handsome to stunning. He swallowed, willing his dick to behave. "Truth, man."

Felix rolled his shoulders. "All I wanted was a damned sandwich."

"I just wanted a coffee." Nick grinned. Suddenly,

Felix didn't seem so unapproachable. "Shit happens."

"That it does." Felix nodded at him, then turned back towards the mini mart. "Take care." He strode away before Nick could respond.

Well damn. He sure knows how to end a conversation. Nick watched him head inside and grab some food, drop a few bills on the counter, and head out to a black pickup in under five minutes. On his way out of the parking lot, Felix tapped his forehead in a rough salute to Nick from the open window of his truck, and then he drove off down the road.

"And there goes any chance at ever asking out the man of my dreams," Nick said under his breath, half smiling.

"What did you say?" Fat Cop asked him.

Nick startled, not realizing the cop had walked back over to him. *Shit. Pay attention to your surroundings, Nick. You know better than that*, he told himself. "Was just wondering if there's anywhere else I could get a coffee around here. It looks like the cashier isn't going to be able to take my order anytime soon." He nodded to the girl still quietly sobbing on the back of the ambulance rig. "It's been a while since I've been in town."

Fat Cop frowned. "Try Daisy's. That's where I go." He held out a small business card. "Call me if you remember anything more from today."

Nick took the card and pocketed it without looking at it. Given his line of work, it'd be a cold day in hell before he'd call the police, but there was no need to be rude about it. "Daisy's. Got it." He'd been there before. In fact, he'd been there plenty of times, all throughout high school. He remembered the old red and white checked tile and the shiny leather booths quite well. He remembered that one winter when he'd come home on break from college, boyfriend in tow, eager to show his new guy his favorite childhood places. And he also remembered being thrown out of the diner, bits of egg literally stuck to his face, when his buddies from high school had discovered he was gay. *Yeah, nope. Not a fucking chance am I going to set foot in that place.*

Fat Cop nodded. "Take care, Mr. Banner." He walked back to his patrol vehicle and got in on the driver's side.

Nick stared at the cop car as it pulled away, remembering how the local officers had done absolutely nothing to help him when he'd tried to file assault charges all those years ago. "Good times," he muttered, abruptly feeling a lot less optimistic about the next few months.

Chapter Two

Felix cursed himself all the way back to the house. He'd fucked up, big time. He'd given Nick his real name. The cops had one of his aliases, John Cooper, but he'd screwed up with Nick. He hadn't expected the guy to offer to shake his hand. Most people gave him a wide berth. He wasn't sure why: he took pains to blend in. He dressed in neutral colors, he made sure to act polite, and he never loomed over anyone unless they deserved it. Even so, he could count on one hand the number of people who'd offered to shake his hand.

He pulled into the driveway of his rental house, gathered his food, and stepped out of the truck. His usual scan of the property showed him nothing out of the ordinary, except the rental sign on the neighbor's lawn was gone. The houses all down the street were quiet. Since it was late afternoon, he knew that most of the people in this neighborhood were still at work. It was a normal Wednesday, except for the part where he'd instinctively intervened in a robbery because he had a soft spot for the poor girl at the mini mart. She'd always been nice to him.

"Damned idiot," he said to himself as he unlocked the front door. He headed inside, walking through the living room to the kitchen in the back of the small cape house. He dropped his sandwich on the table, and checked the back yard for any intruders. The trees had managed to dump a few more yellow leaves on the lawn, but nothing he needed to deal with yet. He kicked off his boots, sat at the table, and sighed. "Shit."

Nick's hand had been slightly cool, but strong. The guy had clearly been in pain from his wound, but it hadn't seemed to really faze him. Felix respected that. "Not that you should even be thinking about him." He pulled his sandwich over and devoured it with a few quick bites. He filled a glass with water and drank it down, then looked longingly at the refrigerator.

No. No beer tonight. You've got to keep your head straight. He threw out the food packaging, and then he ran a hand over his face as he tried to figure out just what it was about Nick that unsettled him so much. He leaned back against the counter, but after a moment he pushed off and started pacing. He felt keyed up, which was odd. He wasn't the kind of guy who worried about shit he had no control over. The image of Nick holding out his hand stuck in his mind like a video on replay.

He's young. Healthy. Haven't seen him in this area before. Forcing himself to stop walking in circles, Felix stood in the center of the kitchen, running down a list of details. *He wasn't terrified by the robbery, but he wasn't happy either. Could he be in the business?*

The sound of his cell phone beeping saved him from further rumination. He slid his personal phone out of his pocket and checked the screen.

Zero: **Money has been transferred, minus my usual fee.**

Felix: **New contracts?**

Zero: **One in your area, two that require travel to Europe.**

Felix sighed, debating on whether he wanted to hop a flight in the next few days. After a moment, he replied. **Who is the close request client?**

Zero: **You know I don't share.**

Felix scowled. He'd known Zero for years, and it wasn't like him to be reticent with Felix, of all people. **Who?**

Zero: **Why does it matter?**

Felix: **Call it curiosity.** The truth was Felix wasn't sure he wanted to do any contracts anymore. He'd been thinking about retiring for a while now. If the job were something messy, he'd just as soon not bother. It wasn't as though he were hurting for cash, after all.

Zero: **Robert Edwards.**

Felix's eyebrows went up. Edwards was a fixture in the organized crime scene on the east coast. He didn't usually farm out his work to freelancers because he employed more than enough specialists to do any job he required in-house. Interesting. Maybe the job would chip into the boredom that seemed to have permanently set up residence in his life. **Set me up with the close contract.**

Zero: **Details emailed.**

Felix: **Will reply email as per usual when complete.**

Zero: **Roger that.**

Felix slid his phone back into his pocket and headed to the bedroom on the first floor that he used as an office. He sat down at his desk and slid his laptop toward him. Sure enough, his email already had the contract from Zero. He opened the file and scanned the details. *Quincy Edwards, white male, thirty-three, alias "Q," two million USD upon confirmation of completion, contract interval two weeks, last known residence 448 Peace Road, Waldwick, NJ.*

Felix rubbed his chin. "Huh. No wonder Edwards is farming out this job. He wants someone in his own family gone. Interesting." He hadn't really planned on doing another job in this area, but what the hell else did he have to do? He hit *confirm* in the email and watched his browser open with an acceptance authorization code. He memorized it, then cleared his browser's history and cookies, and sat back.

"Two weeks. I can be done and gone in two weeks," he murmured, glancing around the room. He hadn't bothered to decorate the place. He never did, so it wasn't difficult to pack up and move on. Hell, a few times he hadn't bothered to pack. He'd just grabbed his go-bag and left all the furniture and other assorted crap behind, buying new supplies when he landed at his next six-month residence. Anything he really wanted to keep was stored at his cabin in the middle of rural New York. The only one who knew about it was Zero, because he'd helped him buy the property and set up security on the place.

He shook his head and stood up. "Getting soft," he muttered under his breath. He thought of Nick with the strong hands. "Going crazy, too," he added as he headed upstairs. He'd take a short nap, and then head back out to the storage unit for some gear to begin basic overnight surveillance. The time frame was tight, but he had enough wiggle room to observe the mark for a few days. He might be going soft, but he wasn't about to make a rookie mistake that got him caught. Soft was one thing. Stupid was quite another.

****

Nick stared at his sister as rage flared through his gut. "He what?" They stood in the bedroom she shared with her boyfriend, Quincy, and Nick clenched his fists in an attempt to not break anything. The throb of his left arm told him he needed to relax. That damned bullet wound was going to plague him for weeks. He uncurled his fingers. *Flesh wound. Bah.*

Jenna wiped the tears from her face, smearing her mascara everywhere. "He didn't mean to, Nick. It was my fault."

The bruise on her upper right arm told him that Quincy most certainly *did* mean to shove her against the dresser she currently leaned against. He stared at the white paint and cute little pink flowers curling around the brass drawer pulls as if the feminine design would somehow mitigate the absolute fucking bullshit she'd just tried to tell him. His sister loved that dresser because it had been a gift from their grandmother, and now she'd never be able to look at it again without remembering the bruises. He swallowed a growl. He didn't want to add to Jenna's misery.

"I shouldn't have gone out with Sara the other night," Jenna said, tucking tangled blonde hair behind her ears. "I knew it would upset him when I told him I wouldn't be home for dinner. It's my fault," she repeated.

Nick carefully took a deep breath, counted to three, and then exhaled. It didn't help calm him as much as he'd hoped. "Jenna," he said, speaking slowly so his voice wouldn't shake with anger. "Your boyfriend treats you like shit. It's time to ditch him, and you know it. I can't put it any more clearly than that. You're twenty-two. You have your whole life ahead of you, and this—" He gestured to her arm, and the dresser. "Is fucking bullshit. You know it. I know it." He ran a hand over his face. "Please. Let me help you. That's why I'm here, right? It's time to get out."

Jenna shook her head and backed away, out into the living room just off the master bedroom. "No, no, I can't. Not now. He'll go crazy. You don't understand." She started pacing the small space, nearly knocking over a lamp in the process. "I know I said I wanted to leave, but I've changed my mind."

"I understand all too well." Nick walked over to his sister and cupped her elbow. "Look at your arm, Jenna." He smoothed a gentle finger over the palm-sized bruise. The dark purple color against her skin made him feel sick to his stomach. "This isn't the first time this has happened, is it?" He wanted to take her in his arms and drag her away from her asshole abuser, but he knew, from awful personal experience, that people needed to make their own choices.

Jenna started crying again. "Nick, look—"

"Jenna. You called me, remember? You told me you needed help. You told me you wanted to leave him." Nick pulled her into a hug, wondering when his sister had started to feel so fragile. *She's lost weight,* he realized worriedly. "I'm here. I'm working remotely at my job, so I am here for as long as it takes to get you out of this situation." He leaned back and forced a smile. "You're just lucky I'm an awesome web developer who can work from anywhere."

"I don't know, Nick…" Jenna trailed off, looking out the front window of her and Quincy's house. "You don't know Q like I do."

"I know enough," Nick said again, wishing his parents weren't such bigoted idiots that they couldn't see his sister's situation clearly. "I know Mom and Dad urged you to stay with him—"

"He's my fiancé! I can't just up and leave. Mom and Dad were so happy when he asked me to marry him. It was like everything was okay again." She stared down at the diamond ring on her left hand as if it held all the answers.

A chill went down Nick's spine at those words. He knew why everything hadn't been okay with his parents: because he'd come out as gay in his senior year of college. That was the year they'd thrown him out of the house. That was the year they'd pinned all of their hopes for a "normal" family on his sister. He'd known exactly how his religious parents would react to his sexuality, and that was why he'd waited to come out. He wanted Jenna to be old enough to know her own mind, so that if his parents clamped down on her, she'd have the means to get out, too.

But clearly my plans didn't go the way I'd hoped. If he'd just stayed in the closet, none of this would've happened to Jenna. *Of course, if I'd stayed in the closet, I would've gone mad with misery.* He sighed, wishing life weren't always such a clusterfuck. "He doesn't deserve you, Jenna, and you know it."

His sister walked to a side table and tore open a box of tissues. She scraped at her face with a thick wad, and then started ripping the thin tissue to shreds. "I don't know what to do."

Nick frowned at her, sick with guilt. *She's scared. She wants to leave, but she's scared to death. I need to fix this.* He rolled his shoulders, trying to ease the crick in his neck. "Ok, here's what we're going to do, Jenna. We're going to pack up your stuff, and I'm going to take you home with me."

"Nick—"

"No." He cut her off, knowing that if he gave her a choice, she'd just sink down even deeper into her boyfriend's clutches. "You called me last week, begging me to come help you get out of here. We texted every day, remember? And I know this has been building for a while. You're going to leave him, and I'm going to help you. No more changing your mind." Nick grabbed two of the boxes he'd brought and headed back to the bedroom. He ignored the stab of pain in his arm as he lifted the box onto his hip. The last thing he wanted to do was worry his sister, so he'd covered up his injury with a long-sleeved shirt. "You can either come pack your stuff or you can watch me do it, but you know I'll probably shove all of your underwear in with your shoes." He risked a wink at her, trying to lighten the mood. *That ought to rile her up.*

"Oh my God, what kind of gay man are you? That's a sacrilege," Jenna said, following him into the room. She didn't argue when he dropped the boxes at the foot of the bed and started opening her dresser drawers.

Nick smirked. "I'm the kind of gay man who doesn't buy into all the stereotypes, remember?" He plunged a hand into a pile of socks and grabbed a bunch. When he tossed them into the box, his sister rolled her eyes and hurried forward to rearrange them in the box.

"Uh-huh. Whatever you say, Mr. Snazzy Dresser. I see those designer sneakers you're wearing. And your shirt is cashmere. So just shut up." She headed for the armoire in the far corner of the room and opened the top cabinet.

Nick watched her slowly gather an armful of tops, relieved that she was finally moving in the right direction. He'd get her out of here, and then she would be able to heal. He emptied the rest of her socks into the box, and then folded the flaps closed and put it on the bed. When he looked up, he realized Jenna was standing with her shoulders slumped, hands full of sweaters as she watched him.

Shit. She's second-guessing herself.

"Nick—" Her face twisted.

"I know it's hard, Jenna." He walked over to her and gave her a hug, then took the sweaters and packed them away for her. It didn't take long.

"I just thought he was the one, you know? I don't understand what happened." Jenna wiped at her eyes again as she wandered over to the dresser. "Why can't I stop crying?"

"It's going to take a while, sis." Nick put a box at her feet. "Just start with one drawer. When you're done, start on the next. That's all there is to it."

"But I don't want him to hurt you," she whispered, looking up at him with red eyes. "He's got a really bad temper."

Nick's heart broke. "Oh, Jenna. He won't touch me. He's a coward at heart." He touched her shoulder, then headed for the closet. "I'm going to toss all of your shoes in this box. You deal with your clothes. Okay?" She nodded, and he watched her start to drop underwear and t-shirts into an empty box. *Good. She's moving.*

"This is real, isn't it?" she said quietly, after a few minutes had passed. "He really is awful. I don't understand any of this."

Nick knew she didn't mean the bruises on her arm. "Yeah, but you'll be okay now. I promise." His voice came out gruff. To fend off his sadness, he started shoving his sister's insane collection of shoes into his box.

"How do you know who to trust, Nick?" Jenna asked, opening the next drawer. "I mean, Quincy was so nice to me in the beginning. I don't understand how I could've been so stupid."

"Jenna, you're not stupid. You're young. There's a difference." Nick closed his box and headed over to her. He didn't mention that the weird, manipulative dynamics of their parents' marriage hadn't been the best example for either of them. He hadn't yet managed a successful long-term relationship, and he wasn't sure if he ever would. "And knowing who to trust… Well, that's a tough question."

"You're not that much older than I am," she said, opening the next drawer. She started dumping her stuff into the box willy-nilly. "How do *you* know how to trust? Do you trust anyone?"

"Trust?" He snorted. "Have you ever seen me with a boyfriend?"

Jenna shook her head. "No." Her face crumpled. "Are we always going to be alone?"

Nick's heart broke all over again. "No. We'll

figure it out. And if we don't, we'll still always have each other," he said, willing her to believe him. *And I'll do better. I'll see her more often. Make sure she's okay, instead of just phoning it in.*

"Yeah. I guess you're stuck with me. Loser." Jenna wiped at her face again as she attempted a smile. "Okay. Those are all my clothes." She closed the box she'd filled and nudged it with her foot. "It's not much, is it?"

Nick's eyebrows rose. "Wait, what?" He glanced up at the rack of dresses hanging in the closet. "What about these?"

"Those are clothes Quincy bought me and made me wear to his stupid business dinners with his family. I don't want them. They're too much. His father would stare at me all through the meal." Jenna shuddered. "It was creepy as hell." She turned her back on the racks of fabric. "I just need to get my laptop and I'm done."

Nick ran a hand through his hair, angry at himself all over again. He hadn't realized how bad it had gotten for her. "I should've come home sooner," he muttered, closing the closet door on the dresses.

"No. There was nothing you could've done," Jenna said, rubbing at the bruise on her arm. "I wouldn't have listened to you. I barely listened to you ten minutes ago."

Nick watched her skin turn red where she scrubbed at it. He walked over to her and took her hands in his. "Stop that." He pressed her hands together between his palms. "It's all in the past. We're going to move forward now." He hugged her again. For the first time since he'd shown up today, she hugged him back, and he swallowed against the relief threatening to choke him.

"Okay," she said in a small voice. "Let me get the

rest of my stuff."

Nick nodded and picked up the box of shoes. After stowing it and the other boxes in the back of his SUV, he went back inside to do a quick scan of the place with his sister. "You sure you got everything?"

She nodded, adjusting the strap of her laptop on her shoulder. "Yeah. That's all of it." She scowled at the magazines and dirty ashtrays littering the coffee table. "He can burn the rest of it for all I care."

"We can come back for the dresser," Nick offered.

Jenna shook her head. "No. I don't want it anymore." She turned her back on the room. "I have other keepsakes from Grandmom."

Nick nodded, not surprised. "I'm sorry."

She shrugged. "It is what it is."

Nick watched a dozen emotions chase their way across his sister's face, none of them good. *Time to get her away from this place*, he thought, hoping that a change in scenery would make her feel better. "Okay. Let's get the hell out of here before your asshole ex comes home," he said, guiding his sister to the front of the house. Before he could open the door, keys scraped in the lock and it swung open, banging against the wall.

Well, isn't that just shitty timing, Nick thought sourly, shoving his sister behind his back as he stared at the man in the doorway. *Fucking Quincy Edwards himself.* He sighed as the confusion on Quincy's face twisted into fury in less than a second. Nick knew exactly what was going to happen next, and it wasn't going to be pretty.

****

Felix pulled out his binoculars and settled in for a long night of surveillance. He'd grabbed a quick bite to eat, and then headed to the block where Quincy Edwards lived with his girlfriend. He'd parked his truck several houses down, behind a few old trees growing from the sidewalks. It was a nice neighborhood. Not somewhere you'd expect to find a drug dealer and money runner, but he supposed that was the point. Criminals didn't live in abandoned warehouses and yachts, like in the movies. They lived in everyday neighborhoods, where they could better fly under the radar. Well, except for Zero, but his friend had built his career around the warehouses he owned. Zero had always been a loner who didn't give a flying fuck what other people thought. Felix had rarely met a more independent operator, not that it mattered to him.

You won't find me living in a warehouse, though. Too fucking grim, he thought, a half smile curling his lips up. No one would ever suspect that a man in his line of work would live in a random suburban neighborhood, and he always made it a point to try to seem as outwardly normal as possible. He couldn't do a damn thing about the inside of his head, but his life depended on him blending in with all of the ordinary people he lived among and worked around. *And if you ask me, I'm a damn sight more "normal" than they are. Or maybe just more honest.*

He scanned the street in both directions, and then focused on the house he'd come to watch. He'd just put the binoculars up to his eyes when he froze, surprise curling around the base of his spine. Quincy Edwards had just gotten home, and from the looks of it, he was confronting his girlfriend and her new man. And the new guy just happened to be Mr. Nick Banner, the guy he'd met at the mini mart robbery earlier.

"Shit." Felix frowned, as he considered aborting the entire contract. He didn't need random connections fouling up his work. Instead of starting the truck and getting the hell out of there, however, he continued to watch the scene unfold, like a man who couldn't eat just one bite of candy. Something about Nick intrigued him, much to his disgust. He cocked his head, watching with interest as Edwards slammed his fist on the front door. It swung in, nearly hitting Nick in the face. To Felix's surprise, Nick got right up in Edwards's space, eyes flat with anger. He hadn't thought Nick would be so aggressive, but then he saw the small woman cowering behind him.

That must be Edwards's girlfriend. Is she cheating on him with Nick? he wondered, ignoring the pang of regret he felt at the thought of Nick hooking up with some woman. He couldn't afford to care about shit like that. He pressed his lips together, keeping the binoculars steady.

Edwards started yelling. From the few words Felix could make out at this distance, the man was upset the woman was leaving. *That would explain the boxes on the sidewalk.* Edwards banged on the door again, and Felix thought Nick might back down, but instead, he said something. It must've really pissed off his target, because Edwards lunged for Nick. Felix nearly got out of his car to help before he remembered he didn't do things like that. He watched Nick neatly sidestep the attack, using Edwards' momentum against him.

"Huh." Felix rubbed his chin. Nick could handle himself pretty damned well. He couldn't deny the rush of pleasure he felt at the sight of Nick shoving Edwards past him like some sort of Kung Fu genius, especially considering the bullet wound in his arm. Edwards crashed into something just inside the door, and Nick hustled the girl out of the house, handing her the keys to a car. She dashed to the SUV parked in front and dove into the passenger side.

"This is either going to get very ugly, or very interesting," Felix murmured, lips twisting. He had no desire to see Nick hurt, or the woman, but he also wasn't about to go play hero again. He'd only intervened at the mini mart because he was hungry, and he tended to do dumb things when people screwed with his meals. And that poor cashier didn't deserve that kind of shit. He sighed, annoyed with himself all over again. He really needed to fucking retire before he lost his edge entirely.

You're not bored now, a small voice whispered at the back of his mind. He scowled, and rolled his shoulders, focusing on the house again. He wasn't surprised to see Edwards come barreling out of the house, red-faced and yelling. Nick stood on the front walk with feet spread, hands relaxed. The moment Edwards lunged for him, Nick took him down with one judicial punch to the head. Edwards dropped like a sack of bricks.

"Fuck me," Felix breathed. His cock hardened, as it so often did when he had the pleasure of watching good work being done. He watched Nick scowl down at Edwards, but the guy wasn't getting up. Nick had knocked him out cold with one hit. Nick shook out his hands, picked up the two boxes, and then headed for the SUV. Felix hurriedly put down the binoculars and hunched down in his truck. One minute later, their vehicle passed him, and he couldn't resist a peek over the dashboard. He got a good look at the woman and frowned when he realized that she could be Nick's twin: same color hair, same bone structure.

"Siblings. She's gotta be his sister," Felix said, picking up the binoculars again once the SUV turned the corner. He looked back towards the house, but Edwards was still out cold in the front yard. "Well, shit. I should do the job right now. Easy-peasy." He could walk up, put his boot on the man's throat, and collect a cool couple million. He considered it. Nick would get the rap for the job, and Felix would be free to head west. "Fuck," he muttered, not moving. For some reason, he didn't want to see the man go down for murder.

"Goddammit." Before he could change his mind, Felix started his truck and pulled away, cursing himself under his breath. He should be driving back there to run Edwards over. Or he could put a round in the man's head. He could break his neck. Any number of ways to finish the contract filed through his mind, but instead of going closer, he drove away, like a dumb shit who didn't know his way around the block anymore. He needed to retire, like, right the fuck now. The moment you went soft was the day someone else took your place, usually with a bullet to your brain to seal the end of your career.

Chapter Three

"You can stay in this bedroom. I set it up just the way you like it," Nick said as he dumped the last box on the floor near the closet, suppressing a wince as the movement taxed his injured arm. His sister had no idea he'd been shot, and he'd like to keep it that way. What she didn't know wouldn't hurt her.

"Thanks," Jenna said. Her voice barely made it above a whisper.

Nick looked at her, worried about the exhaustion in her expression. "I pushed the bed next to the wall. There's only the one window with wooden shutters on the inside, but it's got a great view. And you've got your own bathroom." He gestured to the door near the closet. "This house has two master bedrooms, and each has its own bath. How cool is that? My room is just down the hall." He forced a smile for his sister. He knew she wasn't really up for his whole spiel, but it didn't matter. They had to play the hand they were dealt. It was a lesson he'd had beaten into him on the streets, not that she knew that.

"It's great, Nick. Really." She moved to the bed and fingered the comforter he'd bought for her. "Where on Earth did you find this? I had one just like it when I was a girl." She traced a finger over the antique roses embroidered into the cloth. "And then Mom sold it at the garage sale."

"I have my ways," Nick winked at her, ignoring the comment about their mother. Their parents sucked, and always had. Talking about them wouldn't change a damn thing. "Just enjoy the blanket, and don't worry about where it came from," he added. Really, online shopping made everything easy, but she didn't have to know the details. There were actually a hell of a lot of things she didn't need to know about his life, up to and including his job, his money situation, and how hard he'd tried to keep from tangling her up in his business. *But right now, it's more dangerous for her to be with fucking Quincy Edwards than it is for her to be with me. Which is seriously screwed up.* He shook his head, pushing those thoughts to the back of his mind.

"How did you take Quincy down so fast?" Jenna asked, sitting on the bed.

Nick inhaled. He'd known she was going to ask. He had an answer all ready, but whether or not she believed him... "I started taking mixed martial arts in college," he said, shrugging. *Getting thrown out of your hometown diner with egg on your face kind of motivates a guy to learn how to fight,* he thought, but he didn't feel like describing the whole scenario. She had enough problems of her own without worrying over his past drama. "I liked it, so I continued." He leaned back against the doorjamb. "It's relaxing."

His sister's eyes widened. "Fighting is relaxing? I had no idea." Her gaze went to his fists. "You're not even bruised."

"If you fuck up your hands, you're not doing it right," Nick told her. He flexed his fingers. "I gotta keep these babies in good shape. Can't type without them." He couldn't do the other things he needed to do, either, but that was yet another thing his sister didn't need to know.

Jenna cocked her head. "Could I learn? How to fight?"

Nick blinked, astonished and oddly pleased. "Of course," he said. He had *not* seen that question coming. "It can take a long time to really get good at it. I've been doing it for five years, and I still don't know everything."

"Even so. A little is better than nothing, right?" Her hands went to the bruises on her arms.

ERIN M. LEAF

Nick nodded slowly, realizing where her sudden interest came from. "I can start you off with some simple self-defense techniques."

She smiled. "Okay."

Nick grinned at her. "I can't wait to see my little sister throw a grown man over her shoulder."

Jenna crossed her arms, looking suddenly apprehensive. "I'm not strong enough to do that."

"It's all about momentum, sis," Nick told her, miming a move. "You don't need to be muscular or tall. You just need to be in reasonably good shape, and you need to understand the physics of motion." He saw the uncertainty on her face. "We can start in a few days, after you get some rest." He pushed off from the doorjamb and walked over to her. "I don't want you to worry about anything for at least a week, okay? You deserve a break." He smoothed a hand down her hair. "You're safe now."

Jenna sighed. "Quincy came to my job at the consignment shop. He got me fired." She rubbed her forehead, and then pushed his hands away. "There's no way I'm going to be able to relax, Nick. I need to find a job. Maybe I should've sold that diamond ring Quincy gave me instead of leaving it in the house."

The "diamond" Quincy had given her was a fake, and wouldn't fetch ten bucks on the gem market. Nick grabbed her hands and quieted their restless motion. He needed to redirect her train of thought, pronto. "Shh. It's okay, Jenna. I've got plenty of money. I can afford to have you mooch off of me for a while." He forced a grin. "What else are siblings for?"

"But—" she protested, but Nick cut her off.

"Nope. It's no big deal. You are going to rest and be happy, because I said so." He tucked a strand of her hair behind her ear, gratified that she didn't push him off again. "Now, unpack and settle in. I'm going to head out

35

for some dinner. I'm totally cool with you staying here, but as you know, I am terrible in the kitchen." He smiled at her. "We need food we can actually eat, and my attempts to cook aren't worth it."

His sister snorted as her expression eased. "Yeah, I remember that time you burned a pot black when you tried to boil water. Dad was beyond pissed. So, can we have pizza? With mushrooms? And maybe anchovies?"

Nick made a face. He hated mushrooms, and she knew it, but he was willing to cut her some slack. "Of course. If that's what you want."

Jenna hugged him. "You do love me. You hate mushrooms."

Nick rolled his eyes. "Duh." He hugged her back, trying not to frown over her too-thin shoulders beneath his hands.

She leaned back. "So, are you going to tell Mom and Dad you're in town?"

"No." Nick didn't elaborate. She knew him well enough to know that he wanted nothing to do with the man and woman who'd thrown him out of their house. The year after they'd disowned him had been the hardest of his entire life. He'd owed nearly one hundred thousand in student loans, had no place to live, and his boyfriend had dumped him a mere month after the diner incident. He'd barely managed to graduate from college. The year after that … well. He'd figured out a way to survive, but it wasn't anything he could talk about to anyone, and he sure as shit didn't want Jenna to know about it.

"They're going to ask me where I'm living, Nick," Jenna said reasonably.

"So tell them." Nick stood up and started pacing. If he didn't, he'd go crazy. "Or don't. It's up to you." He could save her from her abusive boyfriend, but he couldn't save her from her own deluded love for their parents.

Jenna frowned. "They ask me about you."

I'm sure they do, he thought, suddenly pissed. "They have my number if they ever want to talk to me," he told her, struggling to keep his voice even. The last thing he wanted to do was scare her. "They don't call. They don't text." He shrugged angrily. "This is not my problem. Hell, it's not *your* problem. It's theirs."

Jenna wrapped her arms around herself again, eyes on the floor. "I don't know what to do."

Nick sighed and forced himself to stop pacing in front of her. "I can't tell you how to handle them," he said, voice tight. "I know you still love them. I know they say they care about you." He rolled his shoulders, trying to get the crick out of his neck. "But they sure as hell don't want me around anymore. They made that clear the last time I tried to talk to them." He shook his head, remembering how his father had thrown Nick's laptop through the doorway. The metal and plastic had shattered all over the front walkway of their house. The neighbors had enjoyed the show. "They don't care to speak to me." *And they sure as hell don't seem to care that their only daughter was stuck in an abusive relationship and desperately needed help.* His parents were terrible human beings. Nick knew criminals who treated their families better than his mother and father did.

Jenna nodded. "I know. It's just difficult, right now."

Nick grimaced, understanding that her misery was rooted deeper than his bad history with their parents. He should've gotten her away from that asshole sooner. Maybe he should've taken her away from their parents, too, but hindsight was always twenty-twenty.

"I'm sorry, Nick."

Nick inhaled deeply, and then exhaled slowly before replying. "Look. Just give yourself a break, okay? Don't think about all the hard things for at least a week. Try and remember who you are, without worrying about what other people think." He crossed his arms in frustration, and then grimaced as his bicep throbbed. He ran a hand over the wound. It still hurt, but at least no one could see the gauze he'd wrapped around his arm under his shirt.

"I can't help it." Jenna scowled. "I have a lot to deal with."

Nick frowned and dropped his arms. "Okay, then give yourself a break for one day. Or for an hour." He tapped her on the shoulder, emphasizing his point. "The only way to get through the shit times in life is to move forward. You can't dwell on the past. And you can't fix everything that's gone wrong all at once. You need to take it one step at a time. Right?" He smiled. It felt a little forced, but at least he was trying. That had to count for something. "Listen to someone who's been there, done that, and bought the t-shirt. You need to do normal things so that your body and brain can remember how it feels. You weren't with him for so long that you can't recover who you are." He put a fist to his heart. "I know this, in here. You are a good person, Jenna."

"You're the only one who thinks so."

Nick scowled at her, and she sighed, but then she nodded.

"I can try."

"Good." Nick walked to the door. "I'm going out for some food. Relax. Read a book. Paint your nails or something. Call a girlfriend to come over. Do normal things."

Jenna made a face at him. "You hate the smell of

nail polish."

"I'll deal with it." Nick gave her a little salute, and headed out. Truthfully, he needed a few minutes alone to get his head calm again. He loved his sister, but she reminded him of all those things he thought he'd left behind years ago: family, love, acceptance, responsibility. And anger. He remembered a hell of a lot of conflict and anger. He could never go back, and he'd made a habit of never dwelling on the things he couldn't change, but he would never abandon his sister. She was the only real family he had left.

So, get a grip, Nick. Now is not the time to psychoanalyze your life. He grabbed his keys from the side table near the front door, and set his mind on the task in front of him. *Pizza, first. Then maybe rent a movie to watch with Jenna, get her mind off her shit. And then, after she's asleep, you can email Zero about the new items you've got for him to sell.*

****

Felix yawned as he pulled into his driveway. He parked outside the garage, and then sat in the truck, listening to the hot engine tick down. He needed sleep, but he was too hungry to just go to bed. He'd heat up some leftovers, and then reassess the new contract before getting some shut-eye. He didn't really need the money, and for some reason, the thought of getting Nick embroiled in a murder investigation just didn't sit well with him. Still thinking over the problem, he scanned the neighborhood, doing his usual check for anything out of the ordinary. He narrowed his eyes when he realized the house next door had lights on inside. He got out of his truck, still watching the windows.

"New neighbors. Need to check them out." He added that to the list of tasks in his head. He kept his job as far away from his living space as he possibly could, and this was a safe, boring area, but it wouldn't do to get cocky. He ran checks on all the people who lived near him. He opened the truck door and got out, then froze when he saw Nick fucking Banner walk out of the house that had just been rented.

"Fuck me sideways," he breathed, mind racing. If Nick had rented the house next door, that must mean that his sister was here, too. His fucking mark's ex-girlfriend was probably living next door. What the hell was he supposed to do with that?

Too many damned roads lead all the way back to me, he thought, once again considering dismissal of the contract all together. Zero would bitch and moan about cancellation fees, but whatever. Felix could afford it. He watched Nick walk down the front sidewalk to his SUV. He didn't seem to be favoring his arm, which inexplicably pleased Felix, but then Nick ran a hand over his face as if exhausted.

Fuck. What do I care if he's tired? Felix shook his head at himself and closed the truck door.

Nick looked up at the sound and caught Felix's gaze. His eyebrows flew up in surprise, but then he smiled and strode over the tiny lawn to Felix's truck.

Aw, hell. Now I have to make small talk, Felix thought, even as he admired Nick's efficient strides. The man moved like a predator, and Felix remembered how easily he'd taken down Edwards. Clearly, Nick wasn't someone who sat around all day. For some reason, Felix liked that about him.

"Hey. I didn't expect to see you here." Nick shook his head and his longish blond hair fell over his eyes. He brushed it back. "Small world." He held out his hand.

Felix couldn't hold back a smile. "Hell, yeah, it's a small fucking world." He shook Nick's hand, and then nodded toward where the rental sign used to be. "You just move in? I haven't seen you here before." His gaze strayed down Nick's body, assessing him for weapons. Nick wore hip-hugging jeans and a soft pullover sweater that hid his bandaged left arm. No bulges or outlines of any weaponry marred the toned lines of his body. He lingered on the sculpted muscles of Nick's chest. The man probably packed a hell of a punch. No wonder Quincy Edwards had dropped like a stone.

Nick nodded. "Yeah. Just got my sister moved in with me, too. It should be interesting. Her ex is a real jerk." He sighed and shook his head. "I'm here to help her get back on her feet and away from that psycho."

Felix wasn't surprised that Edwards was an abusive bastard. "That sucks for her," he merely said, not wanting to tip off how much he knew about the guy.

"Yeah, but I'm here now. I can protect her." Nick smiled again.

Protect her from a slick gangster? Felix mused, but before he could speak, Nick nodded towards Felix's truck.

"Nice wheels."

Felix blinked, momentarily at a loss for words. He'd never in his life got caught up in a random, pointless conversation about vehicles. "It gets me around," he said, not even trying to elaborate. Instead, he changed the topic, weirdly reluctant to shut down the small talk. "So, how's your arm?"

Nick made a face. "Fine, just sore. I'm still pissed, though." He shrugged, wincing slightly. "I hope those bastards rot in jail. The poor girl at the checkout counter looked like she was going to stroke out."

"I think she'll be okay. She's tough. As for the losers who scared her, well, they'll be in lockup for a while. Addicts can't usually post bail." Felix paused, considering. "Unless they have someone who enables their habit, in which case, all bets are off." It wouldn't surprise him if those two goons worked for Edwards. Stranger things had happened. *Case in point: my newest job is to kill the ex-boyfriend of Nick's sister.*

"True that," Nick said, lips twisting. "So, I'm off to get some pizza. Want to join my sister and me when I get back? She could use some normal company." He smiled. "So can I."

He thinks I'm normal? If he knew what I did for a living, he'd be running the opposite direction. Amused, Felix shook his head. "I can't." He didn't explain that he had no time for socializing when he needed to figure out why the hell he felt so tempted into saying "yes". He wouldn't mind getting to know Nick better. It had been decades since he'd just hung out with a buddy. *But that way lies madness.*

Nick waited a moment, as if expecting an explanation for Felix's refusal. "You don't sound all that sure to me. Come on. I'm even getting mushrooms, which are disgusting." He tilted his head. "Do you like mushrooms?"

Felix stared at the guy. He *did* like mushrooms. He hadn't eaten them on a pizza in ages. *Shit.* "Well, since you promised mushrooms…" He trailed off, not quite believing what was saying, even as the words dropped from his mouth. *Did I just agree to have dinner with the brother of my mark's ex-girlfriend? What the fuck is wrong with me?* His gaze flicked down Nick's body again. The man really did keep himself in great shape. *What would it be like to spar with him?*

"Excellent." Nick grinned, rocking back on his heels. "I'll be back in a half hour. Just come to the front door." He nodded at Felix, and then headed back across the grass to his vehicle.

Felix watched him go, mind racing with rationalizations. "This is a good thing," he murmured to himself as Nick's SUV pulled out of his driveway. "It's good to socialize. People need interaction or they turn into nutjobs." He snorted softly to himself. Nick waved at him as he passed by. "Plus, I can get to know more about Edwards if I talk to his ex. Good for business. Right?"

He shook his head, fully aware that his mental gymnastics bordered on the absurd. He ran a hand through his hair, then scrubbed at his short beard. "Jesus. I'm a stupid fucking idiot." He headed inside to take a quick shower. Maybe some hot water would wash some sense back into his brain. God knew he could use a dose of pragmatism right now.

Chapter Four

"Wait, you what? You invited the neighbor to dinner?" Jenna asked, the astonishment clear in her voice. "Are you serious?"

"He's nice. You'll like him," Nick said, putting the pizza boxes down on the kitchen breakfast bar. "He hasn't been here long."

Jenna ran a hand over her hair. "I dunno. I'm kind of tired."

"It'll be okay," Nick said, pulling her into a hug. "It'll be good for you to see that not all guys are raging lunatics. Live a normal life, remember?"

She rolled her eyes. "The fact that you invited him over, today, kind of points the opposite direction, Nick. It's not normal for you to invite random guys to dinner. In fact, I don't remember the last time you even went on a date, unless there's something you're not telling me?"

Nick shook his head. "I would tell you if I met someone."

"Exactly." Jenna pointed at him. "What happened to chilling, painting my nails?"

Nick sighed, wondering if he'd made a mistake. He wanted to help his sister, but at the same time, there was something about Felix that interested him. "He stopped a robbery at the gas station this morning. I think he works in law enforcement or something," Nick said before his brain could catch up with his mouth. He clamped his lips shut, wondering what the hell had got into him. *The man's gorgeous. You're thinking with your dick, dumbass,* his brain informed him in no uncertain terms.

"What? There was a robbery? You didn't tell me that." Jenna stopped in the center of the kitchen, hands full of plates. "Are you okay? What happened?"

Nick grimaced, annoyed with himself for bringing it up. "I'm fine. It was nothing. It happened just as I was going in for coffee, and it was over in under five minutes, thanks to Felix." He took the plates from her and set them on the table. "Relax. He's one of the good guys. I promise." He eyed his sister's expression, hoping she couldn't tell he was lying through his teeth. He didn't know the first damn thing about Felix except that he wanted to fuck him into the wall. "Just … you know. Roll with it. Okay?"

Jenna stared at him for a moment. "Roll with it," she repeated, sitting down. She pressed her thumb between her eyebrows. "God knows my sense of people isn't always reliable, but you always know how to read someone. You always have." She took a deep breath. "If this is important to you, I can deal." She tilted her head, and narrowed her eyes. "Is he cute?"

Dammit. Nick flushed. "Maybe."

"Ha!" Jenna pointed at him. "You want in his pants."

Nick rolled his shoulders, not sure if he was more pleased that his sister was showing some animation after the trauma of the day, or upset that she'd figured out his true motivation for inviting Felix over. "He's straight."

"Uh huh."

"What? You know I don't mess around with straight guys." Nick defended himself.

"If you thought he was straight, what are you doing asking him to dinner, tonight of all nights?" his sister pointed out, very perceptively.

Nick knew she was right, but Felix felt like a good person to him. A little intimidating, maybe, but still good people. He shrugged, as if his mind weren't racing with a thousand conflicting thoughts. "It's just pizza. No big deal."

"You realize he lives next door," Jenna replied, a hint of tartness in her voice. "If he turns out to be a nut case, there's no getting away, and then we're both screwed."

"He's not crazy, and I have no intention of asking him out," Nick said, just as the doorbell rang. *I'd just like to fuck him into next week.* "And it's too late to back out now. He's here," he told his sister, heading for the front door. He swung it open. "Hey, there. Glad you could come." He looked Felix up and down. The man had showered, and his dark hair curled wetly over his forehead and the nape of his neck. Nick wanted to run his fingers through it and lick off the water. *Damn it, get your mind out of the gutter.*

"Thanks for having me." Felix's gaze flicked over the room as if assessing the exits, then landed on Jenna.

Nick waved him in and shut the door. "It's not much, but it's home, for now." He glanced at the cool blue walls and modern furniture. He'd decorated it so it would be soothing, and he quite liked the uncluttered space. He led Felix to Jenna. She'd taken the stool closest to the wall at the breakfast bar that jutted into the living room. "Jenna, this is Felix Cooper, our neighbor. Felix, my sister, Jenna."

"It's Felix Zamaro, actually," Felix said.

Nick blinked, confused. *The hell? I know the cop called him Mr. Cooper.*

"The cop heard wrong," Felix said, clearly interpreting Nick's confusion.

"Uh, okay," Nick said, glancing at his sister.

The look on Jenna's face after she got a good look at their neighbor told Nick she knew *exactly* why he'd invited Felix over, and it wasn't because the man was *nice.* She smirked at Nick, and he narrowed his gaze at her. Their sibling communication seemed to be functioning perfectly, even after years living apart, because she grinned at him before turning to Felix.

"Hey," she said. "Pleased to meet you." She offered him a little wave.

"Sorry if I'm imposing," Felix said, his voice quiet and non-threatening.

Jenna straightened up. "It's no problem."

Nick was happy to see his sister making an effort. He smiled at her. She gave him a look that told him he'd owe her for this. *Whatever. I got her away from that asshole.* She *owes* me.

"Nick told me he just moved you in today," Felix continued, lifting a shoulder. "If you're tired, I can go. I know what it's like to haul boxes."

Jenna shook her head "No, no. It's fine. Have a seat."

Felix took the stool farthest from her, and handed Nick a six-pack of cola. "Least I can do."

"Thanks," Nick said, strangely tongue-tied. Felix had changed into skin-hugging jeans and a green t-shirt that stretched across an impressive-as-hell chest. The color gave his hazel eyes a mesmerizing glow. Nick tore his gaze away, relieved when his sister took up the conversational ball, because he suddenly couldn't string three words together. *Stop staring at him,* he admonished himself.

"So, have you lived here long?" Jenna asked, opening the boxes of pizza. She handed Felix a plate.

"Not really. I moved here about six months ago." Felix held out his plate as Nick began pulling the pizza slices apart. "I rent the house. It's a nice neighborhood."

Nick grabbed a slice with mushrooms and slid it onto the plate. "Fungus pizza, just like I promised."

Jenna laughed. "I like mushrooms, even though Nick hates them. And anchovies." She helped herself to the pizza.

Nick flashed her a grateful smile. Suddenly, she seemed to be reacting much more like the sister he remembered. Maybe just being out of that asshole's house and away from his influence would help her more than he'd expected.

"Nick doesn't like anchovies?" Felix asked.

"Ha." She made a sound in the back of her throat. "No."

"It's the crunch of the bones." Nick shuddered. "So. Gross."

"The bones are too tiny and soft to crunch." Felix laughed, taking a big bite. Nick watched him chew. Even that motion made the guy look sexy as all fuck. *Shit, I've got it bad.* He wanted to rub his forehead, but he knew it would make him look like an idiot. "So, you've been here six months? I grew up here, but I only just came back."

Felix eyed him around his slice of pizza for a moment, and then placed it down on his plate. "I move around a lot." He shrugged. "My job requires travel."

"Really? My brother's job is like that, too," Jenna said, opening a can of soda. "He hasn't come back home to stay for longer than a day or two in years."

Nick kept his body language relaxed, even as his internal alarms started beeping. His sister only *thought* she knew what he did for a living. Steering the conversation this direction always held a chance of exposure. He glanced at Felix. Fortunately, not a hint of suspicion marred the man's face.

"He does something with computers." Jenna sipped her drink, then coughed. "Ugh, too much fizz."

Nick shook his head, smiling through his unease.

He'd practiced the expression in the mirror. No one would be able to tell that he had to force it. *Time to deflect.* "I'm a lowly consultant. I just go where they tell me," he explained, hoping to God the man didn't ask for more details. His sister was going to be the death of him.

"Computer work is a good career, so I hear," Felix said, a hint of amusement in his tone.

Nick nodded and stuffed a bite of food in his mouth so he wouldn't have to expound on his only somewhat-true explanation. The man's good looks were scrambling his brains. Even the bit of tomato sauce on Felix's lower lip looked sexy.

"So, Nick said something about you saving him from a robbery?" Jenna gestured at Felix. The pizza in her hand flopped down, so she folded the piece over itself before taking another large bite. When she'd finished chewing, she looked expectantly at Felix.

Felix turned to Nick. "Did you tell her about your arm?"

Really? That's the direction he goes? We could be talking about the weather right now. Nick scowled at Felix. "No, I did not. Thank you very much." He glanced at his sister. Sure enough, she'd dumped her pizza on her plate and was standing up, eyes haunted. Clearly, her control over her emotions wasn't as stable as he'd hoped.

"Your arm? What happened to your arm?" Jenna grabbed for him, and of course, her fingers closed around the bandage on his left bicep.

Nick winced slightly, and unwound her grip. No way was he going to show her how much her fingers hurt. "Easy. It's just a graze, and I'm fine. No worries."

"No worries? Jesus, Nick." Jenna began shoving at his sleeve. "Let me see."

"Jenna, I'm fine. Seriously. I carried all your boxes out of the house for you, remember?" Nick battled her hands down. "I wouldn't have been able to do that if I'd been hurt bad."

Jenna gripped his fingers. "I hate you. Let me go."

Nick rolled his eyes at her, but he released her hands. "Go eat your pizza."

"It's true. He's fine. He didn't even faint," Felix said, openly laughing now.

Nick gave him his best death-glare as his sister tried again to shove up his sleeve, ignoring his plea to sit down. "Jenna, Jenna! I'm fine. I was in the wrong place at the wrong time." He pushed up his sleeve. "See? It's nothing." He peeled back the gauze." I could've fallen down and done the same thing. The bullet skimmed me. That's it."

"Someone *shot* at you?" Jenna grabbed his forearm as her expression crumpled.

Nick pressed the bandage back over the wound and pulled her into his arms. "I'm fine." Over her head, he glared at Felix. The man didn't even have the decency to look sorry. *You're going to pay for this,* he mouthed at the man.

Jenna reared back and smacked Nick on his uninjured arm. "You jerk! I can't believe you didn't tell me!"

"Ow." Nick frowned at her. "I didn't want to worry you. And stop with the hitting." He caught her hands again.

"I'm your sister! Of course, I'll worry." Jenna hugged him tightly. Nick hugged her back, and then urged her to sit back down.

"Chill out, sis. I keep forgetting it's even there. It barely hurts."

"Geez, Nick," she said, looking as if she was going to start freaking out again. Nick hurriedly cut her off.

"I'm fine, Jenna." He looked at Felix. "Thanks a lot, man."

Felix was watching Jenna the way a man looks at a particularly complicated puzzle, and for a moment, Nick thought maybe he'd misread the man's inherent decency, but then Felix glanced up. "Sorry." His expression smoothed into a rueful smile.

"No, you're not," Nick muttered, taking another bite of his pizza. *You're a damned idiot, Nick,* he thought, wondering why the hell he'd imagined exposing his sister to a new person today of all days would be a good idea. Clearly her emotions were on a rollercoaster, not that he could blame her for it.

"My brother's gay," Jenna abruptly said.

Nick choked on the bite he'd just swallowed. After a minute of coughing, he managed to wipe his eyes. "Jenna, my God. I can't take you anywhere." He glared at her. From the corner of his eye, he could see Felix's perplexed expression.

"You didn't take me anywhere. We're eating in tonight," she replied, too seriously for him to believe she wasn't trolling him.

Ignoring her, Nick rubbed a hand across his face, willing himself towards calm, because what the hell? People didn't just blurt shit like that out. "My sister likes dudes, too, not that that information matters one freaking bit." He scowled at her. She smirked at him.

Unexpectedly, Felix smiled. "I know."

Nick transferred his stare from his sister to his neighbor. "Um, what?" Felix already knew he was gay? It wasn't like anyone could tell just by looking at him. He didn't prance around in rainbow leggings, for Christ's sake. *Maybe he meant he already knew Jenna was straight? I mentioned her ex-boyfriend to Felix, didn't I?*

"I'm a good judge of character," Felix said, biting into the crust of his pizza.

Nick watched him chew for a hot second. Felix's lips were full and pouty, and fuck. Nick couldn't seem to keep his mind out of the damned gutter. "Sexuality and character are two entirely separate things," he finally said, wondering when the conversation had veered off into the woods, and how quickly he could steer it back onto a nice, paved road.

"That's true," Jenna said, her voice quieter now. "And I would know."

Nick frowned, knowing she was thinking about that asshole Quincy. "Hey, no worries." He touched her arm. She gave him a crooked smile. "You're done with him, remember?"

"Ex trouble?" Felix asked.

"Ugh." Jenna hopped off her stool and headed to the kitchen. "Is it that obvious?" She tossed her pizza crust into the trash. "My former boyfriend is a supreme asshole." She glanced at Nick, then nodded and added. "That's why I moved in with Nick. I had to get away from him."

"How long were you together?" Felix asked, finishing off his slice of pizza and sliding another onto his plate.

"Too long," Nick muttered, finding Felix's calm unnerving. What kind of guy could calmly eat pizza while throwing metaphorical bombs into a conversation like that?

"About a year," Jenna said, starting to pace. "I didn't realize at first what a manipulative bastard he really was. Things got weird after a while."

"What did he do for a living?" Felix took a sip of his drink, then continued. "Was he gone a lot, for work?"

Jenna snorted. "I wish." She paced into the

kitchen and began compulsively loading Nick's dirty dishes into the dishwasher. "No, actually, he was around more than most guys. He worked from home, doing some kind of buying and selling or something for his father. I don't know exactly. He had a lot of friends who were really business partners in disguise." She shuddered. "I didn't like most of them. His father was really creepy, too."

Felix frowned. "Sounds like a bad situation."

"Yeah, kind of." Jenna lifted a shoulder. "Thank God, he mostly kept his business away from me. *He* was the problem, not the people stopping by all the time." She slammed the dishwasher door shut a little too recklessly. Glass rattled.

"Hey, you don't have to talk about it, Jenna," Nick said, glancing at Felix. He wouldn't want to listen to her troubles, would he? Except, Felix's face showed nothing but compassion. Nick pursed his lips.

"It's okay, Nick," Jenna said.

"Was your ex abusive?" Felix put down his drink, frowning slightly as he watched Jenna.

Nick sat up. He did *not* expect Felix to ask that. "Hey," he said again, this time to Felix. When the man glanced at him, Nick shook his head at him. *Don't interrogate my sister,* he thought at him, hoping the guy would get his meaning.

Felix nodded minutely, but before Nick could change the subject, Jenna let out an explosive breath.

"Yeah, he hit me. But I hated the emotional abuse more than the physical stuff. He wouldn't let me go out; he monitored my cell phone and my email. He told me everything he did was my fault." She crossed her arms, hair flying. "Not fucking likely. *He* was the one with the weird business meetings in the middle of the night, and the drugs, and the asshole gangsters in my kitchen at four

AM."

Jesus. It was worse than I thought. Nick sucked in a harsh breath. "Jenna, it's done, I promise. He's old news." He glanced at Felix again, but the man's expression wasn't giving him any clues about why he'd steered the conversation in this direction. "You don't have to talk about this," he reassured his sister. He'd never expected her to just blow up like that. *Shit. Maybe I shouldn't have invited Felix over.*

"No." Jenna made a cutting motion with her arm. "I'm okay. I'm good, actually. Maybe I can finally see it all better, now that I'm out of that damned house." She ran a hand over her hair, pulling it back into a ponytail. "I'm never going back to him, Nick," she said, anger snapping in her gaze.

Nick shook his head. "Well, of course, you're not." While he was happy to see her finally remember that she was a strong woman, and not some pushover, he couldn't help but wonder if she was heading for a cliff. She'd been exhausted when he picked her up. The stress of Quincy shoving his way in to grab her, and then quickly packing, and *then* meeting Felix had to mean she was at the end of her rope, or very nearly there.

"No man has a right to dictate a damned thing to me," she said, voice hard and low.

"That is true," Felix said quietly. "Man or woman. Abuse is never right."

Jenna looked at him for a long moment while Nick held his breath, and then her shoulders drooped. "Shit. I'm really tired." She glanced at her brother.

Nick nodded, getting up and going around the bar. "Hey, it's okay. You can rest now." He put an arm around her shoulders. She felt so fragile, he almost worried he'd break her if he squeezed too hard.

"If I see some asshole coming into the

neighborhood, you can be damn sure I'm not going to stand by and let him barge in," Felix said, unexpectedly.

Nick raised his eyebrows at him. *I did* not *expect that. Felix doesn't seem like the kind of guy to butt into someone else's business,* he thought, but then he remembered him taking down the two losers at the gas station. *Huh.*

Felix shrugged. "No man should ever treat a woman with that kind of disrespect." He pushed his plate away. "And I'm not without a few resources of my own."

Nick didn't know what the hell Felix meant by that, but he appreciated the sentiment. "Thanks, man."

Felix nodded.

Jenna sighed, hugging Nick tightly, and then she pushed away. "Okay." She fussed with her ponytail, winding it into a loose knot. "I'm going to bed, Nick. And I'm never going to put up with Q again. If he comes near me, I'll bash him with a frying pan or something." She squared her shoulders.

Nick smiled. "A frying pan can do a lot of damage." He made a mental note to purchase a cast iron pan immediately.

"Yeah." Jenna glanced at Felix. "Sorry I ruined dinner with my crazy meltdown." She rubbed her eyes.

Felix shook his head. "It's understandable."

"Thanks," Jenna said, yawning. "You should stay. Hang out with Nick. God knows he needs someone normal to talk to after helping me today." She smiled crookedly at Felix, then hugged Nick. "Good night." She slipped out from under Nick's arm.

"Sleep well," Felix offered.

"Good night, Jenna," Nick said. She nodded, and he watched Felix watch his sister as she headed toward her bedroom. When her door shut behind her, he rounded on his neighbor. "What the hell, man?" He wanted to know just what Felix thought he was doing, steering the conversation towards Jenna's breakup. "I wasn't born yesterday, you know. She did *not* need to talk about that. What are you after?"

"Nothing." Felix sighed and ran a hand through his hair. "I'm sorry. She looked like she was about to fall apart, and I just wanted to help. Sometimes it helps to talk about it." He twisted his lips. "I've had some experience with trauma."

"Yeah, and sometimes it doesn't help. It's too fucking soon." Nick wanted to smack the guy, or maybe kiss him, and for a second, he couldn't decide which one to choose, but then he let out a breath and sat down. "Shit." He massaged the back of his neck. "You're lucky I like you." He rubbed his eyes, suddenly exhausted. He knew that Jenna's ex was going to show up again, and he knew the bastard would probably be nursing a grudge. He shouldn't have punched him, but at the time, it was all Nick could think of to do to keep Quincy from attacking his sister. And Felix had no idea what he'd walked into, just by coming over. He needed to go home, and get far away from the mess Nick was here to extricate his sister from. "Fuck." *I don't want him to leave.*

"I'm sorry," Felix said again.

"No, no. It's fine." Nick opened his eyes. Felix sat on the stool, looking completely at ease. Nick frowned, but then he caught the barest flicker of regret flash over Felix's expression. *Damn. The man has an insane amount of self-control.*

"I should go," Felix said, jerking a thumb at the front door.

"No." Nick said, even as he wondered what the hell he was doing. He did *not* need to feed this damn crush. And Felix did *not* need to get caught up in his drama. He walked back over and sat down again.

"No?" Felix raised an eyebrow, looking impossibly sexy.

Dammit. I'm so fucking screwed. "No." Nick nodded towards Felix's plate as if he wasn't at war with himself. He knew he should check on Jenna, but instead, he sat there, looking at Felix like some lovesick puppy. Nick wanted him to stay. Hell, he just plain wanted the man. Felix leaned his elbows on the counter, and muscles flexed in his biceps. Nick swallowed, eyes riveted. "Finish your pizza," he forced out, too distracted to say more. When Felix pushed the plate away from him, Nick exhaled, focusing on relaxing the muscles that the conversation with his sister had tightened.

"She's going to be okay, you know." Felix's light hazel eyes steadily watched him.

Is he comforting me? What the hell? Nick took a moment before replying. He didn't want his voice to display his uncertainty. "You don't know that." Nick stared him down. His erection throbbed against the front of his pants. He liked the contradiction: arousal and frustration made for an interesting sensation.

Felix shrugged, breaking their stare-down. "Just saying."

Nick tilted his head. "Do you have a sister?"

"No." Felix stood up.

Nick didn't stop him this time. "A brother?"

"No."

Nick sat back in his chair and crossed his arms over his chest as frustration slowly won out over arousal. What the hell did Felix know about his situation? Absolutely nothing. "Then you don't know dick about my sister and her ex."

Felix stepped closer to him, making Nick crane his neck to keep eye contact. "I know that men like

Quincy Edwards have a lot of enemies." He put a hand on the table and leaned in. "And men with enemies tend to die young."

Nick froze as Felix's soft tone went right to his cock, chasing his anger away with an irrational surge of heat. Felix stood close enough that Nick could feel Felix's body heat on his skin. He stood close enough to kiss. All Nick had to do was lean up and—

Felix straightened up. "I'll be seeing you around," he said, and then he headed to the front door.

"Shit," Nick muttered, watching him go. He couldn't think straight. His cock pushed against his jeans again, thick and annoying. The scent of pizza lingered in the air. It wasn't until Felix closed the door behind him that Nick realized what bothered him about what the man had said.

I never told him the name of Jenna's ex-boyfriend.

Chapter Five

"Fuck." Felix pushed into his house. He'd realized almost immediately that he'd screwed up. Nick had never told him Quincy's full name. Felix shouldn't know it. He shouldn't have said it out loud. "Fuck!" He threw his keys down on the chair near the front door, and leaned back against the thick wood. He felt hot. Uncomfortable. To add to his anger, his dick had been half-hard the entire time he'd been at Nick's house, and it wasn't because he was attracted to Jenna. No. It was Nick. He couldn't forget the way the man had taken down Edwards with one punch.

"Fuck," he said again, more quietly this time. He liked the guy. And he might have to kill him to cover his tracks. And what was with the arousal? He'd been straight his entire life, and had no intention of changing sexual orientation now. He pressed his fist against his cock, hard, hoping the pain would help. It didn't. All it did was fucking hurt.

Felix cursed again, scrubbing a hand across his face. He headed to the window that faced Nick's place, and looked out. Another SUV had pulled into the driveway. He frowned, and then froze when Quincy Edwards got out of the driver's seat. When four more goons exited the vehicle, he knew he had a bigger fucking problem than his persistent hard-on. The moment Edwards kicked in Nick's front door, Felix headed for the cabinet next to the sofa. Crouching down, he grabbed his go-bag and the duffel with his emergency weapons. Felix shouldered the bag, unzipped the duffel, and grabbed his shotgun. He set it down with extra shells on the coffee table in his living room. Hurrying outside before he could question his motives, he stuffed the rest of his equipment in the truck he'd parked in front of the garage. When he glanced over at Nick's place, he saw no sign of Edwards or his men.

"Shit. They're inside." Felix retrieved his shotgun, and then headed for the back door. When he stepped out into his back yard, faint gunshots sounded across the property border. "This is a bad idea," he murmured, even as he slipped between the forsythia hedges that grew along the perimeter of Nick's rental. He crouched down, grateful that it was nearly full dark. He slowly made his way to the back door, then eased it open. One of Edwards's thugs stood in the kitchen with his back to the door like a fucking idiot. Felix didn't hesitate. He rushed in and punched his favorite knife between the man's ribs several times. The guy choked as he fell, but Felix was already moving past him.

He ran into Jenna in the hallway. She had blood on her face. "Get behind me," he rasped, grabbing her arm. She stared at him, eyes wild, and he growled. "Get a hold of yourself. There's no time for hysterics." He pushed her behind his back as he slid his blade back into its sheath at his waist. "Where's Nick?"

"My bedroom," Jenna said, voice shaking. "What are you doing here?"

"Good fucking question," Felix said, angrier at himself than at her. His contract was now screwed up beyond all belief. He might as well paint a goddamn sign on his forehead that read: fuck me sideways. No way he could claim the kill, even if he took down Edwards. Clients paid for quiet, simple removal, not messy shootouts in suburban neighborhoods. He mentally kissed the money goodbye, and slid along the wall to the bedroom. He knew there were at least three other men in the house besides Edwards.

"Nick told me to run," Jenna said, hand twisted in Felix's shirt.

"And we will, just as soon as I get him out of there," he said to her. He eased up to the bedroom, then pulled her hand free. "Stay right here. There are three left, along with your ex."

Jenna nodded, pressing herself against the wall. Felix crouched down again and rolled into the room. One shot took down the man in the corner. The next one took down the thug near the window. Grapeshot flared past the body, but the crash of glass barely registered as Felix watched Nick twist and snap the neck of the goon holding a pistol to his head. The man collapsed, and Nick handily caught the guy's weapon as the guy slid down, bringing it up and aiming at Felix.

"Whoa, easy," Felix said, lifting his shotgun to the side. Nick's hair stood on end. Gunshots littered the wall behind him.

Nick glared at Felix. "What the fuck are you doing here?" He held his purloined weapon steady. Felix knew one wrong move meant death. He could see it in Nick's gaze, and damned if that didn't turn him on. This was a man who wasn't a stranger to violence. "Talk fast," Nick said.

"I'm here to help." Felix nodded to the men he'd killed. He watched Nick glance at the bodies. "I heard gunshots. I came in through the back door."

Nick inhaled sharply, then lowered his gun. "He tried to kill my sister, God only knows why. The vindictive bastard went out the bathroom window." He ran a hand through his hair, messing it further. "Fuck." His gaze lifted, pinning Felix in place. "How the fuck do you know Quincy's full name? I didn't tell you. And what's with the bullshit over your last name? I know you didn't tell the cop Zamaro," Nick spit out.

Felix made a decision that he hoped wouldn't come back to bite him in the ass. "I accepted a contract on Quincy Edwards. And yes, you're right about my last name. I don't give cops my real name. However, I gave it to you."

Nick's eyes narrowed.

Interesting. He knows exactly what I mean by that. Felix watched Nick's body language. Surprisingly, Nick didn't tense up.

"Obviously, the job is blown to shit, right now," Felix added, strangely sanguine about the entire clusterfuck.

"Why should I trust you?" Swinging the pistol down to point at the floor, Nick nodded to the bodies on the ground. "Clearly, you have anger management issues."

Felix bit back a smile as he shrugged. "You're not dead, are you?" He watched Nick's hands. The body always gave away the next move. He didn't want to hurt Nick, and the best way to ensure that he wouldn't have to was to head off any unfortunate outburst before it happened.

Fortunately, Nick merely snorted as he flicked the safety on the gun. "I have good instincts about people." He shoved the weapon into the waistband of his jeans. "Don't prove me wrong."

"I'm not going to shoot you in your sleep, Nick." Felix relaxed his arms, bringing the shotgun around. He ejected the hulls and pocketed them. "Jenna's in the hall."

Nick scowled. "I told her to go out the back."

"There was a man in the kitchen. She had no safe egress."

After a moment, Nick grunted. "Fair enough."

Felix wasn't surprised when Nick opened the closet and extracted a large bag. Whatever Nick did for a living, it sure as shit wasn't just web design, because that looked like a go-bag to him.

"We need to move. This house is compromised," Felix said. His instincts told him they had minutes, not hours, to get the hell out of here.

"We?" Nick lifted an eyebrow. He unzipped the outer compartment on his duffel and shoved the pistol inside.

Felix nodded. "I have a safe house."

Nick tilted his head. "There's help, and then there's *help*. What am I going to owe you if we go with you? You don't strike me as the kind of guy who does favors for free."

Felix pursed his lips. "We can discuss that later." Truth was, he didn't want Nick to feel like he owed him anything, and that was enough of a departure from his regular modus operandi that he wasn't feeling too confident about his decision to fuck the contract all to hell. "Shit." He sighed. "Let's just agree that you owe me one and leave it at that."

"Uh-uh. Not a chance." Nick scanned the room, then crouched down by the man whose neck he'd snapped. He rifled through the goon's pockets. "No ID."

"Not surprising. Edwards has a lot of unsavory colleagues." Felix quickly searched the other two bodies. "Nothing here either."

"Whatever. Let's move," Nick said, heading for the doorway. He paused, looking back at Felix. "I'll owe you one, but I get to decide on the value of the favor."

Felix frowned, but then he nodded, short and sharp. He'd already decided not to collect. Nick's condition on the agreement didn't mean a damn thing to him. He didn't need money. He already intended to retire soon, so he didn't need help with any business. There was literally nothing Nick had that Felix wanted.

Except an explanation for why I'm suddenly so

fucking desperate for his frigging company, Felix thought, abruptly frustrated with himself.

"Hey."

Felix stood up from his crouch. "What?"

"Thanks," Nick said quietly. "That was a shit situation."

Felix stared at him for a long moment. "Yeah, it was. Why aren't you more upset about it?" He already knew Nick wasn't the upright citizen he pretended to be, but he wanted to see what the man said when directly confronted with that fact.

"Because you're not the only man in this room with a few unusual and not necessarily legal extracurricular talents," Nick replied, and then he slipped into the hallway.

****

Nick found Jenna sitting on the floor, knees drawn up and arms wrapped around her legs. "Hey, it's okay." He crouched down. "You're okay, sis."

Jenna hurled herself into his arms. "Oh my God, Nick! He could've killed you." She pushed her wet cheeks into his shoulder.

"But he didn't. I'm fine." Nick ran a hand down her hair, wishing he could take away her fear. He'd never expected Quincy to follow them here with a bunch of goons. He cursed himself for not doing any research on the guy. If he had, he'd have found out that her ex wasn't just a run of the mill dick-wad.

"I'm sorry," Jenna sobbed.

"Shh. I'm fine. We need to get out of here, though." He wondered what she'd think when she discovered he'd agreed to let Felix take them to his hideout. He barely knew the guy. *And he kills people entirely too easily,* Nick thought, remembering the boom of Felix's shotgun. *Not that I'm much better.* He grimaced as he recalled how easy it had been to snap the neck of the thug who'd held him at gunpoint. *I don't really have a leg to stand on when it comes to killing, do I?*

"Where are we going to go?" Jenna leaned back, wiping her face. "I have no money. I have nowhere to go." Her tone grew increasingly hysterical.

"Hey, hey, I've got you, and I have a plan," Nick said, urging her to her feet. "It's going to work out."

"You don't know that," she said, voice shaking.

"I do know that." Nick glanced back at the bedroom. Felix stood in the doorway. When he caught Nick's gaze, he nodded towards the back of the house. "Okay. We're going to go with Felix, now. Do you have anything you need to grab?" Nick asked his sister.

"Wait, what? Felix?" She whipped her head around. "We don't even know him!"

"I have an off the grid cabin," Felix said softly, walking closer.

Jenna stared at him. "Why should we trust you?" she asked, uncannily echoing Nick's question of a few minutes ago.

"Because he helped us, and he doesn't work for your ex," Nick said, trying to head off any further questions. He didn't have any answers for her, but their options right now were limited. In survival mode, you went with gut instincts more often than not, and his gut told him to go with Felix. "Do you need to gather anything before we go?" he asked his sister again.

She shook her head. "I put some clothes and stuff in the duffel earlier, like you told me to." She plucked at the bag Nick had slung over his shoulder. "And you said I couldn't take my phone, so…" She shrugged, eyes welling up. "This sucks."

"It's temporary. A few days or weeks from now

you'll wake up and the world will make sense again," Felix said, walking down the hall.

Nick raised his eyebrows at Felix, but the man didn't elaborate as he passed them.

"What does *he* know?" Jenna muttered. "He's not being attacked by an insane ex."

"It doesn't matter what he knows or not," Nick told her, guiding her towards the kitchen. "He's got a place, and we need out of here, like, yesterday." He inhaled. "And I trust him."

Jenna nodded, letting him tow her past the body in the kitchen. "Oh, God," she said, staring fixedly at the blood on the floor.

"Don't look." Nick pushed open the back door and hustled her down the steps. Felix waited for them near the hedges bordering the backyard.

"Too late," Jenna said, shoulders hunched. "I knew Q was crazy, but I didn't think he'd try to kill me. My God."

"Freak out later when there's time and space for it. Right now, we need to move, sis," Nick said, tucking his fingers around her elbow. He hustled her across the yard, wishing he didn't have to drag her out again, but they had no choice. God only knew where the hell Quincy had taken himself off to, the asshole.

When they reached Felix, he pulled them through the forsythia and pointed to the far side of his house. "We'll go around that side. I parked in front of my garage."

"You sure about this?" Nick asked, grabbing Felix's arm before he could lope away. "We don't want to rain on your parade, so to speak." He thought about Felix's contract on Quincy, and decided then and there to not mention it to his sister if he could manage it. She'd never trust Felix if she knew what he did for a living.

And she'd never trust me again, either, if she knew I'd been lying to her about my job. God help me if she finds out what I really do.

"Positive." Felix smiled slightly. "My parade was already cancelled due to rain."

Nick smiled back at him, surprising himself. "The contract?"

Felix nodded, then shrugged. "I was getting bored with my life, anyway. It's time to shake things up a bit."

"What are you guys talking about?" Jenna asked.

Nick tucked his sister under his arm. He could feel her trembling, and a stab of guilt shot through him for joking around with Felix. "Felix has a few unusual talents that can help us, that's all." He urged her across Felix's yard. Dew from the grass wet the bottom of his pants, but he barely noticed. "Let's get going. We can talk about it later." He aimed a look at Felix with those words.

Felix nodded. "Yes." He unlocked the door of his truck, and Nick helped his sister into the backseat. "Duck down, so no one can see you," he told her.

She nodded, stretching out on the seat. "I'm sorry. I don't mean to be such a pain in the ass."

"You're not a pain in the ass. You're my sister. That's worse." Nick smiled when she snorted, and then he covered her with the quilt he found on the seat. "Just relax. You're safe." He kissed her forehead, willing her to calm down and let him take care of her for once.

She pulled the blanket up over her shoulders. "Cold."

"She's in shock," Felix said quietly from the front seat.

Nick sighed, knowing Felix was right. "Try and sleep, Jenna," he said, dropping his go-bag on the floor. He tucked the quilt up around her neck. She smiled tremulously at him, then closed her eyes.

"We need to hurry," Felix said, scanning the perimeter. "Won't be long before Edwards sends more men here. Vindictive bastard. I can't imagine that killing his ex-girlfriend is a sanctioned hit in the circles he runs in."

"Yeah, I don't think so either. He's just a bitter sonofabitch. Can't stand to let a woman get the best of him." Nick climbed into the passenger side, and buckled up, then gave Felix a hard stare. "You'd better not be screwing with me," he said in a low voice.

It didn't matter how hot the guy was, he couldn't afford to think with his dick right now. He was trusting Felix with his sister's life. He pressed his lips together before he could say anymore. He thought about the knife he'd tucked into his pocket, and the gun in his waistband, but after seeing the way Felix dispatched those men with a freaking shotgun, he wasn't so sure going head to head with the guy was the way to play this situation. If Felix's offer to help went pear shaped, he'd have to get Jenna out of there quietly. He nodded. Direct confrontation wasn't his favorite option, anyway.

"Trust me," Felix said, as if he could read Nick's mind. He pulled his seatbelt on. "I'm not screwing with you."

"Trust, huh?" Nick exhaled. "Not an easy thing to do, man." He glanced back over his shoulder. His sister looked exhausted. Dark circles ringed her eyes.

"I know." Felix started the truck. "We'll be driving for a while. Get comfortable."

"What, you want me to take off my shoes? Prop my feet on the dash?" Nick couldn't help the snark. Tension thrummed through him like electricity in a livewire.

Felix just smiled as he drove down the street.

"Fuck." Nick rubbed his eyes, letting the smile slide from his face. "This situation is bullshit." He noticed that Felix hadn't put on his headlights, despite the darkening shadows.

"Yeah, but at least I'm not bored anymore," Felix said a few minutes later. He'd just pulled onto the interstate, and they were headed north. His wry tone had Nick laughing out loud despite himself.

"That's good? Not being bored?" Nick asked, thinking about his life the past few years. "I could use a little boredom right about now." Hell, if he could retire tomorrow, he would.

"Not being bored is good," Felix assured him, flicking on the headlights after they'd driven a few miles. "Boredom leads to sloppiness. Sloppiness leads to death."

"You sound like a pessimistic Yoda," Nick said. He shook his head and twisted around. His sister was out, head lolling to the side with the rhythm of the vehicle. He looked out the rear window, watching the other cars on the road. "I don't see anyone tailing us. Good call with the lights, earlier."

"I would've taken a different route if we'd been tailed," Felix said, giving him a sardonic look. "This isn't my first rodeo."

No shit. As if that weren't completely obvious, Nick thought, but he didn't say it out loud. He wasn't sure he wanted to know the nitty gritty details of Felix's profession. *Bullshit. You already know he's not an upstanding citizen,* a little voice in the back of his head whispered. The image of the bodies on the floor of his rental house floated to the front of his skull. He wasn't squeamish, but damn. That was a lot of carnage. "Why the shotgun?" he asked, before he could wrestle his curiosity into silence.

Felix glanced at him, and then shrugged. "It's a very common weapon. Everyone and their mother has a shotgun, especially in this area." He checked his rearview mirror, then slowly sped up, shifting into the fast lane of the interstate. "Bears, you know."

"Bears," Nick repeated, then he laughed out loud. Felix had a point. North Jersey had one of the highest black bear densities in the country. "There's no way they're going to think a bear broke into the house."

"Doesn't matter. The cops won't be able to trace anything. There are a million and one Remington Wingmasters just in the Mid-Atlantic states. No one is going to be able to track the shotgun I used in your house to us."

Nick nodded reluctantly. Felix knew his shit. They drove in silence for the next few hours, and then Felix took an exit that led into the Catskills. Rolling mountain roads gave way to a dirt track.

Feels like the forest just swallowed us whole, Nick thought, squinting as he tried to see through the trees on either side.

"Don't even bother. There are thousands of acres of nothing around us," Felix said, once again reading Nick's mind. "My cabin isn't much further."

"You'd better not be a serial killer," Nick joked, feeling the exhaustion of the day and the fight finally catching up to him. *Even if he is a killer, I'm not sure I care. I just want a place to fucking sleep at this point.*

Felix turned an expressionless face to him. "Depends on the definition of serial."

Nick stared at him, and then his lips twitched into a grin as he caught the almost invisible smirk in Felix's gaze. "Ha. Funny." *The man is a contract killer, you idiot. Technically, that could be defined as being a serial killer,* he thought, amused.

"I get your worry. You can't be too picky about your friends," Felix said, smiling.

Nick shook his head. "I'm not that picky. As long as you brush your teeth regularly, wear deodorant, and don't fart inside a nice restaurant, I'm good." He saw Felix's surprise, and smiled wider. "And I'm too fucking tired to fake being straight any longer." He sighed, running his hand through his hair. "Damn. I need sleep."

"I already knew you weren't straight," Felix said, slowing the truck. He turned onto an almost not-there path, and Nick gripped the oh-shit bar above the window so he wouldn't get thrown off the seat. "What are you faking?"

"Clearly, not much," Nick muttered, feeling almost punch drunk with weariness at this point. He didn't care if flirting made Felix uncomfortable. His don't-tease-the-straight-boys rule was long gone—buried under his fuck-it, you-only-live-once exhaustion. "What about you, then? Do *you* know you're not straight?" he asked provocatively, but before Felix could answer, Jenna woke up.

"Are we almost there?" she asked before Felix could respond. Her voice sounded rough. "Ugh. I need to sit up."

Nick turned around, vaguely disappointed. There was no way Felix could answer his question now. "Yeah, we're almost there, sis." He looked at Felix. The man gave no indication that Nick's flirting had cracked his composed exterior. *The man's a robot. Jesus. Isn't he tired?*

"You can sit up, now," Felix said quietly, interrupting Nick's internal griping. "We're almost there. In five more minutes you'll be able to stretch out in an actual bed."

"Oh, thank God," Jenna said, pushing off the

quilt. It fell to the floor as the truck lurched, and she grabbed for the seat in front of her. "Good lord, is this even a road?"

"It's enough of a road for my needs." Felix slowed the truck. "The harder it is to find and drive on, the harder it is for anyone to track me here."

"Huh. Good point," Jenna said, reaching for her seatbelt. Before she could get it on, Felix pulled to a stop.

Nick frowned. He couldn't see a cabin. Hell, he couldn't see fuck-all. "Where in the wilderness are we, Daniel Boone?"

Felix snorted. "Look to your right."

Nick squinted out the window. Nestled in the trees was a dark blob. "That's a cabin?" He opened the door and stepped out of the truck. A chorus of crickets and frogs greeted him. He swatted at a mosquito that buzzed near his ear. "Jesus. This is horror movie territory." He stretched his aching muscles. "I hope to God you have some kind of plumbing."

"Don't worry, the cabin has solar and a bank of batteries. I supplement with a small wind turbine. There's a well, and even a toilet," Felix said, a hint of amusement in his voice. "Come on." He got out of the truck and helped Jenna down from the rear seat. He clicked on a small flashlight and led the way along an overgrown path to the front door. Nick followed him, staying close to his sister.

"You sure about this guy?" she whispered to Nick.

Nick watched Felix unlock the heavy wooden door. When the man glanced back at them, a hint of uncertainty flashed across his face. Nick's instincts, honed over years of survival on the streets, buzzed. Felix was a killer, yes, but he was also a man dying of loneliness.

"Yeah. I'm sure," he told her, voice hoarse with the sudden arousal he couldn't seem to suppress. Nothing seemed to touch it: not worry for his sister's life, not the man whose neck he'd broken, and not the mad dash into the unknown with a guy who wasn't shy about blowing people to bits when the situation warranted it.

"I hope you're right. Because there's no going back now," Jenna said, squeezing his arm. "We're in the middle of nowhere."

Nick nodded slowly. "I know," he told her, leading her up the stairs. *We may be in the middle of nowhere, but I don't want to go back. I want to dive in deeper.*

Chapter Six

Felix opened up the cabin, grateful he'd visited it a few weeks ago and stocked it up with supplies. They had plenty of food, water, and warmth, and that was all that they needed for now. "There are two bedrooms upstairs, that way." He pointed across the living space to the stairs as he flicked on the light switches, then checked the security panel installed next to the door. It hadn't registered any attempted break-ins, not that he'd expected otherwise. He'd have been alerted via text if there'd been any problem.

"Wow," Jenna said, stopping just inside the door.

Felix glanced at her, strangely pleased at the expression of surprise on her face. He'd never brought anyone here before, and hadn't really ever thought about what it might look like to someone else. He'd built it for comfort. He'd built it for himself. He rented houses all up and down the east coast to live in, six months at a time, but this cabin had been his safe house for several years. He wasn't looking forward to abandoning it when he headed west, but he supposed he could always build another one in Oregon or some other western state.

"Make yourself at home," he said, not wanting to dwell too closely on why he'd suddenly broken his self-imposed isolation. He headed for the kitchen, wanting to check the freezer. All the food was still frozen, not that he'd expected anything else. He checked the plumbing next, nodding when he heard the pump click on as he ran the faucet. Everything seemed to be in working order.

"You can take the first bedroom upstairs," he told Jenna. "The guest bathroom is across the hall from the bedroom." He glanced at Nick as Jenna nodded and headed up to the loft. "We'll have to share the other room, unless you want to bunk with your sister." He lifted a shoulder. "The guest bedroom only has a full-sized bed, though. You'll end up on the floor if you stay in her room."

Nick made a face. "I can sleep on the sofa." He walked further into the large room, then dropped his heavy duffel next to the coffee table. He poked a finger at the old leather cushion slumped down against the wooden frame of the sofa.

Felix shrugged. "Whatever you want." He locked the door and threw the bolt. "I don't mind sharing." He gestured to the sofa. "The sofa is old and lumpy. I've been meaning to buy a new one."

Nick gave him an odd look, then headed for the stairs. "I'll take a look." He disappeared up the stairs.

Felix ran a hand over his face. What the fuck was he doing? Did he really want to share a bed with a complete stranger? *Yes,* a small voice in the back of his head told him. His cock lay thick and heavy against the front placket of his pants. He wasn't quite hard, but he also wasn't quite soft. The fight and the flight out of town had been the most excitement he'd had in months. Years of killing for a living seemed to have degraded his sense of ... what? Fear? Excitement? He had no fucking clue, except for some reason, since meeting Nick, he felt alive again.

"Maybe I should get out of the assassination business and try protection for a while," he muttered, imagining the complicated mess of trying to keep someone alive instead of dead. The puzzle of it appealed to him. How to protect someone without getting killed? Without getting caught? He pressed his fist against his dick, enjoying the way he hardened into a full erection. *Interesting.*

"Your bed is enormous," Nick said from the loft landing, startling him out of his self-pleasure.

Felix smiled up at him. "Yeah. I don't like being confined."

"I can tell," Nick said, hands on his hips. "So, I'm officially taking you up on your offer. We'll share the bed." Nick disappeared back into Felix's bedroom.

Felix smirked. He knew his king-sized mattress would appeal to Nick. Somehow, he had the feeling that the other man enjoyed the finer things in life. And Felix had more than enough money to provide them. He grabbed Nick's duffel and headed up the stairs.

"Jesus Christ, are these silk sheets?" Nick was sitting on the bed, one hand tucked underneath the duvet.

"No. Fifteen hundred thread count Egyptian cotton." Felix set the bag down near the dresser.

"Expensive sheets and a pickup truck." Nick lifted an eyebrow. "You are a hell of a contradiction, my friend."

"Nick, I'm going to go to bed," Jenna said from the doorway.

Felix turned, smiling when he saw her in an oversized Wonder Woman t-shirt. *At least she hasn't completely lost her sense of self,* he mused.

"Sleep tight," Nick said, walking over to her and hugging her. "Everything's going to be okay, Jenna."

She shook her head, glancing at Felix. "Is there anything I should be worried about? Should I lock the windows or something?" She held onto her brother tightly for a moment, and then she stepped back. "I mean, it looks like we're in the middle of nowhere, but it was dark when we got here."

"You can sleep easy. No one knows about this property, and I have a security system set up. No one can get in without my knowing about it," Felix assured her.

She stared at him for a moment, the worry clear in her gaze, and then she nodded. "Okay. Because I have a feeling I'm going to be unconscious in like, five minutes. I'm so freaking tired." She rubbed the back of her neck.

Felix smiled at her, willing her to trust him. "You are safe here. I promise."

After another searching look, Jenna sighed. "It's not like I have a choice."

Felix frowned, trying to understand her wariness. *She's vulnerable, and she doesn't know me. She doesn't know that I don't kill innocents. She doesn't know that I kill people at all.*

"I'll walk you to bed," Nick said, slinging an arm around her shoulders. "I want to check out the room." He gave Felix a look that said, *Let me handle this.*

Felix nodded slightly, hoping that Nick understood that he meant no harm.

Jenna ran a hand over her face. "Okay." She yawned. "You going to tuck me in, too?"

Nick rolled his eyes. "God forbid." They headed out of the bedroom.

Felix sighed, then strode to the master bathroom and shut the door behind him. "What the fuck are you doing?" he asked himself in the mirror. Tired hazel eyes stared back at him accusingly, and he snorted and turned on the water. His erection hadn't subsided one bit. He washed his face in ice cold water, but it didn't help. No way was he sleeping anytime soon.

****

Four hours later, the soft sounds of Nick's slow breathing sounded in Felix's head like a metronome of doom. "Fuck," he whispered, not for the first time. He'd already been to the bathroom twice, once to take a piss, and once to try to deal with the arousal that seemed to simmer along his nerves. He'd jacked off fast and furious, but almost as soon as he'd climbed back into bed, his erection had returned. He'd give it five more minutes, and then if he couldn't fall asleep, he'd go outside and walk the perimeter. At least he could do something useful with this excess energy.

"Can't sleep?" Nick murmured, rolling over.

Felix grunted. What the fuck was wrong with him? Just the sound of Nick's low, sleepy voice sparked another surge of heat.

"Still trying to convince yourself that you're straight?" Nick asked, sounding more awake.

Felix frowned, head turning towards Nick. "What the hell are you talking about?"

Nick sighed, pushing the covers down to his waist. "I've seen you looking at me."

Felix sat up and swung his legs over the side of the bed. "I'm going out to walk the perimeter."

Before he could stand up, Nick's hand landed on his shoulder. "No, you're not." His voice was low and soft. Unthreatening.

Felix's muscles tightened anyway. Nick's hand was warm and heavy. His training told him that he could grab Nick's wrist and break his elbow, or twist him around and rip out his throat, but the strange tension flaring through his body wouldn't let him move. "You don't want to do this, Nick," he said, gritting his teeth.

"Do what?" Nick pulled him back down to the mattress. "Touch you? Make you feel good?" He pressed Felix's wrists down, hard.

Felix flexed his biceps. In the dark, Nick was a dark shape looming over him. Instead of fear, or anger, Felix's emotions jumped wildly from arousal to confusion. "I could break your neck."

"That knowledge just makes it sweeter," Nick murmured.

"Makes what sweeter?" Felix asked, voice raspy.

He couldn't seem to breathe right. *Is this a panic attack?* he asked himself. He'd never experienced anything like this. His entire life had been a systematic observation of facts and rational decisions. Nothing much bothered him—not killing, not violence, not sex. Boredom was a problem, but he certainly wasn't fucking bored at the moment. *I'm screwed,* he thought, still not throwing Nick's ass to the floor.

"This," Nick said, leaning down and kissing the side of Felix's jaw. "Jesus, you smell good."

Felix flexed his arms, pushing up against Nick. "Stop. You know I'm straight."

"Make me." Nick moved his lips down Felix's shoulder and pressed his lips to the crook of his elbow.

Felix froze. He couldn't breathe. Couldn't think.

"You're not straight, and you don't want me to stop, Felix," Nick said, and then he bit the soft skin of his arm.

Felix groaned. Just that one sharp touch brought him right to the edge. "Fuck." His hips strained upwards as his balls drew into his body. His cock hurt.

"No, no fucking yet. Tonight, I'm going to blow you." Nick shoved down Felix's sweatpants and took his cock in his hand. "I can't wait to suck you off. I bet you'll try and keep quiet. I bet I can make you come so hard you won't know where you are anymore."

"Jesus Christ." Felix gripped the sheets. He'd never wanted a mouth on his dick so bad before. Nick's *voice* had him shaking. "What the hell are you doing to me?"

Nick chuckled. "I'm not doing anything yet." He leaned in and blew along Felix's erection. "This isn't just about me, straight boy. This is about you. You've suppressed your sexuality for so long that you don't have a damn clue about what you like and don't like. You've been fucking the wrong gender your whole life."

"Screw you. I've been straight for decades. I've fucked plenty of women," Felix ground out, not wanting to admit how hot Nick's touch made him. *You're going to eat your words,* a small voice in the back of his head told him.

Nick slid his thumb over the top of Felix's erection and rubbed the pre-cum welling from the tip in a tight circle. "And every one of those women left you empty. Missing something. I bet you haven't even bothered to pick someone up for the past few years. You haven't hooked up with anyone lately, have you?"

Felix shuddered, but didn't reply. Nick was right. He hadn't even attempted to get laid recently. Why bother? The women always wanted more from him than he was willing to give, and the rote mechanics of sex bored him lately. "Just get on with it," he grated out, not in the mood for a psychoanalytical mind-fuck at the moment.

Nick laughed. "Oh no, my friend. My blowjobs are works of art. I am going to go slow, and I am going to drive you out of your fucking mind." He leaned down and licked a stripe up the length of Felix's dick. Nick's gunshot wound didn't seem to be holding him back from being aggressive in bed. Felix liked that. *He's a badass. Of course I like that*, he thought, still somewhat dazed by the intensity of his arousal for Nick.

Felix growled, hands twisting in the sheets. He waited for Nick to slip him inside his mouth, but Nick scooted down further and began to suck his balls. "What the hell are you doing?" He grabbed Nick by the hair and tried to move him away. No one had ever touched him there before.

Nick let him pull him up, but then he dug his fingers into Felix's wrists, hitting the nerve points. Felix released him, not because of the searing pain, but because he didn't want to fight. He wanted Nick's mouth on his cock. Instead of obliging, Nick immediately pinned his hands to the mattress.

"Oh, no you don't," Nick muttered, and put his mouth on the delicate skin behind Felix's ball sac.

Felix squirmed. He could break free of Nick's hold if he wanted to, and he knew that Nick knew it. The man wasn't even holding him down very hard anymore. "Fuck, Nick." He closed his eyes and inhaled, striving for calm. It was no use. Nick moved further down, pushing Felix's legs open wide. The moment his tongue touched his asshole, Felix bucked. "Jesus!"

Nick grabbed his thighs and held on. "I'm just getting started, Felix."

Felix threw an arm over his face. He'd never in his life felt such pleasure. He'd never fucking *wanted* to feel like this. A cascade of lukewarm sexual encounters flitted through his mind, and he gritted his teeth. How the hell had he been so fucking clueless? He was fucking forty-five years old, for fuck's sake. He reached down, desperate to touch himself, but Nick somehow intercepted his hands.

"No. Keep your hands away from your cock. I'm not done yet," Nick said, and then he went back to tonguing Felix's hole.

Felix groaned, and then suddenly, Nick moved up and sucked the tip of his erection into his mouth. Felix sucked in a hard breath, hips jerking. He was right on the edge of orgasm, but then Nick wrapped tight fingers around the base of his dick. "Not yet."

Felix grabbed Nick by the hair again. "Stop fucking around."

Nick smiled at him, and then he deliberately slid a slick finger into Felix's ass. Felix gasped, going completely still. "What the fuck are you doing?" He tried to sound angry, but his words came out more like an astonished whisper. His face heated, with embarrassment or arousal, or some sick combination of the two.

"I'm making you lose your goddamn mind," Nick replied, adding another slick finger.

Felix didn't know where the hell Nick had found the lube, or if he was just using spit, and he didn't care. "Christ," he moaned when Nick began sliding his fingers in and out. "Why the hell does that feel so good?"

"Just wait," Nick said, and Felix frowned, but then the fingers hit something like an electric wire in his body and his entire nervous system lit up like a damned Christmas tree. Felix bucked despite his resolve to be calm.

Fuck me, Felix thought, mostly incoherent, and then Nick sucked his cock back into his mouth, blowing him completely away. Felix's dick swelled harder. Nick's fingers relentlessly pressed on the spot inside his body as his mouth worked Felix's erection, and suddenly it was all over. Felix flexed his spine as his orgasm hit him like a fucking train. His mind whited out as pleasure rushed through him. His cock jerked as his toes curled and his hands made fists around the sheets. He couldn't do a damned thing except thrust into Nick's mouth until his body gave up trying to turn itself inside out.

A long time later, he felt Nick easing his fingers out. Felix forced his eyes open. The middle of the night darkness kept him from seeing Nick's expression, but the lack of spunk all over the fucking place told him that the man had swallowed every last drop. "Fuck," he muttered, strangely aroused by the thought. The shock he heard in his voice had him clamping his mouth shut before he could say anything else.

"Yeah, fucking sounds good," Nick said, a hint of

amusement coloring his voice. "Maybe we can try that tomorrow." He slid up next to Felix with his boxers pushed down. Felix could feel Nick jacking himself. "I'd love it if you fucked me," Nick added.

"Jesus Christ," Felix heard himself say, mentally imagining himself pounding into Nick's hole. He shuddered, and then roughly shoved Nick's hands aside. He cupped Nick's dick, and then started stroking him the same way he did it to himself. Nick's erection felt hard and hot and silky smooth. He leaned over the man, pressing him down onto the bed with his body. If his cock would cooperate, he'd fuck Nick right now, but he was completely spent. He opened his mouth and bit down on Nick's shoulder. Felix wanted to hurt him, and arouse him, and everything in between. *I'm losing my mind,* he thought, mind racing over all of the pointless, lukewarm sex he'd experienced for the past several decades. *How did I not know this about myself?*

"Oh God, yeah," Nick groaned, startling him out of his thoughts. "Just like that." His hips started moving. Sweat slicked his torso.

Felix closed his eyes and mentally kissed his heterosexuality goodbye. Nick writhing beneath his hands was the hottest thing he'd ever experienced. Felix rolled over until he was completely on top of him, still stroking his cock, and then he kissed him. Nick opened to him immediately, moaning into his mouth. Felix seized the opportunity and bit Nick's lower lip. His cock twitched against Nick's hip, super sensitive after the ridiculous orgasm Nick had given him. Felix grunted, hands twisting around Nick's erection. "Come on, Nick. Give it up to me. I want to see you fuck my hand."

Nick groaned, and then his cock hardened and jerked. Felix stroked him through his climax, not trying to be gentle at all. Nick seemed to like the roughness. He grabbed onto Felix's shoulders and shoved his hips up through Felix's fingers.

"Aw, fuck," he finally said, collapsing back down in a boneless sprawl. His dick twitched, jetting yet more spunk into the mess between their bodies.

Felix gentled his touch, then stopped when Nick angled away.

"Hell. You're a natural," Nick said, voice breaking.

Felix rolled off him and onto his back. "Shit." He ran a hand over his face, and then flinched when he realized it was covered with Nick's jizz. "Shit."

"You've started repeating yourself," Nick said, leaning over him to grab some tissues from the box on the nightstand. "I'm good, but I didn't know I was that good." He laughed.

"Turn on the light," Felix said, needing to see Nick's face.

Nick hesitated, but then did as Felix asked.

Felix stared up at him. Nick's blue eyes had gone dark. For some reason, Felix liked the way his hair looked: wrecked. *God, I'm so fucked.*

"You all right?" Nick asked settling back down on the bed. He swiped at the mess on his stomach halfheartedly, and then tossed the damp tissues onto Felix. He pulled off his damp t-shirt and threw it down over the foot of the bed.

Felix scowled, but then used the tissues to mop up some of the stickiness gluing his body hair to his skin. "Yeah. I'm fine."

"You don't look fine."

Felix wiped his hands and tossed the tissues to the floor. "I just fucking figured out that I'm gay. Give me a goddamn break."

Nick grinned. "Maybe you're bi."

Not likely, he thought, but he wasn't in the mood to argue. Felix rolled his eyes. "Whatever. I don't fucking care."

Nick settled down, then stroked a hand down Felix's arm. "You can totally fuck me when I recover from this." He waved at his limp dick. "Tomorrow morning, hopefully." He yawned. "But now I'm going to crash."

Felix took in Nick's bare torso, and the answering spark of arousal in his core was all the confirmation he needed. "Shit."

Nick laughed as he settled in next to Felix. "You need a new swear word." He rolled partly onto his side and slid a leg over Felix's.

Felix flicked off the light. Nick's warmth felt good. He heard him yawn again, and that spurred an answering wave of tiredness. *I can figure out all this shit tomorrow,* he promised himself, closing his eyes.

Chapter Seven

"Wake up."

Felix's eyes snapped open. His cock was hard, and someone was stroking him. Instinctively, he pushed his hips up into the perfect grip even as he rolled and immobilized the man in his bed. His hands went around the guy's neck and he opened his legs, pinning him to the mattress. Sunlight streamed into the room because he'd forgotten to close the shades. He judged it to be around seven AM.

"Easy there, Felix," Nick said, a hint of amusement in his voice. His hands had stilled. "Remember me?"

Bright blue eyes looked up at him, and Felix's fuzzy brain finally jerked into gear. "Nick?"

"Yeah." Nick twisted his fingers, sending sparks of pleasure down Felix's spine.

Felix let out a harsh breath. "Christ, I could've killed you." His fingers tightened around Nick's throat. He could feel the man breathing. The power he held over Nick aroused him. Nick's hands aroused him. *I'm a sick fuck,* he thought, even as he rolled his hips, thrusting into Nick's palms. He made his fingers loosen. God forbid he accidentally strangle the man giving him pleasure.

"But you didn't kill me. At least, not yet," Nick said, hands cupping Felix's erection. "Fuck my hands."

Felix closed his eyes and rested his forehead on Nick's shoulder. "This is not how I imagined waking up." His hips pushed into Nick's grip again. And again.

"This is *exactly* how I imagined waking up," Nick replied. He let go and shoved Felix's shirt up. "Take this off. I can't believe you're still wearing it."

Felix leaned up and pulled the fabric over his head. Nick was already naked. "This what you want?"

"Oh yeah. Perfect." Nick was already pulling him back down. "Here. Like this." He lined up their cocks and stroked them together. "Come on. Fuck my hands."

Felix groaned, then did as Nick asked. He was already close to coming, and then Nick let go and grabbed his ass.

"Harder. Push down," Nick said, breathless.

Felix couldn't do a damn thing except comply. His hips jerked faster, chasing the sensation of Nick's swollen erection sliding past his. "Fuck."

"Yeah. You feel fucking fantastic, too," Nick muttered, fingers digging into Felix's ass. "So close."

Felix leaned down and kissed him savagely, hips moving faster. Nick sucked his lower lip into his mouth, then bit down. The pain shot through Felix like a bolt of lightning, and his cock swelled. "Nick," he gasped.

Nick pushed up, cock hot and wet. When he groaned, spine flexing, Felix shuddered. His orgasm came out of nowhere. He dropped his head into Nick's neck as his body took over. Heat spread between them, and he thrust, no longer able to keep a steady rhythm. His cock swelled, then softened. When Nick wrapped his arms around him, Felix finally let himself slump down, breathing much faster than he would have expected from such a simple sexual act.

"Yeah. That's what I'm talking about," Nick murmured.

Felix snorted, and rolled off of him with a supreme act of will. "I thought you were going to let me fuck you?"

"No time. Jenna will be awake in, like, five minutes." Nick grabbed the sheet and mopped them both off.

Felix flinched as Nick brushed over his cock. "Easy, there. Are you trying to break me?"

"Yeah, yeah, you're okay, stop complaining." Nick tossed the sheet to the floor. "I hope you have more bedding."

Felix rolled his eyes. "Of course. I also have this thing called a washing machine."

Nick smirked and rolled out of bed.

Felix watched Nick stride to the bathroom, distracted by his perfectly shaped ass, and then his mind reasserted control. "I'm going to take you and Jenna to a guy I know who can help."

Nick paused, just inside the doorway to the bathroom. "Help, how?"

"He can protect Jenna while we hunt her bastard ex down." Felix liked that solution. He'd fulfill his contract and help Nick out at the same time. He didn't mind cancelling the contract, but he didn't want Edwards indefinitely hanging over Nick and Jenna like a damned curse. He might as well do the job and collect the money, especially since it looked like he might be hanging out with Nick for a while. He wasn't anywhere near done exploring his newfound sexuality.

Nick pursed his lips. "So, we hunt him down. Then what?"

Felix raised his eyebrows. "You know what."

Nick tilted his head. "You're going to let me tag along with you?"

He's got a point. I've always worked alone, Felix thought, but then his mouth opened and words he'd never in a million years ever imagined he would say came out. "Yeah, you're coming with me. We nullify the problem, collect payment, and Jenna lives happily ever after without some loser ex on her tail. You got a problem with that?"

Nick shook his head slowly. "Nope."

Felix smiled, feeling strangely at peace for the

first time in years. "We leave in a half hour."

****

Nick stepped out of Felix's truck, then turned to help his sister down from the back.

"We're here?" Jenna yawned as she hopped down. "Damn. We're still in the middle of nowhere, except this time it's an abandoned warehouse graveyard instead of a forest." She glanced around. "This is some kind of cliché weirdness, isn't it? I feel like I'm walking into a bad suspense movie." She frowned. "Maybe this isn't such a good idea, Nick. They always kill people in giant warehouses, you know?"

"This isn't the movies, though. It's real life." Nick reached in to grab her bag. "Felix says this is the place." He looked around. His sister was right. Old brick warehouses with broken windows surrounded them. The faintest tang of water told him that there was a river somewhere beyond the cluster of buildings, but he had no desire to go exploring. Gang tags and trash littered the ground. Potholes pocked the asphalt, and weeds poked up through the cracks. If the sun hadn't been shining down on them, the place would probably look like something out of a dystopian movie, not a thriller, like his sister said. He rolled his shoulders, glad he'd managed to grab his favorite knife on the rush out of his rental house. He could feel it along his forearm, cool and useful. He also still had the pistol one of Q's goons had left behind. He readjusted it in the waistband of his pants, wishing he had a holster. He did *not* want to shoot off his own dick by carrying it like this for too long. *Maybe Felix's contact will have something better I can use,* he mused.

"This *is* the place. And you will keep your mouth shut about it," Felix said, locking his truck. "My contact doesn't like people knowing where he lives. Hell, I'm

89

taking a risk just bringing you here."

Jenna looked down at her feet. "I have no one to tell. And you're helping me. I would never squeal on you."

Felix's hazel eyes softened as he glanced at her. "Good."

Nick suppressed a wave of affection. He liked the way Felix treated his sister. He liked the way the man hadn't freaked out after his first gay sex. And he really fucking liked Felix's competence with nasty situations. *No falling in love, Nick. You had some fun with him, and maybe you'll have some more fun, but that's it,* he reminded himself. *No attachments in your line of work. It's not smart.*

"Follow me," Felix said, heading for one of the warehouses. Halfway there, he stopped and changed direction. After a few minutes of seemingly random wandering, Felix led them into a dank alley and stopped halfway down. The far end held a chain link fence, so their only exit was the way they'd come in.

"You sure this guy isn't going to shoot us on sight?" Nick asked as the hairs on the back of his neck stood up. He knew that someone was watching them. He'd been in too many hairy situations to ignore his instincts now. He grabbed his sister and put her behind him, not that that would do much good. In these close quarters, the threat could come from behind or above just as easily as it could from in front of them.

"Yeah. I'm sure. I helped him out of a shit situation a while back. He owes me." Felix pulled out a cell phone and punched in a few random looking characters, and then he waited.

Nick frowned. He recognized a code when he saw one.

When Felix's phone buzzed, his shoulders

relaxed, and he slipped his phone back into his pocket. "Okay. We can go in." He opened the heavy metal door set deep into the crumbling brick wall in front of them.

Nick followed Felix into the dark building, keeping Jenna behind him. His spidey-sense told him that the shit was about to hit the fan, but Felix's ease contradicted his worries. "Dammit," he muttered, drawing his blade. He didn't want to shoot someone by accident, but he sure as shit didn't like walking into a dark hole controlled by no one he knew.

"This way," Felix said, leading them into a hallway on the far side of the vast space. At the end of the hall, a bare light bulb buzzed against the wall, illuminating a newer looking door. Felix tapped on it.

When it opened, Nick froze. The muscular man standing behind the door was someone he knew well, even though he'd only met the guy in person once. *And now I'm completely fucked. Who knew Felix's friend would be my fence?* He stepped back instinctively, even though he knew it wouldn't help. The man's eyebrows went up, and then he grinned.

"Nick Banner, well, well. What a surprise," Zero said, dark eyes flicking past Felix to land on Nick.

Felix went perfectly still. "You two know each other?

"We do, indeed, Felix." Zero smiled as he stepped back to usher them in. "Welcome to my humble abode."

"Interesting," Felix said in a low voice, staring at Nick. "You didn't mention that to me when I told you his name, Zero."

Nick nearly flinched back at the cold tone, but then he reminded himself that even if Felix turned on them, he wasn't without skills of his own. He already had his knife in his hand. *And I've had his cock in my mouth,* he thought, hoping that the pleasure he'd given Felix would be enough to convince him that Nick meant him no harm. He made sure Jenna was still behind him. She didn't deserve to get trapped in the middle of this if it all went to shit. *And it's probably too much to hope that I get through this without her finding out about my real career.*

"Oh yes, it *is* very interesting, isn't it? Nick is one of the best thieves on the east coast," Zero said smoothly. "And why would I mention it to you? You know my clients have perfect anonymity, Felix. And, too, I didn't want to ruin the surprise." Zero smiled, dark eyes twinkling evilly. "We make a lot of money together, don't we, Nick?"

Nick grunted as Jenna's hands tightened painfully around his arm, pulling on the healing wound of his bicep. *Yep, and now I'm completely outed,* he thought, almost laughing at the irony. His sister had known he was gay since he was twelve, but this? She didn't know about this. He'd never wanted her to know. *What are the fucking odds that Felix's contact would be my fucking fence?*

"A thief," Felix said, an odd note in his voice. "Yes, very interesting."

"Nick, what is he talking about?" Jenna asked, fingers digging into his arm.

"I told you that I work from home," Nick said tightly. "It's not a big deal."

"I thought you did something with computers," Jenna replied, not sounding in the least convinced.

"And he does. We do all of our business together online. He 'discovers' the product," Zero explained, using air quotes to convey a multitude of meanings with the word. "And I sell what he so carefully finds. It's a win-win situation."

"Nick?" Jenna sounded like she wanted to make a run for it.

Judging her survival more important than keeping his true career a secret, he turned. "I only steal things that people won't miss."

"Precisely, like expensive art and jewelry," Zero said, stepping back. "And sometimes very protected information stored on private servers. Nick finds all the stuff that people want most to hide, and it's all insured to the gills. It makes for a very tidy business, you must understand."

"Oh my God, Nick. Is this true?" Jenna shook her head. "I don't get it. Why would you do that? I thought you were a web designer or something."

Nick rubbed his face. The top of his head had begun to throb. "I ended up on the streets with a shitload of student loans and nothing except the clothes on my back, Jenna. What's there to understand? Our parents kicked me out. I got hungry. Things happen." Nick was losing patience. He'd come here to help her, and she was freaking out over his fucking job. "Deal with it, sis. It is what it is." He knew he wasn't being very nice, but he'd reached his limit of patience.

Jenna stared up at him, eyes wide. "If you're a thief, what is Felix?" She glanced at the man quietly waiting in the doorway.

"Ah. That is also a very interesting question, my dear, but it's better answered inside, where the walls don't have ears." Zero motioned them through the doorway.

Nick nudged her inside. As soon as the metal door shut behind them, lights flashed on, nearly blinding him. He blinked and cursed. "Jesus, Zero. You're a paranoid fuck."

"Yes, I am, and it has kept me alive all these

many years. Come," Zero said, tapping at a security display on the wall. "This way." He led them down another hallway. At the end, a polished wooden door sat ajar. Zero eyed Nick's weapon. "You won't need that in here, Nick." He ushered them into a lavishly decorated apartment.

Nick fingered his blade as he followed Zero into the apartment. He stopped just inside the door and whistled when he saw the original Harper painting hanging on the wall over Zero's flashy red sofa. "Damn. I thought a client bought that last year?"

"He did." Zero chuckled. "I was the client. I liked that one too much to let it fall into some grubby drug dealer's ignorant hands."

Ignoring them, Felix headed towards the bar on the far wall.

"Make yourself at home, Felix," Zero said, watching Felix attack the glasses on the bar. "No need to be polite and wait for me to offer refreshments."

"We've known each other for decades, Zero. Give it a rest." Felix poured himself a shot of something, then turned and lifted his glass in question. "Thirsty?"

Zero sighed, clearly pushing away his annoyance. He shook his head. "Nothing for me, especially not if I'm to provide protection to this lovely lady." He took Jenna's hand and bowed over it. "Can I offer you a drink? Water? Vodka?"

Jenna stared at him, visibly confused. "No, thank you."

"So polite." Zero grinned at her. "This favor of yours I am doing…" He paused, turning to Felix. "After this, we will be even-steven, yes?"

Felix laughed. "Not a chance, and you know it."

Zero frowned. "So dramatic, even after all this time."

"You know as well as I do that neither of us can keep track of who owes the other what anymore, Zero," Felix said.

Zero smirked. "True."

Nick slid his blade back into its sheath, feeling silly for walking around with it. He ran a hand over his face, still trying to wrap his head around the fact that Felix and Zero knew each other, and knew each other quite well, at that. "How the hell do you two know each other?"

"He handles my contracts," Felix said, not really answering Nick's question.

"And I handle them very well, indeed," Zero added, sitting on the sofa. "There is a great deal of money to be made in the business of killing people." He ignored Jenna's gasp, and continued. "However, I fear dear Felix is losing interest in his profession, yes?"

Felix grimaced. "Perhaps."

"Retirement, then?" Zero cocked his head delicately. "That might be very challenging for you, Felix. You grow bored rather easily."

The man is at least two-hundred fifty pounds of pure muscle. How the hell does he manage to look feminine? Nick wondered, staring at Zero. The man wore black jeans, thick boots, and a tight t-shirt. *Well, not exactly feminine. Refined, maybe.* In another situation, he might have tried hitting on Zero, but after meeting Felix, he had no interest in it.

Felix shrugged, but didn't speak.

"Wait. Felix kills people?" Jenna whispered, gaze darting from Felix to Nick.

Nick sighed at the expression on her face. He'd worried she'd be upset about this. "Yeah."

"Oh my God." Jenna tried to pull away from him, but Nick wouldn't let her go.

"Calm down. He's not going to kill you," Nick said, suddenly annoyed with the entire situation.

"Listen to your brother, my dear. Felix is definitely *not* going to kill you," Zero said, smiling. "He's going to kill your boyfriend, Quincy Edwards."

****

Felix eyed the bottle of whiskey, tempted to knock back another shot. The first one still burned in his gut, and he sighed, knowing that he couldn't afford the lack of focus. *Not now, not ever,* he mused, gaze drifting back to Nick. He'd had sex with a man, and that didn't upset him nearly as much as finding out that Nick wasn't some innocent bystander in the world. *He robs people. And he's very good at it, or I would've picked up on his choice of careers when I first met him.* He ran a finger along the bar. "How long?" he asked, unable to stop himself. He had to know.

Nick frowned at him. He'd just managed to get his sister to sit down next to Zero.

Maybe she's decided that Zero is the least dangerous of all of us, Felix thought, bitterly amused. *If only she knew the truth.*

"What?" Nick asked him, settling down on the sofa's arm. His sister looked like she didn't know whether to lean into her brother, or away from him.

"How long have you been in the business?" Felix asked, already knowing that it didn't fucking matter. *I should be relieved, not angry,* he told himself. Nick's easy acceptance of Felix's profession made sense, now. Nick's dishonesty … well. That could be what had Felix's guts in such a fucking twist.

"Five, almost six years," Nick replied, rubbing his arm. Felix figured that his gunshot wound had started to itch, so he knew it was healing, but it annoyed him to see Nick fussing with it. He should never have been shot in the first place.

"What does it matter how long I've been working?" Nick asked, narrowing his eyes.

"Do you like it?" Felix wanted to take the question back as soon as they left his mouth. What did he care? He'd see Nick and his sister through their little problem, collect the money owed him for Edwards's head, and disappear.

Nick blinked. "Yeah," he said roughly. "I do. There are worse ways to make a living."

"Oh God," Jenna whispered, clearly distraught. She leaned away from her brother. Nick frowned at her.

Felix shook his head. "Don't judge, Jenna. It's not nice."

Zero burst out laughing. "Not nice? You sound like my Aunt Millie, scolding her for stealing a cookie."

Felix scowled at Zero. "Nick busted his ass to help her. He disrupted his business to help her. He deserves her respect."

"Well, now. This situation becomes ever more interesting with every word you utter," Zero said, still smiling. "This is the most animated I've seen you in years, Felix. Why is that, I wonder."

Ignoring Zero and his irritating speculations, Felix chanced a glance at Nick. The man was looking at him with a strange expression on his face. Heat seeped into Felix's cheeks, but he ignored that, too. It didn't matter what he thought. Ultimately, it was up to Jenna how she wanted to treat her brother, and it was up to Nick how he wanted to deal with it. *Dammit. Get your mind back in the game,* he told himself, exasperated. *You can't afford to get hung up on this shit right now.*

"Okay," Zero said, clapping his hands together. "This is how it will go. You will leave sweet Jenna in my care. I will provide protection for several days." He patted her hand. "Felix and Nick will hunt down the very, very stupid Quincy Edwards, and nullify his participation in Jenna's life. I will collect my fee, and we will all live happily ever after, yes?"

Jenna shrank back. "Nullify?"

"Why, yes. That is what Felix does, my dear," Zero said, still smiling. "Felix removes problems for our clients. He's very good at it. And from what I've heard, Quincy Edwards is a problem for more than one person."

Jenna looked at her brother, but Nick didn't offer any fake consolation. "The man beat you. He would've killed you. As far as I'm concerned, your ex doesn't have a good reason to live anymore, sis," Nick said.

"We could call the police," she offered tentatively. "Death seems a bit excessive." She bit her lip and looked down. "I can't believe we're actually talking about this."

Felix was already shaking his head before she finished speaking. "Do you know what the statistics are for abused women getting help from the cops?"

Jenna didn't look up. "Yeah."

Felix sighed. "Look. Quincy Edwards is into some rough shit, and you know it. You may not have seen it firsthand, but you knew something wasn't right with him. I've got a contract to take care of the situation. You'll be free to live your life, and he will never bother you again. If you go to the cops, you'll what? Maybe get a restraining order?" He rolled his shoulders, exasperated with her hesitation.

"I know, but still, this is crazy." Jenna frowned, eyes darting from him to her brother and back to the floor. "And I know that I let this happen to me, and it's all my fault, but that should mean I get a say in how to handle it, right?"

"No, you don't. And you didn't let any of this

happen to you. You are not at fault for someone else's stupid, evil life choices," Nick said, pulling her in for a hug.

Felix watched the siblings, sensing that Nick was talking about far more than just Jenna's ex-boyfriend.

"Your ex is an abusive dick," Nick continued to speak. "You had nothing to do with the way he chose to handle his business or personal life, and you didn't provoke him. If anyone is to blame, it's Mom and Dad for being such shitty parents that you thought moving in with Quincy was a better idea than staying with them." Nick sighed and ran a hand over his face. "Hell, *I'm* more at fault than you. I should've let you move in with me the moment you graduated high school."

"Yeah, like that would've worked. You're only four years older than me, Nick. You were living in a dorm. You say this isn't my fault, but it's not yours, either," Jenna said.

"It is no one's fault, but you must deal with the fallout anyway," Zero offered mildly. "It does no good to talk about blame." He stood up. "Go. Rid the girl of her problem. I will keep her safe. We will watch a fun movie together, yes?" He smiled down at Jenna.

She smiled tentatively back at him. "You're sure it's safe here?"

"I set the security system up myself. I am the best." Zero waved a hand at the open space. "We are half underground; the walls are soundproof and lined with steel. I have cameras everywhere. You will be safe here," he said.

Jenna looked at Nick questioningly. He nodded at her. "I trust him."

"As do I," Felix added, not that she'd believe a word he said.

Jenna inhaled, then let out a shaky breath.

"Okay."

"Excellent. It is time for lunch. I am making sourdough and ham sandwiches. You will help me, Jenna." Zero put out his hand to her. When Jenna put hers in it, he hauled her up and towed her to the kitchen area. When he reached the counter, he frowned, staring at Nick and Felix. "You are still here? Go, go." He flapped his hands at them. "I am not feeding the two of you, too."

Felix snorted. "I will check in later tonight."

Zero nodded. "Of course."

Nick walked over to his sister and gave her another hug. "Take care, sis. You know I love you."

"I love you, too." She held onto him tightly for a moment. "Don't get killed."

Nick smiled. "Not a chance. I'm very, very careful."

"Let's go," Felix said, itching to get away. Too much affection on display made him cranky. He'd led a solitary life for a reason.

"I'll text Zero tonight, too, to see how you're doing," Nick told his sister.

"Okay." Jenna smiled at him, then looked at Felix. "Don't let my brother die."

Felix raised his eyebrows. "You're asking me to protect him?"

She frowned. "Yes."

"I can take care of myself, Jenna," Nick said, heading for the door. He opened it and waited, clearly expecting Felix to follow him.

Jenna rolled her eyes, then fixed her gaze back on Felix. "Promise me."

Felix regarded her fierce expression and had to smile. He didn't often make promises, especially ones he couldn't guarantee he'd be able to keep, but in this case, he'd make an exception. He wanted to keep Nick alive, too, as strange as the sentiment felt. He didn't form attachments. He didn't need them, but after last night, he couldn't deny the curiosity that had him wishing for another night with Nick, and maybe even more than one night.

"I will do my best," he said to Jenna, and then, contrary to everything he'd ever done in his solitary life as a killer, he followed Nick out to help him hunt.

Chapter Eight

Nick sat in the passenger seat of the truck, wondering when the hell he'd grown so attached to Felix's continued survival. "You don't have to come with me," he said, angling his body towards Felix. "I can take Quincy down by myself." He still couldn't believe his sister had asked Felix to protect him. *I can take care of myself, but she doesn't really know that, does she?* He wondered if he should've told her about his nonstandard career sooner.

Felix didn't respond immediately, instead smoothly passing a slower vehicle to their right. Just when Nick was about to repeat himself, Felix shook his head. "I have a contract on him, remember?"

"Wait? You were serious about that?" Nick asked, struggling to make sense of Felix's words.

Felix shrugged. "Didn't you hear Zero mention his fee?"

I thought he was talking more generally. Shit. Nick stared at Felix as a chilling thought came to him. "Is that all it is to you? A contract?"

"Yes." Felix glanced at him, then shifted into the leftmost lane of the interstate. "No." He exhaled roughly, hands tightening on the steering wheel. "Fuck. I don't know what you're asking me."

Nick waited for more, but when Felix remained silent, he sighed. "Talking to you is like pulling teeth." He couldn't really blame Felix for being so uncommunicative. It wasn't like *he* enjoyed talking about his feelings. He sighed again, wondering what the fuck he thought he was doing. After Quincy was dealt with, what then? Were he and Felix going to date? Hook up? Go their separate ways? *Shit. I've got to get it together.*

Felix suddenly spoke, interrupting Nick's

thoughts. "What more do you need to know? I'm going to kill Quincy Edwards. You can help. I'll split the payment with you if you want. The end."

"Jesus, Felix." Nick ran a hand through his hair. "That's not what I mean," he said, exasperated with himself *and* Felix. "And I don't want your damned money. I don't *need* your fucking money. I'm just trying to figure out what the fuck we think we're doing." He inhaled. "I mean, don't get me wrong. I had a great time fooling around with you. But what's next? I don't know the first thing about you, and that sure as shit didn't feel like a simple hookup to me." Nick's face heated as he ran through what he'd just said. *I sound like a girl begging her boyfriend to pay attention to her. Jesus.*

Felix gave no indication that Nick's outburst bothered him in any way. He shifted back into the slow lane, and then he took the next exit onto a smaller highway dotted with houses and businesses before he spoke. "I grew up in an abusive household. My father killed my mother when I was eighteen. It wasn't a surprise. He'd been heading that way for a while, and since he was a cop, no one did anything. It was ruled accidental. She fell down the stairs, with help in the form of my dear old man's hand between her shoulder blades." Felix laughed bitterly.

"God, Felix," Nick muttered, shocked.

Felix ignored him and kept talking. "I knew if I didn't keep my mouth shut, he'd kill me, too. The moment I graduated high school I signed up for the Marines. I didn't set foot anywhere near my father again until he managed to kill himself with booze and a particularly violent gang confrontation in the Bronx. He died a fucking hero, or so everyone thought. I paid for his funeral, retired from the service, and went into business for myself right after, a little over fifteen years ago."

Fuck. That's grim, Nick thought, not sure what to say. "You were a sniper, weren't you?" he finally asked, still struggling with what Felix had just told him. He thought he'd had it bad when his parents disowned him, but at least his parents were still alive. *And my father never hit my mother, let alone killed her. And they weren't abusive, not really. Not like that.*

"Yeah." He glanced at Nick. "I'm a lot older than you. I've had time to learn how to forget about all that shit."

I don't think he's forgotten as much as he thinks he has. Nick rubbed his face, but didn't point that out. "My parents disowned me during my senior year of college, when I told them I was gay." He didn't feel all that much younger than Felix, though he knew the man had at least twenty years on him. *Getting kicked out and living on the street tends to age you.*

"I know," Felix said, glancing at him. "I assumed that was the case, after what you said to your sister back at Zero's."

Nick wasn't sure if he was hearing sympathy in Felix's voice, or just indifference. "Yeah," he said, tiredly. "It sucked, but at least they weren't violent. They're just crazy conservatives."

"Kicking a kid out of the house isn't violent?" Felix asked, sounding surprised. "You were homeless. I never had to deal with that."

"I was twenty. Older than you were when you signed up," Nick pointed out. "I did fine."

After a long pause, Felix spoke again. "So, we both had a shit situation to deal with when we were young. We survived." Felix put on his turn signal and turned right onto a residential street. "It doesn't matter, anyway. It was a long time ago for me. Decades."

"It wasn't that long ago for me," Nick muttered,

thinking about his sister and his parents. It'd been six years, and he still hated them. He wasn't sure that would ever change.

Felix gave him a look. Nick supposed Felix was right to try to repress everything. God knew he didn't really need all the fucking bitterness littering up his skull. It wasn't like he kept in touch with his parents. They were out of his life, and he had no intention of ever letting them back inside.

"Why didn't you stay in the Marines?" he asked, instead of dwelling on his past. He wanted to know more about Felix.

"Boredom. And I was tired of dumping sand out of my fucking boots." Felix slowed, then parked the truck under the canopy of three enormous trees. "We're here."

Nick glanced around. "This is the street where Quincy lives. You really think he'll still be here? Seems like a stretch, to me."

"Dunno, but it's worth casing his place." Felix leaned down and pulled a folder out from under his seat. He tossed it onto Nick's lap.

"What's this?"

"Take a look," Felix said.

Nick paged through the papers, then whistled. "Fuck. He's Robert Edwards's nephew? How did I not know this?" Robert Edwards was into real estate scams, arms dealing, and a dozen other shady activities. Everyone in the business knew who he was, but not so many people knew he had a nephew. Nick hadn't. He knew Zero sold a few of his goods to the older man, but Nick had made sure to stay far away from that side of things. The best thief was the one no one knew existed. "Shit. My sister was dating his nephew and I had no clue." He kept reading. "Quincy was thirty-three? Jesus, he was eleven years older than Jenna."

"What the fuck does that matter? I'm forty-five. Didn't stop you and me from screwing around, did it?" Felix said.

Nick pursed his lips. "That's different."

"How?"

I'm not a naive young girl, and I wasn't planning on sticking around, Nick thought, but he didn't say it out loud. "It just is."

"Whatever," Felix grunted. "You done with that?"

Nick gathered the papers and tucked them back into the folder. "Robert Edwards isn't going to take it at all well when his nephew turns up dead." He handed the folder back to Felix. "And you know they're gonna be looking at me."

"Not my problem. It won't be your problem, either, as long as we do it nice and neat." Felix shoved the packet back under the seat. "You ready to go in?"

Nice and neat, he says, as if it will be that easy. Ha, Nick thought, mind running through what he'd need to do to keep every last trace of himself away from the scene of the crime. "What are we looking for?" Nick said, checking his borrowed pistol. The clip was full, but he had no more ammunition. His knife, as always, sat tucked against his forearm. He pulled out a pair of vinyl gloves. He had no intention of leaving any prints inside.

Felix shrugged. "Information. Phone numbers. Maybe we'll get lucky, and Quincy will be sitting on his toilet, like a stupid motherfucker."

Nick laughed. "Yeah. In your dreams."

Felix gave him a tight smile and got out of the truck. Nick followed him.

****

"Nothing. There's not a goddamned thing here."

Disgusted, Nick kicked a half-packed box of random junk across the room. Packages of instant noodles, two paperbacks, and a handful of cutlery scattered across the dirty carpet. "He's long gone, Felix."

Felix scanned the living space one last time. "Fuck." He tugged off his leather gloves irritably.

Nick agreed with the sentiment as he tucked his disposable gloves in his pocket. They had no leads. Quincy had taken off for good, and he'd left nothing useful behind. "I bet his uncle helped him clear this place out. He doesn't have enough brains to be this thorough. The place is clean as a whistle."

"Hmm." Felix looked around one last time, then exhaled. "We'll pick up the trail in the morning." He headed for the door.

"What makes you think we'll be able to do that? We got nothing. No leads. Not even a fucking breadcrumb." Nick followed him out of the house. Late afternoon shadows fell across the sidewalks as they headed for Felix's truck. The residential neighborhood looked quiet and ordinary, when Quincy's business was anything but. *That's how it goes, though. Drugs and guns are everywhere, these days.*

"I know where Robert Edwards has a bolthole. We'll check in with Zero tonight, and head there in the morning." Felix unlocked the truck and climbed in.

"Why not go there now?" Nick had a serious hard-on about fucking Quincy up. He wasn't normally the kind of guy who wanted to break a man's bones, but this time he'd make an exception. The memory of his sister crying into his neck would haunt him forever, as would her bruises.

"I'm tired. You're tired. We need a plan." Felix pulled out and slowly drove away from the neighborhood. "It's never a good idea to storm in with guns blazing." He shook his head. "We don't even know if Edwards is where I'm thinking he's at, let alone if he's got his nephew with him. He doesn't stay in one place for long. He moves around. We'll get Zero to check his network for information on his whereabouts."

"Why the hell would Zero help us so much, anyway?" Nick asked. When he worked with Zero, it was a strictly business relationship. He fenced the shit Nick stole, and took a modest fee off the top. Obviously, Felix's relationship with the guy was different. Felix had walked into Zero's place as though he'd been there before.

"We went to high school together. One day, a few assholes thought it would be fun to permanently remove Zero from the planet by using him as a punching bag. I disagreed." Felix eased onto the highway. "Zero was never shy about his choice of dating partners. And I don't like bullies, especially homophobic ones with tire irons." He glanced at Nick. "Don't read too much into it. We've been doing business together for decades."

Not surprising Felix would react like that, given the way his dad treated him. And at least now I know Zero won't be hitting on Jenna. Nick leaned his head back against the seat. "So, Zero owes you, huh? Is that like how I owe you?"

"No. You owe me something entirely different." Felix smiled at Nick, then turned his attention back to the road. "Zero owes me for saving his skin that time, and a few other things over the years." He sighed. "I owe him, too. Neither of us can keep track anymore."

"Still. We have a few hours of light left. We could check this bolthole you mentioned and still have time for dinner before it gets dark. No need to bother Zero yet." Nick really wanted to exhaust their options before turning in for the night. Every moment Quincy was out walking around, healthy and stupid, worried Nick. Zero wasn't infallible, no matter how sturdy he thought his bunker was. *And I should know. I make a living by breaking into impregnable places.*

"Not without more info." Felix pursed his lips, head turning to look at him. "Let it go, Nick. I promise you, Edwards will be dead within twenty-four hours."

Nick frowned. Felix wasn't budging on this, and since he was in the man's truck, and at the man's mercy... *Fuck it. Felix knows a lot more about killing people than you do, and you know it,* he told himself. He'd always been impulsive, and he wanted to get this over with, but not at the expense of his life. *Or Felix's life. Or my sister's.* He reached up and massaged the wound on his arm. It itched more than it hurt.

"Stop messing with it. You'll tear open the stitches," Felix said, knocking his hand down.

Nick scowled at him. "What do you care?"

Felix didn't respond.

Nick sighed, and closed his eyes. They had a long drive back to Felix's cabin. He might as well get some shut-eye.

****

A few hours later, Nick shoved the empty bags of fast food into the trash in Felix's kitchen. "Did you hear from Zero?" He was tired, but not so tired he'd forget to check up on Jenna.

Felix held up his phone. "He says your sister is fine. She fell asleep in the middle of the movie."

"Did you ask him about Quincy? And his mobster uncle?" Nick leaned back against the kitchen counter. The edge dug into his lower back, but he didn't care. A little pain here and there kept him focused. He poked at his arm again, ignoring Felix's scowl of disapproval. "What did he say?"

"He's got nothing on either of them," Felix said.
Nick frowned. "Let me see."

After an exasperated sigh, Felix walked over and held out his phone. Nick grabbed it, scanning the messages.

Felix: **Info on Edwards?**

Zero: **Neither one in usual holes.**

Zero: **Tasked a minion with search and stalk, nothing yet.**

Felix: **Status on Jenna?**

Zero: **Sleeping, poor thing.**

Felix: **Send update in AM.**

Zero: **Roger that.**

"A minion?" Nick asked, confused. He handed Felix's phone back to him. "Is that wise?"

"Zero has a lot of contacts in odd places," Felix said. He put the phone on the counter. "Whoever he asked to help out will either be paid, or owes Zero a favor. Don't worry about it."

Nick ran a hand over the back of his neck. His muscles hurt, but there wasn't a lot he could do about it. He'd never take pain medicine in the middle of a job. The pain would keep him alert, at the very least. "At least Zero seems cool with Jenna."

"He's a good man," Felix said, looking out the window.

Night had fallen, and Nick couldn't figure out what Felix could possibly see through the glass. Even the trees across the small clearing had vanished into the dark. If Felix hadn't had a phenomenal security system, complete with infrared cameras, Nick would never be able to sleep here. He hated not being able to see his surroundings. "You realize, having a cabin in the middle of nowhere puts you into the creepy killer category. You could star in your own reality television show. 'Killer in the Dark' airs at nine," he joked.

Felix turned to him, eyebrows raised. He wasn't smiling. "If the shoe fits."

Nick laughed. "You're not the least bit upset about being called a killer, are you?"

Felix stalked over to him and boxed him in, arms on the counter to either side. Nick blinked. *Huh. I didn't expect him to do that.*

"I *am* a killer. And I'm very, very good at it," Felix said, leaning in. Warm breath puffed across his cheek. "Question is, do you even know what that means?"

Nick's cock hardened so fast he felt lightheaded. "Jesus, Felix." Felix brushed his lips across Nick's jaw, and Nick abruptly realized that he wasn't the only one with an erection. The knowledge did nothing for his self-control. He wanted more of Felix, and the sooner, the better.

"I never dress up a peach and call it an apple, Nick. I am what I am." Felix's hazel eyes had darkened. "I am a contract killer."

Nick licked his lips, more turned on than he could remember being ever before. Felix really pushed all of his buttons in exactly the right way. "Fuck." Felix didn't seem the least bit bothered by his sudden attraction to another man. Nick knew he'd enjoyed the blowjob, and the rubbing one out against each other this morning, but he'd expected some straight guy blowback at some point. "You jumping into the gay side of the pool again?"

"You're the one who pointed out my not-so-straight tendencies, Nick." Felix pressed against him harder. "Why so surprised now?"

Nick shuddered. "Just making sure that a punch to the face isn't in my immediate future. It tends to ruin the mood." He reached up and grabbed Felix's arms as he thrust his hips forward. The pressure of his cock against his jeans fucking hurt. "What do you want?" He wouldn't mind blowing the guy again. Felix's cock was the perfect size for his mouth. *It'd be the perfect size for my ass, too,* he thought, swallowing hard.

Felix reached up and pulled Nick's arms down, trapping him against the counter. "It's not obvious?"

Nick shivered. He'd gotten so used to topping that no guy ever seemed to take the initiative with him anymore. He didn't know if he gave off too many tough-guy vibes or what, but the truth was, he liked it when a man showed his strength. He *liked* it that Felix wasn't afraid to shove him around. He flexed his wrists, but didn't try to break free.

"You like that, hmm?" Felix pressed harder.

Nick's arm wound throbbed as the counter cut into his wrists. "Yeah."

"You want me to fuck you, don't you?"

Nick swallowed, hard. Felix's voice wound itself around his spine in the best possible way. "Yeah, I do."

Chapter Nine

Felix bared his teeth, once again grinding his cock into Nick's groin. Ever since Nick mentioned fucking, he'd been thinking about it in the back of his head. Nick's perfect ass, splayed open to him, was an image he couldn't seem to shake, and he wanted to see if the reality matched his imagination. "Let's take this to the bedroom," he said, releasing Nick's wrists.

Nick grabbed him. "No."

Felix raised his eyebrows. "No?" Had he completely misinterpreted Nick's interest? *No, he's just as fucking turned on as me,* he thought, staring at the other man's blown pupils.

"Here. Now." Nick reached back and pulled his shirt off, back to front. He tossed it on the tile floor. "You got any olive oil? Shortening?"

Felix made a sound in the back of his throat. "You want me to fuck you bareback?" He inhaled, trying to keep from coming in his fucking pants. "Risky," he said tightly.

"I like risk, in case you haven't noticed," Nick said, shoving down his jeans. His cock sprang out, hard and red and wet at the tip. His blond pubic hair framed it perfectly.

Felix stared at Nick's erection, inexplicably curious about how it would taste. He imagined the weight of Nick's cock on his tongue, and almost went to his knees, but Nick's yanking on his shirt interrupted his focus.

"Earth to Felix." Nick roughly undressed him. When his hands tried to yank down Felix's pants, Felix snapped out of it, and took over, kicking off his boots.

"Calm the fuck down," he growled, opening a cabinet. He grabbed the shortening and slammed it down on the counter. "You want me to fuck you? Then you will do as I say." Felix had never fucked a man before, but he'd done anal with women. And he knew from the way Nick's breathing hitched that the man liked it when Felix took the lead. *I can take the lead twenty-four seven, as long as it ends up with me balls deep in Nick's ass.*

"Jesus, fuck, Felix." Nick grabbed himself and squeezed, eyes on Felix's erection.

Felix narrowed his eyes. "Hands off the goods. Don't touch yourself unless I say so."

Nick glared at him. "Then stop staring at me and get to it."

Felix shed the rest of his clothes, then grabbed Nick by the wrists again. "You like it when I hold you down."

Nick closed his eyes and exhaled sharply. "Yeah. I do."

"You'll like it even more with my cock inside you." Felix leaned in and bit Nick's lip, hard. "When I have you pushed up against the counter, you won't be able to move. I'll do whatever the fuck I want with you."

Nick gasped, leaning in. "Fucking tease. Lotta words there, Felix. Show me some action."

Felix grinned. He rubbed their erections together, strangely not the least bit freaked out by it. He'd enjoyed sex with women, but the sensation of Nick's hard body against his was on an entirely different level. Nick was leaner than Felix, and he liked the way the younger man's smooth skin felt against his rougher, hairier chest. He liked everything about Nick. He liked the small tattoo of an open lock on the other man's lower right hip. He liked the way Nick's hair felt under his fingertips. He liked Nick's mouth. Felix flashed back to the memory of Nick sucking his cock, and shuddered. He cupped Nick's face, and then rubbed on thumb across his lips. "Open up for me."

Nick smiled, then sucked Felix's thumb inside. Felix swayed, but then Nick bit down, hard. The stinging pain made him smile. "Feisty, aren't you?"

Nick laughed. Felix moved in, grabbing him by the ass. "I'm going to fuck you right here." He turned Nick around, then opened the shortening and scooped out a generous portion.

"I like pain," Nick said, obligingly spreading his legs.

Felix eyed Nick's hole, liking the way his balls looked from this direction. "I know you do." He smeared the white slick stuff on Nick's ass, then rubbed a generous portion on himself. "I'm going to open you up with my cock. You got a problem with that?"

Nick's shoulders tensed. "Nope."

Felix grunted, then slid his slick erection between Nick's legs, bumping his balls with his cockhead, avoiding his hole. "Good." He grabbed Nick by the hips, and began pumping. He meant to drive him insane before he ever got close to the fucking part. "You're not going to come until I say."

Nick groaned, hands going down to touch himself again.

"Oh no, you don't," Felix muttered, grabbing Nick's arms. He wrenched them back up, holding them against the counter.

"Fuck, Felix," Nick panted.

Felix kept slowly pumping his hips. Nick's ass crack felt hot as hell, and every time he bumped Nick's balls with the head of his shaft, pleasure shot up Felix's spine. "You're hot as fuck."

Nick hung his head down. "And you're a fucking tease."

Felix bit Nick's shoulder. "Yeah. I am." He

leaned back and gripped himself. He started pushing at Nick's hole, but didn't press in. He wanted Nick to open up for him. He wanted Nick to beg. "You got a problem with that?"

"Depends on the situation," Nick ground out, trying to lunge back.

Felix used his free hand to press Nick's head and shoulders down on the counter. "You don't get to rush this, Nick."

Nick groaned, but he let Felix hold him down. "God, you're a prick."

"That also depends on the situation." Felix pressed harder with his cock. Nick's hole looked puffy and red, and he could feel the muscle starting to relax. "You're a perfect fucking bottom, aren't you?"

"Not always," Nick countered, breathing heavier.

Felix let his free hand slide down, and he gripped Nick's cock. Nick groaned, hips jerking. Felix pushed his own cock at Nick's hole again, and then again. "I got you," he murmured, slowly stroking Nick's dick. He wanted Nick on the edge, but not over. Not yet.

Nick shuddered, hands clenching into fists. "I'm close."

"No, you're not," Felix said, tightening his grip around Nick's erection. He pushed in, hard, and the head of his cock slipped inside Nick's body. He exhaled harshly, fighting for control as Nick clenched his muscles. "Fuck."

"Yeah, that's what we're doing," Nick managed to say.

"If you're coherent enough to speak, I'm not doing my job properly," Felix told him, pushing in slowly. He'd had to wait a moment so he wouldn't just pop off. He wanted to fuck Nick long and hard.

"Truth," Nick managed, voice cracking.

Felix bared his teeth, then pulled out and shoved back in, faster this time. Nick grunted. Felix let go of Nick's dick and cupped the man's balls. "Interesting. You didn't go soft at all."

"I like pain, remember?" Nick shook his head. "And you went too fucking slow."

Felix snorted. "No. I went just fucking right." He may not have ever done this with a man before, but it wasn't fucking rocket science. He knew what he was doing. "Hold on."

Nick grabbed the edge of the counter. "Come on, Felix. I'm not a goddamn porcelain doll. Do it."

Felix exhaled, and then he grabbed Nick's hips and began fucking him in earnest. He adjusted his angle until he felt Nick's muscles seize up. *That's the spot,* he thought, grinning. "I'm going to make you come, Nick, just from this." He fucked harder. "And you're not going to touch yourself. You're going to just take it. You're going to take me so fucking deep you'll be able to taste me on the back of your throat."

Nick didn't speak as he hung onto the counter. A fine sheen of sweat slicked his back, and Felix felt his own body heat up as Nick's hole tightened around his dick. He moved faster and faster, until he couldn't keep track of anything: all that mattered was fucking Nick hard enough to make them both forget their names. He shoved in, going up on his toes, and then finally Nick cried out. "God!"

Felix bared his teeth in a hard grin as Nick's spine bowed. Warm jets of cum coated the counter beneath them, and he hammered into Nick faster, holding his hips so tightly he knew he'd leave finger-shaped bruises. Nick's asshole squeezed him again, and then again, and then it was all over. Pleasure shot through Felix like a fucking freight train. His hips jerked hard, slapping into Nick's ass so roughly he worried he'd hurt the younger man, but when Nick grunted, pushing back to meet him, he knew he could let go. His climax raced through his body, and he leaned his head down on Nick's back, almost crying with the intensity of it.

A long time later, his softening cock slowly slipped out and Felix forced himself to step back on shaky legs. He didn't want to let go, but Nick had put his head down on his arms on the counter, and snuggling while standing up was just not an option. *Snuggling at all is not an option,* Felix reminded himself, but then he looked down and saw his jizz leaking from Nick's ass. Slowly fading handprints marred Nick's hips. "Fuck," he muttered as his cock gave one last twitch. Satisfaction and something stronger, more primal, swept through him at the sight. He liked that he'd marked Nick up. He liked his fucking cum dripping out of Nick's ass. "Fuck," he said again, not entirely sure where the hell his head was going. He took a deep breath, trying to gather some semblance of control.

Nick snorted as if he knew exactly what Felix was thinking. "Yeah. That was … huh. Something." He stood up and cracked his neck. When he turned around, Felix reached out. Nick pulled him in and gave him a tight hug, not seeming the least bit surprised at Felix's desire for connection. "Jesus Christ, Felix. What the fuck was that?"

Felix closed his eyes and held on. He knew exactly what Nick was asking, and he had no answer. He just knew he was totally, completely fucked.

****

Several hours later, Nick stared at the steady rise and fall of Felix's back from his side of the bed. The man breathed deep and easy, but Nick knew he wasn't asleep. "We could do jobs together. Didn't Zero say something about you being tired of your career?"

After a long, silent moment, Felix sighed and rolled over. "It's frigging two AM. Do you really want to have this conversation right now?" He rubbed his eyes tiredly, and shoved the covers down to his waist. "Shit, we should have pulled the shades down."

Nick made a face. "I can't sleep either." The light from the full moon shone down into the bedroom. It was bright enough to read. Bright enough to keep him awake. *Yeah, that's why I'm tossing and turning. The moon,* he thought sarcastically. *And it has nothing to do with my sudden and stupid interest in staying with Felix after we take care of removing Quincy Edwards from the face of the Earth.*

"I thought you were only sticking around for your sister," Felix said, scratching a hand through his short beard. His eyes told Nick he knew exactly what direction this discussion was headed, and he didn't like it.

Nick let his gaze move from Felix's face to his insanely muscular torso. The man was built for brawling. *And fucking,* he thought, flushing as his body remembered with it was like to have Felix looming over him. Pressing into him. He'd never in his life enjoyed a fuck that much. No man had ever been strong enough to hold him down before.

"Not too many jobs for a thief in rural Jersey, you know," Felix continued as if Nick hadn't just been chasing that same damn thought in a mental loop inside his brain over the past few hours.

"North Jersey isn't the back of beyond. My rental is only an hour or so from the city." Nick pointed out after he forced his brain to think about what Felix was saying and not what he looked like.

Felix exhaled. "What are you really asking me, Nick?"

Nick pursed his lips. "Just saying I wouldn't mind hanging out with you some more." He lifted a shoulder. "You know what I do for a living. I know what you do. It's nice not having to lie and explain away the hours I spend doing jobs at night. I like that freedom."

"Freedom?" Felix eyed him, then put his arms behind his head. "You're talking about dating," he said flatly. "That's the opposite of freedom. And I thought you didn't date. Didn't have the time, or something."

He sees right through me. Nick shrugged. "I could change my mind. Try dating, or whatever you want to call it." He schooled his face to blankness. No way was he going to let on the way his heart pounded against his ribs right now. "You seem cool with the gay thing, so…" He trailed off.

Felix rolled over on top of Nick. "I'd planned on heading out west after this last job."

Nick shuddered as Felix's warm, nude body slid across his. "Heading out?"

"Across country. I want to build another cabin in Oregon. Or maybe Washington." His lips quirked. "The state, not the capitol." Felix rolled his hips, grinding his erection into Nick's junk.

Nick's cock rapidly hardened. "Jesus, Felix. I can't think straight when you do that."

Felix smirked. "You've *never* been able to think straight, from what I can see. You've been a homo your whole life."

Nick groaned. "That was bad. No more puns from you." He grabbed Felix's ass and pushed up into him. "Fuck. You feel good."

Felix kissed him, hot and slow and filthy. By the time he lifted his head, Nick couldn't remember his own name, let alone focus on what they'd been talking about. "You bastard. You're trying to distract me."

"Is it working?" Felix's hips moved in a slow grind.

Nick swallowed, hard. "Yeah."

"Good." Felix dipped his head down again and bit into Nick's neck.

"Fuck. What are you, a vampire?" Nick rolled them until he was on top. He wanted Felix to fuck him again. *Hell. If he takes off for the west coast, I'm fucking following him. He's too damned hot for me to let him get away.*

"You think too much," Felix said, hand suddenly on Nick's cock.

"Says the man who insisted we not go storming into Edwards's bolthole because we needed to approach the situation more carefully," Nick managed to gasp out. He thrust his cock into Felix's perfect grip half a dozen times before he got control of himself. He pushed Felix's hand away. "Stop, or I'm going to come all over you."

"That's kind of the point," Felix said.

Nick scowled, and lifted up. He took Felix's erection in hand and positioned it at his hole. Felix went still. "Yeah. You're starting to see *my* point, aren't you?" He slowly lowered himself down, not caring that he hadn't prepped at all. His ass was still loose and slick from earlier, and Felix's dick slid right in with only a little bit of an ache. "Admit it. We make a good team." Nick exhaled, enjoyed the feeling of fullness. In this position, Felix's cock was hitting right on his prostate. He lifted up slightly, and then waited, watching Felix's face.

"I'm not used to having a partner," Felix said, voice breaking as Nick screwed himself down very slowly.

Nick bared his teeth. "It's too late for regrets. If you move across the country, I'm fucking following you." He moved up and down, gritting his teeth. He was so fucking close, and they hadn't even done anything vigorous. In a moment of clarity, he realized that this was what he'd been looking for all along, even when he hadn't known he'd been searching. "Jesus." His hair dampened as pleasure curled through him. "What the hell are we doing?"

"You're asking me?" Felix started thrusting. All Nick could do was hang on. "I wasn't in the market for a boyfriend."

Nick choked on a laugh. "Because you thought you were *straight*, you dumb motherfucker." And Nick didn't know how the hell Felix had ever believed that. No straight man ever fucked another dude like this. *The kissing is what really gives it away.*

Instead of answering, Felix closed his eyes and arched his back. Veins stood out in his neck. Nick frowned, gripping Felix's arms. "Don't do that. Fucking look at me while you're balls deep in my ass."

Felix opened his eyes.

Nick's breathing hitched. The intensity of Felix's arousal seared Nick to the bone. He couldn't breathe. Couldn't imagine his life without this anymore, even though he'd only known Felix for a few short days. "I'm right here, Felix. This is you and me."

"I know," Felix said, hips moving faster. "Don't you think I fucking know?"

"Don't you fucking forget it," Nick gasped, even as his climax abruptly pushed through him. His cock jerked, and hot spunk coated Felix's chest, and then his chin. Nick shuddered, riding out the pleasure. Felix clenched his teeth and thrust up one last time, and then he, too, let go. His gaze never left Nick's as his hips pushed up, screwing hard. Warmth spread inside Nick, and he didn't regret barebacking a bit. He wanted this connection.

"Jesus Christ," Felix moaned, hips still jerking. He held onto Nick's hips with the strength of a maniac.

"Yeah. Fuck me hard." Nick tightened his fingers around Felix's biceps in return. The slight sting of the stitches from his gunshot wound pulling at his skin barely registered. He stared into Felix's eyes until he knew that the other man would never, ever forget this moment. "This is it, Felix. This kind of shit happens once in a lifetime, if that, and you know it."

Felix slowly unclenched his fingers and relaxed onto the mattress. He didn't speak, but his eyes said volumes.

Nick waited for Felix to say something, but when he didn't, he finally let go and rolled to the side. He sensed Felix's bone-deep exhaustion, but also his worry. "Don't sweat it." He put a hand on Felix's shoulder. "It's not like I'm going to do something stupid."

"Too late." Felix snorted. "We are so fucked. You know that, right? This…" He waved at them twisted up together on the bed with a free hand. "Is a liability."

After a moment, Nick shrugged. "So what? I like to live dangerously."

"I kill people for a living, Nick. I can't afford liabilities."

"Uh-huh. You do know who you're talking to, right?" Nick laughed. "I'm a thief, Felix. I'm used to living on the edge of disaster."

Felix sighed.

Nick rolled into him, snaking an arm around his waist. "Anyway, you're going to retire, right after we find Quincy and make him pay for terrorizing my sister."

"You seem very sure of that," Felix said, voice low.

Nick stared out the window. The moon had

finally slipped below the tree line, plunging the room in darkness. "I have good instincts." He very carefully did *not* mention to Felix that those good instincts of his were telling him that his sister wasn't safe right now. There wasn't anything else they could do, and he knew it, but he hated leaving her at Zero's. The guy had insane security, and had been in business for decades, but still … Jenna was his sister. He couldn't help but worry.

And maybe that's what Felix means by liability, Nick thought, even as sleep dragged him down into the night.

Chapter Ten

Felix watched Nick from the corner of his eye. The younger man frowned at the highway, and Felix increased their speed. The day had dawned warm and sunny, but the clear blue skies didn't at all calm Nick down. He'd woken up this morning with one goal in mind, and he'd made sure Felix knew about it. Nick was worried about his sister. Strangely, Felix understood that.

If anything happened to Nick, I'd be more than fucking upset. I'd be enraged, he admitted, wondering how the hell he'd managed to fall in love with a man in the space of a few days. He shook his head, alternately pissed at himself, and amazed. After his mother died, and he'd left home, his emotions had sort of flattened out. Nothing jarred him—not boot camp, not sniper school, not his service overseas. His career as an assassin had been one of calculation, not excitement. As the years passed, he'd begun to believe himself incapable of stronger emotion, but not anymore. Nick had shown up in his life and all of his preconceived notions about attachment had been thrown into a dumpster and set on fire.

"Why didn't Zero respond this morning?" Nick asked, for the third time.

"I don't know." Felix took the next exit, and headed for the warehouse. He'd known Zero for decades, and it wasn't like the man to ignore his texts, particularly given how few he sent. Zero wasn't generally awake this early, but he had to know that this situation was a special case. For all his talk of it, Felix didn't call in favors. He especially didn't show up at his old friend's hidden apartment bunker with a girl and her brother, asking for help. He glanced at Nick. His blond hair had slipped across his face, and Nick shoved it back impatiently.

Worry etched lines into his forehead.

"We'll be there soon," Felix said, trying to soothe him. Clearly, he sucked at it, because Nick gave him a look that spoke volumes. "I'm driving as fast as I can. If I go any faster, some random cop with a quota to fill is going to pull us over," Felix added.

"Yeah, yeah. I know," Nick muttered, staring out the window. He fingered the knife strapped to his arm.

Felix suppressed a sigh as he took the exit they needed to get to Zero's place. After another tense half hour of driving, he pulled up and parked in the alley. "Looks fine," he said, knowing even as the words left his mouth that the relative calm of the place meant nothing.

Nick tossed him a disgusted look as he got out of the truck. Felix shook his head. He deserved that. He followed Nick to the door.

"Shit." Nick was staring at the ground. A smear of old blood decorated the crumbled cement of the stoop.

"Doesn't necessarily mean anything. It's old," Felix pointed out, shoving open the door. The darkness of the warehouse felt good after the bright daylight. He edged inside, keeping his back to the wall.

"It wasn't there yesterday," Nick said softly, following him inside. "It's not *that* old."

Felix didn't reply. Something about the warehouse felt wrong. He headed for the hall on the far side the space, taking care to muffle his footsteps. When he reached the door, he frowned. It wasn't like Zero to leave it even slightly ajar. He drew his Glock, holding it down by his thigh. He had no intention of going off half-cocked and running into the corridor shooting like a villain from a shitty suspense novel. He'd been a killer for years. He didn't make messes. He didn't make any drama, if he could help it. Quick and clean was his motto. A soft sound from Nick had him freezing in his tracks. "What?" he asked softly.

"The door," Nick said, just as quietly.

Felix looked. Bloody fingerprints marred the edges. "Fuck." He moved forward as the hair on the back of his neck prickled. When Nick tried to rush past him, he grabbed him and shoved him back. "Stay behind me." He glared at his lover until Nick nodded, short and sharp. The man wasn't happy about it, but Felix didn't care. This was what he did. Nick might be an excellent thief, but he wasn't a killer. *Well, at least not like I am,* Felix amended. He knew damn well Nick could take someone out if necessary, but he wasn't a contract assassin like Felix.

He slid inside Zero's door, pausing to let his eyes adjust. Every light in the place was on, blazing down on a scene straight out of a fucking disaster movie. Furniture lay on its side. Broken glass littered the floor. Felix's glanced over the place, absently registering the damage to Zero's favorite painting, and then his gaze locked onto the small foot sticking out from behind the sofa. He walked forward, crouched low to present a smaller target. His heart slammed into his ribs when he saw the tiny hole centered in Jenna's forehead. He looked up, meeting Nick's gaze.

"No," Nick said, face twisting. He rushed forward, landing on his knees next to his sister. "No, no, no…"

Felix took a deep breath. He hadn't secured the rest of the place. He put a hand on Nick's shoulder, wishing he could do something. Nick's pain radiated through his muscles. Felix squeezed, but he didn't think Nick even noticed, so he stood up and headed for the bathroom. It was clear of intruders, and a total fucking mess. Blood streaked the side of the tub. He shook his head and went to the bedroom, cautiously edging inside the door.

"Took you long enough," Zero said from the floor at the foot of the large bed. His voice sounded weak. Sticky.

Felix glanced at him, ruthlessly suppressing his emotions. He didn't have time to have a fucking breakdown, even if Zero was his oldest friend. He looked at the closet. Blood pooled near the door. He walked closer, then sighed. The closet was empty. The apartment was safe, at least for now. He grabbed a handful of towels and hurried back to Zero. "What happened?"

"They fucking broke in, is what happened," Zero said, coughing. Blood speckled his chin. "Made a goddamn mess."

"Yeah. Hold still." Felix carefully eased his friend's hands up and away from the wound in his chest. "It missed your heart." He was afraid to roll him and check for an exit wound. The man had lost a lot of blood.

"No shit. Nicked my lung, though," Zero said, voice thready. "Clean through and through."

"Hmm." Felix pressed a wad of towels to Zero's injury. "You might live if you stop trying to talk."

"It was Quincy Edwards. Fucking little prick." Zero coughed again. He looked even grayer now than he had just a few short minutes ago.

Felix holstered his pistol and pulled out his phone. He dialed nine-one-one, but then Zero grabbed his arm. "No. Call Ariana."

"You have a fucking hole in your lung," Felix protested, but he was already redialing.

"He shot poor Jenna, and he and his goddamn loser friends decided to make a mess of my home before he left." Zero squeezed Felix's arm. "Promise me…" He broke off, wheezing.

Felix gave terse instructions to Zero's doctor

friend. When he hung up, he nodded. "She's on her way."

"Promise me," Zero tried again.

Felix pressed on Zero's wound. "You know I'll fucking kill him and his crew, Zero. Take it easy."

Zero's expression eased. "Good."

"Is he all right?" Nick asked from the doorway.

"The bullet got his lung." Felix looked down at his friend. "Tough bastard probably twisted out of the way of the killing shot."

Zero smiled faintly.

"Did he say who did it?" Nick asked.

Felix looked at him. "You know who did it."

"How the fuck did he get past the security?" Nick sounded like a man on the edge of a killing rampage. "I make a living breaking into places like this, and it isn't fucking easy."

"Hacked into my system," Zero said. He sounded like he was drowning. "Brought a fucking army. Outnumbered three to one."

"Fucking shut up," Felix said. Even his iron control couldn't contain the rage welling up in his gut. "Shit."

Nick came closer. "You said she would be safe."

Zero's face sagged. "Was wrong." He looked away. "Sorry."

"You saw his security, Nick," Felix said, low and angry. "You know Edwards had help. This isn't Zero's fault."

"I know that it's not Zero's fault. It's mine for leaving her here. I should've kept her with me," Nick bit out. "I should've stayed here with her."

"And then you would've died, too," Felix pointed out. "Because Edwards brought help." He glanced around. "A lot of help."

"We could've run," Nick said.

Felix inhaled, but didn't speak. Nick's point made sense in a rational world, but that's not where they lived. If Edwards was willing to go this far to kill Jenna, he'd have gotten to her no matter what Nick did. And if Nick and his sister had run, then Felix would never have had the chance to make love with him. *Frig it. I'm really losing it.* He stared at Nick, wishing he could say something that would help.

Nick let out a harsh laugh, clearly interpreting Felix's frustration. "Yeah, whatever. Hindsight and all that." He glanced at Zero, eyes dark. "Quincy and his fucking uncle need to die."

Zero gripped Felix's hand tighter. "No. Mine."

"What the hell's he talking about?" Nick asked, obviously short-tempered.

Felix didn't blame him. "He wants to kill the uncle." He smiled grimly. "Zero doesn't take kindly to betrayal, and the only way Quincy Edwards would be able to get his crew in here was if he had help." He glanced around. "Expert fucking help, and that means the uncle. For some reason, Robert Edwards decided to fuck Zero and his operation all to hell." He shook his head. "Stupid business decision, but that asshole isn't the sharpest knife in the drawer."

"Bastard wanted me to work for him," Zero croaked. "Always said no. I won't be his lackey." He coughed, then stared at Felix. "He's mine to kill."

Nick eyed Zero, and then snorted. "Sure. If you live, dude."

Zero glared at him. Felix was surprised his friend had the strength to look so angry. *But then again, he really is a tough bastard. And maybe that was Nick's plan. Get him pissed enough to hang on.*

"Anyway, what the fuck was Robert Edwards

doing helping his fucking nephew break in here, anyway? I thought he put out a hit on Quincy," Nick pointed out. "Robert Edwards has no reason to help a guy he wanted dead."

"Robert Edwards probably figured that he'd win however it ended up. Either Quincy killed Zero and Jenna, or Zero killed Quincy. With any luck, they'd kill each other and he'd be free of both of them, and he'd be able to take over Zero's business with a minimum of overhead. He doesn't give a shit about anyone, so the goons he sent to help his nephew would be acceptable losses if they died."

"That's fucked up," Nick said, frowning.

Felix shrugged. "No one ever said the Edwards family was nice." He turned to Zero. "Do you know where the nephew went?"

Zero coughed again. "Headed for your shack in the woods."

Felix raised his eyebrows. "And how did he find out about that place?" He already knew the answer.

Zero smiled through his pain. "I sent them there, of course."

"Shit. We missed them?" Nick said, running a hand through his hair.

"Mines," Zero said, wheezing again.

"Okay, enough talking," Felix said, keeping pressure on his wound.

"Mines. Oh, that's delicious," Nick murmured.

Felix bit back a smile, and then a female voice called out. "Zero?"

"In here," Felix yelled.

An older woman dressed in scrubs hurried into the room. Felix nodded, recognizing her from the pictures Zero had shown him over the years. Zero only let a very select few people into his close circle, and

Felix tried to keep track of every one. Ariana had married one of Zero's buddies from the military. A younger man with auburn hair followed her. He moved like someone trained in martial arts. Felix watched him carefully, but he didn't seem to have any weapons. *He looks like a younger, male version of Ariana. Zero never mentioned her son.* He wondered if Zero had ever met him before.

"Jesus, Zero," Ariana slid a huge backpack off her shoulders. "Good thing I brought help. I'm going to need another set of hands to deal with this."

"It nicked his right lung. Zero says it's a clean through and through, but I was afraid to move him to check," Felix said, still pressing the towels on the wound. "I think the blood loss is more of a problem than the lung."

"It's possible." Ariana nodded curtly. "You did good, whoever you are. I'll take it from here." She eased her hands under Felix's, and then jerked her head at her son as Felix sat back on his heels. "Julian, get the pressure bandage, the one with the petroleum jelly." The younger man nodded, lips pressed together as he quickly unzipped the large backpack.

"Go," Zero said, flapping his hand weakly. "The trap is set, but you need to spring it."

Felix hesitated. He didn't want to leave Zero here unprotected. He eyed Ariana's son again. The guy looked like he could handle himself, but he was an unknown variable in an already volatile situation.

"You can't help me," Ariana said, glancing up. "Also, I called my brother. He's a cop. I don't think you want to be here when he arrives."

"Fuck, Ariana. No cops here," Zero said, trying to sit up.

"Too late, my friend. He's already on his way." She put her hand flat on his chest and pushed him down.

"No moving, Zero. You'll do as I say until I'm sure you're not going to die."

"The cops will keep you safe," Felix said, impressed with the woman's quick thinking. "No one will come around if they're here."

"Fuck." Zero coughed. "That's the end of this place, then." He closed his eyes.

"Are we staying or going?" Nick demanded, hovering in the doorway.

Felix sighed. "Get better, Zero." He glanced at Ariana. "Will he end up at the hospital?"

She nodded. "Most likely. I can stabilize him, but he'll probably need surgery I can't do here with this equipment."

Zero tried to protest again, but Felix shook his head. "Do as she says, Zero." He stood up. "I'll check back in with you later."

"What about my sister?" Nick asked in a low voice when Felix joined him. "I can't leave her like this."

Felix glanced at Ariana. Her son was watching them. "You never saw us here, understand?" he said to the young man.

The guy nodded, frowning. "I know when to keep my mouth shut." He glanced at his mother. "I'll take care of them."

Felix frowned at him, then turned to Nick. "Jenna Banner ran to Zero for help when she left her boyfriend. Zero did his best, but you can see what happened. The cops will take it from here."

Nick shook his head. "I've got to call my parents."

Felix grabbed his arms and shook him. "No. That is the worst possible thing to do, Nick. You don't want to be anywhere around here when the cops come. You don't want to have any clue that Jenna went to Zero." He loosened his hold when he saw Nick wince. The bandage under his fingertips told him Nick's wound was still tender. "And we have work to do," he said, more softly.

Nick's expression went from grief, to anger, and then back again. "Yeah." He swallowed, then took a deep breath, running a hand over his face. "Okay. You're right."

Felix let go and stepped back. "Get your head in the game, Nick." He headed out of the bedroom, careful not to disturb any of the mess. He avoided Jenna's body, wishing she hadn't had to die. After a last, tortured look at his sister, Nick followed him. When they reached the darkness of the warehouse, Nick finally spoke.

"This is no fucking game, Felix. This is a hunt, and I'm not stopping until Quincy Edwards is nothing but a goddamn smear on the ground."

Chapter Eleven

Nick swallowed down the horrible mix of grief and rage he felt about Jenna's death as Felix drove back to the cabin. He wanted to scream and yell and break shit, but he knew that if they were going to catch Quincy, he needed to control himself.

"Almost there," Felix murmured.

Nick fingered his blade. If he could, he planned on skinning the bastard who'd killed his sister. "What exactly did Zero mean about mines?" he asked, instead of grinding his teeth again. He had an inkling, but he wanted to hear what Felix had to say.

"I have the entire forest around my cabin seeded with mines." Felix glanced at him, then shrugged. "Military surplus."

"We should've just brought Jenna here," Nick growled.

Felix sighed. "Maybe. And maybe we would've died, too, along with her." He glanced at Nick, face unreadable, then focused on the road again.

"I thought you were some kind of super fucking assassin," Nick said bitterly, glaring at the side of his head.

"One against many is never good odds," Felix replied. His voice was smooth and steady, and Nick felt his rage well up again. How could the man be so fucking calm after what happened?

"Yet here we are," he bit out, trying not to blame Felix for everything. *He had no idea that Quincy's uncle would help him penetrate Zero's place,* he reminded himself. *He had no idea that Zero's bunker was vulnerable. They showed you the security. You know it was damn near impenetrable.* Talking himself down from the edge of rage wasn't really working. He took a deep breath and held it for a few seconds, and then let it out again. He might know rationally that neither Felix nor Zero were to blame for Jenna's death, but that didn't seem to matter. He wanted to hurt someone. He wanted someone to pay. *And admit it. Deep down, you blame yourself.*

"Yes. Here we are. And we're going to fucking wipe the floor with them. I no longer give a shit about the odds. They shot my best friend. They killed your sister." Felix's hands gripped the steering wheel like a man driving on the edge of a cliff. The display of emotion, as subdued as it was, soothed Nick. He'd only known the man for a short time, but he knew that Felix wasn't given to strong emotions. His career demanded steady nerves and detachment. Knowing that Felix wasn't nearly as unemotional as he pretended to be calmed Nick considerably.

Nick nodded. "Yeah. They did. So, what are we going to do about it?"

Felix gave him a look. "You know exactly what we're going to do about it. Edwards and his crew need to know that there are some people you just don't fuck with." Felix slowed the truck, then pulled into a clearing and cut the engine. "This is about a half a mile from the house. You good to go?"

Nick looked at his lover. God help him, but he liked the cold calculation in Felix's gaze. Despite his grief, his cock twitched. He'd fuck Felix right here and now, if only to affirm that they were still fucking alive, but they had a task to complete. Steely determination filled him in place of the rage. "Hell, yeah. I'm good to fucking go." He slid his knife back into its sheath, then hefted the shotgun Felix had given him. "This is going to tear them to pieces, isn't it?"

Felix nodded. "It is."

"Good." Nick opened the truck door and hopped lightly to the ground. He scanned their surroundings. Late afternoon sunlight glittered through the canopy like a goddamn Disney movie. Nick glared at a bird singing on a branch just overhead. "Which way?"

Felix came around the front of the truck. "Follow me."

Ten minutes later, Felix paused, looking around. "Something's not—"

Boom.

Nick tensed, every muscle in his body going into high alert as the sound of an explosion cut off Felix's words. "One of your mines?"

Felix nodded, eyes squinting through the trees. "This way. Follow me precisely." He plunged off the trail and into the brush. Leaves shivered as he passed, but nothing rustled underfoot.

Nick followed, putting his years of burglary to good use. He knew how to move around a forest quietly. He knew how to move *everywhere* quietly. When Felix stopped short, Nick halted, muscles quivering. Felix pointed. Nick tilted his head, then nodded when he saw blood and bone spattered on the ground. Five feet away lay the remains of an intruder. Some small part of him knew he should be freaking the fuck out—he wasn't a killer, for fuck's sake—but most of him felt weirdly pleased by the carnage. These assholes had a hand in killing his sister for no good reason. All she'd wanted was to get the hell away from Quincy, and that psycho fuck had decided to hunt her down.

"This way to the house," Felix murmured. "Stay close."

Nick nodded. "No problem."

Felix melted into the trees. When they emerged at the edge of the clearing where the cabin stood, Nick took a deep breath. They'd discovered three more tripped mines in the forest. Two of them had killed someone, but there was no way of knowing how many more men were here.

Felix pointed to a large SUV parked in front of the steps. "If that's their only vehicle, maybe three more guys, tops."

"Quincy pissed off the wrong guy," Nick said, grimly satisfied. "Not too bright, is he?"

"Indeed." Felix smiled coldly. "He has no idea I'm involved in this."

Nick returned the smile, thinking of his sister. She didn't deserve to die, but Quincy sure as fuck did. "Don't kill him," he told Felix.

Felix pursed his lips.

"He's mine, Felix," Nick hissed, leaning in. He grabbed his lover's arm. Warmth seeped through the soft fabric into his palms. "He's *my* fucking kill."

After a moment that stretched too long for Nick's liking, Felix nodded, easing away from Nick's grip. "He's yours."

Nick inhaled, then let it out slowly. He didn't want nerves and adrenaline to fuck this up. "They must be inside." They'd done a quick survey of the perimeter, and they'd found no one, aside from the dead guys littering the forest floor.

"You ready?"

"Hell, yeah." Nick snorted. "You have to ask?"

Felix touched his shoulder. "Don't fucking die in there."

Nick put a hand over Felix's, then leaned in for a quick, bruising kiss. "You too. We've got things to do, places to see."

Felix's fierce grin warmed Nick down to his toes.

****

"Clear," Felix mouthed from the foot of the stairs. They'd checked the downstairs bathroom and laundry room and found nothing. The great room and kitchen were empty. That meant any intruders had to be in the loft. He pointed up, and Nick silently nodded, moving in front of him. Felix followed, somewhat concerned that they hadn't found Edwards yet. Nick made short work of the stairs. When he reached the guest bedroom, he gestured to Felix.

Felix nodded, knowing Nick wanted him on the other side of the door. He silently moved across the frame, and then slowly eased the door open. Nick crouched down, pointing the shotgun inside. When he shook his head, Felix nodded and headed inside, moving to the guest bathroom. Nothing. Even the shower-tub combination was clear. They headed back to the hall, and he stared at the closed master bedroom door. *Edwards must be in there. Fucking coward, hiding from us.*

Nick pointed at it. Felix nodded again, and they mirrored their previous stance. When Felix slowly turned the doorknob and eased it open, the wood suddenly splintered right above his hand. He dropped to the floor, pleased to see Nick doing the same.

"I know you're out there! Come on in. I can't wait to kill the bitch's brother, too. I like to tie up all my loose ends," Quincy Edwards yelled.

Felix grimaced as the ringing in his ears slowly faded. Edwards's voice didn't sound quite right. "Drugs?" he mouthed at Nick.

Nick nodded, then rolled his eyes.

Yeah, yeah. I know it doesn't matter, Felix thought. He counted down from three on his fingers, pleased that Nick was watching him closely so they could coordinate their entry, and then he rolled inside shooting.

The hollow boom of the shotgun sounded, and Felix saw a shell hit the wooden floor just inches from his hand. *Nick's only got one more shot left, and then he has to reload.* Felix squeezed off a few more shots as distraction as his gaze ranged the room. *There! By the fucking window.* He shot Edward's shin. The asshole screamed and dropped to the floor. Felix rolled into a squat, gaze darting around the bedroom. He didn't see any other men, but that didn't mean someone wasn't hiding in the bathroom. He looked at Nick, then pointed to the bathroom. The door was ajar.

Nick nodded, and then he strode forward. "You thought you'd get away with it, huh, asshole?"

Felix stood up in a rush, and crossed the room. A shot rang out, and he ducked instinctively. Glass shards cut his neck as the mirror mounted on the wall shattered. He kicked the bathroom door wide, and shot the man standing near the toilet. Blood spattered the window. The body slumped over the windowsill, knocking a candle to the floor. Felix pivoted, his Glock pointed at the shower, but no one was there. He let out the breath he hadn't realized he'd been holding.

"Sloppy work," he muttered to himself. He should've insisted that Nick wait until he'd cleared the bath. He should've checked the shower faster.

"You're a stupid fuck," Nick said from the bedroom.

Felix looked out the window. No men loitered in the clearing. With the three in the woods, and the one on the floor of the bathroom, he figured they'd got them all. Five men fit comfortably in the SUV parked outside. The only man left alive right now was Quincy Edwards, and he wouldn't be for long.

"You're the stupid fucking asshole. If you kill me, my uncle will wipe your entire family from existence," Quincy said.

Felix walked to the doorway. Nick stood over Edwards with the shotgun pressed to the man's gut. The sneer on Edwards's face confused Felix. *No one can be this fucking dumb.* He stared at the man, then shook his head. Not even a flicker of intelligence crossed the guy's face.

"You're assuming that I give a flying fuck about the rest of my family, Quincy," Nick said, shaking his head. "You didn't do your homework, did you?" He pressed the barrel of the gun into Quincy's soft stomach, showing teeth when the man tried to crawl away. "You are the dumbest motherfucker on the planet."

"Faggot," Edwards spat.

Nick laughed. "You bet." And then he pulled the trigger.

Edwards gasped, then tried to take a breath and coughed, his face going grey.

"You know that gut wounds are a terrible way to die," Nick said conversationally. "Mostly you bleed out, but it hurts like crazy while it's happening."

Edwards tried to reach up, but couldn't raise his arm more than an inch. "Fucker," he whispered, coughing again. Blood fountained from the ragged wound in his torso.

Felix walked over. "I saw you fingering your blade earlier," he said to Nick. "I'm surprised you didn't skin him." He liked the way Edwards flinched when he overheard his words. *Good. He deserves to die in fear.*

Nick shrugged. "This was easier. Didn't feel like getting my hands dirty on this loser."

Edwards gurgled, but couldn't seem to get his voice to work.

Nick prodded him with his toe. "You're not dead yet? Jesus. Taking a long time." He tilted his head. "That must hurt like hell."

Edwards glared at him. Nick crouched down. "You know your uncle is going to die, too. And he's going to go down begging for his life. Zero doesn't take kindly to having his business disrupted, dumbass."

Edwards blinked.

"Your uncle hired me to kill you, by the way," Felix said casually. "Your own fucking blood wanted you dead and gone. Interesting."

Edwards's eyes widened.

Felix nodded. "'Too stupid. Too much of a liability,' were Robert Edwards' words on the contract, I believe. Most people don't bother with explanations, so that was an interesting detail to put in writing." Felix bared his teeth at the man bleeding out in his cabin. "Guess I'm going to have to give Nick the money for the job, though." He shook his head. "First time for everything, I suppose."

Nick chuckled. "You can keep the fee, Felix. I did this one for free." Edwards opened his mouth as if to protest, but then he slumped down, eyes stuck open.

"Well." Nick stood up, wiping his free hand on his pants. "That's it, I guess."

"Kind of a letdown, isn't it?" Felix took the shotgun from him.

Nick scrubbed his face with both hands. "Yeah." He glanced around. "Shit. What a fucking mess."

Felix shrugged. "Time to torch the place." He liked the area, and the privacy, but he'd gotten used to leaving places over the years. He'd find somewhere else to set up his life, and maybe this time he'd really retire instead of just thinking about it.

"Why bother? We could get a cleaner in." Nick headed to the window. "It's got a good view. And it's quiet." He grimaced. "Most of the time."

"Too many people know it's here," Felix said, thinking of Zero and Robert Edwards. "Zero is going to be making a big fucking mess, too, as soon as he recovers." He ran a hand through his hair. "Time to put some miles between me and here."

"Don't you mean, 'us and here'?" Nick asked.

Felix raised his eyebrows.

"I plan on stalking you." Nick walked over, crowding into Felix's personal space. "And I'm good at my job. I'll find you, no matter where you go, so why not just save us both the fucking bother and let me come with you?"

Felix inhaled. Nick smelled good, like crushed leaves and gunpowder. He thought of never smelling him again, and the sudden awful dismay that welled up in his gut shocked him. He licked his lips. He wanted to kiss Nick. He wanted to grab him and never let go. "I thought you might have a funeral to deal with." He hated to bring it up, but it had to be said. "And some other loose ends."

Nick's expression went dark. "I'll say goodbye to Jenna in my own time. There's no goddamn way I'm going to stand in line with my parents, and pretend that everything is fucking fine with our family."

Felix got what Nick was saying. Even grief didn't heal wounds like that. "I hear you."

"Anyway, they'd probably throw me out if I even tried to go to Jenna's funeral." Nick exhaled violently. "Fuck them." He stepped back.

No. Felix grabbed Nick and pulled him into a rough hug. *He's not walking away from me.* Nick's muscles felt like rocks, and Felix wished he hadn't had to bring up Jenna's death. "You don't have to stalk me."

Nick leaned back, but didn't try to get away. "No?"

"You can come with me." Felix fought to control

his breathing. He hadn't felt this overwhelmed in decades. For the first time in his life, he was offering another person a hand into his life, and it fucking terrified him. He shook his head. Emotions he'd thought long dead and buried rushed through him, and Nick stood there, not saying a fucking word. "You hear me?"

Nick looked at him so long, Felix thought maybe he wasn't going to reply, but then he smiled. "Okay."

Felix swallowed down the rush of relief. "Good."

"That's all you have to say?" Nick rolled his eyes and kissed him softly.

Felix groaned into Nick's mouth as his cock went from soft to hard in three seconds. Nick's body was hot as hell against his. "Jesus, Nick."

"I'm no savior," Nick muttered, sliding fingers into Felix's hair. "In fact, I'm pretty fucking screwed up." He kissed Felix again, this time brutally. "I shouldn't even be doing this right now, right over the body of my sister's killer."

"Who gives a shit about that? It's just dead meat." Felix asked, wrestling him around. He pushed Nick up against the wall and thrust into him. "Christ. You have no idea, do you?"

"What?" Nick shoved his hands under Felix's shirt, growling when the tactical vest resisted his efforts to get it off.

"Your sister might be dead, but you're not, Nick," Felix said, wanting him to understand. "You're *not* dead." He put his hands on Nick's biceps and shook him. "You're fucking alive right now. And it doesn't matter where we are. Doesn't matter what you did." He took a deep breath. "All that counts is what you do next."

Nick stared at him. "You getting all sentimental on me?"

Felix shook him again. "No. I'm being practical.

If you want to live in this world, you've got to choose to live in it. No frigging limping along, half-assed, reacting to the shit that happens. And if you come with me, you have to understand that it won't always be pretty." He stepped back, waiting. He wanted Nick to choose him again, this time with a full understanding of what that meant. "I'm a killer, Nick. And nothing is going to change that, even if I retire. Even if I never pull another trigger."

Chapter Twelve

Nick stared at Felix, not sure if he was pissed or pleased that the man had forced him to consider precisely who and what he was. *Felix is a killer, but what am I?* Nick glanced at the body on the floor. Edwards's eyes stared through him. He didn't feel even a shred of remorse, and that more than anything else told him how to answer. He looked back at Felix. "I'm a killer, too."

Felix's fierce expression eased. "You sure about that?"

Nick nodded. "Maybe something's broken inside my head. Maybe I'm just a vindictive motherfucker. Either way, the only thing I feel about killing my sister's killer is satisfaction."

Felix exhaled slowly. "That happens. And sometimes you realize you're good at it."

Nick frowned. "I'm a better thief than I am an assassin."

"Hmm, true," Felix said, looking over the mess on the floor. "And it's never good to combine specialties in a relationship. Avoids arguments about technique." Felix smiled, slow and cocky. His hazel eyes had gone dark with lust.

Nick groaned, then grabbed him and dragged him downstairs. "We are not fucking on top of a body," he gritted out. He might be seriously lacking in fucking morals, but there were limits.

Felix let Nick shove him onto the sofa. Nick made short work of Felix's vest, then started on his own. "This is going to be quick." He tried to take off his knife, but the sheath's buckle defeated him and he left it strapped to his arm.

"Stop talking," Felix said, taking off his shirt. He unbuttoned his jeans. The tip of his cock pushed against the zipper.

"Fuck," Nick muttered, going to his knees. He nosed in, needing to taste him. Felix smelled hot and dangerous, but more importantly, he smelled alive, and Nick needed that reassurance right now. Grief welled up again, but he shoved it away. *Not now. Grieve later*, he told himself. He licked the tip of Felix's shaft, and then he shoved down his jeans, trapping Felix at the thighs. "I have no control around you. We should be getting the hell away from here." He wrapped a hand around Felix's cock. Heat seeped into Nick's palm, and he leaned down again, licking and sucking.

Felix groaned, hips jerking. Nick let him shove his erection all the way in, relaxing his throat. When he swallowed, Felix made a sound, hips straining. Nick backed off, rolling Felix's balls in his fingers. "I'm going to fuck you."

"Never done that," Felix said.

"There's a first time for everything." Nick stood up and undressed, watching as Felix worked his jeans off. The moment he was free, Nick went back to his knees, pushing Felix's legs back. "God, you taste good." He sucked Felix's cock down again, then slid down, licking as he went. When he reached Felix's hole, he swirled his tongue around the pucker.

"The fuck, that again?" Felix shoved him away.

"Shut up." Nick grabbed his wrists and held him down. "I'm blowing your fucking mind." He bent back to his task, loving the sounds Felix made. When he slid a spit-slick finger inside, Felix shuddered.

"Fuck." Felix shoved himself down on Nick's finger.

"Yeah." Nick slid another one in, licking around them. Felix's muscles had relaxed, and he could probably fit his cock inside now, but the last thing he wanted to do hurt him. "Wait here," he said, easing his fingers out.

"Christ." Felix lay boneless on the sofa. He touched his cock, then jacked himself slowly. "Lube is in the cabinet." He pointed to the door just off the mud room.

Nick nodded. When he returned, Felix had his eyes closed and head thrown back. "God, look at you. You're killing me," he said.

Felix smiled. "Slip of the tongue?"

Nick choked back a laugh. "Shut up." He dribbled too much lube over his hand and cupped Felix's balls. Slick wetness dripped down on the floor. Nick didn't give a shit.

Felix's eyes snapped open. "Fuck!"

"Yeah. That's exactly right." Nick pushed and shoved at Felix until his ass hung off the sofa, then lined his cock up. "Feel that?" He pushed the tip of his erection at Felix's hole. "Relax." He slung Felix's legs over his shoulders and pressed in, not letting up until the head of his dick was inside. Felix made a sound somewhere between a growl and a groan, but Nick had no intention of stopping. "God, you're tight." Felix felt like a burning ring of fire around his cock.

"Nick." Felix scrabbled at the sofa, trying to hang on.

Nick sucked in a breath and pressed in some more. Felix's leg rubbed against his still-healing gunshot wound, and the pain of friction made him grit his teeth. "Take it. Come on."

Felix finally exhaled, and Nick sank balls-deep into his body. "Hang on, Felix. I'm getting there."

His lover glared at him. "Fuck you."

Nick didn't reply. He couldn't speak. He could barely fucking move. He swallowed, hard, and then began thrusting his hips. He'd never be able fuck anyone else ever again. Felix was everything he'd ever wanted: tough, dangerous, and fucking sexy as hell. Even the blood from the broken glass that had cut him along his neck and face turned him on. "Never again," he chanted as he began to move in earnest.

"What?" Felix hung onto the edge of the sofa, muscles straining.

"I'm never going to fuck anyone else again. This is it," Nick managed to force out. His dick was on fire, and his balls were so tight, he knew he was holding onto his orgasm by sheer luck. "Fuck. Come on, Felix." He reached down and began to jack his lover fast and hard.

Felix snapped his hips up, then down again, hair wild as his body took over.

Nick squeezed him harder, hips working his cock deeper and deeper. The burn in his thighs didn't matter. The pain in his arm didn't matter. The only thing he wanted was to see Felix lose his fucking mind. The cock in his hand swelled thicker, and then Felix froze, hips and legs and torso trembling as his cock jerked. Thick ropes of spunk jetted out, coating them both. The pressure on Nick's erection sent him over the edge, and he groaned, falling down into Felix as he climaxed.

A long time later, he peeled himself off of Felix and slumped down on the floor. The hard wood pushed into his bones, and abruptly he felt about a thousand years too old for screwing on a sofa. He glanced up at Felix. His lover looked good. Better than good, even with the lines on his face and the bit of silver in his stubble.

"God, we're a mess." Nick felt like he had to say something. Nothing ever happened the way he expected. He thought he'd feel better with Quincy dead. He thought he'd never fall in love, and now he knew that neither of those things was true. *Fuck. I'm losing it, which is absurd, after everything that's happened to me.*

How is this *the breaking point?*

Felix groaned, stretching out on the sofa. "And I'm not as young as I used to be." He ran a hand over his face. "We need to clean up and get out of here." He dropped a hand on Nick's head, combing through his hair as if all of the killing earlier was just a job. As if the blood was ordinary.

And maybe for him it is. Nick nodded, willing himself to get up as the sensation of being completely outside of his body started to finally fade. He felt boneless. Satisfied, but not happy. He thought of his sister, and sighed.

"It will take a while to get used to what's happened," Felix said, as if reading his mind. "Don't fuck with it. It's like picking at a cut. You just leave it alone and it'll get better."

"Yeah." Nick got up, then offered Felix a hand. "Yeah. I guess." Felix took his hand, and Nick hauled him up. "You sure you want to torch this place?" He glanced around. "It's a nice cabin."

Felix shrugged. "Seems prudent."

"We could deal with Quincy's uncle. Put an end to this entire fucking situation." Nick thought about it, trying to weigh the pros and cons. Part of him wanted to do it, if only to give himself closure, but the rest of him knew that it likely wouldn't end there. If they killed Robert Edwards, then someone else would come after them. And someone else after that.

"No. Zero will want to handle that situation." Felix headed for the stairs. He didn't bother to get dressed. "And he's got the leverage to limit any collateral damage."

Nick watched him walk up to the loft. The juxtaposition of his nudity against the wooden walls left his dick feebly twitching in hopes of a second go at sex.

Nick shook his head, then rolled his shoulders and grabbed his pants. He shoved his feet into the legs, and then habit took over and before he knew it, he was dressed. He hadn't bothered to wipe up. The musky smell of sex reassured him. He went over the last twenty-four hours in his head, trying to normalize the situation. *I fucked an assassin. I killed the asshole who murdered my sister. I'm with Felix now, and where he goes, I go.* He rubbed his eyes. "Jesus. When will I learn not to jump head first into a giant clusterfuck?"

Felix reappeared fully clothed, with a large duffel slung over his shoulder. "You ready?" Clearly, he hadn't heard Nick mumbling to himself. He dropped the duffel near the door.

Nick nodded, not bothering to look around. He didn't have anything here to gather up. "Yeah. Let's blow this pop stand."

Felix half smiled, then walked to the kitchen area. He reached behind the stove and fiddled with something. "It'll burn fast. I have it set up to blow." He went to the fireplace and yanked open a panel set into the floor right in front of the hearth. "Gas makes this almost too easy." He twisted something, then popped the panel back into place.

"A gas explosion?" Nick had to hand it to him: Felix knew his shit.

"If we're lucky, they might even think we died in the mess." Felix pointed upstairs. "It's a nice way to get rid of bodies. And it will be a perfect explanation for the mess in the woods. Lowlife drug dealer bites off more than he can chew when he invades rival's bunker. The cops will love it."

Nick nodded. It all seemed too fucking easy. "So, how many states are we really talking about? Still fixated on the west coast?" He didn't care how far they went, but he needed to know so he could reorganize his contacts and keep his business intact.

"Yes." Felix rubbed his jaw. "This place is going to be crawling with law enforcement in a week or so. I'm thinking about Oregon."

Nick raised his eyebrows. "You sure about that?"

"We'll check in with Zero, first. Maybe give it a few days, but yeah. I'm sure." Felix walked closer. "Are you having second thoughts?"

"Fuck, no." Nick stood his ground. Felix walked right up to him, looking like sex and danger and bad news. *And if there's one thing I can't resist, it's a man with those qualities.* "I told you. If you try to leave without me, I'll stalk you."

Felix smiled. "You may regret this."

"That's not your problem," Nick replied.

Felix reached out, then gently brushed Nick's hair out of his eyes.

Nick held still. The look on Felix's face worried him.

"This is your last chance to back out." Felix slowly and deliberately tightened his fingers in Nick's hair until he couldn't move his head. "I'm not in the mood for games."

Astonishingly, Nick's cock hardened again. "What makes you think I'm playing?" he whispered, not even trying to fight Felix's grip. He could break free, but it would hurt. Maybe that was symbolism for their entire fucking relationship. He smirked.

"It would be so easy to fucking kill you," Felix murmured, leaning in as if to kiss him.

"And I'd kill you right back." Nick's hand twitched, and the blade he kept at his wrist popped into his hand. He pressed it right up against Felix's heart. "You don't scare me."

Felix inhaled sharply. "Fuck."

Nick smiled and leaned in, capturing Felix's mouth in a soft kiss. "Admit it. We're perfect for each other."

Felix groaned, releasing his grip on Nick's head. "I guess so." He pressed closer, until the tip of Nick's blade bit through his clothes.

Nick eased up the pressure, not wanting to actually cut his lover. Felix fought him, pushing in harder.

"Jesus, Christ, what the fuck are you doing, Felix?" Nick couldn't believe how aroused he was. Hadn't they just gotten done fucking?

"Give me your knife," Felix said.

Nick frowned, but Felix let him go. "Why?"

"Just do it."

Nick pressed his lips together, but he offered his right hand. His blade sat on his palm: slim, sharp, deadly.

Felix deftly plucked the blade out of his hand. "Give me your hand."

"So fucking pushy," Nick said, scowling.

"Just do it."

Nick sighed, then raised his left arm and aligned it with Felix's, wrist facing up. He had an inkling of what Felix intended, but he couldn't be sure. He glanced at Felix's expression, but nothing on his face explained what he meant to do. *I don't have to do this,* Nick told himself, but then Felix spoke.

"Good. Hold still."

Nick opened his mouth, about to protest, but then his lover slashed down with the knife. "Fuck!" Pain slammed into him. "That fucking hurt, Felix," Nick said. Before he could snatch back his arm, Felix had grabbed him.

"It won't kill you." Felix was turning his arm,

pressing the shallow wounds he'd made together. "Blood to blood." He gripped Nick's arm right below the elbow.

Nick licked his lips as he slowly let his fingers tighten around Felix's arm. His heart felt like it was going to jump right the fuck out of his chest. The cut on his forearm stung, especially with Felix grinding his own wound against it. If he'd ever had any doubts about Felix, they'd completely disappeared. *No one does this kind of shit anymore,* he thought, staring down at their arms. Blood trickled out from beneath where they were pressed together.

"Blood to blood, Nick," Felix repeated intently.

Nick looked up. Felix's hazel eyes bored into his. A thousand and one questions clamored into the front of his brain, but Nick ignored them all. The only thing that mattered was Felix, standing here waiting for him to reply. "Blood to blood, Felix," he murmured, voice cracking. "You and me. That's all that matters now."

Felix nodded, short and sharp, and then he kissed Nick, hard. "It's done." He released Nick's arm, then pulled a few lengths of gauze out of his pocket. He wrapped Nick's wound first, then did his own.

"You planned this?" Nick asked, knowing this particular wound would scar. Felix had judged the depth perfectly. They didn't need stitches, but it would be a bitch to heal.

Felix lifted a shoulder. "Not quite." He looked around his cabin. "Time to go."

Nick fingered the gauze as he followed Felix to the door. "You have a hell of a way of declaring commitment, Felix."

Felix held up his arm. "This is a lot more permanent than words will ever be."

Nick stared at him, and then snorted. "Good point." Somehow, the sting of the new wound made his grief over losing his sister feel less overwhelming. It was almost as if the pain in his heart had an outlet. *Maybe as it heals, I'll somehow learn how to miss her less,* he mused, fingering the gauze. "All right," he said aloud, mentally feeling his way out of the morass of emotions roiling in his gut. "Let's get the hell out of here."

After a short, sharp nod, Felix turned the knob and opened the door. Outside, late afternoon sunlight slanted across the clearing. It was hard to believe that just a few short hours ago the quiet woods were a scene of carnage. Nick watched the light silhouette Felix's body. Nothing about the man screamed "killer", but his utter competence bled throughout every one of his movements. He'd never looked more fucking hot to Nick. Felix paused, then looked back.

"You ready?" he asked.

"Yeah." Nick smiled, and joined Felix on the stoop. "I've been ready for years."

Epilogue

Six weeks later, somewhere in rural Oregon...

"Zero says that Robert Edwards still has people watching the warehouse," Felix said, looking up from his phone.

Nick pushed the last floorboard into place, hammering down the corner with his fist until he was sure it was wedged in properly. "Yeah?" He ran a hand over his forehead, wiping the sweat away. Laying down a new hardwood floor was a pain in the ass, but neither of them wanted to have a troop of contractors snooping around their new place. Privacy was somewhat of a goal for a retired assassin and a thief. "Zero is living in that souped-up RV of his, right? How is he managing? He just had surgery a few weeks ago."

"According to Ariana, the surgery wasn't complicated. The blood loss was the bigger concern. And Zero is in excellent shape." Felix suddenly grinned. "As for the warehouse, Zero says it's perfect bait. Edwards can't seem to resist poking around in it."

Nick rolled his eyes. "I thought Quincy's uncle was smarter than him, but maybe not."

Felix shrugged. "Not our problem."

"Why doesn't Zero just kill him already? Clearly, he knows exactly where Edwards is. This seems to be taking a hell of a long time," Nick said, frowning down at the floor. The last board was bowing a bit. He banged on it again.

"He's looking to take down the entire organization, not just the head guy," Felix replied. "Again, not our problem."

Nick sat back on his heels. He *almost* wanted it to be their problem: it still pissed him off that Quincy's uncle had helped his idiot nephew kill Jenna. On the other hand, he'd hate to see Felix take up killing again, and he knew that Felix would never let Nick deal with Robert Edwards on his own. If he hunted Edwards down, Felix would come with him. And over the past few weeks, his lover had mellowed to the point where he even cracked a joke occasionally. Nick sighed, once again pushing his frustration away. He knew he would never really get over his sister's death, but he was coping better these days. "Whatever happened to that guy who checked up on Zero for us in the hospital?"

"Ariana's son?" Felix asked. "She said he's staying with Zero to make sure he doesn't overdo it."

"Damn. He isn't on Edwards's radar, is he?" Nick worried that Ariana's son was going to get fingered as one of Zero's acquaintances. Since neither he nor Felix would have moved across the country without some way of getting real updates on Zero's condition, they'd asked Ariana to keep tabs on him. She'd had to hand over Zero's treatment to a surgeon. She'd asked Julian to check in on Zero, who'd still been in the hospital recovering when they'd first headed to Oregon. No one at the hospital knew that Julian was Ariana's son, so it kept him from being noticed by any of Edwards's thugs. No one realized that Julian knew Zero in any way other than as a delivery man for a certain excellent coffee shop near the hospital where Zero had spent a week recuperating.

"He's fine. No one knows anything about him in connection to Zero, although his mother says that he seems pensive these days. Whatever the fuck that means." Felix stood up from where he was fitting in quarter-round molding, and headed over to Nick. "Looks good."

"Pensive, huh." Nick grimaced, then stretched his neck out. "This is a hell of a lot of work." He smoothed a hand over the wood he'd just installed.

Felix shrugged. "It is what it is."

Nick stood up. "That was the last section, thank fuck." He rolled his head, trying to work the kinks out of his neck. Banging down wood planks was murder on his back. "How do you know Julian is okay?"

"Because Zero mentioned him. Again." Felix held out his phone to Nick.

Nick took it and read the email. "Huh. Zero seems strangely cool with Julian's company for a man who supposedly enjoys his solitude." He grinned. In the email, Zero detailed how impressed he was with Julian's calm and competence.

"Zero can use the company after all the years he's spent holed up alone in that warehouse," Felix said, smiling. "At least he doesn't suspect that we had anything to do with sending Julian to him."

"I think there's a bit more than mild approval in that email. Maybe some frustration, too," Nick said, rubbing his chin. "Love is in the air."

Felix barked out a laugh. "Are you fucking serious?"

Nick raised his eyebrows. "Zero is a stoic motherfucker. When was the last time he sent you an email like this?"

Felix scowled. "Never."

Nick smiled. "Precisely."

"Why in the hell are we even discussing this?" Felix asked, unclipping his tool belt from his waist and letting it fall to the newly install floor. "Zero is a grown man. He can handle his own love life."

Nick smiled. "You just don't want to talk about the L word."

Felix stared at him, hazel eyes narrowed.

Nick walked up to him and cupped his cheeks.

"You can't even think about it without getting all pissed off and angry." He leaned in and kissed him.

Felix growled. "You are such a shit." He grabbed Nick by the arms and wrestled him up against the wall. "You know how I feel."

Nick smirked. He *did* know, even if Felix had never said the words out loud. "You love me."

Felix scowled. "Shut. Up." He punctuated his words with two hard kisses.

Nick licked his lips. "Admit it."

"Fuck you."

"Sure thing. After you say you love me," Nick taunted, liking the way Felix's cock grew harder the more belligerent he became. Their relationship might not be all roses and unicorns, but it worked for them. And he liked to rile Felix up. He dismissed Julian from his thoughts.

As Felix likes to say: not my problem, and right now I have more interesting things to think about. Like how long it will take Felix to lose control.

"You know I do." Felix yanked at Nick's jeans, undoing the button and zipper with little finesse.

Nick gasped as his cock sprang out. "I know you do, and I know I do, but you've never said it out loud."

"Jesus Christ, Nick," Felix said, wrapping a fist around Nick's cock.

Nick groaned, pushing his dick into the rough warmth of Felix's palm. "I love you," he said, just to see the flare of heat and irritation in Felix's gaze.

Sure enough, Felix glared at him. "If you don't shut the fuck up—"

"You'll what? Not fuck me?" Nick had Felix's shirt half off now, and he ran the tips of his fingers over his lover's taut abdomen. "Uh huh. Thought so," he said, when Felix didn't reply. He dropped his head down on

Felix's shoulder and opened his lover's pants. Felix's erection slipped right into his hand, hot and heavy. He pressed closer, lining their cocks up together. "God, that's fucking perfect." He cupped them both with his hands, batting Felix's fingers away. "I got this, lover." He stroked them steadily, not wanting to go off too quickly, but everything felt so good, he couldn't help speeding up. Felix smelled like sawdust and sweat and musk. Nick swallowed, hard, trying to keep from coming like a fourteen-year-old boy experiencing his first fucking hand job.

Felix's hips jerked as Nick twisted his thumbs over the tip of his cock. "Shit."

"Yeah," Nick said, rubbing the copious amount of pre-cum all over them. "Yeah, come on, Felix. Do it. Come all over my hand, baby."

Felix groaned, and then he grabbed onto Nick's shoulders so hard it hurt. His erection swelled, and then thick, hot jets of spunk coated Nick's cock. Nick grinned, even as the heat of Felix's pleasure tipped him over the edge, too. He shuddered as he orgasmed, then slumped against Felix, thinking of what else they could get up to that day. It was only mid-morning, after all. They could fuck on the staircase. They could make out in the kitchen. They could even say a fuck you to wearing clothes for the rest of the day, if they wanted to.

"I love you," Felix whispered into Nick's shoulder.

Nick's thoughts fractured. "What?"

"You heard me." Felix leaned back, smiling faintly.

Nick flushed. "Wow." His heart tripped at the expression on Felix's face. He knew how Felix felt, but hearing the words out loud stunned him. "I love you, too."

Felix pulled him in for a hug. "Is this what it's like for all those people out there?"

Nick knew Felix meant people with normal lives. People with regular jobs and spouses and children. "I have no idea," he said, chuckling as he hugged Felix tight. "We are not normal, and we're never going to be normal. And I don't really give a flying fuck about being normal, either."

Felix laughed. "True."

"Let's just be happy we met, and leave it at that," Nick suggested when they'd finally let go of each other. He swiped at the mess on his groin halfheartedly, then gave up. He needed a shower. Looking at his lover, he grinned. So did Felix. Maybe they could fuck in the bathroom.

Felix's eyes twinkled. "So romantic."

Nick rolled his eyes. "I'm a thief, not a romance novelist. You get what you get, and you don't get upset."

Felix snorted. "Come on. Let's go clean up." He slapped Nick on the shoulder, and headed for the stairs.

Nick watched him walk, all contained power and skill wrapped up in a truly excellent body. He didn't care that Felix killed people for a living. He didn't care about their age difference. Even after all these months, he still couldn't believe that Felix was his guy. *My own, personal nullifier.* He almost laughed out loud at his fucking spectacular luck. He felt like he'd pulled the biggest heist of his career. *And all because I broke my rule about not fucking a straight guy.*

"You coming?" Felix asked, looking back at him.

"You bet I'm coming. I'll always come with you, Felix," Nick replied, smirking.

The End

THE CRIMINALS

THE FIXER

The Criminals, 2

Erin M. Leaf

Copyright © 2018

Chapter One

Some big motherfucker was sitting on Zeke Graham's chest, and he didn't like it one bit. He opened his strangely groggy eyes, about to use his considerable strength to shove the fucker onto the floor, when he realized that he couldn't move his arms. Or breathe on his own. A horrible tube stretched from his lips down into his throat, hurting his esophagus. He couldn't swallow. Beeping sounds from his left pierced his skull, setting off a headache worse than any he'd ever had before.

"Zero? Can you hear me? Try and relax. You're in the hospital, and you're on a ventilator. Don't fight it. You're waking up from surgery," a female voice said. Something cool touched his arm.

Zeke, known to most everyone as Zero, struggled

to order his thoughts, but everything seemed to float away from him before he could make sense of it. He tried to turn his head, but the room he was in was dim and blurry, and he couldn't see much. He tried again to lift his arms, but he couldn't move at all. His limbs felt like they'd been squashed underwater, and the sound of the machine breathing for him freaked him the fuck out, not that he'd show it. He counted to ten in his head. In his experience, counting slowly did more to calm him down than any fancy meditation exercise. And given his shit luck for most of his life, he needed something to keep himself from flying off the handle every other day.

"Okay, try and cough as we pull out the tubing. On three," the voice said.

Zero counted silently as the woman counted aloud.

"One, two, and three." She smoothly pulled the tube out of his throat.

Zero choked, then gasped as a searing pain in his chest made his headache seem like a joke. "God," he croaked, but no sound came out.

"Easy. Your throat is still trying to figure out how to work," the woman said, easing an ice chip between his teeth.

Nausea swept through Zero, and he frowned, clenching his teeth. The ice chip cracked in half, then melted. "Sick," he managed to whisper.

"It's from the anesthesia. Hang on, and we'll get you something for that. We don't want you vomiting with that chest wound," the nurse said.

Zero concentrated on lying perfectly still. He must have dozed or something, because when he opened his eyes again, something burned in his arm.

"That's the Zofran. It should help with the nausea," a male voice said. "As soon as it kicks in, you'll feel better."

Somehow, Zero knew that he should be more worried about what was going on, but he couldn't seem to focus. He closed his eyes, and drifted off. A long time later, he woke up again. The pain in his throat was better, and he could see clearly. He was in a hospital bed, in a room with a window on his right. A row of what looked like cloth cells stretched down the left-hand side of the antiseptic space and around the perimeter of the room.

"Hello there." A male nurse bustled into his room, pushing back the curtain. "I see you're awake. Can you tell me your name?"

Zero licked dry lips. "Zero. Zeke to my dead mother."

"Excellent." The man nodded, eyes on the monitor above his bed. "You're awake, and your vitals are stable, so we'll be taking you to your room, now." The man turned to Zero and smiled. "How are you feeling?"

"Like a truck sat on me." Zero tried to lift his arms, and was happy to find that they worked. Sort of. He hadn't liked being so drugged that he couldn't control his body. Nearly all his life, he'd had no one to depend on but himself, and he hadn't been this vulnerable since he was a kid. He needed to be able to defend himself if necessary. "Like shit." He tried clearing his throat, but the pain in his chest put a quick end to that action. He concentrated on breathing, counting in his head until he felt a bit calmer.

The nurse nodded. "I know you feel like crap right now, but believe me, you came through major surgery better than I've seen most people." His gaze flicked down Zero's body. "It's a good thing you're in excellent shape."

Zero wanted to snort, but he had a feeling it

would hurt like hell. "What did they do?" He hadn't expected to feel so bad after surgery. He'd thought the bullet had simply slipped through his body, no biggie. He knew he had an exit wound on his back.

"You had your lung reinflated, and a fragment of a bullet removed. Apparently, a tiny piece had lodged up against one of your ribs. You're a very lucky man." The nurse began to unpeel the stickers and leads stuck to Zero's chest. "Your heart is strong though, so there's that."

"How long?" Zero struggled to make his mouth work. He really needed a drink, but he had a feeling that was off the table for a while.

"How long what? How long were you under? Several hours." The nurse bundled up the EKG wires and shoved them into the cabinet under the machine.

"No." Zeke clenched his teeth in frustration, then tried again. "How long before I can get out of here?"

"It'll be a few days." The nurse smiled. "Depends on how quickly you can be up and walking around. As soon as you can use the toilet by yourself, you'll be good to go." He undid the blood pressure cuff. "They took the catheter out while you were still under, so that's good. As soon as you start to feel like you have to use the toilet, just let your nurse know and they'll help you get there."

"You're not my nurse?" Zero swallowed again, wincing at the soreness in his throat.

"No, I work on the recovery ward. I'll be helping you down to your room, and that's it."

Zero nodded, and let his eyes close again. *Where the hell is Felix? And Ariana?* he wondered. He'd been helping his friend out, protecting Jenna, the sister of Felix's boyfriend, Nick, and then all hell had broken loose. That little prick Quincy Edwards had busted into

Zero's warehouse bunker, probably with the help of both intel and men from his mobster uncle. Zero had taken a shot to the chest, and Jenna had died. He grimaced. The girl had been a sweet thing, and she certainly didn't deserve to lose her life like that. He might've died, too, if Felix and Nick hadn't shown up in time to call Ariana, his doctor on call. She was another one of his favors. He'd helped her out with a problem years ago, and she owed him a house call. She'd shown up, no questions asked, thank God. He'd been in the service with her husband, too, so the connections with her family were tight. He grimaced. He didn't like to call in the favor, but it was a good thing he knew her.

"Ok, there, Mr. Zero, hang on and we'll wheel you down."

"Please, it's just Zero," he said as he opened his eyes to find out that a hospital aide and a new nurse had appeared out of nowhere. A frisson of fear shot through him as he took in their unfamiliar faces. *Hell. I'm really out of it. I'm going to bite it if I don't get my shit together.* He couldn't afford to be drifting in and out of life like this. He had enemies. He had a business to run. Contracts to place, and goods to sell. He wasn't used to being so weak. It wasn't safe.

"So, what do you do for a living?" the nurse asked. Her cheerful demeanor told Zero she didn't mean anything by her question. She unlocked the wheels on the bed and nodded to the aide. The man pushed gently, and the bed began to roll toward the double doors at the end of the ward. "Are you a cop?"

A cop? Amusement rushed through Zero. *She's just making small talk,* he told himself so his mind wouldn't go zooming off into what-ifs. He had no capacity to plan for an exit right now, so he needed to make do with the situation as it was. "Not a cop. What would you say if I told you I was a fence?" he asked, smiling slightly. He flexed his fingers and toes, gratified to feel the weird, groggy tingling recede. The more awake he became, the better he felt about his situation. He could *think* again, which was what had bothered him more than anything else. Pain he could handle. Not having his brain work was a disaster he couldn't bear to contemplate.

"You like to tell tales, don't you?" The woman laughed, and her braids bobbed as she smiled down at him. "Since you're not a policeman, I thought you'd say you were a bouncer. You look like you could bench press a horse." She guided the bed down the hall. "Next you'll be telling me that you're a world-famous assassin, or a spy, like James Bond."

No, being a contract killer is my best friend Felix's job. Zero smiled wider, despite the pain starting to bleed through the fading anesthesia. "I did work as a bouncer once, my dear." If he'd been feeling better, he'd flirt a little. The ladies enjoyed it, and somehow, they always knew he didn't mean anything serious with it. "And I can mix a delightful martini."

"You're a sweet talker, aren't you?" The nurse grinned as she punched the button for the elevator. Her dark skin gleamed even in the harsh hospital light, and Zero suddenly wished he had his camera. He liked taking pictures of people.

Everyone should have a hobby, he mused, thinking about how he'd light her face. Of course, the handsome male aide silently pushing the bed from behind was more his type, but Zero wasn't one to discriminate when it came to art.

"I'm Jacinda. You just lie back and enjoy the ride," the nurse said.

Zero nodded, frowning when the last remnants of

the anesthesia made him dizzy. "Will I have a private room?" he asked as they wheeled him into the empty elevator.

Jacinda looked at him in surprise. "Of course. Doctor Amon arranged everything for you. I thought you knew. They told me you were conscious when you came in for treatment." The elevator binged, and the doors opened. They pushed his bed out.

"I am still waking up," Zero said, wondering if Ariana would make an appearance at his bedside. It would probably be better for her if she didn't. He made a mental note to call her and make sure she stayed far away. If Felix had completed matters like he'd expected, that disgusting twit Quincy would be dead by now, and his uncle, Robert Edwards, would be out for blood. Zero didn't want Ariana getting caught in the crossfire when he eliminated the man. He wasn't keen on anyone breaking into his home. Not only was it bad for business, he also had a reputation to maintain.

"Ah, it looks like you have visitors already," Jacinda said, pushing him into a room. She arranged the bed near a bank of monitors on the wall, then locked the wheels. The aide helping her wandered out, and Jacinda busied herself with letting down the side rail of the bed nearest the bathroom. "Whenever you feel up to it, just push this button and I'll help you to the bathroom."

"Of course," Zero said, and she patted his arm before heading out of the room. He turned his attention to the two men waiting by the window. "How interesting. I thought the two of you would be too busy to come check up on me." His voice still had a hint of rasp to it, but he made an effort to speak clearly. He didn't want anyone to know how weak he felt, even his friends. Felix scowled at his words, and Nick frowned. Zero sensed their exhaustion, even through his own post-surgical weariness.

"We've completed our business," Felix said, not elaborating.

Judging from the shadows under Nick's eyes, Zero knew precisely what that business had been. Quincy Edwards was dead. "Heading west, then?" He thought briefly about apologizing, but the two men already knew how deeply regretful he felt about Jenna's death. Nick looked like a man floundering on the edge of drowning, and didn't need to rehash the circumstances of his sister's death.

"Yes. I don't really want to stick around," Nick said, rubbing his eyes. "Especially since Felix won't let me go after Quincy's uncle."

"Felix knows that villain is my problem to solve," Zero said softly.

"Even though he helped his nephew kill my sister?" Nick demanded angrily. He took a step forward, but then stopped when Felix put a hand on his arm.

Zero sighed, and the pain in his chest reminded him that he wasn't up to hunting anyone at the moment, damn it all to hell. *Patience,* he told himself. "Even so. He invaded my home. He is my responsibility. I don't take kindly to men breaking into my sanctuary. Clearly, he wanted me dead because I would not work for him. Vindictive bastard."

Felix nodded. "We understand."

Zero knew his friend Felix truly did get it. He wasn't so certain about his friend's new boyfriend. "I promise that he will not enjoy my justice, dear Nick."

Nick glared at him, then shrugged off Felix's arm. "I don't have the resources to do what needs to be done, despite my skills. I'd need your help anyway. I'm a thief, not a killer." He started pacing at the foot of the bed.

Zero watched him for a moment, feeling the exhaustion from his surgery dragging at his limbs. "You need rest, and to grieve. I will properly dispose of the criminal, and we will all live happily ever after, yes?" He hoped Nick took the hint. The only thing Zero wanted right now was to sleep some more, and maybe take a piss.

Felix, inscrutable as always, leaned back against the windowsill. "Nick. Let it go. Zero will do what he said."

"Fuck, Felix—" Nick began, but Zero cut him off.

"It is regrettable, what happened to your sister. I will tie up all the loose ends as soon as I am on my feet. Do not fret over it. You know my word is good, and that is precisely why I will handle the situation. My reputation is my business." Zero pushed the button on the side rail, elevating the bed a bit more. He needed to face Nick properly, so the man could see his intention on his face. "We've worked well together for several years, haven't we? We have made a great deal of money."

Nick stopped pacing and stood in the center of the room, hands clenched into fists. "Yes."

"Then trust that I will take care of it," Zero said. He glanced at Felix. "You've explained to him how we met, correct?" He still remembered that day vividly. He'd been barely fourteen, an early freshman in his new high school. The bleachers had stretched above his head like prison bars. The boys holding him down thought it would be funny to rape a "fucking faggot", as they liked to call him. Felix, a senior at the same school, had discovered the boys assaulting Zero, and used his fists to convince them that it was a very bad idea. Since then, Zero's loyalty to Felix for saving him from a brutal rape had never wavered, and he wasn't about to let the man down now, despite the recent debacle.

Felix nodded.

"Good. Then you understand that I keep my word."

Nick shoved his hands into his pockets. "You didn't keep Jenna safe, though, did you?"

Zero would have liked to shake some sense into Nick, but he didn't have the energy for it right now. And, too, the man was clearly grieving deeply. "You know what happened, and you know how deeply I am sorry for her loss," he merely said. He couldn't have predicted that fucking Robert Edwards would give his nephew the manpower to break into Zero's warehouse, especially not when the older Edwards wanted his nephew dead. He cocked his head, thinking about the situation. "I believe that Edwards was simply trying to ensure his nephew's death, above and beyond the contract that he took out on the boy. What better way to do that than to break into my home? Though very few people know where I lived, everyone knows how I feel about threats against me and mine. He would know that I'd retaliate swiftly. Even better if I died during the process. The elder Edwards has never liked my independence, and I would never work for him directly."

"Edwards didn't pay up yet, I noticed," Felix murmured.

Zero nearly smiled at his old friend's single-minded thought process, but held back when he looked at Nick again. The poor man was doing his best to hold it together, but he had a way to go before his grief over his sister's loss ran its course. "I will check into the situation tomorrow," Zero merely said.

"You still expect him to pay for the contract he put out on his nephew's head, after all that happened?" Nick asked.

"But of course," Zero said, surprised that such an experienced thief would need an explanation. "Business is business. The circumstances of the kill do not invalidate the matter of Quincy's death. Felix is owed his money for the job. If Edwards does not pay, the contract will be declared void, and Edwards' ability to do business will be damaged. He dare not risk it." Zero reached up and rubbed his face. He was beginning to feel a lot more pain. He glanced at the nurse's button, then decided against calling her. Pain never killed anyone. Spiraling down into a hole of opioid medication could very well mean his end. He had no intention of becoming addicted to any substance. He would endure, and he would heal, as he had so many other times in his life.

"You act as though Edwards will be able to continue doing business at all. Dead men don't get to fucking do business, Zero," Nick bit out.

At that, Zero had to let his smile out. He knew he didn't look healthy, or happy, and that the smile was more of a baring of teeth than anything else. "I want him to suffer before he dies, Nick." He looked at his old friend, Felix, and saw understanding in his expression. "And for him to suffer, he needs to not quite understand what is coming for him."

Chapter Two

Julian stared at his mother in disbelief. "You want me to what?"

"I just need you to go check up on him a few times for me, that's all," she said, sipping at her coffee as if her request made any sort of sense. The nervous twitch of her fingers as she put the cup back on the table betrayed her, however.

"You're his doctor. And now you're telling me you can't actually go see him in the hospital?" Julian had no idea what the hell was going on with his mother, but he didn't like it. "You literally saved his life, and now he's dismissed you?" Julian remembered the man who'd nearly bled to death quite well: tall, muscular, bald. Even fighting for his life, Zero wasn't the kind of guy who was easy to forget. The circumstances of the situation were even more bizarre: he and his mother had been having a meal together when she'd received a call. Her already fair skin had gone even paler than usual, and the next thing he knew, she'd dragged him out to a row of abandoned warehouses. They'd discovered a dead girl and a man lying on the floor with a punctured lung. Felix, the guy that had called his mother to come help, loomed over them like a creepy statue as his mother worked to save the wounded guy's life. The other dude pacing around the mess of the apartment looked like someone more than ready to commit extreme violence, and Julian had later discovered that the dead girl was his sister, so in retrospect, he understood the man's rage. Even so, going to visit the wounded guy in the hospital, incognito, seemed nuts. "Mom, you're not making any sense. I know a little bit about emergency medical treatment, but I'm not a doctor."

"That's not why I want you to visit him." His

mother pushed her long, red hair over her shoulders and sighed. "He's asked me to stay away. He doesn't want the men who broke in to connect me to him, but I want to make sure he's healing okay. It's important to me."

"Wait, what?" Julian went still as the ramifications of that statement sank in. "His injury wasn't because of a random break-in?" He'd thought the trashed apartment looked a bit more deliberate than a typical robbery, but he'd been too busy helping his mother treat the guy to dwell on the details.

She shook her head. "No. Zero isn't an ordinary man. Nothing about his injury is random." She fiddled with her mug.

What the hell does that mean? Julian wondered, frowning. "What does he do for a living?"

His mother looked away. "He's a fixer."

Well, shit, Julian thought as his gut twisted. "You're going to have to explain that a bit more," he said, as if he didn't already know more than he ever wanted to about that sort of thing. He touched his coffee mug, then thought better of taking a drink. He couldn't guarantee he wouldn't choke on the hot coffee right now.

His mother lifted a shoulder. "Zero is really good at helping people handle difficult problems." She glanced at Julian, eyes dark with worry. "I hate to ask this of you, but it can't be helped." She drew in a deep breath. "And I know you can take care of yourself."

Difficult problems my ass, Julian thought, remembering the way one of his best clients had suddenly dropped off his schedule a year ago, and then turned up dead a few months later. No one had been able to figure out what the hell had happened, but Julian had managed to trace the man's death to a dark web assassination contract. That situation had solidified his desire to get the hell out of the escort business. He knew full well what fixers did, and it was nothing safe. "Doesn't the man have other doctors? He's still in the hospital, right?"

She nodded. "He does, but they won't give me his status now that I've signed off on his case." She pursed her lips. "HIPAA regulations."

"I don't know what you think I'm going to find out," Julian said, running a hand over his jaw. "I'm just a lowly banker."

She snorted. "Please. You think I don't know what you really do for a living?"

Julian went still. "What are you talking about?"

His mother lifted an eyebrow.

Julian's face heated. "Mom."

"Don't 'Mom' me, Julian. I know you were an escort. I also know that you quit about three months ago." His mother picked up her cup and sipped her coffee. "I'm relieved, to be honest. I'd much rather you play with the stock market than with random strange men. It's safer."

"Mom! Jesus," Julian muttered. The sharp pain at the base of his neck told him that he'd tensed his shoulders too much, but the horror of finding out his mom knew about his unorthodox job pushed him from uncomfortable right over the edge into stressed out beyond belief. "How?" He wasn't able to get any other words out. He clenched his jaw, then concentrated on relaxing his muscles. "Shit."

"One of your clients was a surgeon I've worked with. Imagine my surprise when he mentioned that he'd gone out with someone who looked just like me, only young and male." She shook her head. "And this doctor is notorious for using escort services, because he doesn't have the time or the emotional capacity to actually date someone for real." She sighed, then pushed her cup away. "And, too, you asked me test you, what? Every six months or so? Like clockwork. Bit suspicious, and I'm not a stupid woman."

I knew I should've let the agency do the STD testing, dammit. He hadn't trusted them, however, to do a thorough enough job. "Dammit, Mom. You weren't supposed to know. No parent is supposed to know about their kid's sex life." Julian gave up trying to relax and let his shoulder muscles knot up into a giant kink. It would take the services of a top-rate massage professional to help him at this point.

"I know why you did it, Julian," she said evenly.

Julian pinched the bridge of his nose. He supposed he should be happy she wasn't freaking out, but to have her so calmly discuss his former job unnerved him. "Since when are you so nonchalant about this sort of thing?" In his experience, his mother was a dedicated emergency surgeon and upstanding member of the community.

She laughed. "I've been helping Zero for years. And it's hard to stay naive when you're an ER doctor, honey." She tilted her head. "Did you have to sleep with all of them? I hope not."

This is so not a conversation I ever wanted to have with her. Julian grimaced. "No, actually. Most of the clients were just lonely and wanted someone to talk to. I wasn't a prostitute. I was an escort. I went to a lot of charity galas as someone's cousin. And I escorted women, too, not just men." It was true. Of the hundred or so clients he'd entertained while in college and the year after he'd graduated, he'd maybe slept with ten of them.

"Well. That's good, at least." His mother pushed away from the table and stood up.

"Why is that good?" Julian couldn't believe he was asking her this question, but it slipped out before he could stop himself.

She looked at him. "I wouldn't want you to have a skewed perception of sex. It's not always about hooking up, you know. I have no problem with you being bisexual, but I worry that you'll never know about falling in love if you keep flitting from person to person."

Okay, that's it. No more talking about my sex life, Julian vowed, scrubbing his hands over his face. "Yeah, no. I'm done talking about this. Time to change the subject."

His mother laughed. "So, you'll go visit Zero for me? You can bring him coffee or something." His mother started pacing. "He won't let me treat him, or even see him, but it doesn't feel right to just walk away. He's been a friend of mine for years."

Julian tipped his chair back. "How, exactly, did you meet this guy, Mom? He doesn't seem like the type of person you'd decide to hang out with. And you've never mentioned him before."

"We weren't the kind of friends that hung out." She walked to the window and stared out over the backyard. "He was in the military with your Dad. They were good friends. I never told you, but when your father died, I needed help with some things, and Zero stepped up." She waved a hand. "Finances, dealing with the military people. I told him that if there was anything I could do he should give me a call." She trailed off, then shook her head. "A couple years later, he had a nasty cough that wouldn't go away." She glanced at her son. "Bronchitis. No big deal, but he wouldn't go to a regular doctor's office. He preferred to live offline, he said."

Julian's father had died overseas ten years ago, when he was thirteen. That meant Zero was at least fifteen years older than he was, maybe more. "Huh." He couldn't think of anything else to say. The years right after his Dad's death had sucked, and he usually did his best to not remember them. "He was in the service, then?"

"He'd already got out by then. Apparently, your dad and he kept in touch. Something about your Dad saving his life or whatever. I don't know the whole story."

Julian digested this. "Does Uncle Dave know about this guy?" He imagined not. His mother's brother was a cop. *A good one, too. He'd be pissed if he found out about this.*

His mother snorted. "Hell to the no, Julian. He'd have a canary if he knew I was friends with Zero, so please do me a favor and don't mention it at Thanksgiving."

Julian smirked as he let the chair's two front legs fall back down. "I should, just to make you pay for this ridiculous thing you're asking me to do."

"You do that, and I'll bring up your former job. Your Uncle Dave won't approve of that any more than he would of my unorthodox friendship with Zero," she said, one eyebrow raised.

Julian knew when to back down. "Okay, yeah. I call a truce," he said sheepishly.

She laughed. "So, you'll do it, then? Check up on Zero for me?"

His mind shied away from the thought of seeing Zero again. He'd been ridiculously attracted to the guy in the middle of saving his life. What would it be like to interact with him now that the guy wasn't struggling to breathe? Better if he just stayed away, but when his mother looked at him like that, he had no defense. He sighed. "Fine."

His mother walked over to him gave him a hug. "Thank you."

Julian flushed again, awkwardly patting her on the back. "Ugh. You knew I'd cave."

She straightened up, smiling. "Of course."

Julian rubbed his eyes. "Okay. Where is he, and how many times do you want me to pop in on him?" He tentatively took a sip of his coffee. *Yuck. Cold.* He pushed the mug away.

"Holy Name Hospital in Teaneck, and as often as you can," she replied, dropping back down into her chair. "Thanks, Julian."

"Don't mention it." He couldn't deny his mother anything, and she knew it. *Dammit.*

****

"Come in," a man's low voice called out.

"She owes me big time for this," Julian muttered under his breath as he pushed open the door to Zero's private room. "Hey, coffee delivery," he said, hoping he hadn't woken the guy up. *Good thing I'm not shy,* he thought as his gaze took in the half-naked body of the man his mother had cajoled him to check up on. Even covered in bandages the guy looked great. Thick muscles sat on top of more thick muscles. The man's head was slightly stubbled, and Julian could tell Zero hadn't had a chance to shave in at least a week, not that it detracted from his looks. The rough around the edges shtick suited him. Julian yanked his attention away from Zero's full mouth, and his gaze landed on his chest. A tattoo of a horse sat on Zero's left pec. *Wait, no. That's not a horse.* He stopped walking and stared at the weirdly badass unicorn prancing across Zero's chest. He couldn't tear his gaze away.

"Her name is Pointy."

"I—" Julian stuttered, nearly dropping the coffee. "What?" He knew Zero wasn't asleep, but he thought he'd at least be groggy enough not to care about the person delivering his coffee. Steady dark eyes looking at him with a hint of amusement, and no little bit of curiosity, told him that there wasn't a damned thing wrong with Zero's brain. He felt like the man was peering directly into his soul. *Fuck.* Julian's cock hardened, and he barely suppressed a wince as the tight fit of his jeans cut off the circulation to his junk. He tore his gaze away from Zero's face and put it firmly back on the man's tattoo, as if that was any better.

"You're staring at my tattoo. Her name is Pointy," Zero said in his deep voice, as if it was entirely normal for a man of his size and presence to have a fucking unicorn tattooed on his fucking chest.

"Is that a rainbow?" Julian asked before he could stop himself. He stared at the hints of color peeking out from behind the black inked creature. He wanted to touch it. Jesus. He was so fucked.

Zero smiled, then coughed. He grimaced, frowning, and Julian realized the man was still in a lot of pain. "Shit. I'm sorry." He hurried forward and put the coffee tray on the rolling table next to the bed. He grabbed a box of tissues from an ugly nightstand and stood there, futilely wondering what the hell he could do. Hand the guy a tissue? Pound on his back? His mind immediately presented him with images of other things he'd like to pound, and Julian felt his face heat up. *Damn this stupid pale skin.*

Zero slashed a hand at him before Julian could make a decision about what to do. "I'm fine. Still getting used to the hole in my right lung," he rasped, looking Julian up and down. "Do I know you?"

Shit. He recognizes me. Julian put the tissue back down and awkwardly adjusted his baseball cap, hoping it hid most of his hair. Dark red was a pretty damned distinctive color for a man, and people had a tendency to remember him. "No, I don't think so," he said, shoving his left hand in his jeans pocket to disguise his erection. "I'm just the delivery boy." He gestured at the coffee, trying to look relaxed. Hearing Zero's indescribably low voice did weird things to his libido. *Down, boy. This dude is not only a criminal, he's too old for you,* he told his dick. It didn't help.

"I didn't order coffee," Zero said, raising an eyebrow. "In fact, I believe my doctors would likely have a conniption if I ingested caffeine at this point in my recovery. Of course, that might be amusing, so..." He peeled the lid off of one of the cups with his right hand, not seeming to mind the medical line stuck into his forearm. "Hmm. Caramel macchiato?" He sipped at it cautiously. "Lovely flavor."

Julian helplessly stared at the foam dotting Zero's upper lip. *Jesus. Even laid out flat in a hospital he's fucking gorgeous.* "Um, she said that's your favorite."

Zero sipped the coffee delicately, then put it back on the tray. "She?" he asked mildly.

It was at that moment that Julian registered that Zero's left hand wasn't in view, and that in fact, the man had a fucking gun pointed at him from beneath the covers. Julian froze as fear and arousal clashed head on inside his body. Inexplicably, the arousal won, and his breath hitched as he realized that he really, *really* fucking liked this badass dude. "My mother," he said, then cleared his throat as he gave up all pretense of keeping his identity secret. "She said you wouldn't let her come near her, so she sent me." His hard-on was making it really goddamn hard to talk. He wanted nothing more than to undo his jeans and let it all hang out. The thought of what would happen if he did that made him snort. He'd probably end up with a hole in *his* lung.

"Your mother?" Zero pursed his lips, and tilted

his head in a surprisingly delicate manner. "Ah. The delightful doctor." He eased his left hand out of the covers, gun still cocked as he drew it into view. "Interesting." He stared at Julian for a moment more, and then he clicked the safety back on, and put the pistol on the tray next to the coffee. "Why am I not surprised? She is nothing if not persistent."

Julian relaxed minutely. "That is true." The thought of his mother pleading with him to go visit Zero made him shake his head.

"You must be her son." Zero sipped at the coffee again. "Mmmm. You bought this at that lovely little place on the corner, didn't you? The proprietor of that shop is a mean old son of a bitch, but they know how to brew a fine cup of joe."

Julian nodded. "Yeah. They grind their own beans every morning." He licked his lips. He'd bought two coffees, but wasn't sure now if he should dare to drink the other one. Watching Zero lick the foam from his lips ensured that his damned hard-on was going nowhere anytime soon, and he wasn't sure he could sit down at this point. *Get a grip, Julian,* he told himself. *You were a professional escort, for fuck's sake. You have self-control, and you are very, very good at making someone comfortable and relaxed, remember?*

"Are you going to loom over me for the next fifteen minutes then?"

Julian jerked his gaze away from Zero's muscular forearm. "No, of course not." Gathering his wits, he moved closer and extracted the remaining coffee from the disposable tray. "So, how are you feeling?" he asked, feeling like an idiot. "You look better than you did the other day, that's for sure." He sipped his black coffee carefully. God knew he needed the energy boost to jumpstart his brain back into gear.

"Ah, how delightful. Small talk. Just what the doctor ordered," Zero said, narrowing his eyes. "And I remember you, by the way. You pressed your hand on top of my wound like you were trying to shove it through to the other side." His lips quirked up in a half smile. "I suppose I should thank you for helping your mother."

Julian willed himself not to blush. "My mother told me to ask you how you're doing. If I don't, she'll be upset."

"And we don't want the darling Ariana upset, do we?"

Julian scowled. "You can joke all you want, but when my mother asks me to do something, I do it." He took another sip of his coffee. "She doesn't ask very often."

"Hmm." Zero carefully turned his coffee cup one-quarter revolution clockwise. "This is true."

Julian watched Zero touch his weapon, and then he glanced at the monitors beside the bed. "You're off all of the monitors. That's good. It's only been, what? A week and a half?"

"Two weeks. Apparently, I'm a fast healer," Zero said, pushing a button on the side of his bed. The back moved up more, until Zero was basically sitting up. He swung his legs over the side, and pushed away the tray. "Help me with this," he said, fiddling with the transparent medical dressing holding the IV catheter snug against his forearm.

Julian frowned. "Aren't you supposed to let a nurse do that?"

Zero looked up at him, dark eyes once again amused. "And since when do you obey all the rules, Julian?"

Julian stared at him. He hadn't told Zero his name, had he? *My mother must have,* he mused, shaking his head. "Fine." He washed his hands at the sink, then raided the cabinets for some gauze and tape. "I take it this means you're not staying the night?"

Zero smiled. "You are correct." He grabbed the line and yanked it out with one smooth motion.

Julian slapped a gauze pad on Zero's arm, then taped it down, keeping pressure on the small area. Zero's arm felt warm and strong. The man smelled mostly like antiseptic, but an intriguing spicy scent teased his senses, and he found himself leaning closer.

"I will not bleed to death from such a tiny wound, Julian," Zero said softly, the timbre of his voice so low it rumbled.

Julian scowled, but he let go. Water from the IV dripped on the floor, and he reached up to pinch off the line. "If you're leaving, I'm coming with you," he heard himself say, as if from afar. *What the hell are you doing?* he asked himself. *This man is in deep shit, and you want to tag along for the ride?*

"Are you?" Zero asked, standing up.

Julian nodded.

Zero smiled faintly, eyes meeting Julian's gaze, and then he nodded. "Very well." He didn't sway or clutch at the bed rails. Instead, he began to calmly dress himself, pulling on a worn, button-down shirt and arranging it loosely over his soft linen pants. He picked up his pistol and somehow hid it in a pocket. The only thing betraying his injury were the bandages taped to his chest, and those were quickly covered by the shirt.

Julian stared at him as the man slipped his feet into what looked like very expensive leather shoes. When he straightened up, he tilted his head as if in inquiry. Julian narrowed his eyes. Zero wasn't much taller than he was, but the older man probably weighed fifty pounds more, all of it muscle. He wanted to grab him and sink his fingers into Zero's biceps. He wanted to rub himself all over the guy. *Jesus, get a grip, dude.* Fortunately, Zero's voice snapped him out of his reverie.

"Are you ready? Because you're my ride out of here, Julian."

Chapter Three

Zero watched Julian drive his car, impressed with the man's smooth acceptance of his demand for a ride. Despite Julian's youth, not much seemed to rattle him. He liked that. In his admittedly dangerous life, he couldn't let unexpected situations rattle his composure. The secret to being a good fixer was the ability to roll with any given situation, even when it all went to hell. And if Julian was going tag along with him, he needed to not be freaking out over every small thing.

"Want to tell me where we're going?" Julian asked, smoothly downshifting as he approached a stop sign.

"Make a left," Zero said, curious about Julian's level of patience. When the man merely lifted a brow and then did as he said, Zero allowed a small smile to curve his lips.

"I take it you really enjoy playing the role of tall, dark, and mysterious," Julian said, driving down the tree lined street.

Zero snorted softly. "I don't know you, Julian. I don't know if I can trust you with my business."

"I'm driving," Julian immediately replied. "I kind of need to know where we're going."

"We're going to River Edge. I have an item I need to pick up." Zero hoped that Aaron at the storage place had done as he'd asked and filled up the tank on his RV. He needed his backup living space to be ready to roll when he arrived. He had no desire to screw around. He wanted to be up and running within the hour.

"And then?" Julian turned right at the end of the street and eased onto Rt. 4. He drove over the Hackensack River without even asking. "What's my exit?"

"There." Zero pointed.

Julian slowed and exited the highway.

"Take a right," Zero said, resisting the urge to press at his wound. It was healing quite well, but that could change if he fucked around with it. He had more self-control than that. "Okay, slow down."

Julian glanced at him, but did as he said. "How about a hint?"

Zero smiled. "Pull into that parking lot. The storage place." He watched Julian smoothly shift gears, and then do as he asked. The lean muscles rippling in his forearms hinted at a man who wasn't afraid to use his body when the occasion called for it. He liked that about him. He liked Julian's calm, and the way he'd stuffed his dark red hair into his cap. He liked the hint of stubble on Julian's chin. Zero shook his head. *Don't get distracted now, darling. You have work to do.*

"Okay," Julian said, parking in one of the spaces. "What's up with this place?"

Zero debated with himself for approximately one second, and then he gave in to his baser urges. "If you want to know, come along," he said, getting out of the car. He headed for the outside gate leading to an inner courtyard.

"Shit. Wait up," Julian said, locking his car hurriedly.

"Time is precious," Zero said, pressing a hand to his chest. The damned hole in his lung burned, even though the doctor said he was doing well.

"This is crazy," Julian muttered as he loped alongside Zero. "You're going to rip your stitches and bleed to death if you don't slow down."

"The doctor already removed the stitches," Zero informed him, punching the security code into the gate's number pad.

"Whatever." Julian shouldered him aside and opened the gate for him. "For God's sake, my mother will kill me if you collapse. Stop it."

Zero had to laugh. "I could probably bench press you."

"Not right now you couldn't," Julian retorted, holding the gate open. His blue eyes flashed with irritation.

Zero smirked, and walked past him. "Come on. My rig is just past the building." He headed for the sleek RV parked around the corner. He nodded as he saw the dark aluminum gleaming in the afternoon sunlight. Aaron had clearly done his job. Zero's backup home was freshly washed, and, he hoped, stocked with food and the weapons he'd requested.

"Holy shit, is that yours?" Julian asked as they walked up to it.

"Yes." Zero walked around the brand-new motorhome, happy to see that the car trailer he'd requested had been hooked up.

Julian traced a finger down the black stripe that circled the vehicle. "This is seriously dorky."

That forced a laugh out of Zero. "It's practical, not sexy." He typed in the code on the door, pleased when the lock opened on his first try. His memory hadn't failed him, despite all the drugs he'd had pumped into him during surgery. He opened the door, then paused and looked at Julian. The man was frowning at him. "What's the problem?"

Julian pursed his lips. "My mother said you're a fixer."

Zero's eyebrows went up. "Yes." He hadn't expected Ariana to tell her son exactly what he did for a living. *Intriguing,* he thought, staring at Julian. The man didn't seem nervous. He seemed … curious.

"Why are you letting me follow you around?" Julian asked.

Good question, Zero thought, smiling. "I find you interesting." And he did. Julian didn't react at all like he'd expected to any of the things Zero said or did. At least, not so far.

"Interesting? Me?" Julian laughed, lips twisting. "I'm just a guy. Nothing interesting about me. Where are you planning on going, anyway?" he asked, gesturing to the RV. "I can't imagine that will be very comfortable to drive with your chest hurting you."

Zero stepped up into the motorhome. "I won't have to drive it." He checked cabinets and drawers, pleased when he found the pistols he'd requested neatly lined up beneath the kitchen sink. He opened the small closet in the hall and checked the shotgun bolted to the inside wall. He headed for the master bedroom, nodding at the fresh sheets and deep red duvet on the queen-sized bed. He'd have to remember to tell Aaron he no longer owed Zero a favor.

"Jesus. It's like a five-star hotel in here," Julian said, following him to the rear of the motorhome.

Zero chuckled. "Even a gunshot wound is no reason to live like a barbarian." He checked the bathroom, and then headed for the front. "You know I knew your father."

Julian sighed. "Yeah. Mom told me."

"He was a decade older than I, and he had excellent instincts. He knew we were heading into an ambush, and he saved my ass. He kept us from driving the usual route. Everyone lived that day, and that's a minor miracle in that sort of combat situation." Zero finished his inspection and leaned against the built-in breakfast table. Julian was watching him closely, blue eyes giving nothing away. *I like this man,* Zero thought, appreciating Julian's calm composure, even in the face of what might be a very uncomfortable statement.

"So Mom said," Julian merely said.

Zero tilted his head. "I was very sorry to hear of his death."

The faintest hint of tightening in Julian's face betrayed his emotional discomfort. "Yeah. Cancer sucks. Why are we talking about this?"

Zero lifted a shoulder. "I'm wondering if you have the same good instincts as your father." He slipped his hands into his pockets. The cold metal of his gun soothed him, and he drew it out, efficiently ejecting the magazine. He popped the last bullet from the chamber and set the weapon and ammunition on the table.

"I don't know where you're going with this," Julian said, after a long silence.

Zero smiled slightly. He'd known Ariana for ten years now, and he'd kept an eye on her and her son. He knew Julian was way smarter than he let on to people, and he also knew the guy had worked as an escort for a few years. What he didn't know was what Julian was doing now, and for some reason, he wanted to find out. "Since you're coming with me, I decided to speculate on your talents. Nothing sinister, my dear." He watched Julian's face closely. *Hmm. A bit of confusion, and there's that curiosity again. He reminds me of a cat,* he mused, reaching up to touch his bandage through his shirt. He found it interesting that Julian didn't mind the endearment. Most men would've gotten all bent out of shape by now, but not this one. Julian was cool and collected, and clearly sharp as a tack.

"You assume a hell of a lot, Zero," Julian finally said.

Zero let his smile widen. "Am I wrong?"

Julian let out an explosive breath. "No, dammit."

He glanced outside. "What about my car?"

"I have a lovely car hitch on the back of this beauty," Zero said, patting the table. "Surely you noticed it?"

Julian scowled, finally allowing his frustration to show through his control. "Fine. I'm driving."

Zero grinned. "I expected nothing less."

****

Several hours later, Julian stared at the RV neatly slotted into its new home. He'd helped Zero hook it into the plumbing and electricity of the pad set onto an acre of cleared land in the middle of rural north Jersey. Apparently, Zero liked his privacy, because this place wasn't in any normal RV park. Zero owned fifty acres out here, with the cleared section smack dab in the middle of his property. Clearly, he didn't want any neighbors, though he'd had it wired up for utilities. Julian shook his head. It was hard to believe they were only a few hours out from New York City. Trees rustled gently in the late afternoon sunlight across the meadow. His stomach growled.

"Come on inside. I'll make you a sandwich," Zero said, silently appearing by his side.

Damn. The man moves around like a ghost, Julian thought. He didn't startle, but it was a close thing. "You don't have to feed me."

Zero rolled his eyes as he climbed the steps into the motorhome. "Please. I am not so rude a host that I would neglect your obvious need for nourishment. You can call your mother while I get it ready."

Julian sighed, then followed Zero inside. The truth was, he wasn't entirely happy about the attraction he felt for the older man, mostly because the guy knew his mother. He didn't want to crush on a guy who could call up his mom and complain about Julian's manners, or lack thereof. "You know how weird it is that you know my mother, right?"

Zero shrugged as he pulled bread and cheese from the refrigerator. "It is what it is."

Julian wanted to hunch his shoulders, but three years of escorting important people to important functions had trained those tendencies out of him. He settled for rubbing his thumb against his index finger. "I should go."

"Why?"

Julian scowled. "I'm not even sure what I'm doing here."

Zero raised an eyebrow, but said nothing as he grabbed a frying pan from a cabinet.

Julian watched him assemble the ingredients for grilled cheese, and his stomach growled again. He sighed. "I'll call my mom."

Zero nodded. "Tell her that you will be busy for the next few days. Maybe even a couple of weeks."

Julian paused, finger poised over the speed dial on his cell phone. "And why will I be busy?"

"Because you'll be helping me out with some tasks." Zero deftly spread butter on bread, then dropped it into the frying pan. It sizzled as Zero placed slices of cheese on the bread.

"Shit," Julian muttered. He knew he should argue with Zero about drafting him to help with this so-called task, but his damned curiosity got the better of him. He wanted to know what was going on. *I'll give him a day or two, and then I'll get back to my work,* he decided as he held his cell phone to his ear.

"Julian?" his mother's voice sounded muffled through the phone.

"Hey, Mom. I'm with Zero," he said, grimacing as he imagined her reaction to his news. "He checked himself out of the hospital and I gave him a hand getting situated in his new place."

"He checked himself out? You're not serious?" his mother asked, voice rising.

Julian opened his mouth to reply, but she beat him to it.

"No, wait. Never mind," she said, sounding exasperated. "Of course he did. Stubborn fool."

"He seems pretty healthy to me," Julian told her, eyeing Zero's perfectly muscular butt as the man flipped the sandwiches in the pan. "No fainting or spurting blood."

Zero snorted softly, but kept his back to Julian.

Julian's mother sighed loudly. "Tell him to keep the wound clean, and not to do anything strenuous. He needs to heal on the inside, too."

"Sure, Mom." Julian huffed out a short breath. As if Zero would listen to either of them. He'd only interacted with the man for a few hours and he already knew enough about him to know that Zero was a man who pushed himself past his limits. "Listen, I'm going to hang out here and give him a hand with a few things, okay? I won't be around for a few days. Might even be a week." He waited for his mother to yell at him.

"Hmm," she merely said.

Julian blinked. "That's it? No lecture?"

She laughed. "You're a grown man, Julian. Twenty-three years old. Who am I to tell you what to do?"

Julian rubbed his forehead. This made no sense. She *always* had an opinion about his life, which was why he'd never told her about his escorting gig. "Mom, you're freaking me out." He looked up to find Zero smiling at him. Julian made a face at him. *The guy thinks this is funny. It's totally not funny. Dammit.*

"I figure it's about time for Zero to meet someone he can't push over," she said, as if that made any sense.

"Um." Julian considered her words. "He basically railroaded me into helping him, Mom."

She chuckled. "Uh-huh. He twisted your arm, did he? You argued with him and everything?"

Julian pursed his lips. "Well, he obviously needed help."

"And the fact that he looks like a slightly taller version of Vin Diesel has nothing to do with it, right?"

Julian flushed, annoyed that his mother could read him so easily. He'd been able to fool a hundred clients with his self-control, but his mother only had to say a few sentences and he was blushing like a teenager. "I'll check in with you in a few days, okay? Bye, Mom."

"Wait, Julian," she said, voice going low. "Be careful. I know you can take care of yourself, all those mixed martial arts classes saw to that, but Zero runs with a rough crowd. The only reason I'm not freaking out is because I trust him."

Julian dropped his face into his hand. "Mom. I'm not dating the guy. I'm helping an injured dude set up his house."

She laughed. "Um, okay. Sure."

"I'm hanging up now," Julian told her.

"Bye, love. Be careful," she said.

"Love you, too, Mom." Julian cut the connection and slid the phone into his pocket. He looked up to find Zero watching him with amusement. "What?"

"My parents are dead. Enjoy her interest while it lasts," he said, then turned to the stove and flicked off the gas. "Sandwiches are ready."

"I love my mother, but I'd prefer it if she didn't interject herself into my…" Julian trailed off. *Into my what? What the hell do I even call this? A crush?* he mused, then shook his head. At any rate, he certainly didn't want to talk about it with Zero. "You know what? Forget it." He slid into the bench seat and eyed the sandwich Zero placed in front of him. "Wow. That looks fantastic." Melting cheese oozed out of the sides of the bread. Right on cue, his stomach growled.

"It's the least I could do," Zero said, sitting down. "I appreciate your help." He placed two cold beers on the table.

Julian cocked his head. "Are you sure you should be drinking that?"

"I'm not on any drugs." Zero shrugged and took a bite of his sandwich.

"No pain medication?" Julian couldn't imagine recovery from chest surgery without some kind of relief.

"No. Pain never killed anyone, and I need sharp senses," Zero said, nodding at Julian's plate. "Are you going to eat?"

Julian sighed, and picked up his sandwich. "You're a stubborn man, Zero."

Zero laughed. "True."

They ate in silence for a few minutes, and then Zero relaxed on the seat, draping his arm over the back. His healing wound didn't seem to be bothering him at all. Julian didn't understand how the guy could be so stoic after such a terrible injury. Julian had seen the bloody mess firsthand when he'd gone with his mother to Zero's warehouse. The man had lost a *lot* of blood.

"I am impressed," Zero said, after a long moment.

He's impressed? I'm the one who's impressed. Julian raised his eyebrows and took another swig of his beer, carefully looking at Zero's face, and not at his chest. "With what?"

"You haven't asked what I would like you to help me with." Zero smiled slowly. "You are either very patient, or not very bright."

Now he's just screwing with me. Julian carefully set his beer bottle down, not even tempted to rise to Zero's mocking words. Truth was, he wasn't sure he wanted to know what kind of mess the man had stirred up. He'd seen enough over the past few years to know that a fixer didn't exactly do things that were entirely legal, but then again, it didn't seem to matter one bit to his libido. He couldn't deny the attraction he felt for Zero. *Which is insane, because I have no idea what else he's mixed up in*, Julian mused. A guy didn't just end up in the hospital with a gunshot wound. There were always reasons. He remembered the carnage in Zero's warehouse apartment. He especially remembered the dead girl near the sofa. "I'm curious. But I'm also fond of my continued existence on this planet."

Zero lightly tapped a finger on the table. "I can pay you. I have many resources."

"What?" Julian sat up straight. "No. Nope." The last thing he wanted to do was turn this situation into a financial contract. He'd invested every last penny of his escorting money into a fund, and he'd made a fortune off of it in the last year. He didn't need money. He could live off the interest he'd collected for the rest of his life. "No. I don't need your money."

Zero's dark eyes gleamed with interest. "You don't need money. How intriguing."

Julian frowned. "What exactly are you involved in, Zero? Stop making cryptic remarks and just give it to me straight. I don't want to be guessing about it." The image of the dead girl swam into his head again. Maybe hanging out with Zero wasn't such a great idea. His gaze landed on the man's arms: muscular, capable. He'd rolled up his sleeves to cook, and Julian was bemused at how much he enjoyed looking at Zero's smooth skin.

Because I want to do more than look.

Zero inhaled, then let it out. "Very well. I shall explain, but I need assurances that you won't go running to Mommy with the tale. Ariana does not need to know the details. The less she knows, the better for her health."

That sent a trickle of worry through Julian, even through his annoyance. "You ask for confidentiality, and I'll give it to you, but not because you just threw my mother in my face. I'm a grown man, Zero. Don't be an ass." Zero didn't need to talk to him like that. He wasn't a child. He hadn't been a child for a very, very long time. *Not since my father killed himself and left me and my mom to fend for ourselves,* he thought bitterly.

"I know." Zero shook his head, suddenly looking tired. "I am merely being cautious, though I apologize for my harsh words." He tilted his head. "A few weeks ago, my friend Felix brought a friend and his friend's sister to my warehouse, asking for my help protecting her. Her ex, you see, was an abusive prick. How could I say no? I harbor an intense dislike for bullies and abusers."

The way Zero said the word "prick", low and harsh, pinged Julian's instincts. He had a feeling that Zero didn't really show his true character to the world. The way he spoke, slipping in and out of a refined accent, told Julian that Zero put on a show for most people. That he was slipping up now spoke volumes. *The question is, is it deliberate or accidental? The man does almost nothing randomly.* He stared at Zero, and the calculating look on his face told Julian all he needed to know. "Where are you from, Zero?" Maybe if he knew that, he could begin to unravel the mystery of Zero's life.

Zero's eyebrows lifted, and he smiled. "Oh, aren't you clever, Julian."

Julian crossed his arms over his chest. "You dance around people with words. You do it on purpose.

Why?"

Zero turned his hands palm up on the table as if to show he had nothing to hide. "I have been nothing but truthful with you."

Julian didn't reply. *I can wait him out. The question is if it will matter. Obviously, no one can make Zero talk if he doesn't want to. The man was coherent even with a sucking chest wound.*

Zero drew his hands back in. "I attended the same high school as Felix. We grew up in Pennsylvania together."

"That tells me nothing," Julian said, after waiting a moment for more details.

"It answers your question," Zero countered.

Julian ran a finger down his beer bottle. The condensation from the drink had nearly dried. He hated warm beer. He decided to try another angle. "So, this guy's sister, I assume she was the dead girl in your warehouse?" He picked up his drink and took a swig.

Zero's face showed the first stirrings of anger Julian had yet seen. "Yes. They gave her into my protection, but unfortunately, her ex brought help to break into my home."

Julian considered this. "You plan on doing something about the ex?" He didn't expect Zero to go to the cops. The guy was a fixer, for Christ's sake. People like that handled their own problems.

"No. The ex is now dead." Zero picked up his bottle and sipped his beer.

Julian didn't understand. "Okay," he said, drawing out the word. He wasn't sure if his attraction to Zero was enough of a reason to put up with this kind of conversational bullshit. Abruptly, he made a decision. "Look, man. Either spit it out, or I'm leaving. This tit for tat shit is annoying. If you want me to stick around, I need to know the details. If you don't want me here, that's cool, and I know where the door is." He almost held his breath waiting for Zero's answer. Truth was, he didn't *want* to leave. He wanted to stay and decipher what made Zero tick.

Zero cocked his head, then sighed. "I'm not entirely certain I shouldn't just let you go. My situation is quite perilous at the moment." He pushed his beer bottle away from him. "But you intrigue me." He slid out of the seat and walked over to Julian, boxing him in with his arms. "I'm a practical man, Julian. I don't let my dick make decisions for me."

Julian stared at him. Zero was so close he could almost curl his fingers around the warmth that poured from his ridiculously smooth skin. "What are you saying?" he asked, wincing when his voice cracked. *Jesus, man. Get a hold of yourself. You were an escort to far more important people than this guy.* He cleared his throat, about to say more, but then thought better of it. *Wait and see what he does.*

"I'm saying I want to find out what you taste like, darling."

Julian's heart knocked against his ribs, and for a moment he thought Zero was going to kiss him, but then Zero straightened up, warm brown eyes going flat and cold. "But I have a vendetta to execute, and that makes any pursuit of pleasure a secondary consideration for at least a little while." He shook his head. "You don't deserve to become embroiled in my mess."

Julian exhaled the breath he didn't even realize he'd been holding. His cock pressed hard and heavy against his jeans. Something about this guy really revved his fucking engine. "Why don't you let me decide what I deserve and what I don't?"

"Are you certain?"

Julian scowled. "I already told you I'm a fucking adult, Zero. What more do you want from me?"

Zero stared at him for a moment, and then nodded, short and sharp. "So be it."

Chapter Four

Zero closed the door to the bathroom and took off his shirt, suppressing a groan at the deep ache in his chest. His wound was healing, but he was definitely not at one hundred percent yet. He was maybe at fifty percent. Maybe. He snorted.

Who the hell are you kidding, Zero? he asked himself. He wasn't anywhere near healed yet, and he still had to deal with Robert Edwards. He sighed, leaning on the sink as he turned on the water. He splashed some on his face. He didn't want Julian to know how fucking exhausted he felt. *Or how fucking old I am,* he thought, thinking of the younger man's seemingly endless amount of energy. He'd tried to look at Julian as just his old army buddy's kid, but it wasn't working. For one thing, Julian's dad had been at least ten years older than Zero, and he'd been more of a mentor to Zero than a peer. For another thing, there was something about Julian that pushed under his skin. He didn't know if it was the guy's poise at such a young age, or his fucking penetrating stare, or what. He knew Julian was twenty-three, which put Zero right into the old fucking pervert category at his age of forty, but he couldn't seem to help himself. He wanted to strip Julian down and fuck him until neither of them could stand up.

He turned off the faucet, and stared at himself in the mirror. "You're going to be stupid, aren't you?" he asked himself. Rings circled his eyes, and he knew he needed to get some real rest, especially if he was going to make Edwards very fucking sorry he helped his prick nephew Quincy break into Zero's home. "So get your shit together, man."

He stared at himself a moment longer, and then he rubbed his face. He had a business to run. A reputation to protect. He needed to let everyone know that they couldn't just waltz into his space and slaughter one of his guests. The first step towards that goal was letting Edwards understand that Zero wasn't a forgive and forget kind of guy. Edwards was going down, but there was no way he would be able to do what was necessary by himself until he felt better. And that meant he needed help, because he couldn't let the situation fester any longer.

Zero tossed his shirt into the tiny dirty laundry bin, then began to carefully peel at the bandage on his chest. When he'd got it off, he rolled up the used gauze and tossed it in the trash. Sleeping in a hospital sucked, and he hadn't slept through the night since he'd been shot. He also knew he wasn't going to be able to let Julian leave. The guy pushed all of his buttons, in the best possible way. He thought of Julian's soft, dark red hair, brushed back from his face. The piercing blue eyes. His unexpectedly strong hands.

"Fuck." He shook his head, then turned on the faucet and wet a cloth. He knew the dressing on his back wasn't going to come off as easily as the one from the front because he'd been sleeping on it.

"You okay in there?" Julian called.

Zero smiled grimly to himself, then turned off the water again. "I am not dead yet," he replied, opening the door. "I need to get this bandage off." He pointed to the gauze taped to his back. "If the wound looks as good as the one on my chest, I won't have to replace the gauze. I believe it has healed enough." He grabbed a soft towel from the shelf with his free hand and dried his face.

"Jesus Christ, Zero," Julian said, staring at the scar on his right pectoral muscle. "That looks like a dog tried to chew its way clear through you."

Zero smiled. "Yes, well, that's basically what a

bullet does. It's not as pretty as the movies make it out to be." He touched his scar gingerly. When Julian's gaze didn't move, he added, "I'll be fine."

Julian grimaced. "Yeah, well. If it looks that bad on the outside, I shudder to think of what it feels like on the inside."

Zero shrugged, and immediately regretted it when dull pain radiated through his chest and shoulder. Julian had a point. He wasn't quite healed yet. "I need a good night's sleep." He pursed his lips. "Do you know how to use a gun?"

Julian frowned at him. "What does sleep have to do with a gun?"

"I would like you to stay. If you do, I would be happier if you knew how to handle a weapon." Zero didn't add that he would sleep a hell of a lot better if he knew Julian had his back in case things went to shit out here in the middle of nowhere. He'd managed to purchase this property on the down low, and no one should know that he owned it, but he hadn't managed to stay alive this long by being careless.

"Jesus, Zero," Julian said, running a hand over his face. "Yeah. I know how to use a gun."

Zero let some of his relief bleed into his expression. "Excellent. Now, will you please peel this off? The itch of it is making me quite irritable. Soak it with this cloth, first." He handed the wet rag to Julian, and turned his back, waiting for the younger man to move closer. When warm hands touched his shoulder, it was all he could do to keep himself still. The cold cloth soon followed, but it did nothing for the heat swirling in his body. His cock stirred as he met Julian's blue gaze in the bathroom mirror. Julian was staring at him, eyes bright with something he wasn't sure he was ready to label. "How does it look?" Zero asked, trying to nudge

Julian into dealing with the bandage.

Julian dropped both his gaze and the towel. He began to carefully peel away the gauze, much too slowly for Zero's patience level.

"I'm not a delicate flower, Julian. Just peel it off," he said.

Julian gave him a look in the mirror that told Zero he wasn't going to be rushed. "The corner looks about as good as the hole in your chest."

"Good. Just rip the gauze off. I will not break." Zero fought to keep his muscles relaxed. He wanted to turn around and sink his fingers into Julian's hair. *Stupid thoughts, my dear,* he told himself. *Control yourself.*

"The rest of it is looser." Julian tossed the wet cloth onto the sink, and peeled the rest of the tape away from Zero's skin.

"How does the wound look?" Zero asked again, hoping he wouldn't need another bandage. "Is it closed?"

"It looks red and puffy, and it probably hurts like hell," Julian said, but then continued. "It doesn't look infected. The scar looks good. No discharge. It's just very new." He put a finger on it and pressed lightly. "Does this hurt?"

"No." Zero couldn't feel anything, actually. "I likely have nerve damage right around the incision."

"That sucks." Julian let his hand fall.

"No, that's normal." Zero touched his chest wound, then forced his hand down. If he gave into the itch surrounding the wound site, he'd break open the newly healed skin. "I'm going to shower, but first I'll show you where I keep the shotgun." He turned towards the kitchen, but Julian's hand on his arm stopped him.

"It's in the closet," Julian said.

Zero smiled, pleased. "Have you been snooping?" The faintest flush on Julian's high cheekbones betrayed him.

Zero couldn't help it. He leaned in and cupped Julian's cheeks. Fine auburn stubble pricked his palms. He loved it. "Darling, how enterprising of you," he murmured. He *really* liked this man. Julian's delightful combination of youthful innocence married to a startling level of self-confidence flat out did it for him. Instead of jerking his head away from Zero's hands, Julian's skin heated more. Zero watched while the younger man's face flushed a deeper pink. "Lovely," he murmured.

"What the hell, Zero?" Julian stared at him.

Aw, fuck it. Zero moved closer, crowding Julian up against the bathroom door. It didn't take much movement to pin the younger man there. His motorhome might be a luxury model, but it was still a small space for two large men. "Are you quite certain you want to stay here with me, Julian?" he asked, giving the man one last exit possibility. "I can't guarantee that you will remain innocent under my care."

"Innocent?" Julian laughed. "I'm not innocent, and neither am I in your care. For the last time, I'm a grown man. I choose where I want to be." Julian leaned into Zero's touch, eyes going heavy lidded. "You keep making the assumption that I don't know what I want." He put his hands on Zero's wrists. "I'm bisexual. I've never been in anyone's closet, let alone my own. Stop pretending that you're in charge of my life, Zero."

Arousal slammed into Zero, despite his exhaustion. Most men looked at his size and ran the other way. The ones who liked their lovers big ran away when they discovered Zero's brain was just as impressive as the rest of his body. Julian, however, hadn't shied away even once. Delight warred with the violence Zero worked so hard to keep in check. He wanted to grind himself into Julian until they were both dirty and aching. Zero hummed under his breath, and leaned in. "I'm going to kiss you now. And you're going to like it."

"So much talk," Julian whispered, but Zero's mouth shut him up.

****

Julian froze the moment Zero's lips touched his. Instead of devouring him, Zero coaxed him open gently. Instead of biting, Zero licked and nibbled until Julian's need for a solid touch burned through him. He yanked Zero closer, groaning when the man's heavy body pressed him to the wall. "Fuck, Zero. Stop with the teasing."

Zero lifted his head. "Oh, but teasing can lead to such delightful things, Julian."

Julian answered by biting Zero's bottom lip. "You talk too much." He knew he was asking for trouble by hooking up with a guy recovering from a gunshot wound, who also had a lot of unfinished and probably illegal business to deal with, but fuck if he cared right now. He wanted Zero. He hadn't felt this revved up by a simple kiss, like, ever. *So what if I get myself in trouble? I gotta live my life, right?* He licked inside, chasing the fading taste of beer on Zero's breath.

Zero shuddered, hands going around Julian's neck. He threaded his fingers up into Julian's hair. "Mmmm. You taste like a very, very bad idea."

Julian groaned, then ground his cock into Zero's hip. "Don't overthink this, Zero. We could have a good time together." He wasn't a small man, and he knew he was in fantastic shape, but his lean muscles were no match for Zero's bulky frame. Decades of some kind of weight lifting had given Zero enough mass to shoulder his way through just about anything. He locked one hand in Julian's hair, and then he used the other to jerk Julian closer. Julian let him. Hell, Julian *liked* it.

"Someday we're going to fuck and nothing will be the same ever again," Zero murmured.

"Promises, promises." Julian smirked, grinding against Zero until his dick hurt with the pressure. "You feel like a guy in need of some relief."

"Fuck." Zero's eloquence seemed to have completely deserted him. Julian let Zero manhandle him down the hall to the master bedroom.

"You're going to get us both killed," Zero muttered, muscles bulging as he moved.

"But what a sweet way to die," Julian replied, not giving a shit about Zero's paranoia. "You talk too much." He inhaled, catching a hint of the man he knew lay under all the hospital scents.

Zero grunted, lips busy along Julian's jawline. "You don't know what you're fucking with."

"I know you're going to fuck up your incisions if you keep that up," Julian said when Zero shoved him up against yet another wall.

"Shut up." Zero kissed him again, savagely this time.

When the kiss ended, Julian gasped for air. "We definitely doing this then?" he asked, trying to get his bearings.

Zero stared at him, dark eyes gone black with lust. "You better be very sure, my dear."

Julian rolled his eyes and stripped off his t-shirt. "Come on. There's a nice bed here. I'd like to rub off on you." He figured that wouldn't be too strenuous for a man with a healing gunshot wound.

Zero scowled, but Julian was way past being intimidated by this guy. He might be huge, he might be a total badass, but he was also weirdly gentle. "I'm going to figure out what makes you tick," he said, sitting down and urging Zero forward. "Come here." He tucked his fingers in the waistband of Zero's sweatpants and eased them down. "Oh, nice," he breathed when Zero's thick erection sprang out. He caught it against his palm.

Zero grunted, hips quivering. "You look good holding my cock."

Julian grinned up at him. "I'm going to do a hell of a lot more than just hold it."

Zero just stared at him, face going taut. His gaze burned right into Julian's soul, so he leaned in, breathing in the man's musk. The scent of antiseptic caught his nose, and he reminded himself to take it easy on the old guy. He opened his mouth and gently licked the tip of Zero's erection, sliding his hand down to cup his balls.

"Jesus. Now, who's the tease?" Zero said, voice rumbling.

Julian answered him by sucking hard, then sinking down. Zero shuddered, and Julian let his jaw relax. If there was one thing he was really fucking good at, it was giving head. He'd been an escort for three years, and in that time, he'd become a fucking expert at it. A lot of men liked to pretend they were straight, but were totally okay with receiving head. Those were the guys that wouldn't take Julian anywhere in public, but who seemed in desperate need of some kind of companionship in private. He'd blown young men and old men, and he'd enjoyed it. He worked Zero's shaft with his free hand, bobbing up and down his cock until he felt it swell even more. He smiled around the shaft, and that was when he made the fatal mistake of looking up into Zero's gaze again.

Chapter Five

Zero stared down at Julian, liking the way his mouth opened over his erection. The guy looked like he was enjoying the process, but Zero knew he hadn't truly thought through the ramifications of what he was doing. Not really. He let Julian suck him, and he thought about what it meant that he'd gotten so snared up that he'd let a guy he genuinely liked give him a blowjob. Zero preferred to keep his sex quick, hard, and anonymous, yet here he stood, breaking all his fucking rules.

Felix would be laughing his ass off at me if he could see this, Zero thought, but then Julian hit a particularly sensitive spot and he shuddered. Julian looked up, blue eyes luminous.

Zero sucked in a breath, suddenly right at the fucking edge of orgasm. He swallowed, hard, and shoved his hands into Julian's hair. "That's it." He dragged the younger man off his cock and pulled him up.

"Wha—" Julian tried to speak, but Zero shut him the fuck up with his mouth. He didn't want to talk. He could barely even *think*.

Julian shivered under his hand, and when Zero shoved down the younger man's jeans, he groaned. Zero found Julian's dick and stroked him, then maneuvered them both to the bed. "This isn't a fucking date, Julian. And I'm not paying you for sex. Get that shit out of your head right the fuck now." He pushed, and Julian went down, bouncing on the mattress with his jeans around his hips.

"What the fuck, Zero," Julian said, frowning. His cock stood out straight and thick.

Zero shook his head. "I'm not one of your clients." He pulled off Julian's sneakers and flung them down. "I am not fucking easy." He yanked on Julian's pants.

Julian sat up, flexing a truly impressive set of abdominal muscles. "How the hell do you know about that?"

Zero pressed him back down with a hand on his chest. "Who do you think told your mother?"

Julian sucked in a harsh breath, fingers curling into fists. "The fuck?"

Zero climbed on top of him. "I am very, very fucking good at what I do, Julian. I not only deal in goods, I deal in information." He ran his fingers down smooth skin, stopping to admire the tribal tattoo decorating Julian's torso. "I know all about you."

Julian went still. "No, you don't."

Zero wasn't certain what demons flicked through the man's mind, but it didn't matter. He'd find out. "I know more than you realize."

"Get off me," Julian said, face pink.

Anger? Zero mused, leaning back. He'd never force an unwilling lover, not after what he'd been through in his life. He examined Julian's expression more closely. *No. This is arousal.* Julian's hard-on pressed against his ass, hot and delicious and perfect. Zero lifted up and arranged them so that their cocks slid against each other. Julian groaned, hips bucking. Zero leaned down, enjoying the feel of Julian's skin pressed to his.

"Fuck, Zero—" Julian broke off.

"Do you truly want me to get off you?" he whispered into Julian's neck. "I will. I will walk out the door, and we can forget this ever happened."

Julian sighed, then shook his head. "This isn't how it's supposed to go, man." He wrapped his arms around Zero's waist, then slid one leg around his thigh.

Zero smiled. "I told you, I'm not easy." He

leisurely thrust against the younger man. Julian's cock wasn't as thick as his, but it was slightly longer. His height was comparable, so they were perfectly matched for this particular form of sex. He reached down and grabbed Julian's ass, squeezing as his cock slicked Julian's until they were both slippery. He'd always had a generous amount of pre-cum, but today it seemed even more copious than usual. *Too much time spent laying on my ass in the hospital,* he thought. He hadn't even had the opportunity or energy to jack off since the shooting.

"Fuck. I've been almost there for an hour, Zero. Enough." Julian wrapped his other leg around his thighs and began heavy thrusting. "I want to fucking come."

"I want to fucking come all over you," Zero countered, meeting Julian's movements with his own. He pressed down so tightly there was no space between their bodies. He groaned as his dick slid against Julian's hot cock, and squeezed his ass even tighter. He dipped his head down to taste the younger man's neck, but then out of the blue, his climax thundered through him. He gasped, erection jerking.

"Oh man," Julian said, head going back. "Fuck." He bucked up, and then his cock pulsed hot spunk against Zero's already messy groin. "Fuck, yeah," Julian hissed, shuddering. He had his arms wrapped around Zero's shoulders.

Zero sighed, feeling his body go completely boneless. The ache in his chest was worse, but he didn't give a fuck. "Damn." He wasn't sure if he was disappointed that he'd shot off so quickly, or pleased that all the lingering tension of his stay in the hospital seemed to have bled out of him.

"Yeah, that too." Julian rolled his hips one last time. "God, that was perfect. Also, you weigh a fuckton, and I need air." He shifted until Zero slid off to the side.

Zero winced as his healing wound abruptly made itself known via a stabbing pain along his shoulder blade.

"Oh, fuck. Did I hurt you?" Julian leaned up, pushing Zero further onto his back. "Shit."

Zero huffed. "No, you did not hurt me. I am fine." *Or I will be. Just need to catch my breath.* He silently counted to ten, willing his muscles to relax back into his post-orgasm relaxed state.

"Bullshit. Stay there." Julian got out of the bed and headed for the bathroom.

Bemused, Zero watched him walk. The guy really had a fine ass. When Julian reappeared with a wet cloth, Zero sat up, frowning at the burn of heat in his chest.

"No, I said stay there. For God's sake, Zero." Julian gently pushed him back down. "I'm here to help, remember?"

"I think I can wipe up my own jizz," Zero said, wryly.

"No, you can't," Julian replied, gently cleaning him up. "You need sleep. You have bags under your eyes."

Zero grimaced. "Maybe so, but I am not on my deathbed." He tried to grab the cloth, but Julian dodged his hand.

"Shut up and let me do this. Jesus. Stubborn old goat." Julian finished wiping him. "Lift up."

Zero obliged, somewhat amused by the man's fussing. Julian eased the covers out from beneath him, then tossed the used cloth in the direction of the bathroom. "It's early, but I'm fucking wiped." He climbed back into the bed, and pulled the comforter up over them both. "Go to sleep."

"Are you always this bossy after an orgasm?" Zero asked.

"Yes." Julian closed his eyes. "I also snore."

"Aren't I lucky," Zero murmured, watching Julian's body go boneless. He supposed there were worse things than having a young lover snoring against his shoulder. He touched the wound on his chest, then sighed and closed his eyes. He needed a shower. He needed to start moving in on Edwards. But most of all, he needed a full night's worth of shut-eye. He'd never heal properly if he didn't get enough rest. He listened to Julian's breath even out, and slowly let himself fall into sleep.

****

Julian woke up into darkness. For a moment, he couldn't figure out where the hell he was, and then he heard someone breathing next to him. *Who?* he thought for a moment, frowning. He turned his head to see the dark shape of a man sleeping next to him, and then the events of the past afternoon slammed into his head. *Zero. Some truly excellent sex. Grilled cheese,* he grinned, then froze when a clatter sounded from the door of the motorhome.

"Shit," he said under his breath. He put a hand on Zero's shoulder, thinking that would be enough to wake the guy, but Zero didn't stir. He shook him gently, but Zero just inhaled deeper, not waking up. *He's exhausted,* Julian thought, rolling away and sitting up. *Not surprising, given all the shit he's been through.* Julian stood up, straining to hear anything. The sound of cicadas softly droned outside, but he *knew* he'd heard something else.

"Get up," he told himself, thinking of the shotgun a few feet away. It wasn't loaded. He'd need to deal with that if someone was really trying to break in. The thought worried him. He'd had some training in Krav Maga—*Okay, a lot of training,* he thought—but he'd never had to fight a person off in real life.

"Or it could just be a coyote," he murmured,

walking naked to the hallway. The dim light of a nightlight just barely lit the space enough to keep him from walking into things. "We're in the middle of fucking nowhere." He opened the small closet where Zero kept some clothing and grabbed the shotgun racked against the wall. The shells were on the shelf above him, so he grabbed the box and headed closer to the front of the motorhome. He'd just managed to open the box of shells when a man shoved through the door of the RV, deforming the lock near the knob.

"Fuck!" Julian threw the box of the shells at the guy to slow him down, then grabbed the tall pepper mill sitting on the counter. When the guy cursed, Julian smiled grimly and rushed forward. He wasn't going to wait for this asshole to come to him first. He feinted a thrust at the guy's armpit, and then when the man blocked him, he hit him in the temple with the solid wood pepper mill. The man grunted, but he didn't go down. From the corner of his eye, Julian saw another guy enter through the broken door.

"If you want to live, just fucking stand down," the second man said, pointing a pistol at Julian.

Oh, hell no, Julian thought, ducking. He twisted, jamming the pepper mill into his attacker's groin. The man doubled over, coughing and groaning, and then Julian punched him with the wood in the side of his neck. He went down like a stone. Julian rolled, trying to avoid the bullets hitting the side of the hallway. "Shit," he muttered, wondering if Zero was still sleeping it off in the bedroom.

"That is quite enough of that," Zero said, looming like a brick wall in the doorway.

Julian wanted to yell at him to get the fuck down, but suddenly the bullets stopped. He glanced back at the front of the motorhome. In the dim light, he realized the man with the pistol was bleeding from a shot in meaty part of his shoulder. The guy grabbed at his wound, swaying as he dropped the gun. It clattered to the floor.

"Well, shit," Julian said, staring up at Zero. His lover hadn't bothered to put on clothes, either, and he looked like a vengeful mobster with his ridiculous muscles, and the glower, and the black Glock in his fist.

Not to mention that nasty looking scar. Damn, he's hot. Julian took a deep breath, willing his heart rate the calm the fuck down. At this point, he wasn't sure if the adrenaline was from the fight or the sight of Zero standing over him like that.

"Are you hit?" Zero asked, eyes flicking to Julian.

Julian shook his head and stood up. "Nope." He reached over and switched on a low light, then stared at the bastard bleeding all over the floor. The guy looked pasty, not surprising, given how much blood was pumping out of his wound. "Who the fuck are you?"

The guy just looked at him, then glanced past him at Zero.

"Not talking, huh?" Julian pursed his lips. "So much for being safe out in the middle of nowhere, dude." He raised an eyebrow at Zero.

"Indeed," Zero said, looking only mildly irritated, but Julian knew him better by now. Zero was pissed, but he wasn't going to show it to their new friend.

"Here. Have a fucking seat," Julian said, striding forward. He grabbed the guy by the front of his shirt, ignoring the man's groan of pain, and pushed him down onto the floor.

Zero walked forward, not seeming the least bothered by his nudity, or Julian's. He delicately stepped over the guy Julian had taken down. "My dear, you realize you killed the other one, yes?"

Julian glanced at the man on the floor. No, he did *not* fucking realize that, but damned if he was going to show his dismay in front of this prick. The man actually had the balls to reach into his jacket, and Julian grabbed his wrist. "Don't fucking move, asshole." He patted the guy down, and extracted a nice little blade from his inner pocket. "What the hell did you think you were going to do with this? Huh?" He brandished it in front of the man's face. Stringy black hair hung down over the guy's forehead. Julian wrinkled his nose at the stink wafting from him. He touched the blade to the man's chin. "Answer me."

The guy blanched.

"Move back, my dear," Zero said. "You are frightening him."

Julian clenched his teeth, but he did as his lover asked. He was better off further away from this joker, anyway, given his sour mood. He stood up.

"I have a few questions for Mr.—" Zero cocked his head. "Yes. I thought I recognized you. Mr. Jacomo, isn't it?"

The guy's eyes brown widened. "Fuck you."

Zero laughed. "Oh no, only one man gets to fuck me, and he's the gentleman standing over you looking like he very much wants to stick your own blade into your throat."

"Fucking homos," the man said, spitting to the side.

Julian growled, moving in again, but a headshake from Zero stopped him in his tracks. "Fuck." He wanted to smack the guy upside the head. *Clearly, I haven't been as successful as I'd thought in settling my nerves.* He glanced at Zero. His lover was staring down at the wounded guy the same way he'd stare at a bug through a microscope: equal parts annoyance and speculation. *How the hell did Zero know this goon's name?* Julian wondered, clenching his fists, and then carefully unclenching them. *It doesn't matter. I just want him gone. We should have been safe here.* Anger and frustration curled into a hard ball at the pit of Julian's stomach, and then he glanced at the body on the floor.

"Fuck," he said more softly, taking a deep breath as his anger turned to unease. *I killed a man,* he thought, carefully stepping back, closer to Zero. He set the thug's knife down on the counter near the shotgun, and studiously avoided looking into the unmoving eyes of the dead man on the floor. He knew the martial arts he'd enjoyed learning so much could hurt someone, but he'd never expected to be in a situation where he'd actually have to use his skills to kill. He wasn't exactly sure how he felt about it. *And now is not the fucking time to examine your psyche, Julian. Get a fucking grip,* he told himself. They still had to deal with the prick bleeding out on the floor of Zero's motorhome.

"So, what brings you to my humble abode, Mr. Jacomo?" Zero asked, gesturing to his surroundings.

"Screw you," the man replied, still belligerent.

Zero tsked. "Why do thugs react with such a limited vocabulary? Is it a lack of imagination? Do you know, my dear?" He turned to Julian.

Julian noticed that Zero never used his name. *Interesting.* He shrugged. "Lack of intelligence often leads to a lack of imagination. I'd be willing to bet this guy isn't the sharpest knife in the drawer."

Zero smiled, but it looked more like a baring of teeth than anything else. Julian watched the goon on the floor flinch. "And is that indeed the case, Mr. Jacomo? No? Well, then, I suggest you explain to us precisely what you are doing here in my home in the middle of the night. Yes?" Zero moved forward, looming nude over the man. "I don't take kindly to people breaking in and attempting to kill me in my sleep."

The guy's eyes darted around the space, looking everywhere except at Zero's heavily muscled form standing over him. Julian noted with amusement that Zero's softened dick was right at eye level on the guy. The thug didn't seem to like that at all.

"Talk, or you will die," Zero said casually.

The man stared at the floor.

Julian leaned against the counter. "I am not in the mood for this shit, you know." His voice came out harsh. Since they seemed to be playing good cop, bad cop, he might as well continue with his part. He really wanted to put on a pair of pants, but he was afraid to leave Zero alone with the intruder. *Not that he can't handle himself,* he thought, taking in Zero's unwavering focus, despite his healing wound. The arm holding the Glock never wavered. "I was sleeping. I was having a good fucking dream."

The guy looked at Julian, then dropped his gaze back to the floor. "I got nothing to say to you."

"Well, that is a shame," Zero said, and then he abruptly dropped into a crouch and pressed his gun into the man's forehead. Hard. His healing wound didn't seem to be bothering him at all, but then, Julian already knew that Zero's pain tolerance level was insane.

"Boom," Zero whispered.

The man flinched, hard.

"I would really like to get some more sleep," Julian said, when the man still refused to talk.

Zero cast him an amused glance. "Patience, my dear."

Julian made a sound in the back of his throat. The man glanced at him, and then away, visibly trembling. Julian didn't know if it was fear or blood loss.

"I already have one body to dispose of, Mr. Jacomo. One more won't bother me unduly," Zero said to the guy, dark eyes gleaming.

The man shrank back. "He'll kill me!"

"Oh my God, why do the assholes always say that?" Julian asked of no one in particular. He picked up the guy's blade and started tapping the counter with it. He had to do *something* or the excess energy shooting through him would push him into an action he'd regret. "Like, you already have a gun to your head. You're going to die *right now*, you moron. You won't have to wait until your boss gets his hands on you. Is that what you really want?" Julian gestured to the body on the floor while he spoke.

The guy stared at Julian, then looked at Zero. "Mr. Edwards said if we don't kill you he kill us both. I got no choice."

Zero sighed, loudly. "Edwards sent you here to murder me in my bed. I already know he wants me dead. What else can you give me to buy your life?" He leaned back, easing up on the gun a little. "How did Edwards know where to find me?"

The guy swallowed. "Mr. Edwards, he shoot the guy at the storage place after he cuts off his fingers. I was there with him. He make John and me hold the guy down." His eyes flicked to the dead body and back.

Zero went still. "He killed Aaron?"

The thug nodded.

"Jesus, that's your boss?" Julian asked. "Crazy, much? Why the hell would you work for a piece of shit like that?"

"What else?" Zero tapped on the man's skull with the gun, ignoring Julian's outburst.

"I give you the names of Mr. Edwards's top guys! Don't shoot, okay?" The man sounded like he was on the verge of stroking out.

If you had Zero staring at you like that, you'd stroke out, too, Julian thought, fascinated. Zero was a seriously fucking intimidating guy. *Looks like our roles in good-cop, bad-cop just switched around.*

"Who are they?" Zero asked, narrowing his eyes at the thug.

"McMurty, Toome, Shavstri, and Demotov," the man blubbered. "That's all I know."

Zero nodded as if ticking points on a list, and then he stood up. "Mr. Jacomo, you realize that I am going to kill Edwards, slowly and painfully, yes?"

The man just looked at him, like a deer caught in someone's headlights. "No one can kill him. No one." He tilted his head, baring his throat. "Might as well do me now. Get it over with."

"I have already started to kill him, Mr. Jacomo. You might want to think about that if you intend to live," Zero said, jerking his head at Julian.

With an intuition he didn't know he had, Julian moved forward and jerked the guy back to his feet. He ignored the man's moan of pain. "Time to go, dumbass." He dragged the thug to the door and tossed him out onto the grass, not really caring about his gunshot wound. If the man was coherent enough to spew insults at them, he was coherent enough to get up and run away.

"I don't know where you parked, and I don't care, as long as you get the fuck out of here, pronto," Julian said. The light from the night's full moon gave him a clear view of the man's face as the guy stared fearfully up at him. Julian didn't know where this new aggressive persona of his came from, and he didn't care. These fuckers had broken into Zero's home and tried to kill them. He was pissed. *And upset. Don't forget about that,* he thought, mind shying away from the image of the dead guy on Zero's floor.

The guy got to his feet. "You die next. You both die."

Julian snorted. "Everyone dies."

"Not like you." The man shook his head, and then turned and trudged across the clearing, hand on his wounded shoulder.

"Come back inside, Julian," Zero said from behind him. "He won't bother us anymore."

Julian spun around, belatedly realizing he'd stepped down onto the grass. "Shit." He ran his hands through his hair. "What about the guy inside?" He couldn't bring himself to say "the guy I killed". He stared down at his bare feet. Clippings of dew-wet grass stuck to the tops of his toes.

"I have people to clean that up," Zero said, holding the door open for him.

He has people to get rid of dead bodies? Julian swallowed, and scrubbed a hand over the back of his neck. *I don't even know what to think about that.* He looked at Zero. His lover seemed strangely calm. The full moon highlighted the muscles in the arm Zero was using to hold open the door. Julian wanted to roll around inside Zero's preternatural control. He wanted to fuck Zero until he forgot the events of the last hour. He stepped back up into the motorhome, pausing in the doorway.

"Are you okay?" Julian hoped Zero hadn't strained anything. The closer he got, the easier it was to see the way the new scar stretched along Zero's skin. It looked fine, but any more of this kind of drama, and Zero might be looking at a serious setback. Infection sometimes came on fast and hard, even after a wound seemed healed. He would know, after listening to his mother's lectures about stubborn patients enough times over the years. Julian took control of the door, not wanting Zero to strain his chest muscles.

"You're the one who took a man down with your bare hands," Zero said, stepping back inside. "I am fine."

Julian followed him into the motorhome, scowling when the door crunched against the jamb, but didn't latch. "I used your pepper mill, not my bare hands." Julian looked around for the kitchen implement. He hadn't remembered setting it down.

"It's in the corner, by the hall closet," Zero said. He made a move to crouch down, but Julian stopped him, squatting to retrieve the mill. A few stray shells had scattered out of the box he'd thrown at the first intruder, and he scooped them up, too. When he stood up, he caught Zero smiling at him.

"What?"

"I am so very pleased that you are a capable man, Julian." Zero walked to him and took the shells and pepper mill from his hands. He set them on the counter, and then he leaned in and kissed Julian softly. "It is extremely sexy."

Julian blinked. Zero smirked at him and then headed for the bedroom.

What just happened? Julian thought, touching his mouth. His cock had hardened mid-kiss. He knew it wasn't normal for a lover to get turned on by violence, but between his own adrenaline and Zero's words, he had the sinking feeling that his idea of normal was about to change.

Chapter Six

Zero slipped on his sweats and grabbed his phone from the nightstand, ignoring his erection. He needed to contact his cleaner, and get the mess out in the kitchen cleaned up pronto. Much as he'd enjoy screwing Julian up against the wall, they had no time right now for sex. Besides, he sensed Julian's dismay over his own violent competence, and the best way to move the young man past it was to erase the evidence. *He'll always remember, but he doesn't need to stare at a corpse all day long.* He opened the message app on his phone, and tapped out a query.

Zero: **One item to clean up, emergency fee available.**

Georges: **Location?**

Zero grimaced. He didn't have an address. He didn't *want* to have an address. The entire point of moving out here into the middle of nowhere was so he couldn't be contacted. Now he'd have to drop a pin on a map and share the information. He sighed. There was no help for it. His unknown location was no longer unknown anyway, as evidenced by Edwards's thugs breaking in and littering up the place. He opened his map app, took a GPS screenshot, and sent it to Georges. After a moment, his cleaner replied.

Georges: **ETA 30 min. Confirmation Y8WTW**.

Zero: **Acknowledged.**

Zero slipped his phone into his pocket, and headed out of the room to find Julian staring fixedly at the body on the floor. "Julian." His lover looked up attentively enough, but Zero could tell he was preoccupied. *Maybe redirecting his attention will help.* "I would like for you to help me repair the door."

Julian glanced at the broken frame. "You've

slipped back into fancy speak mode." He pursed his lips. "In fact, as soon as those guys broke in, you started talking like someone's butler."

Zero frowned. Now was not the time to discuss his coping mechanisms. On the other hand, perhaps it was better that Julian focused on him rather than the dead guy on the floor. "It's a habit. It calms me down, and unsettles people. I like the dual utility of the mannerism."

"I know." Julian shook his head. "Believe me, I understand." He rolled his shoulders. "When that guy tried to kill me, habit took over, and now he's dead."

"That isn't habit. That's training, and I'm grateful you have it," Zero told him. "We would be dead, otherwise. They meant to shoot us in our sleep. If they hadn't been so incompetent..." He trailed off.

"You sure about that?" Julian asked.

"About what? Their incompetence, or their intention?"

"Their intention. You really think they would have killed us in our sleep?" Julian asked, sounding as if he didn't quite believe Zero.

Zero moved closer. "Yes. And there will be others." He reached under the eye-level cabinet on his left and unlatched the hidden shelf. It opened down, exposing a bank of security monitors.

"Whoa. Where the hell did that come from?" Julian stared at the displays. "You had these all along?"

"Yes." Zero grimaced, though he was pleased to see that his lover had shifted his attention from the body on the floor to the screens. "I should have had these open and active from the moment we arrived here. He flicked a switch, activating the security feeds. One by one, the cameras came on. "There. Do you see? Our Mr. Jacomo parked near the road, down the hill from this property." He pointed to one of the grainier screens. He could switch the cameras over to infrared, but with the light from the moon, he didn't think it was necessary.

Julian moved closer. "His shoulder wound doesn't seem to be bothering him much."

"Adrenaline." Zero knew he hadn't damaged anything vital with his shot, but the man would be feeling the affects of the wound soon enough. He'd lost a lot of blood. He watched Jacomo get into a dark sedan, probably an old Ford, and drive away. "He has maybe ten more minutes before the shakes set in. Let's hope he gets to where he's going without taking down some innocent bystander."

"We're in the middle of the woods. That won't give him enough time to get back to Edwards."

Zero laughed. "He isn't going to Edwards. He is running for his life. He will try to get as far away from here as possible."

Julian snorted. "I should've known."

"It won't do any good, anyway." Zero smiled grimly. "Nowhere is truly far enough from Edwards, which is another reason why I plan on eliminating the bastard. His irrational behavior is threatening the business of many, not just his own organization." Zero scanned the other displays, checking the time. "The cleaner will be here soon. You may want to put on some clothes."

Julian flicked a glance at Zero's pants, then nodded. "Will do." He headed for the bedroom.

Zero could tell by the way he skirted around the body that Julian didn't want to think about what he'd done. And he probably didn't want to think about what Zero planned to do to Edwards, either. He understood. The first time he killed a man wasn't something he'd ever forget, even if the bastard had been beating his mother into a pulp at the time. "And she died anyway, so it was all for nothing. Revenge is never a good enough reason for killing." Zero sighed, putting away the bad memories.

"Who died?" Julian had returned quicker than Zero'd expected. "You look grim." He frowned. "Not that there isn't a lot to be angry about." He gestured to the mess in the RV.

Zero debated lying, but he liked Julian. His instincts told him to trust him. He made a split-second decision. "The first man I ever killed was a dealer who'd come for money my mother didn't have. When he realized that she'd smoked his product without the means to pay him, he beat her to death."

Julian paled. "Jesus. That's terrible."

Zero shrugged. "It was a long time ago, in the middle of the crack cocaine epidemic. I got over it."

Julian was shaking his head. "How the hell do you get over something like that? I didn't get over my dad dying." He ran a hand over his face. "You killed the dealer?"

Zero nodded. "Yes."

"When did this happen?"

Zero could tell Julian was putting the pieces of his life together, and for the first time in his life, he didn't mind someone knowing about his past. *Do I really want to get close to this man?* he mused, as if he still had a choice. He'd already let Julian into his world far deeper than he'd anticipated a mere twenty-four hours ago. "I was twenty. Home on leave from the Army." He watched Julian's expression range from horror to sympathy to confusion. "I came home from the grocery store, and found him standing over her with a hammer."

"A hammer? Jesus. I can't even imagine going through that." Julian shook his head. "I take it that no one ever found out?"

"That I killed him? No. No one ever found out," Zero confirmed. "Who would miss a two-bit crack dealer, high on his own goods? Nobody. The police didn't even open a case on it." He didn't add that he'd dumped the body in the river. Julian didn't need to know those details.

"What happened then?" Julian looked as though he expected a lot more to the story, but there was no story. Just life, with all of its cruel mediocrity.

"I went back to my unit, and we shipped out to the Middle East. Nothing else happened," Zero said, pushing the memory of the dealer's face back down into the depths of his skull. No need to relive that again. Not now. Not ever. "I buried my mother. I put it behind me."

"Do you regret it?" Julian asked, almost in a whisper. His face showed his concern.

Regret killing the man who destroyed my mother? Zero nearly growled, but then he took a deep breath. Julian needed the truth, but he didn't need Zero's bitterness. He'd been nothing but kind. Julian was one of those rare individuals who seemed to truly be able to empathize with someone else's trauma. *And here I am dragging him into my mess,* Zero thought, sadly. "No, I don't regret what I did. He needed to be dead. I facilitated that need." Zero turned back to the monitors. "Some people are more useful dead than alive, but that knowledge doesn't necessarily make it easier for those of us who are the instrument of their fate."

"You're speaking fancy again," Julian said.

Zero sighed, and ran a hand over his bald head. Stubble pricked his palm. He really needed to shave. "It gives me time to gather my thoughts. Unnecessary words lead to trouble. And that leads to regret," he added.

"That's it? That's why you talk like you're on the way to an afternoon tea party?"

"I also enjoy watching the consternation on the faces of my enemies," Zero pointed out, half smiling. He turned and leaned back against the counter. He wanted to scratch at his scar, so he folded his arms over his chest. Best to leave it alone, or it would never finish healing properly. It already ached more than he liked.

Julian choked on a laugh. "How can you joke at a time like this?"

"These are the times when humor is most important," Zero said, straightening up. "Come. I have some tools with which we can repair the door." He headed for the front of the RV, and opened the alcove cabinet set above the passenger's seat. He pulled out a pair of pliers and a clamp. "We have maybe fifteen minutes until the cleaner arrives. Let's make it count." He handed Julian the pliers, and they got to work. After a few minutes' work, the door handle moved smoothly again.

Julian pulled the door shut, and used the pliers to bend the jamb back into place. "It's not perfect."

Zero shrugged. "It doesn't need to be perfect. It simply needs to keep the bugs outside."

"You were hoping the solitude would provide enough security. That's why you didn't bother armoring this thing." Julian tossed the pliers back into the cabinet, and crossed his arms. The position highlighted his toned arms, not that Zero was complaining about the view. "There are more secure hideouts, you know."

"Yes, I know." Zero glanced at the monitors, then nodded. The cleaner had arrived. "Don't fixate on the little things, Julian. We can only move forward from any given situation, not back." He stood up and opened the door. Two men dressed in disposable coveralls stood just outside.

"Y8WTW," the taller of the two men said.

Zero showed him his phone screen with the confirmation code. The man grunted. Zero held open the door. The men filed in and got to work. Zero glanced at Julian. His lover was staring at the cleaners who'd begun wrapping the body into a large bag.

No. This will not do, Zero thought, recognizing the younger man's guilt. "Julian."

Julian's head snapped up.

"I need to set up some contracts. Would you like to see how it's done?" Zero asked him.

"Are you sure that's something I should know?"

Zero considered Julian's words. *He has already killed someone on my behalf,* he thought, eyeing the younger man. Julian had put on his jeans, and the fabric clung in all the right places. He knew he should feel worse about dragging Julian into his current predicament, but he'd left that sort of morality behind decades ago. "It would be best if you understood how these things are arranged." He watched Julian's expression closely, and saw the precise moment his young lover realized all the implications behind Zero's words. He also watched Julian swallow the information, and almost imperceptibly straighten his stance.

That is strength. This is a man I wish to keep, Zero thought, more surprised by the suddenness of his attraction, than by the strength. Men like Julian came into one's life maybe once in a lifetime. Zero had long ago learned to recognize when it was time to hold on to something precious, and when it was best to let go. *And I have no intention of letting go of this man sooner than I must.*

****

Julian followed Zero into the bedroom and watched his lover open the roll cover of the corner desk built into the back wall. It barely fit with the queen-sized bed taking up almost all of the space, but since Zero had only a stool and not a chair, it seemed to function well enough as a workspace.

"Here. This is how I run my business," Zero explained, opening the laptop and logging onto a secure browser. He clicked easily through a login window, and then the desktop abruptly shifted into a new screen, and another browser Julian had never seen before opened up. "This is my private corner of the internet," Zero murmured, clicking into a site. He typed in an administrator password, and it opened up on a list of names. It looked like some sort of interactive database. "These are the available contractors." He ran a finger down the screen. "Hmm. Good. Felix has taken himself off the board."

"Felix?" Julian's eyebrows rose. "That's the guy who found you in your warehouse, right?"

Zero nodded. "He has been a top-rated contract killer for decades. He has just retired." He laughed. "I wonder if he'll be able to handle the boredom."

"Wow." Julian rubbed his face. "My mother mentioned him to me a few times. I had no idea about his job. I mean, I *knew*, but I didn't know, at the same time." He sat down on the bed, feeling as though his entire worldview had suddenly shifted on its axis. It had all started with the day he'd gone with his mother to help her treat a patient in his home: Zero. And now, with the guy he'd killed, and the knowledge Zero was freely sharing with him... He inhaled as a dozen unrelated pieces of information slotted into place in his mind. "You're a fixer. You work with criminals." He knew saying it out loud made him sound slow, but he needed to hear it.

"You knew that," Zero said gently. "I am a criminal, my dear. I make no excuses for my choice of career." He turned to look at Julian. His dark brown eyes were warm, but then his gaze shifted to just beyond Julian's shoulder and turned cold. Julian twisted around.

"We're done, Mr. Zero." One of the men who'd come to clean up stood in the doorway.

"Excellent. The usual fee will be applied to your employer's account, plus fifty percent bonus for the immediate service." Zero rose and rummaged in a box set into the alcove above the nightstand. "And here is something for you and your partner." He handed the man several hundred-dollar bills.

"Pleasure," the man said, tipping his head and leaving.

"They don't say much." Julian stared as the man and his partner disappeared from the motorhome. He hadn't even heard them cleaning up.

"I don't pay them to speak," Zero murmured, replacing the small box where he'd removed the cash.

Julian stared into the hallway and kitchen area. He couldn't even tell there had been a fight. The space looked pristine. *God, I'm losing it,* he thought, rubbing his eyes. Outside, the first faint glimmers of dawn had begun to stain the sky with light. They'd left the window in the back of the RV open for the breeze, and he could hear some birds beginning to wake up.

"Julian. Don't fret," Zero said quietly. "All will be well."

Julian spun around. "Are you fucking kidding me? I killed a guy, and it's like the whole thing has been completely erased." He sank his fingers into his hair, yanking on the strands. "Shit."

Zero sat back down on his stool. "Has it truly been erased, Julian?"

Julian looked at him. Zero's steady gaze told him all he needed to know. "No," he whispered. His brain shied away from the image of the body sprawled on the floor.

"And it never will. But don't let yourself spiral down into a hole. You merely did what you had to in order to defend your life."

Julian was about to protest when Zero swiveled around on the stool and clicked over to a different page on the open browser.

"Look. Mr. Jacomo's companion was a man named John Podeste. He is wanted in three states for larceny, armed robbery, and hmm... Interesting. Murder. Domestic violence. He violated the terms of his parole, too." Zero pointed at the screen. "That is the man you killed."

"Does that make my murder of him justified?" Julian demanded. He had to admit, he felt a tiny bit better, and he felt guilty over *that*. There seemed to be no direction his thoughts could go that didn't result in him feeling like shit.

"Only you can answer that question," Zero replied, closing the window and opening a new one. He typed in a query at the top, and four names scrolled down the page.

"Those are the guys Jacomo said were Edwards's top men," Julian said, frowning. He focused on the information filling in on the screen in an effort to distract himself from what he'd done.

"Yes." Zero typed in another query, and the four names zoomed to the top right corner. Zero typed a number into the space where the cursor blinked, then hit return. A long list of contractors scrolled up, some shifting from black to dark green.

"Is that what I think it is?" Julian asked.

Zero closed down the window and shut the laptop. "Edwards won't have the comfort of his men

233

helping him with his empire for very long."

"You just put out a hit on those men." Julian stared at the closed laptop. "It only took you, like, a couple seconds. Jesus." He knew he had to get it together. He'd known what Zero was before he got into bed with the man, and dwelling on the situation wasn't going to change anything. Even more importantly, he'd volunteered to help. He'd decided to sleep with Zero. No one forced him into it. Anything that happened did so with his full knowledge. Zero had made certain of that. *And, too, you find his lifestyle intriguing. Or you did, until you had to defend yourself. And the reason you're upset over that is because you're not as upset over it as you think you should be. Fuck. I'm acting like an idiot.* Julian stood up. "I understand. I suppose it's better than you going after him personally."

Zero smiled. "Oh, but I *am* going after Edwards personally. I simply prefer to pull up some of the weeds before I venture into an overgrown yard. It cuts down on the ticks, you see."

Julian had to laugh. "You and your metaphors." He eyed Zero's self-satisfied smile. Zero's jawline had begun to sport some serious stubble. "Okay. That's enough serious talk. You need a shower. You were in that hospital, what? A week? Two? And I know they didn't let you shower."

Zero's eyebrows rose. "You are suddenly very impatient."

"You stink. And so do I." Julian tried to tug Zero to his feet.

Zero shook his head. "One moment, my dear." He pulled out his cell phone and dialed a number, keeping eye contact with Julian. "My dear Banner. You did not warn me that your boss knew about my lovely motorhome, and I am upset with you. You accepted my money. You are supposed to send me regular updates about the situation."

Julian sat back down. "A spy?" he mouthed at Zero. He shouldn't be surprised. Zero was the kind of man who had connections in places Julian didn't even know existed.

Zero nodded at Julian, but didn't lower the phone. "Despite your protestations, Banner, your text did not arrive. Perhaps you feel it would be better to betray me? Perhaps you prefer to stay with Edwards indefinitely? I know how much you enjoy working for the man who destroyed your father." He paused, lips pursed. "No? Well then, I suggest you do your job."

After those words, Julian watched Zero's face go from calm to angry in the space of two seconds. For some reason, he seemed to be able to interpret Zero's expressions easier than when he'd first met the man. *Is he more relaxed in front of me? Or am I just learning to read him better?* He thought of the moment when Zero had needed him to haul Jacomo off the floor. Zero had shifted his shoulders the slightest bit, and Julian had immediately known what he wanted him to do.

"No, my confused friend. You are quite wrong," Zero said, voice going low. Threatening. Julian shivered. Zero was a certified badass. He'd always been attracted to those kinds of men. *And don't forget the women,* he thought, remembering one lady in particular he'd escorted to a number of events. Cassandra Mortisimer had rung all of his bells, but she'd been married, and too far out of his sphere of life for him to ever even consider pursuing her outside of his escort assignments. *I might have, though, except she also scared the shit out of me. Even Zero doesn't make my blood run cold the way she did on occasion.* He hadn't regretted that he'd never see her again once he'd quit that job.

Zero continued speaking. "Edwards might tear off your fingers, but I will simply kill you without warning, in the dead of night. This, you know. This, you have always known." Zero moved as if to hang up, but Julian could hear a man yelling frantically through the phone's tiny speakers. He sounded upset, which was not surprising, given Zero's assurance of death.

It's the calm voice. When Zero threatens you, he makes it seem as if he's checking a point off of a list of options. It's as if you mean no more to him than a simple task to be handled as efficiently as possible. It's disturbing and creepy and I love it, Julian thought, even more turned on. He ran his hands down his thighs, then forced himself to sit still. He had it bad for this guy. *This crush of mine isn't going to end well,* he thought, then tucked that worry into the back of his mind. He wasn't sure he cared. Zero was the kind of man he never thought he'd get to touch. *He's like a white-hot ember, and I'm the moth diving into the inferno. I legitimately can't help myself.*

Zero listened for a moment, face impassive. Julian could tell that Zero had the guy exactly where he wanted him. Something about the angle of his head, or maybe it was the nearly imperceptible curl of Zero's upper lip that told him everything he needed to know.

"Very well. See that it does not happen again. You know the consequences of failure," Zero stated, and he tapped the screen, ending the call. He carefully placed the phone on the desk.

"I should be terrified of you," Julian said softly, too aroused to care that his face was flushed. Watching Zero threaten people was hot. It shouldn't be, but it was. Julian shifted his weight on the bed. His cock was hard, and pushing against his jeans.

"But you are not, are you? You are not at all

frightened of me, because you know I will not harm you." Zero stood up. "My spy won't forget to send a text the next time he has information that I need." He shook his head. "Sheer incompetence, but he was the only one willing to be led astray in Edwards' employ."

"You have fingers in every frigging pot." Julian tilted his head back. From what he could see, Zero's cock wasn't soft, either. He almost reached out to pull him closer, but then he remembered how desperately they both needed a shower. *Focus. Let the man clean the stink of the hospital off before you attack him, Julian.*

"Information is what makes the world go 'round, my dear," Zero said, standing over him. "The man who has the most information does not need to worry about life running over him, because he is in control of the vehicle."

"Are you always in perfect control?" Julian asked Zero, knowing even as the words came out of his mouth that he meant them as a goad. He wanted Zero to trust him. He wanted to see Zero without the perfect diction and controlled emotions. He wanted Zero to show him who he truly was, inside. *You're asking for too much, too soon,* he told himself. *It hasn't even been twenty-four hours since you first met the guy again. And the first time you saw him, he was drowning in his own blood. Not the most auspicious first meeting.*

Zero touched the scar on his chest. "I wish I were perfect, but you of all people know that I am not."

Chapter Seven

Zero knew that Julian wasn't trying to remind him of his gunshot wound. From the troubled look on his lover's face, he could see Julian wasn't referring to that terrible incident. He put a finger over Julian's mouth just as the man opened it to speak. "I realize that's not what you meant."

"Even so," Julian said against his finger.

Zero cursed himself, then hauled Julian up, ignoring the burning ache in his chest. "You destroy my control. My careless words prove this." He kissed Julian softly, wondering what the hell he thought he was doing. He had no room in his life for love, but he also couldn't turn away from it when it walked in his door, all unasked for. Julian was a wild card. Even after only one day, Zero knew that what Julian offered, what Julian didn't realize *himself* that he offered, wasn't a one-time deal.

Julian's rigid stance relaxed. "Shit, man. I'm sorry."

"It doesn't matter." Zero glanced at the bathroom. Come sit with me while I shower. This is a luxury motorhome, but sadly we both won't fit in the stall." He walked to the bathroom and opened the door. The way the RV was constructed, he could latch the door to the hallway's opposite wall, opening the bathroom to the master bedroom. It was quite a clever design. The stock model also had an additional single bed over the kitchen table, but Zero had changed that out for more storage. Julian had no choice except to sleep in his bed, with him.

"You're asking me to watch you shower?" Julian sounded breathless.

"Yes. Is that a problem?" Zero stripped off his sweatpants, and kicked them to the corner. At this point, he wasn't inclined to ever wear them again. He'd worn them in the hospital for several days, and he preferred to not be reminded of that place. He opened the shower door and glanced at Julian. His lover had drifted closer, face still slightly flushed. Zero smirked. "You can sit on the toilet." He pointed.

Julian swallowed, but he sat down.

Zero turned on the water, and stepped into the spray. His hard-on didn't subside, even with the slightly cool water. "It's been over a week since I have been able to shower." He sighed, wetting his face. The water felt divine. "Sponge baths don't quite do the job."

"Fuck."

Zero glanced at his lover. Even through the wet glass door he could see Julian cupping his erection. "You like what you see?" Zero grabbed his soap and scrubbed the hospital stink off his body. He took his time, savoring the feeling. When he reached his cock, he used the soap as a lubricant, and pumped his hand over his length, exhaling with the pleasure.

"You're a tease, Zero," Julian said, voice gone low. He gripped the edge of the toilet seat with his free hand.

Zero laughed. "No. You know I will gladly fuck you." He rinsed off, and decided to ignore the stubble on his face and head. He was too tired to deal with it right now, and Julian didn't seem to mind. He turned off the water, and opened the door. Steam billowed out as he grabbed a towel from the shelf.

"The only reason I'm not all over you is because I know how badly you needed to wash," Julian said.

"You could use a shower, too," Zero said, smiling. He dried off, then slung the towel around his neck. He'd never be able to secure it around his waist with the erection he sported. "Come on. Strip." He stepped back, leaving room for Julian in front of the shower stall. "Don't take too long. The hot water tank is small."

Julian stood up. A slight flush rode his cheekbones, and Zero knew that meant his lover was right on the edge.

"You really think I can take a shower at this point?" Julian asked.

Zero nodded. "Yes. I want to see you."

Julian inhaled, then slowly slid his pants down. His thick cock sprang out. Zero wanted to go to his knees and suck him off, but the deep twinge in his chest told him it would probably not be a good idea. "Wash up," he said instead.

Julian stepped into the shower and turned on the water. It cascaded over his head, wetting his hair down. Zero stared at him. The water delineated every muscle on his body, and darkened the tattoo on his chest. "Hurry," Zero said hoarsely.

Julian smiled, then slowly soaped up. "This what you want?" He smoothed his hands down his chest. Soap bubbles drifted south, into his dark pubic hair.

Zero touched himself again, shuddering as his cock swelled even more. He hadn't felt this randy since he was young, and those days were long gone. "That's exactly what I want," he said, already imagining what it would be like to run his hands down Julian's wet skin.

"Fuck. If you keep looking at me like that, I won't be able to hold on, Zero," Julian said, rinsing off. "I'll come right here in the shower." He squeezed his cock. "You really want to waste this?"

In answer, Zero got up and shut off the water. "Don't bother drying off." He reached in and pulled Julian out of the shower, then swung him around and pushed him against the sink. "You smell like my soap." He leaned in and licked a strip up Julian's neck.

"Delicious."

"Christ." Julian wrapped strong hands around Zero's biceps. "If you don't fuck me, I won't be responsible for what I do."

Zero leaned back. "Well, we can't have that." He put his towel on Julian's head and roughly dried his hair, then skimmed it down his body. He knew he missed some water, but he didn't give a shit. "Come on." He pulled Julian out past the kitchen, then pushed him up against the table.

"What, here? There's a nice soft bed just over there." Julian pointed.

Zero didn't want Julian in bed. He wanted him spread open and vulnerable, right here. Right now. "Don't fucking move," he said, kicking Julian's legs apart a bit more. He rummaged in a cabinet to the left of the table, and finally found the lube he'd stashed there months ago. "I'm going to fuck you until you can't remember your own name."

Julian gripped the edges of the table, hard. "Promises, promises."

Zero smiled, then dribbled slick gel down Julian's ass crack. "I'll rim you someday," he said aloud. He silently cursed his damn gunshot wound. He couldn't risk injuring himself further. "You won't be able to fucking move." He gripped Julian's hips. For all his talk, he had the feeling he was the one who was losing control right now, not Julian.

"I don't need anything except your cock, Zero," Julian said, sounding way too coherent for Zero's taste.

Zero groaned, then slotted his erection between Julian's legs. He might not be able to do all the things he wanted, but he could give Julian a ride to remember. They were almost the same height, and he could feel the younger man's balls nestle against the tip of his cock. He rested his forehead in between Julian's shoulder blades. "You're gorgeous," he murmured, thrusting gently. He reached around and grabbed his lover's erection, thumbing over the tip.

Julian shuddered. "Likewise."

Zero snorted. "Not right now, I'm not." He slid a hand down and began to tease at Julian's hole. Julian groaned, pushing back against him. "Uh-uh, not so fast," Zero murmured against his skin. "Slowly, my dear."

"Fuck slow." Julian pushed back again. "I want you fast and hard."

"Patience," Zero said, as much to himself as to his lover. He let go of Julian's cock and spread his lover's legs further. "Don't fucking move."

"Or what?" Julian twisted around to smirk at him.

Zero huffed, then leaned over and grabbed two zip ties from the still open cabinet. "Or this." Before Julian caught on, Zero managed to secure his wrists to the table's legs.

"Oh, shit," Julian said, yanking. The table didn't budge, and neither did he. "You fucking tied me up?"

Zero leaned in again, grabbing Julian's hips. "You wouldn't listen."

Julian looked at him over his shoulder. "You're a pervert."

Zero grinned at the lust on Julian's face. "That, too." He slipped a hand around Julian's hard-on. "If you say 'red,' I'll stop and undo the restraints. I'm not a barbarian."

Julian snorted. "Not fucking likely I'll call uncle, Zero, and you know that."

Zero raised his eyebrows, then reached over again and grabbed the knife Julian had left on the counter. "Hold very still." He traced the tip of the knife down Julian's spine.

"Oh, Christ. What the fuck are you doing?" Julian's voice shook.

"Do you trust me?" Zero asked. He set the knife tip against the swell of Julian's ass. He wanted to mark him as his, but he also didn't want to hurt him. Warring instincts raged inside his head. Holding a blade against Julian's skin was dangerous, mostly because of how much Zero loved to cut people up. He rarely allowed himself the pleasure, because he knew how easily he could slip over the edge into brutality. Not even his oldest friend Felix knew how much he liked to play with knives. He kept a very careful leash on those desires. "You look fucking beautiful with this blade against you," he whispered, drawing it down Julian's skin. The contrast of the slick metal against Julian's body had him inhaling shakily. *Someday I will photograph him just like this*, he promised himself. "Do you trust me?" he asked again, voice rough.

"Yeah." Julian shivered. "God knows why, because you're a crazy motherfucker, but I trust you."

"Good." Zero turned the blade around, using the handle to tease at Julian's asshole. He coated the end with lube, making sure there were no hard edges. "This hilt is smooth. It's a nice Micarta handle. Just the right size." He pushed, and the tip slid into Julian's ass.

Julian groaned, head thunking down on the table. "Fuck, Zero. What the hell are you doing?"

"You know exactly what I'm doing. Don't move," Zero warned him again. "One slip, and it'll cut you."

Julian held himself rigid. "Fuck." Sweat slicked his back, but Zero could see how hard Julian's cock was. This turned him on, big time. "You're a fucking lunatic, Zero."

True. Zero slid the knife in further, gently

stretching the ring of muscles. He wasn't sure if he wanted to make Julian come with the knife, or fuck him with his cock. "Trust goes both ways, Julian. I'm trusting you to have control, and not move. You're trusting me to have control and not hurt you."

"This is sick," Julian croaked. He banged his head on the table.

"Do you call 'red'?" Zero asked, watching his lover try not to squirm. The knife in his ass didn't move, and that was a testament to Julian's impressive control. Zero inhaled, willing himself to calm.

"Hell, no," Julian replied immediately, looking over his shoulder. "I'm green. Fuck me."

Zero reached around and stroked Julian's cock. It was dripping with pre-cum. "If you move, you'll cut yourself." He kept a hand on the knife, fingers wrapped around the crossguard to make sure it didn't slip too far. He stroked Julian's erection with his other hand.

"Fuck." Julian dropped his head on the table again.

Zero slowly drew the knife out, then pushed it back in. Julian grunted, breathing harder. Zero jacked him faster. "Are you close?"

Julian groaned. "I don't know."

Zero grinned. "We'll keep going, then." His own erection was so hard it hurt. He couldn't imagine holding out long enough to fuck Julian, but he had no intention of losing control now. He eased the knife's hilt in again, then pulled it out, teasing Julian's hole. Julian's hip bucked, and Zero froze. "No moving." He kept his eyes on the blade and squeezed his fist around Julian's cock.

"I need to come," Julian said, sounding wrecked.

Zero fucked him a few more times with the knife, then pulled it out suddenly and set it on the table so Julian could see it clearly. "That was inside you," he said roughly. "I fucked you with a knife."

Julian jerked his hands, straining against the ties. "Zero, come on." The muscles in his arms stood out. "Stop playing around."

"You sure?"

"Fuck, yes."

Abruptly, Zero surged forward, shoving his cock inside Julian's willing asshole with one hard thrust. Julian's body felt like an inferno.

Julian let out a harsh groan, and Zero went still, fighting back his climax. "Someday I'll let you fuck me with that same knife," he murmured. "I bet it felt good inside. I bet you liked wondering if I'd go too far."

"Jesus, Zero," Julian panted. "If you don't fucking move, I'm going to kill you with my bare hands."

Zero kissed Julian's back, then started to thrust. He went slow at first, and then faster. "This what you want?" He ignored the deep ache in his chest. He didn't care in this moment if he hurt himself. Fucking Julian was more important.

"More," Julian growled, voice cracking. "Harder."

Zero grabbed the knife and cut through Julian's restraints, then tossed it away. He was tempted to carve into Julian's arms. He wanted to carve into his *own* arms, and they didn't need more blood on the floor today. "Take it, Julian. Take me." He fucked harder, fighting for purchase on Julian's sweat-dampened skin.

"I am fucking taking it," Julian said, pushing back as Zero thrust into him. "Come on. Give it to me."

Zero pulled out, breathing heavily. If he kept going, he was going to blow, and he didn't want to come just yet.

Julian turned around and yanked him in for a

bruising kiss. "You sick motherfucker. Come on." He dragged Zero to the bedroom and pushed him onto the bed.

Zero gasped, hand against his chest, but Julian climbed on top of him before he could breathe properly. *Whatever. I don't need air as much as I need Julian right now,* he thought.

"You fucked me with a knife, you crazy man," Julian said. He licked his lips as grasped Zero's cock and sank down on it.

Zero stared at the younger man. Julian looked like a warrior, all muscle and attitude and purpose. "I did. So what? You liked it. We both liked it." Just the memory of the knife sticking out of Julian's ass revved him up higher. He grabbed the comforter and made fists in the fabric.

"Yeah, I did." Julian gritted his teeth. "You could've really hurt me."

Zero narrowed his eyes, trying to hold onto his control. He wanted to grab Julian's hips and force him down until neither of them could move. "But I didn't."

Julian lifted up and then very deliberately screwed himself down again, not touching his erection. The tip was deep red. Wet. Zero stared at it as Julian moved on his cock. He wanted to touch it, and force Julian to climax, but if he moved even an inch right now, he'd break.

"I loved every second of it." Julian lifted up again.

Fuck, Zero thought, as his control broke. He didn't care about his fucking wound. He didn't care about hurting Julian anymore. He grabbed the younger man's wrists and yanked him down, thrusting hard up inside him again and again. "You can take it," he muttered, fucking hard. "You can take it."

Julian threw back his head and growled, just as his cock jerked. Thick streams of spunk jetted out, coating his chest and Zero's abdomen. The sharp smell of semen wafted through the room, and Zero breathed it in, loving everything about this man.

"Zero—" Julian tried to speak, but his voice broke before he could get any more words out.

"Yeah, you can take it, can't you? Just like that," Zero said, as his cock swelled. His orgasm crashed through him so hard he thought for a moment his heart had stopped, but then Julian twisted down harder. Zero moaned, letting his body take over. He climaxed for what seemed to be an hour, and he couldn't breathe, and he didn't care. Then Julian collapsed on top of him and Zero wrapped his arms around the love he'd never expected to show up in his life.

Chapter Eight

Julian sat at Zero's computer, checking up on the contracts his lover had set up a week ago. So far, three of Edwards's top five men had been eliminated. Julian sat back, rubbing at his chin. What the hell did it mean that it didn't bother him that those men were dead? He'd checked into their backgrounds, and they weren't good guys, but it shouldn't matter. Murder was wrong, the end. His mother was a doctor, for Christ's sake. *Then again, I'm not a good guy, either, am I?* he mused, mind shying away yet again from the image of the dead body on the floor.

"What have we got?" Zero said from behind him.

Julian swiveled around. His lover lounged in the doorway, looking like sin personified. Zero wore jeans and a tight t-shirt, and no shoes. He'd shaved his head, but left the stubble on his face. Julian's cock twitched, which was ridiculous. He'd had more sex the past week than he'd ever had before in his entire frigging life. He should be exhausted. He shouldn't want to tackle Zero and strip him naked. He took a deep breath, willing his overactive libido to calm the fuck down. "Three dead. Two to go," he said, eyes going to the bulge at Zero's groin.

Zero nodded. "Felix called. I updated him on the situation." He absently rubbed at the scar on his chest.

Julian couldn't see it through the t-shirt Zero wore, but he knew that the injury wasn't healing nearly as well as either of them had hoped it would. *Probably because we shouldn't be fucking on every available surface,* he thought, feeling a pang of guilt. He knew Zero should have been resting, and instead, the two of them were screwing around, every spare minute. "My mother texted, too," he said, instead of putting his worry about Zero's wound into words. He shouldn't be worrying. Zero was a big boy. And it wasn't like they were in love, or anything. They could stop at any time, right? *In your dreams,* a small voice at the back of his head accused. Julian ignored it. He couldn't face the thought that he might be falling for a killer. *No, not a killer. A fixer, which is almost worse. A killer does one thing very well. A fixer enables multiple levels of criminality. And Zero, well... He isn't going to change, because he's entirely okay with what he is. Hell, you don't* want *him to change.*

"Oh?" Zero's tone encouraged an explanation.

Julian pulled himself together. "No one seems to be following her," he said, shrugging. "Which is a relief." He pushed away his unease. He liked Zero. And he wasn't committing to anything by hanging around for a few more weeks. His apartment was paid through the next month. His investments were doing well. He had nowhere else he needed to be. As long as his Uncle Dave, the cop, didn't find out about any of this, he was golden.

Zero smiled, sexy as fuck, even though Julian knew he wasn't trying to be. "Good. I tried to be careful with her. I would never want to see your mother harmed."

"I know," Julian said. He looked at his lover. Zero looked back at him. The silence stretched out, and then Julian shook his head. "How long will it take the last two guys to disappear?" He turned and shut Zero's laptop, cutting the connection to the browser.

"Another day, maybe. Could be sooner." Zero stalked over to him. "That works for me. I need the rest, and I want Edwards to suffer. Watching his guys go down will make him crazy." He slid his fingers into Julian's hair and tilted his head for a kiss.

Julian frowned at him, even as his body relaxed into Zero's hold. "We haven't been resting, Zero," he said sardonically. "Far from it."

Zero snorted, then bit Julian's lower lip. "Resting enough," he murmured against Julian's mouth. "Resting is for pussies."

God, I want him again. Julian kissed him back, then pulled away, despite the throb in his cock. "You need *more* rest, not less. I know your wound is bothering you."

Zero scowled. "I'm not dead yet."

"Yeah, and I'd like to keep it that way," Julian said, touching Zero's chest lightly.

Zero glared at him.

"Behave yourself," Julian said, knowing that Zero would be amused by the command.

"You like it when I'm bad." Zero smirked.

"Even so. We can't fuck around all day long." Julian shrugged off Zero's hold. *I don't know what the hell I'm doing here,* he thought, opening the laptop again. The browser refreshed. "Huh." Julian scanned the screen again, not sure if what he was reading was real.

Zero leaned down. "What?"

"The final two men have been taken care of." Julian pointed to the list of names with his fingers. "Jesus. That was fucking fast. I didn't expect that. Not two minutes ago the contracts were still active." He sat back, slightly stunned. He should be more upset that the men were dead at all, and not be concerned with the speed of their demise, but he just couldn't bring himself to feel guilty. Taken aback, yes. Guilty, not so much. *I'm definitely going to hell.* He rubbed his face.

"With the amount of money I coughed up, I'm not surprised," Zero said, sounding pleased. "Good. This is precisely what I wanted." Zero sat down on the bed.

Julian started to scroll through the list of known associates of Edwards to take his mind off the killings. The names blurred across the screen, and then one practically leaped out at him. He lifted his finger off the keyboard, staring at the glowing letters. "Well, shit." He didn't know how many more shocks his system could take.

"Find something interesting?" Zero leaned in.

Julian tapped the screen. "I know her. Cassandra Mortisimer." He looked up at Zero. "Why is she on this list?" He'd taken her to a few charity events. Even now, the memory of her cold eyes and lush body forced a shiver down his spine. He'd liked her, sort of, when she wasn't scaring the shit out of him. "She's bad news, for sure, and I had no idea she knew Edwards."

"She's his wife, Julian," Zero said, tapping a command on the keyboard. A paragraph opened below her name, giving details. "She never took his last name." Zero smiled. "I bet that pissed Edwards off." He looked at Julian curiously. "How did you know her?"

"She was one of the women I escorted." Julian ran a hand over the back of his neck. "I liked her. She scared the crap out of me. The combination of those two things…" He trailed off, shaking his head.

Zero laughed. "You liked a woman who frightened you? Why am I not surprised?"

Julian frowned at the computer screen. "She requested my services several times." He remembered her sleek blonde hair and her penchant for cinnamon breath mints. Now, every time he smelled cinnamon, he thought of the way she threw her head back when she orgasmed. She was one of the clients who'd insisted on sex. Even though she had to be at least thirty years older than he was, he hadn't minded. She was hot. She paid extremely well. Her cold, cold eyes turned him on, because he was clearly a sick fucker who needed therapy. "Shit." Julian leaned back on his chair and ran his hand over his face again.

"You slept with her."

Julian looked at his lover. Zero's words were a statement, not a question. "Yeah. I did."

Zero's mouth twisted. "Not lately, I hope."

Julian shook his head. "I quit escorting, remember? I didn't need the money anymore."

"I've met Ms. Mortisimer. I can see the appeal, even if you don't need the cash," Zero said.

"She's in fantastic shape, yeah," Julian said, thinking of her toned thighs and her smooth skin. She'd called him a few times after he'd quit. He'd explained that he no longer worked as an escort, and she understood, but seemed to be waiting for something. For him to cave in and fuck her again? He looked at Zero's stubble, and the muscles in his arms. His lover wasn't toned, he was a fucking brick wall. He wasn't smooth, he was scarred. Well-worn, yet underneath all of that, Zero had a sophistication and edge of danger that even Cassandra Mortisimer couldn't top. "I prefer you, Zero," he said, knowing he was exposing something even as the words left his mouth.

Zero smiled, slow and deliberate. "Good."

"She's called me a few times. I don't know how the hell she got my private cell phone number," Julian said, thinking through the implications. "Jesus. I knew she was married, but I didn't know she was a *mobster's* woman." He wasn't sure how he felt about that. On the one hand, what did it matter? He was an escort. He did his job, and he did it well. On the other hand, Julian liked her a lot more than he'd liked some of the other people he'd slept with during the course of his career. What did that say about him when the kind of people who revved his engine tended towards criminality? *It means I haven't been entirely honest with myself. Ugh.*

"I am not surprised she called, Julian." Zero ran his hand down Julian's arm. "You are quite beautiful."

That wasn't the first time Zero had said something about his looks. Julian blushed, to his annoyance. *Why does he think I'm beautiful?* "No, way. I'm a dude. Guys aren't beautiful."

Zero laughed. "You have the most gorgeous skin. I want to mark you up." He sat back and shook his head. "I won't, though. Not unless you ask me to."

Julian stared at Zero. He remembered the knife. He remembered their first fuck on the kitchen table. They hadn't done anything quite that edgy since then, but he remembered it well. Too well. His cock throbbed, and he shifted his weight, not wanting to adjust himself and call attention to his erection. "What exactly do you mean by 'mark me up'?"

Zero's eyes darkened. "I would love to spank you again. Maybe tie hemp ropes around you, just to see the pattern once I take them back off again." His stare bored holes into Julian's soul. "And I like to cut." He slowly extended his arms, showing Julian the inside of his forearms. "See?"

Julian had noticed the faint slashes on Zero's skin, but he'd had no idea they were self-inflicted. He raised a finger, then touched one. It was a very old scar. He ran a finger down Zero's arm, telling himself that cutting wasn't sexy. His libido didn't agree. "You did this to yourself?"

Zero nodded. "See the pattern? I had an obsession. I stopped myself before I got carried away."

"You haven't cut in a very long time. These are old." He ran his finger down Zero's skin to his palm, then forced himself to stop. "I never would have guessed." He curled his fingers into a fist.

"It is not a healthy hobby," Zero said, drawing away. "I took up photography, instead." He snorted. "It is not quite the same."

They stared at each other for longer than was completely comfortable. *I would probably enjoy it if he cut me,* Julian realized, thinking of how much he'd enjoyed the restraints and the knife play. "Fucking hell."

Zero smiled faintly.

Julian shook his head, pushing the images in his mind away. "I could contact Cassandra. See if she'd help us."

Zero's eyebrows rose. "You believe she would help you?"

"Yeah. She liked me." He shrugged. "I liked her. We didn't part on bad terms." He thought about Cassandra, and suppressed a shiver. He liked her, but in the way you liked a dangerous large cat: hopeful she either liked you back, or you made sure to never poke her with a sharp stick. "She's a bit scary."

Zero pursed his lips, amusement swimming into his gaze. "Call her."

"For real?" Julian was still trying to think through all the possible repercussions of contacting her.

"Yes. If she will help, it will make Edwards's downfall even sweeter." Zero smiled again, but this time, the expression chilled Julian to the bone. "If even his wife will betray him, well…" He stood up. "We should take every advantage we can of this situation."

Julian leaned back in the chair. The thought of talking to Cassandra while Zero watched him did absolutely *nothing* to abolish his hard-on. "Okay." He slid his cell phone out of his pocket, watching Zero. His lover was looking at the outline of his cock pushing against the zipper of his jeans. Zero clearly didn't mind the view. Julian took a deep breath. He didn't want to call Cassandra and sound like he was on the verge of a climax. She'd find it amusing, but she might also get the wrong impression. He exhaled as he scrolled back through his recent calls until he found her number, then tapped the screen. The phone only rang once before she picked up.

"Julian Amon. How unexpected of you to call," Cassandra said in a silky tone.

"Hello, Ms. Mortisimer," Julian managed, voice husky. Zero was watching him with an intensity that made Julian want to strip them both naked. *Focus, man.*

"It's an interesting day for you to suddenly contact me, darling."

Julian knew she was referring to her husband's dead men, but he couldn't very well tell her that he knew what was going on straight out. Although, he *was* relieved to find out that she was alive and well. "Why didn't you tell me you were married to a mobster?" he said instead, letting her know he wasn't as in the dark as he had been. *Low key is the way to handle this,* he decided.

She chuckled. "You were an exemplary escort. Would it have mattered?"

Julian half smiled. Zero's expression told him he knew exactly what Cassandra was saying, despite him not putting the call on speaker. "It might have."

"Water under the bridge, particularly now that you have retired from that profession," she said breezily. "Now, what can I do for you, Julian? Surely you didn't call to complain about such an inconsequential thing."

Julian pursed his lips, then decided to give her a little something. "I'm dating an interesting fellow, these days."

"A man, hmm?" She didn't sound surprised.

"That's right. Your file said you were bisexual."

"Yes, a man." Julian watched Zero smooth a hand down his thigh. His lover's erection was entirely visible through his clothes. "And he has an interesting profession."

"Is he there with you now?" Cassandra asked.

"He is." Julian swallowed at the husky tone in her voice. Or was it the way Zero suddenly cupped himself, hips moving under his own hand? *Doesn't matter. I'm totally fucked, either way.* Julian took a shaky breath, willing himself to not come in his damned pants like a teenager.

"What's his name?"

Julian frowned, not sure what to say. "She wants to know your name," he told Zero.

His lover nodded. "Tell her. Put the phone on speaker."

Cassandra inhaled sharp enough for Julian to hear it through the phone. "I recognize that voice."

Julian went still, not sure what to do.

"Do what he says, Julian. Put the phone on speaker," Cassandra said, sounding exactly the way she did in the middle of sex: excited. Breathy.

Jesus. Are we all total fucking perverts? Why does this turn me on so much? Julian shifted his weight. His cock actually *hurt* now, from being trapped so long. "Should I tell her your name?" he said, after he'd tapped the screen and placed his phone next to Zero on the bed.

"I don't think names are necessary," Zero replied, hand still on his erection. He'd popped the button on his jeans.

"No, they aren't," Cassandra echoed.

Julian shook his head, exasperated with himself. With Zero. "I was hoping you might be able to help us, Ms. Mortisimer."

"Oh, so formal, Julian? After all, you've had your mouth on my cunt. Call me Cassandra, hmm?" She laughed, low and rich, and then she continued. "I'm not sure what I could possibly do to help your new boyfriend, if he is who I think he is. He's in an excellent position to do a great deal of damage."

"Think of it as a mutual exchange of favors, my dear," Zero said, speaking towards the phone. He looked pleased.

Julian wasn't exactly sure what Zero wanted, but he was willing to play along. *This is what amazing sex does to a guy,* he thought, not regretting a moment of it. *It makes you do crazy shit.*

"So, you would like a favor from me, correct? And then you would owe me a favor. I like that," Cassandra said slowly. "What do you think, Julian. Is he a man of his word?"

Julian leaned in. "He is." He thought about Zero tying his hands to the kitchen table. "He definitely is a man of his word."

"What is it that you want from me?" Cassandra asked.

Zero smiled, all teeth. Julian caught his breath. His lover looked like a man who'd just won the lottery.

"We would like for you to introduce us to your husband, Cassandra," Zero said softly. "Face to face. In person."

Silence.

"Cassandra?" Julian hoped she hadn't cut the connection.

"You are asking for much more than a simple meeting, I suspect," she said, sounding wary for the first time.

"Yes." Zero didn't explain.

Julian swallowed at the threat running through

Zero's tone.

"I have one condition," Cassandra said slowly.

"What is it?" Julian asked, when he saw that Zero wasn't going to respond.

"If things go as I expect, I may not have the opportunity to collect my favor after this meeting. I would like to collect it ahead of time," Cassandra said, a hint of steel in her voice.

Zero leaned forward, eyes intent on the phone. "What is the favor?"

Julian noticed that Zero didn't even hesitate.

"I wish to meet you both, in person, at a place of my choosing," Cassandra said.

Julian shook his head. *No way,* he mouthed to Zero. *Too dangerous.*

Zero ignored him. "Done."

"I'm not finished." Cassandra cut in. "I also want a kiss from each of you. And I want to watch you together."

Julian sat back, confused. "What?" She couldn't possibly mean—

"You heard me, darling. If I am going to face my demise, and granting this favor may definitely be my last, I want a moment of pleasure for my trouble."

Zero rubbed his chin. "I am not attracted to women."

Cassandra huffed. "I don't care."

Zero looked up at Julian. "One moment." He tapped the mute icon on the cell phone. "Is she trustworthy?"

Julian snorted. "I have no idea. She never tried to do anything that fell outside the purview of the agreed upon contract when I escorted her, but I wouldn't go so far as to say she's safe. There's something about her that's very, very calculating."

"Hmm. One could argue the same about me."
Zero nodded. "Are you willing to put on a show for her?"
He glanced down at Julian's erection. "Your body is, but
are *you*?"

Julian swallowed, hard. "Shit." He imagined Zero
fucking him while Cassandra watched, and his damned
hard-on swelled even more. He reached down and undid
his jeans, sighing in relief when his cock finally had a bit
more room.

Zero smiled and unmuted the phone. "We agree,
Ms. Mortisimer."

"Excellent."

Julian could swear he could hear her smiling
through the phone.

She continued. "One o'clock tomorrow. The
Hyatt in Paramus. Don't be late."

Julian stared at the phone as the connection went
dead. "Did we just agree to what I think we did?" He
went over her words, and shook his head. What the hell
had he just gotten himself into? He looked at Zero, but
the arousal on the older man's face was anything but
reassuring.

"Don't overthink it," Zero growled, standing up
and looming over him. He shoved down his pants, letting
his cock spring out right in front of Julian's face. "Are
you going to deny that you like the idea of sucking me
off in front of your old lover?" Zero fisted his cock, and
pointed it at Julian's mouth. "Because in my business,
my dear, the moment you start lying to yourself is the
moment you die."

Chapter Nine

Zero waited. He knew Julian wouldn't refuse him.

"You want me to suck your cock? Right now?" Julian looked up at him, blue eyes nearly black.

"Yes." Zero noted the flush on Julian's cheekbones. His fair skin couldn't really hide how turned on he was.

"And you want me to suck you in front of Cassandra Mortisimer, tomorrow." Julian licked his lips.

Zero nearly groaned. "Precisely."

"You're a sick fuck, Zero," Julian said.

Zero bared his teeth. "So are you, because you are going to do it, aren't you, Julian?"

Julian leaned in, shoving Zero's hand away from his cock. "Yeah. I am." He closed his lips around the crown of Zero's erection and sucked, looking up through his eyelashes.

Zero did groan this time. There was no way he could remain silent, not with his dick sliding into Julian's perfect mouth. "That's it. Fucking suck me." He locked his knees as Julian opened his throat and took him in all the way to the root. His lover did this so well. "Oh, fuck."

Julian reached up and fondled Zero's balls, then slid his cock back out. "She might betray us. Set a trap at the hotel." His lips were already slightly puffy.

"I don't give a fuck," Zero said, shoving his cock back into Julian's mouth.

Julian smiled around him, and then he started sucking him in earnest.

Zero sank his fingers into Julian's messy red hair, shuddering when his lover scrubbed his tongue along his length. "Jesus Christ. You are so goddamn good at this,

Julian."

"Practice," Julian murmured, licking the tip.

Zero growled, suddenly jealous. "The only man you practice on from now on is *me*."

Julian paused, one hand on Zero's erection, and the other cupping his balls. "Exclusivity?"

"Where the hell did you think we were going?" Zero said, struggling to keep his voice even. He wasn't about to let Julian go, not now. Not after everything the younger man had done for him the past week. He'd even killed a guy, and Zero *knew* Julian was still bothered by it.

"I wasn't sure," Julian replied, sounding uncertain.

Instead of saying more, Zero pushed in again. Julian deep-throated him with ease. When he swallowed around Zero's erection, Zero cursed and pulled out, jacking himself rapidly. Thick jets of cum spattered Julian's face and hair. "Fuck."

Julian licked his lips, eyes gleaming. "Mmm."

Zero stared at him, then abruptly took off his shirt. "You can fuck me." They hadn't done that yet, but suddenly, Zero needed to feel his young lover inside him.

"What?" Julian looked surprised.

Zero shucked his pants, then yanked at Julian's clothes. "You heard me."

"Oh, Jesus," Julian muttered, pushing Zero's hands away and stripping. "You'd better be fucking sure."

Zero rolled his eyes and leaned over to grab the lube. "Do I look like a shrinking virgin to you?"

Julian shook his head, then climbed on the bed. "No, but that doesn't mean dick, and you know it. I didn't think you liked to bottom."

"I like what I fucking like," Zero said, not

bothering to explain that he *didn't* usually like to bottom. Something about Julian changed all of his perceptions about himself: that he was a loner, that he couldn't afford to get close to anyone, and most importantly, that he was always the top in any sex. He poured the lube onto his hand and reached back, prepping himself. It had been a long damned time since he'd done this.

"Oh, God," Julian breathed.

Zero looked up to find his lover fixated on his fingers.

"That's the hottest fucking thing I've ever seen," Julian said, pushing his hand away and taking over the prep.

Zero sucked in when Julian's fingers breached his hole. "It's been a while," he managed to croak.

Julian nodded. "I know."

What's that supposed to mean? Zero wondered, but then Julian leaned down and sucked his still soft cock into his mouth. His hips came off the bed as not enough stimulation warred with too much. "Fuck, Julian." He wasn't sure if he wanted to flip the younger man over and start all over again by fucking him, or just lie back and let Julian do his thing.

"Shut up. You have more stamina than three other men combined," Julian said, and then he sucked his cock back inside.

Zero shut his eyes as Julian's talented mouth coaxed an erection out of him faster than he thought possible. "More," he said, screwing himself down on Julian's fingers.

"Bossy," Julian murmured, but he obliged, adding another finger.

Zero grunted, breathing through the burn. He knew it would hurt. He liked the pain. He liked it *too* much, and he didn't enjoy whoever he happened to be in bed with seeing him look vulnerable, but Julian had pushed past all of his barriers. *And he doesn't quite realize it yet, does he?* he thought. He propped himself on his elbows and watched Julian suck his cock and finger-fuck him. It was fucking fantastic. "Enough." He tugged on Julian's hair. "I'm loose. Fuck me."

Julian let Zero haul him up. "You sure?"

Zero glared at him. "Yes."

"I don't think I've ever heard you sound so desperate."

Zero growled wordlessly, and Julian grinned. "Fine." He lined up his erection and pushed inside, then froze, eyes closed as he gritted his teeth. "Oh, God. Don't move, Zero. Please don't fucking move."

Zero shuddered. "Don't stop." His ass ached, but he wanted more. He reached up over his head and grabbed a pillow. He needed to hang onto something, and he was afraid he'd hurt Julian if he let himself go.

"I have to, or I'm going to lose it," Julian said grimly, face strained.

Zero smiled. "Don't wait too long."

Julian glared at him, then reached down with one hand and stroked Zero's erection. "You talk too much."

Zero bucked, nearly dislodging Julian. His still sensitive cock jerked, and he couldn't keep himself still.

"Yeah, that's more like it," Julian muttered, thrusting inside.

Zero groaned as the double stimulation hammered all of his nerves. He squeezed his fingers into fists, not caring if he wrecked the sheets.

"Fuck," Julian said, hips thrusting in, then out, as if he had all the time in the fucking world. His hand stroked Zero slow and steady.

Zero wanted to tell him to go faster, but he could barely breathe, let alone talk. He squeezed his muscles.

Julian gasped, letting go of Zero's cock.

Zero bared his teeth, looking Julian right in the eyes. "Fuck me. Stop pussyfooting around."

Julian lost it. He pressed in, eyes dark with lust as his hips hammered Zero faster and faster. Sweat gathered along his hairline.

"Yeah. That's it," Zero muttered, hands against the headboard. Julian had shoved him up the bed until there was nowhere else to go.

"You. Drive. Me. Crazy." Julian panted out the words in between thrusts. He hit an angle that sent lightning up Zero's spine.

Zero moaned, spine arching. "Julian."

"Yeah, I got you," Julian said, fucking hard and fast at the perfect angle. He managed to reach down and strip Zero's cock as he did so.

Zero cried out as an orgasm came out of nowhere. Every one of his muscles seized up with pleasure.

"Jesus Christ," Julian said, and then he was bowed down over Zero, hips jerking erratically.

Zero felt warmth slide into him as Julian climaxed, and then his lover collapsed. Zero caught him, frowning when a deep ache in his chest told him that they'd definitely overdone it. He tried to take a deep breath, but pain stabbed at him. He forced himself to relax. *It's okay. It was fucking worth it,* he told himself.

"You okay?" Julian asked.

"Yeah." Zero stroked a hand down the younger man's back. "You?"

Julian snorted softly. "Hell, yeah."

Zero smiled. He could live without deep breaths. He wasn't so sure he could live without Julian.

****

Julian sat in the passenger's seat of Zero's truck, watching his lover drive them to the hotel. He knew

Zero's injury was bothering him, but he wouldn't let Julian drive, the stubborn bastard. "You sure you're up to this?" he asked, again.

Zero gave him an exasperated look. "That is the third time you've asked me that question."

"Yeah, well. You've been favoring your right side since yesterday." Julian shook his head. They shouldn't have fucked so vigorously, but he'd kind of lost his damn mind when Zero had let him top. His lover was strong and healthy, but he was also still recovering from a serious chest wound. "I'm sorry."

Zero glanced at him, one eyebrow raised. "You're apologizing for fucking me?"

Julian scowled. "I'm apologizing for going a little overboard. I can tell your chest is bothering you."

"It's not bothering me that much." Zero laughed. "And it's not like I minded."

"We should have rescheduled this meeting with Cassandra." Julian tapped a finger on the seat. "God knows what she'll really want from us." He wasn't looking forward to kissing her, that's for sure. And he *really* wasn't looking forward to Zero kissing her. Somewhere along the way, he'd fallen hard for the older man. The thought of Zero kissing *anyone* except him made his blood boil.

"Relax. I'm not going to fall in love with Edwards' wife, my dear. I'm gay."

"I'm not," Julian muttered, still worried. "And that's not the point."

Zero took the next exit. "If anything, I am the one who should be worried, yes?"

"What? No." Julian crossed his arms over his chest. Was Zero joking? He eyed his lover. Zero was concentrating on driving, and Julian couldn't tell what he meant by that statement. *I'm not in love with Cassandra.*

She's hot, sure, but that's all it is. That's all it ever was with the people I escorted. Zero is different.

"Hmm." Zero eased onto the road that led to the hotel. The traffic was terrible, but it didn't seem to faze him, even when Julian grabbed the edge of the seat, sure they would die before ever getting to the hotel. When Zero finally pulled into the parking lot, Julian breathed a sigh of relief. Zero parked in the back and turned off the car.

Julian stared at the dash. He didn't want to get out. He didn't want to see Cassandra again. He didn't want to kiss her, no matter how much he'd been attracted to her in the past. He'd put that part of his life behind him. *But you promised Zero you would do this. How fucked up is that? I promised my current lover that I would kiss my former lover.*

"Julian."

Julian ignored the older man. He didn't need a damn pep talk.

"Julian. I can't force you to help me," Zero said, unexpectedly.

"You're not forcing me," Julian said, unlatching his seatbelt. He got out of the truck. The midday sun shined down on them, cheerful and bright, everything he wasn't feeling at the moment. Julian shaded his eyes as he stared at the hotel. Zero walked around the vehicle and leaned against it. Julian could feel the older man watching him. "I'm not a fucking show pony," Julian said finally. "I don't like this deal we made."

"This is nothing except an exchange of favors," Zero said mildly.

Julian shook his head. "She's a shark, Zero. She's always got some ulterior motive."

"Do we not also have an ulterior motive?" Zero pointed out.

Since when does this sort of thing make me lose my cool? I never had this much trouble handling my emotions when I escorted. Is this what falling in love does to a man? Julian sighed, running a hand through his hair. He finally looked at his lover. Zero lounged against the truck as if he hadn't a care in the world. He wore all black, as if it weren't hot as hell out, and he looked cool and collected. *Like a mobster,* Julian thought, feeling a pulse of arousal shoot through him, despite his anxiety. Zero looked fucking dangerous. "She's bad news," he said, trying one last time.

"Indeed," Zero said, half smiling. "But so am I, Julian."

Julian had to laugh at that. "True." Zero was definitely not your average dude with an office job. "Did you bring any weapons?"

Zero smirked. "You need to ask?"

Julian shook his head, then glanced at his phone. "It's twelve-fifty. We should get going if we want to be on time."

Zero nodded, then started for the doors. Julian followed him. By the time they stood outside Cassandra Mortisimer's door on the third floor at precisely one o'clock, Julian had managed to calm the worst of his jitters.

Zero glanced at him, then knocked on the door. Julian tensed when it swung open, but to his surprise, Cassandra was the one standing in the doorway, not one of her minions. Her long blonde hair cascaded over her shoulders in a soft cloud, almost hiding the fact that she was at least fifty years old if not older. Julian had rarely seen a woman her age look so fantastic. He stared at her, willing himself to look at this situation as nothing more than a business transaction. *I have more than enough experience with clients. I should be fine,* he reminded himself.

"Julian." She smiled. "How lovely to see you again." Her eyes flicked to Zero, and then she stepped back, holding the door open. "Come in."

"No bodyguards?" Zero asked. He stepped inside before Julian could move, eyes assessing every corner of the space. He pursed his lips, then moved in further. Julian followed, surprised that Cassandra had rented a suite for a simple afternoon meeting. *But then, do we really want to be kissing each other in public? No. No, we do not.*

"Do you intend on killing me?" Cassandra asked, nodding at Zero.

Zero only raised an eyebrow in response.

"Good. We understand each other." Cassandra smiled as she walked to the mini bar. "Therefore, no bodyguards are necessary. I prefer to keep our conversation private, anyway." She opened a bottle of something and poured it into a glass, then raised it to her lips, smiling faintly. "Some risks are worth taking."

Julian let the door shut behind him, then leaned back against it. Cassandra wore an elegant, cream sheath dress, but he wasn't deceived by her simple appearance. Edwards's wife wasn't an ordinary woman. He looked at her smooth blonde hair, at the curve of her waist, and then he met her gaze. Cool blue eyes stared back at him.

"Why don't you come in, Julian? I promise I'm not going to bite you," she said, then raised the glass to her lips.

Julian grimaced, but did as she asked, moving to stand near Zero. "Ms. Mortisimer. You're looking well."

"Thank you. Call me Cassandra. No need to be that formal, is there?" She held out her hand to him. "You are looking quite fine as well, Julian."

He took her hand held it gently for a moment,

then smiled and bent over, kissing her wrist. He'd been an escort, for fuck's sake. It was time for him to put on his mask and use some of the skills he'd learned. "The new bracelet is lovely," he said, slowly lowering her hand. Diamonds and emeralds glittered from the platinum strand that fell across her wrist.

"A gift from my husband," she said, shrugging. "Will you introduce your friend?" She turned to Zero.

Julian kept his smile firmly fixed upon his face, and forced himself to step into the role he'd fulfilled so many times. "Cassandra, this is Zero Graham," he said. He'd asked Zero on the ride over what name he'd wanted to use, and his lover had told him to use his real one. Julian hadn't understood, because he knew Zero's birth name was Zeke, but then he'd figured out what his lover meant. The older man had been living with the name Zero for decades. He'd only use his given name if he had to go legit somewhere, and that wasn't fucking likely.

"Ah. The infamous fixer. A pleasure," Cassandra said, holding her hand out to him.

Zero took it, and stood there, fingers wrapped loosely around Cassandra's wrist. Zero could probably fracture every bone in her arm without breaking a sweat, and from the flash of wariness in her eyes, quickly hidden, Cassandra knew it, too.

"I have heard that you don't often meet clients in person." Cassandra slid her arm free, then gestured at the mini bar. "Would you like a drink?"

"No, thank you, my dear," Zero said, walking to the window. He looked outside, then drew the curtains shut.

Cassandra tilted her head, but made no objection about Zero's obvious desire for privacy.

"Shall we get to the point?" Zero said, crossing the room. He pulled out the desk chair and settled into it.

Julian took a deep breath, feeling the tension ratchet up in the suite.

"I can arrange for you to meet with my husband tonight at six." Cassandra settled lightly on the sofa set near the desk. "I hope that is acceptable."

Zero nodded. "It is. I am surprised that you could set it up so soon."

"I don't like to procrastinate, particularly not when the situation concerns my future." Cassandra sipped at her drink, slowly draining half the glass.

Julian stepped up to Zero and leaned back against the desk. "Do you know what will happen when we meet your husband?" He had to ask. He couldn't let her do this unless she understood exactly what Zero had in mind. She might be a shark, but *he* wasn't.

Cassandra drained her glass, then set it aside. Her blue eyes looked hard as steel when she finally turned her gaze on him. "I know precisely what will happen, Julian. I am eager to be of assistance."

Julian inhaled, willing calm into his core. "I'm surprised."

She huffed out a breath. "Don't be. I didn't marry the bastard willingly."

Zero frowned.

Cassandra nodded. "Yes. It has been every bit as unpleasant as you imagine. My father insisted on it. I was sixteen at the time. My father is dead now, and I made certain he didn't die easily." She looked at Julian. "I used to have a son. He would've been several years older than you this past May if he'd lived."

Julian went still at the implication she didn't voice aloud. "I'm sorry."

"Condolences are not what I want."

"What do you want?" Zero asked, leaning forward. His arms dangled from his knees, and he looked completely at ease.

Julian knew better.

"I already told you. I would like a kiss, from each of you, and then I would like to watch you two together." Her eyes flashed. "And I would like to be there when you meet my husband tonight." She stood up and walked over to Zero. "I want to stand over him and watch the knowledge of his downfall sink into his thick skull." She looked down at Zero, then glanced at Julian. "I have plans for the future."

Zero reached out and took her wrists. When she didn't protest, he yanked her down onto his lap. "Agreed."

Cassandra didn't even try to struggle. "You didn't even bargain."

"As far as I'm concerned, you can have whatever you want," Zero said, voice rough.

Cassandra tilted her head. "And what if the price is you?"

Zero laughed. "It's difficult to get blood out of a stone."

Julian watched the knowledge of Zero's sexual preferences swim into Cassandra's expression.

"Ah. Pity." She pulled her wrists from Zero's grasp and cupped his face.

Julian tensed.

"I'm going to collect my fee anyway." With those words, Cassandra leaned down and kissed Zero.

Julian clenched his fingers into fists. *You knew this would happen going in,* he told himself. *You agreed to this.* It didn't help. When he saw Zero reach up and sink his hands into Cassandra's hair, he stood up and started pacing. He couldn't watch this. No fucking way.

"Julian," Cassandra said.

He spun around. Her mouth was puffy. He knew

full well how Zero kissed, and he had no desire to see the results on another person's face. He'd thought he might find it sexy. Arousing. Judging from the anger raging through him, he was definitely not into voyeurism. *Good to know, right?*

"Your turn," she said, sliding off Zero's lap.

Julian frowned at Zero, then took a deep breath. His lover looked calm. Completely unaffected. Then Cassandra was at Julian's side, and she touched his shoulder.

"Don't look at him," she demanded. "Look at me."

Julian shook his head at her. "This isn't going to end well for you."

"That is not your problem, is it, Julian? Let me worry about what might happen. All you have to do is make me happy, just as you have so many times before." She smiled, and he well remembered that look on her face. He'd seen her completely flushed with arousal. He'd seen her cry out in the midst of an orgasm. She looked, if anything, even better today than she had the last time he'd seen her, but he wasn't even a little bit interested. "You're going to thank me for this, Julian," she said, her voice husky. "Mark my words."

He was going to argue, but she drew his head down. The moment she touched her mouth to his, he remembered how much she liked it when he nibbled on her lips. His body remembered exactly what to do with her, and his hands automatically slid around her waist. She kissed him, and Julian remembered that she tasted like cinnamon more often than not. He remembered everything, but he had absolutely no desire to follow through on any of it.

"Kiss me back, Julian, or the deal is off." Cassandra looked angry for the first time.

Julian glanced at Zero. His lover nodded at him. Julian was about to refuse, but then he saw how frozen Zero held himself. Muscles bunched under Zero's shirt, and abruptly, Julian realized that Zero wasn't even a little bit calm. His lover had his fingers curled into fists. Julian blinked as relief sent a surge of adrenaline through him.

"Julian." Cassandra's voice hardened.

He turned back to her, and dipped his head down, kissing her almost violently. His cock hardened, but it had nothing to do with her and everything to do with the man who watched him kiss a woman he didn't want with barely restrained violence.

****

Zero forced himself to take long, slow breaths, but it didn't do a damned thing to calm the jealousy stuck in his craw like a stone. He could see that Julian didn't want to kiss Cassandra Mortisimer. He could tell that his lover was well and truly done with her, but it didn't matter. She had her arms wrapped around Julian's shoulders, and his lover kissed her with a single-minded concentration that told Zero he wanted to be anywhere but here, doing this distasteful favor. He kissed her with his mind, not his body. When Cassandra finally released him, Julian immediately stepped back.

Cassandra laughed, low and pleased. "Interesting." She touched her mouth.

"You got what you wanted," Julian said, running a hand over his face.

He glanced at Zero, and the anger in Julian's gaze hit Zero mid-chest. Zero's cock stirred for the first time. Julian looked like a man who could happily spill blood right now. Violence always inspired lust in Zero, and the combination of heat and fury in Julian revved him to near breaking. Julian looked back at Cassandra, and Zero breathed a silent sigh. A few more seconds of that look and he wasn't sure what he'd do. *Yank him away from her and fuck the consequences,* he realized.

"We done here?" Julian asked, staring hard at Cassandra. Zero hoped Julian's lack of a filter wouldn't sour the deal. He needed to eliminate Edwards, and he couldn't afford to piss off Cassandra, because he had a feeling he would be dealing with her for many years to come.

"Not entirely, no," Cassandra said, settling back on the bed. "I'm not done. If you'll recall, I also want to watch you two together."

Julian swallowed, his gaze swinging back to Zero.

Oh, that has him riled up even more, Zero thought, but the truth was, he was grateful she didn't ask for more for herself. He didn't think he could touch her again and successfully fake interest. He stood up, ignoring the deep ache in his chest. His wound wasn't healing properly, but he didn't have the time to see to it. Not now. Not until this thing with Edwards was finished. "And we will fulfill that part of the bargain, as agreed." He walked over to Julian and cupped his lover's face. "Won't we?"

Julian bared his teeth at Zero. "This is insane."

Zero yanked him close, not at all surprised to feel Julian's hard-on against his hip. "But you like it," he whispered in Julian's ear. He slid his hands down until he cupped his lover's ass, and then he pressed their groins together. His wound protested, but he didn't care. "You like knowing you have to do this while she watches."

Julian tried to pull away, but Zero wouldn't let him.

"I'm not into voyeurism," Julian gritted out.

"Oh, that's delicious," Cassandra said, smiling languidly. "Because you could have fooled me. You certainly look interested." She let her gaze rest on Julian's ass.

Zero leaned in and kissed Julian gently before his lover said anything else. "You don't care if she watches me fuck you, Julian, because you want her to know that you don't belong to her. You never belonged to her." He whispered the words into Julian's ear. "You belong to me."

Julian groaned softly, then gave in, sliding his arms around Zero. "Screw you."

Zero laughed, backing Julian up to the bed where Cassandra sat. When Julian's knees bent against the mattress, he followed his lover down, climbing up his body. He ignored the burn in his chest that told him he was overdoing it. It didn't matter. It didn't matter that Cassandra sat close enough to touch. It didn't matter that his hip bumped hers as he devoured Julian's mouth. When he finally came up for air, Julian looked wrecked. "See?" Zero told him.

Julian narrowed his eyes at Zero, licking his lips.

Before the younger man could reply, Zero yanked Julian's shirt open, and then slid his hands down over his erection.

Julian bucked up into his palm, and Zero bared his teeth. "I can fuck you right here. Right now. While she watches." He left out the words *while she watches me take what she can never have again,* but he had a feeling Julian caught his unspoken meaning loud and clear. He leaned in again. "Would you like that, darling?"

Julian didn't reply, but Zero saw the answer on his face. He knelt up over his lover and took off his shirt, then undid the buttons on his pants. He knew the waist holster of his handgun would be visible to Cassandra, but he also knew she wouldn't dare try to reach for it. She probably had a weapon of her own, anyway. He unbuttoned Julian's jeans, and reached inside, stroking the younger man's erection, palm to skin.

"That's enough," Cassandra said in a soft voice.

Zero froze. He didn't really want to stop, but he looked over at her. She stared at them with an unreadable expression on her face. "Are you backing out of the deal?" Zero asked her, fighting to keep his voice steady. His erection throbbed, but he did his best to ignore it for the moment. Julian's cock in his hand felt hot and ready, and he wanted nothing more than to suck his lover into his mouth. He eased his hand away.

"No." Cassandra stood up, straightening her dress as she walked to the desk. "Six o'clock tonight, come to this address." She bent over and scribbled something onto the hotel stationary.

Zero nodded. He'd had a feeling she wouldn't see this part of her favor through to the end. *Because she knows what love looks like, and she doesn't have it. No one wants to stare that truth in the face.*

"Why the hell did you want to see us together?" Julian asked Cassandra.

Zero glanced at his lover. Julian had his fingers twisted into the hotel bed's coverlet. "She wished to prove something to herself, Julian," he said gently. Anger swam through Julian's expression, then faded as Zero rolled off him. "And she has."

"That's absurd," Julian said, propping himself up on his elbows.

"No. Not absurd. Sadly, it's the truth," Cassandra said, walking to the door.

Zero put a hand on Julian's arm when the younger man would've stood up. "Don't." He saw that Cassandra's eyes had thawed from cold steel to warm blue.

She shook her head. "Someone deserves a

happily ever after, don't you think, Julian?" She opened the door. "The suite is paid for through tomorrow. Please enjoy it as long as you wish," she said, and then she walked out of the room.

Chapter Ten

Julian watched the door close behind her. "What the fuck just happened?"

"A very intelligent woman saw precisely what she'd hoped, and didn't enjoy it at all," Zero said.

Julian stared at his lover. "That makes no fucking sense at all."

Zero shrugged out of his shirt and tossed it aside. "It will."

Julian wasn't sure he cared. He hadn't liked kissing Cassandra. He hadn't liked watching Zero kiss her, either. But somehow, the moment Zero touched *him,* he forgot to care. His cock still throbbed, reminding him that they'd stopped in the middle of foreplay. "Are we going to have sex now? Here?" He glanced around. "After all that? We don't have much time if we're going to meet her at six o'clock."

"We'll manage." Zero shoved down his pants, then climbed back on the bed. His wound looked redder than Julian remembered, but then Zero slid a hand back inside his jeans and onto his erection. His thoughts scattered.

"Fuck." Julian thrust up into Zero's perfect grip.

"Yes. Let's," Zero said, sliding his hand up, then down again.

Julian gritted his teeth, then took off his shirt. He shoved at his pants, relieved when Zero helped him take them off. "I didn't bring anything," he said, wishing he'd remembered lube.

"I did." Zero leaned over and extracted a packet of slick from his pocket.

Julian blinked, then rolled over.

"God, look at you," Zero said.

Julian heard the packet crinkle, then cold gel

dripped down his crack. "I don't need foreplay." He could barely keep it together as it was.

"Too bad." Zero rubbed the gel into Julian's hole, slipping one, then two fingers inside.

"Just do it," Julian gritted out, resting his head on his wrists. He wanted to feel Zero lose it. He wanted to stop thinking about Cassandra.

"Breathe," Zero instructed.

Julian tensed as the blunt tip of Zero's cock nudged at him. "Come on."

"Relax, my dear." Zero pressed in, and he didn't stop.

Julian hissed at the burn. "Yeah. Come on." He huffed out a harsh breath, taking the pain. Having Zero just push inside like that felt like a wall had slammed into him. When the older man reached around and cupped his balls, Julian's hips jerked. "Christ!"

"You look so good like this," Zero said, bottoming out. He leaned over Julian's back, hot and hard.

"Don't stop." Right now, Julian needed a good fuck, not a slow walk to the edge. "Please."

Zero exhaled. Then he began to move, slowly and then harder.

"God, yeah. That's it," Julian said, and then he gasped when Zero found the perfect angle. He hammered into Julian's prostrate. Julian gripped the covers, beyond words.

"This what you want?" Zero asked, fucking him hard. "I own you, Julian. You're mine. No one else touches you ever again."

Julian nodded, feeling the truth of Zero's words in his bones. Their bodies slapped together, but Julian didn't care. He didn't care about anything right now except getting off. He needed to erase the memory of

Cassandra's smug expression when he'd finished kissing her. "You can cut me if you want," he said suddenly, imagining the thrill of it.

Zero froze. "Julian…" His voice cracked, and then he pulled out.

Julian rolled over to find Zero staring at him like a man possessed.

"Do it, Zero." Julian drew a line down his right pec. "Right here." He imagined what it would feel like, and felt his erection jerk. "I want it."

Zero shook his head, then grabbed Julian's legs and pushed back inside, hard and violent. "You don't know what you're asking."

"I do." Julian could feel his lover shaking. Zero's thrusts weren't controlled anymore. Zero's expression wasn't controlled, either. "I know exactly what it would feel like," he said, struggling to get the words out. Zero's grip on his thighs felt like iron. He reached down and cupped himself, knowing that if he did anything more he'd climax immediately. "I know it would burn, no matter how careful you were. I know the blood would feel warm."

Zero groaned, leaning down. His eyes were so dark they were black. "Are you trying to make me hurt you?"

Julian shook his head. "No. Just the opposite." He squeezed his erection, holding back. "It would probably take a while to heal. It would scar."

Zero growled, thrusting so hard his balls hit Julian's ass. "Shut up."

Julian bared his teeth. "Make me."

Zero slapped Julian's hand away, and violently stroked his erection. Julian howled, spine bowing as his orgasm hit him all at once, like a train smashing into a wall. His cock jerked, and then Zero grunted as he climaxed, too, hips shoving him hard. Warmth spread throughout his body as he kept climaxing, longer than he thought possible.

"Fuck," he wheezed, grabbing Zero's shoulders and pulling him down. He didn't care that his spunk covered his chest, or that they'd be glued together. He needed Zero to ground him right now, because he felt like he was about to fly apart.

Zero collapsed on top of him, shaking and shuddering. Julian held him as tight as he dared. Zero's erection slowly softened, and then it slipped out of him.

A long moment later, Zero lifted his head. "What the fuck, Julian?"

Julian smiled. "What?"

Zero stared at him. "Someday I'm going to take you up on your offer."

Julian went still. *Someday? That implies we have a future.*

"Don't panic." Zero touched Julian's cheek. "Not now."

"What the hell are we doing, Zero?" Julian forced himself to take a breath, and then another. He thought about what his life would be like without Zero, and anxiety twisted down his spine.

Instead of answering, Zero kissed him, then rolled off. "We should make plans." He stood up and walked over to the note Cassandra had scribbled on the desk.

Julian watched his lover touch his scar, frowning as he read the address.

"Apparently, Edwards owns a gym." He looked up. "Cassandra said to meet her in the back, and she will let us in." He sighed. "Seems too easy."

Julian grimaced. "Nothing about this is easy." He stood up, ignoring the drying jizz all over his chest. He walked over to Zero and touched his gunshot wound.

"Does this hurt?"

Zero shrugged. "A little."

Julian looked closer. "I think it's infected." The flesh around the pink scar looked red, and Julian worried that Zero might have a deeper problem with the healing than just a surface infection. "You don't want to screw around with it, Zero."

Zero stepped back. "I'll get your mother to look at it tomorrow." He put the note back on the desk. "Tonight, we have business to attend to." He looked at Julian, then tilted his head. "You don't have to come."

"Zero—" Julian began, but Zero slashed a hand through the air. The last thing Julian was going to do now was leave Zero on his own. *Not with that wound. Not with everything.*

"No. It will keep until tomorrow, Julian." Zero gathered his clothes and headed for the bathroom. "We have a lot to do this afternoon." He paused in the doorway. "This is almost over." He shut the door.

Julian listened to the sound of water running. "Yeah, it's almost over. And then what?" He rubbed his face. "I'm so fucked."

****

Julian stared at Zero as he drove, somewhat amazed at the older man's calm demeanor. "You're not worried about swinging by your warehouse?" He wished Zero had let him take him to his mother instead of going to collect weapons, but the man was stubborn. *He looks pale.* Julian frowned, concerned that his lover was hiding his pain levels from him.

"No." Zero tapped the phone he'd placed in a holder on the dashboard. "The security feeds show no one around. It looks like Edwards has finally given up surveillance of the building and surroundings. It's a risk to go there, but one I'm willing to take." He snorted. "He is probably short of manpower. He can't really afford to have men sitting around staring at an empty building all day."

Julian smiled tightly. "What a surprise."

Zero nodded, smirking. "Indeed. Best three million I've ever spent."

Julian swallowed. He wasn't poor, by any definition of wealth. He'd made a fortune investing his funds, but he still couldn't imagine blowing that kind of money on a hit. "I'm going to assume that you didn't spend all your assets."

Zero gave him a look. "No, my dear. Of course not." He took the next exit off the interstate and slowed down, grimacing as the truck lurched over a pothole.

"Why don't you let me drive?" Julian said, noting Zero's heavy grip on the steering wheel. "I hope we didn't make it worse." He shouldn't have let Zero fuck him so vigorously.

"I am fine," Zero replied, heading for his warehouse. "We don't have time to stop."

Julian sighed, knowing Zero wouldn't appreciate it if he nagged him. "Promise me you'll tell me if you start to feel worse."

Zero glanced at him, but didn't reply as he drove into the alley of his warehouse.

Julian reached out, but Zero ducked his hand. "I just want to see if you're running a fever."

Zero scowled at him as he parked. "You can fuss all you want tomorrow." He turned off the engine. "Today, I have plans." He got out of the truck.

Julian sighed, then followed him, noting the blood still smeared on the outer door of the warehouse. "Grim." He tapped the metal.

Zero pushed it open. "It adds to the ambience. I do not want anyone believing there is much value to breaking in here."

"You'll end up with squatters." Julian followed him into the vast, dark space.

"No chance of that. I have ways to discourage anyone from hanging around." Zero walked along the wall, heading for the door to his underground bunker. "This particular building is too far from most shelters and other amenities, so very few people try to enter." He shrugged, then winced. "It has never been a problem."

"What are we here for?" Julian asked as Zero flicked on a light switch just inside the hallway that led to his apartment.

"Weapons. Specifically, I want my favorite shotgun." Zero entered a code into the keypad near the door at the far end of the hall, then pressed a thumb to the screen. The doors nicked open.

"A shotgun?" Julian rubbed his chin. "That doesn't sound very efficient."

"Efficient is too merciful." Zero headed into his apartment.

That's a pretty fucking brutal plan, Julian thought. He followed Zero, carefully picking his way past overturned furniture and smashed lamps. "Wow. It's really trashed. I mean, I knew it was bad, but I was too busy the last time I was here to really notice." He stared at the sofa. He remembered the girl who'd died just behind it. Her blood smeared the leather, and Julian shook his head. *What a waste.*

Zero had stopped in front of a blank wall. "They destroyed my favorite painting." He kicked at something on the floor. "Barbarians." He touched the sofa. "Not to mention what they did to poor Jenna. She was a sweet girl."

"We should hurry." Julian checked his phone. They needed to be at the address Cassandra had given them in an hour. They didn't have time to sightsee, and he sure as shit didn't feel like remembering that day. He'd only seen the aftermath of the carnage, but that was enough to give him nightmares for the rest of his life.

"I know." Zero leaned down, hand pressed to his shoulder, then pushed on a section of the wall. A slot sprang open, and he reached inside, extracting a long case. "Let's go." He looked around. "I do not think I will live here after my business with Edwards is through. It is time to build another home. Somewhere more convenient, perhaps."

"I won't argue with that." Julian took the case from him, noting Zero's hastily suppressed wince of discomfort. "You're in pain. This is stupid, Zero."

"You can drive," the older man said, handing him the keys to the truck. "But I will finish this business today."

Julian scowled, but didn't argue. He'd see this through with Zero, and then he was dragging his lover off to see his mother. "You need antibiotics. And to sleep for an entire week."

Zero closed and locked the door to the apartment, then leaned back against the wall. "I'm fine. Just tired." He ran a hand over his face. "I need to get this done." He sighed.

Julian propped the case against the wall. "Maybe just sit for a minute." He checked his phone again, frowning when he saw the time. When he looked up, Zero was sliding down onto the floor. "Shit!" He grabbed for him. "Zero!" The older man didn't respond, closing his eyes. Julian eased him to the floor, cursing. He checked Zero's pulse. It was steady and strong.

"I'll be fine," Zero said, voice slurring. "I'm just tired."

"You're a stubborn ass." Julian slung his arm

over his shoulders. "Can you stand?" He glanced at the shotgun case, then decided to leave it. He couldn't carry both his lover and the equipment, and Zero wasn't going to see Edwards today, not if Julian could help it.

Zero nodded. "I'm fine. Just give me a minute to catch my breath."

"Okay. On three. One, two, three." Julian hauled him up. "Come on."

"Don't have time for this," Zero gasped out, letting Julian drag him out to the truck.

"Shut the fuck up. You have time to live, Zero. That's more important than some revenge." Julian got him into the front passenger's seat, and then buckled him in.

"It's more than revenge. My business depends—" Zero broke off, coughing.

"You've been running your fucking business for how many years?" Julian asked him, but didn't wait for an answer. "It'll survive for one day longer." He hurried to the driver's side and started the truck. "I'm taking you to my mother."

"Not the way a boyfriend usually meets the family," Zero said weakly.

"You already know my mother." Julian frowned. "And you sound like shit."

Zero closed his eyes.

Now I know he really feels awful. He'd never let that go, normally, Julian thought, starting the truck and pulling out of the parking spot. He thought about taking Zero to his apartment—it would certainly be safer for his mother, but he discarded the idea almost immediately. Zero needed care he couldn't provide. *What about a hospital?* He considered it, then shook his head. Zero had already had thugs break into his motorhome. If he took his lover to a hospital, it would be too easy for someone to track him there. *Christ, this is a disaster.*

Fifteen minutes later he pulled into the driveway of his mother's small house. "Come on," he muttered, helping his lover out of the truck. "One foot in front of the other, Zero." He got to the front door and banged on the glass. "Mom!"

His mother hurriedly opened the door. "Julian? What happened? Jesus. Get him inside." She helped Julian into the house, directing him to put him on the sofa. "God, he looks terrible."

"I think his wound is infected. I don't know how bad," Julian said, ripping Zero's shirt open. He sighed when he saw the wound didn't look any worse. "No streaking, thank God."

"That doesn't mean he isn't very sick," his mother said, grabbing her bag from the hall closet. "I don't have an IV here. We should get him to a hospital." She extracted a stethoscope.

Zero opened his eyes. "No. No more hospitals."

"Zero, you probably need strong antibiotics," she said, checking his pulse. "And blood tests. Now breathe."

"No." Zero coughed, and made as if to get up off the couch.

"Sit down." Julian pushed him back down. "Are you insane?"

"Edwards," Zero said, staring hard at Julian. His gaze shifted to Julian's mother. "Not safe."

"Fuck. Stop worrying about that," Julian said, helping his mother put a blood pressure cuff on Zero's arm. *Is Zero right? Will my mother be okay with Zero here? Maybe I shouldn't have brought him.* He shook his head. *Too late now for second-guesses. We're already here.*

She glanced at him, then at Zero. "What's he babbling about?"

"Meeting," Zero said.

Julian's mother shook her head. "No. No way are you going anywhere except a hospital."

Zero grabbed her wrist. "No hospital. Too dangerous. Too many people."

Julian grimaced. Zero saying it aloud confirmed what he'd already gone over in his head. What would happen if Edwards's thugs tracked him to a public place? "Zero's right. Nobody knows he's here. It's safer that way." *I hope,* he added to himself, not sure he believed his own words.

His mother huffed out an irritated breath. "Fine. I have to make a call. He needs medications I don't keep in the house." She stood up and headed for the kitchen.

"Call Cassandra. Explain the situation," Zero said, handing Julian his phone.

Julian handed it right back to him. "I don't need your damned phone."

Zero glared at him. "I need to reschedule."

"You need to rest." Julian stood up.

His mother came back into the room. "I have a friend dropping off the supplies. Help me get him into your old room, Julian."

Julian nodded, grabbing Zero and hauling him back up. Zero groaned.

"Sorry," Julian muttered. He and his mother got him into his room and into his narrow bed, still pushed up against the wall just as it was when he was a teen. "Stay there," he told his lover as his mother went back out to the hall.

Zero sighed, but nodded his head.

Julian joined his mother. "Is he going to be okay?" he asked her, mind racing a thousand directions at once. *I need to make sure both my mother and Zero are safe.*

She nodded. "Yeah. I think he's more exhausted than anything else, honestly." She gave her son a sharp glance. "What have the two of you been doing?"

His face burned. *No way am I answering that question.*

"Good God, never mind. Don't answer that." She looked toward the room where they'd put Zero. "I need to get some fluids into him."

"Will you be okay here with him if I head out?" Julian asked, feeling torn in opposite directions. He didn't want to burden his mother, but he also knew that the opportunity to deal with Edwards might not happen again. Cassandra was going out on a limb for them, and if they didn't hold up their end of the deal, she might very well end up dead. *Along with me, and Zero, and my mother.*

"What? Are you going somewhere?" His mother had already moved down the hall to the kitchen.

Julian scrubbed a hand over his face. "There's this meeting we set up. It's important." His mind shied away from the details of exactly what he'd have to do at this meeting.

His mother frowned. "He should be okay. He's exhausted. The slight fever he has is more a reaction to his body burning fuel he doesn't have in reserve than a severe infection, I think." She glanced into the room at Zero, then gestured for Julian to follow her. When they reached the kitchen, she sighed. "This meeting. It's important?"

Julian nodded, not knowing how to explain it to his mother. He didn't really want her to know how dangerous it would be to confront Edwards.

"And you think you can handle it without Zero?" She poured water into a glass. "Are you doing business with him?"

"Sort of." Julian exhaled, thinking of the shotgun he'd stupidly left in Zero's apartment. "Yeah. I can handle it." He'd *have* to handle it, and he'd have to be creative about it.

His mother eyed him, then nodded. "Okay. I'll take care of Zero. You do what you have to do."

Julian started to explain more, but she cut him off.

"No. The less I know, the better."

Julian stared at her. "You sure?" He didn't expect his mother to be so calm about the situation. She *knew* what had happened with Zero. She was the one who'd helped him after he'd been shot all those weeks ago.

She snorted. "I'm not young, and I'm not naive, Julian."

He grimaced. "Fine." He didn't really want to talk to her about it. *I should just cut my losses and get the hell out of here while I still can.*

She smiled and put a hand on his arm. "Julian. Honey, I know you and Zero are together. And I'm happy about that. Zero helped me a lot over the past decade, and it's good to see him finally fall for a good guy, but I'm under no illusions about what he does for a living."

"How can you be so calm about this?" Julian didn't understand this side of his mother.

"I've been an ER doctor for over a decade. And your father told me some things he'd had to do…" She trailed off, then shook her head. "Hell. I had to make some awful choices in my life, too. Life isn't as black and white as people think. I love you, Julian, but you're a grown man who has to make his own path in the world. You basically told me that when you decided to become an escort."

"But I didn't tell you about that," Julian

protested, still uneasy with his mother knowing about his former job.

She huffed. "Please. You didn't have to tell me. Anyway, you could do worse than to stay with Zero. He might be into some unsavory things, but he'd never hurt an innocent. He's done his best to protect quite a few people he didn't have to help."

Julian stared at her as his resolve to keep her and Zero safe strengthened. "I love you, Mom. You know that, right?" He pulled her into a hug. *I know what I have to do.*

"I love you, too, Julian," she said.

Chapter Eleven

Julian parked the truck in the street. He was near the alley that ran behind the building Cassandra indicated on her note, and his mind was stuck on one thing, and one thing only. *Get to the gym.* If he tried to think beyond that, he'd choke, and the people he loved would probably die. He'd rushed out of his mother's house without saying goodbye to Zero. He didn't need the distraction of his lover talking him out of what he knew he had to do.

When he got out of the truck, he walked down the street at a normal pace, and headed for the alley. Halfway down, his eyes went to the door propped open in the back of the brick building. It was painted bright yellow for some reason he didn't have the patience to reason out right now, but it didn't matter. That's how he knew he had the right place. In this section of town, people liked to hang out for a smoke during their breaks, and he scanned the street, but right now, this was the only open door. The bookstore on the corner was open. He'd checked. The restaurant two buildings down was open. The bank, the cleaners, and the secondhand clothing store were all open, because it was barely dinnertime, and the evening rush hour had just begun. The coffee shop next door looked busy, though, and he knew his time to do this thing was limited. If he didn't get in there and deal with Edwards, he'd be facing the slew of people who came to the gym after work.

"Go, Julian," he murmured, squaring his shoulders. "No witnesses. No noise." He glanced at his cheap burner phone. He'd texted Cassandra, requesting a picture of her husband, and she'd obliged with several different shots, no questions asked. She'd also told him she wouldn't be at the gym to meet him, which relieved him considerably. He'd been nervous about her being there, but now he didn't have to worry. She'd told him that she'd managed to draw away two of her husband's remaining bodyguards into the coffee shop with her, but that he'd have to act quickly, because she couldn't keep them there longer than an hour. She'd told him there were only three left, which didn't seem like a lot to Julian for someone in Edwards' position, but then, Zero *had* managed to eliminate a lot of the mobster's most trusted people. Julian stared at the photo, memorizing the outline of the guy's face, then turned the phone off and put it away. "No distractions."

He slid his hands into his pockets and sauntered up to the door. When he entered, he made sure not to touch anything. Just inside the hallway, another open door stood ajar, lights on. He drew gloves from his pocket and pulled them on as he glanced inside. Edwards sat at a cruddy old desk with a stack of bills piled on one side and a money counter on the other. A couple bags of crystal meth sat right in front of him. He had his head bent over a notebook.

Paper books? Talk about old school, Julian thought. *And where is the last bodyguard?* He glanced down the hall. The door to a men's bathroom was shut, but light bled out from around the edges. *If he's in there, I'd better hurry.*

"Luther, what the fuck are you doing out there? How long does it take you to take a fucking piss?" Edwards shouted, startling Julian out of his hesitation. He walked into the office and shut the door behind him with his foot.

"Finally," Edwards muttered, and then he looked up, presenting Julian with an excellent view of his face. He looked just like the photos Cassandra had sent, so there was no worry about Julian getting the wrong guy.

Edwards' expression morphed from irritation to anger. "You're not Luther," he said, lunging for something beneath the desk.

He was too late. Julian had already grabbed him by the neck. "No, I'm not Luther."

"Do you know who I am? I run the biggest organization on the east coast, you little punk." Edwards struggled, face turning red as Julian squeezed. "What do you want? I'll give you money, drugs—" Edwards's words choked off as Julian squeezed tighter, putting what he'd learned in all those years of training to good use. He tensed his muscles, then jerked his arms in opposite directions. Edwards's neck snapped. Julian stared at him as the old bastard's eyes went vacant, and then he let go and stepped back. His hands were slick with sweat inside his thin gloves.

"Fuck," he whispered, gorge rising, but he swallowed it down. It was time to go. He pivoted, then eased open the door. The men's room door was still closed, so Julian hurried down the hall and slipped out through the back. He checked the alley once again, but saw no cameras. Most of the places didn't have surveillance back here. He walked to the street, taking out his burner phone. He removed the sim card and crushed it under his heel, then tossed the phone into a garbage bin. He reached the truck and drove away. A mile down the highway, he peeled off his gloves and pulled into a gas station where he flushed the thin plastic down the toilet. It was only after he drove away that the full implications of what he'd done hit him. He pulled over to the side of the road, and quietly allowed himself to have the nervous breakdown he'd been suppressing for the last hour.

****

Zero sat up and swung his legs over the side of

the bed, pissed off and worried. "What do you mean he went to a meeting?" If he didn't owe Ariana his life, he'd be doing a lot more than asking the question. *Like shaking her until the answers I want come rattling out.*

"Do *not* stand up, Zero. You need antibiotics and rest. Julian will be fine." Ariana pushed him back down as he tried to rise.

"You have no idea what meeting he is going to, Ariana," Zero said, barely keeping his temper in check. His gaze darted around the room and landed on the poster taped to the faded blue wall over the wooden dresser. It was from some action movie that had been released over a decade ago. Zero wondered if the teenage Julian had any idea back then what he'd get himself into as a grown man. Maybe that was why he'd taken up martial arts. Maybe that movie was why he hadn't hesitated to hook up with Zero. He scowled.

"I know enough," she said, checking the IV line. She'd hung the bag on a hanger that she'd hooked over the headboard. "He's a big boy, Zero. He can handle himself."

"Jesus, woman. You have no idea what's going on." Panic rose as he tried to get up again, but Ariana pushed him down more firmly this time.

"The fact that I can keep you down is proof enough that you need to stay in bed, you stubborn idiot. You outweigh me by a hundred pounds, and you can't even push off my hand." She poked him in the chest, and he sucked in a pained breath. "Yeah, and there's that, too. You're nursing a barely healed wound that could easily turn into sepsis, so just stay down."

"Ariana—"

She cut him off. "You realize Julian left two hours ago?" She glanced at the clock on the nightstand. "No, I'm wrong. It's two and a half hours now. You only woke up because the fluid I pumped into you rehydrated your body. You need to rest and take care of yourself, Zero."

Zero stared at her, aghast. *Julian could be dead right now, and she's babbling about my health? And I can't even stand up.*

"You don't even realize you were out cold, do you?" Ariana asked him.

He swallowed, wondering how the hell he was going to break it to her that her son was dead. He gripped the blankets, surprised to find his eyes burning. He cursed his wound and his weakness. Never before in his life had he ever felt so helpless, not even when he was a child. Getting beaten up by bullies was nothing compared to this.

"Mom?"

The sound of Julian's voice pushed Zero back onto the mattress. He struggled to move, but he couldn't get up. "Fuck," he whispered. Relief rushed through him so hard he couldn't think straight. "Fuck."

"In here, Julian," Ariana called. "Zero just woke up."

Julian appeared in the doorway. "Have a good nap?" he asked, smiling.

Zero stared at him. Julian's tone might be light, but he saw the truth in his lover's eyes. Julian's normally bright gaze looked haunted. Julian had done Zero's job for him. "Julian," he croaked, his vision going blurry.

"Hey." Julian gave his mother a quick hug, and then he sat down next to Zero. He barely fit on the narrow mattress. "Shut up. I'm fine."

Zero grabbed his wrists. "What the fuck did you do?" Anger began to trickle back in alongside the relief.

Julian glanced at him mother, then met Zero's gaze, blue eyes shadowed but steady. "I handled the meeting, just like we discussed. It's done." He shrugged. "Cassandra bailed at the last minute, not that I minded."

Zero stared at his lover, fighting to make sense of his words. Before he could reply, Ariana spoke.

"Now that Julian's back, I have to go to work. I have the evening shift for the next week," she said. "I left a list of instructions in the kitchen, honey. You've had some training, so you know what to do with the antibiotics and IV." She patted Julian on the head.

Julian nodded. "Thanks, Mom. I'll take care of him, no problem."

"Take care." She squeezed Julian's shoulder and left the room.

"Julian." Zero squeezed, digging his fingers into his lover's forearms. He barely noticed Ariana leaving the house. "What. Did. You. Do."

Julian pulled away, grimacing. "I had to make sure my mother would be safe." He rubbed his face. "And you, too, of course. You know Edwards isn't the kind of man to let things slide. The mess at your apartment is proof of that."

Zero couldn't think of a damn thing to say. "Fuck." Guilt sat like a damned boulder in the center of his body. It hurt a hell of a lot worse than his stupid gunshot wound.

Julian smiled briefly. "You said that already."

"You never should have gotten into the middle of this," Zero said, angrily. "This wasn't your fight. Jesus Christ, Julian." He struggled to a sitting position. "You had no business going to meet Edwards alone. Hell, I should never have let you come with me when I left the hospital. Your mother should never have sent you to check up on me."

"Yeah, like you could've stopped me from going with you," Julian said, frowning. "And if my mother hadn't sent me, we would never have met." He seemed to deflate. "And that would've sucked."

"Would it?" Zero asked, meaningfully. Julian should never have had to spill blood for him. He'd always handled his own messes.

"Jesus, Zero. How can you say that?" Julian glared at him. "You fucking asshole."

Zero looked away, faintly nauseated. The thought of never making love with Julian… He shook his head. *Julian's right,* he realized, but he couldn't bring himself to say it out loud. "Does Cassandra know what you did?"

Julian stared hard at him for a moment, then finally shrugged again. "No idea, but probably. She was at the coffee shop next door to the gym with the last two bodyguards. She's the reason I was able to get to Edwards so easily."

Zero flinched when his cell phone buzzed. He reached out and picked it up, wincing as the movement put pressure on his wound. Cassandra had just sent him a text. "She knows." He tapped out an acknowledgement. "She's pleased."

Julian took the phone from Zero and turned it off. Zero was going to protest, but one look from Julian shut him up. *He deserves my complete attention, especially after everything he's done for me.*

Julian put the phone back on the nightstand. "Good. You shouldn't have any more problems then, right?"

"What precisely did you do?" Zero had to ask. He needed to know, for his own peace of mind, but he also didn't want Julian to carry the burden alone. *Also, I'll never fucking forget what it felt like when I thought he'd gone to his death.* He suppressed a shudder.

"I snapped his neck."

Zero inhaled, immediately angry all over again.

Julian wasn't a killer. He shouldn't have gone to the gym without Zero. "You should not have gone without me. This was not for you to do. It was my responsibility."

"Really? Is this how you're going to handle the situation?" Julian stood up and started pacing. "Bullshit." He pointed at Zero. "You don't get to decide what I will or won't do, Zero."

"Julian—"

"No." Julian slashed a hand through the air. "You knew the moment I brought you here, my mother was at risk. Cassandra sent us the info and helped set up the hit, and you know damned well the window of opportunity was short. You'd already played this situation out to the point where there was no time left. You saw to that, not me."

Zero stood up, cursing as stars scattered across his vision. He would *not* fucking pass out now. "Even so, it was not your problem." He hated that Julian had solved dealt with Edwards for him. He *hated* that he was responsible for the blood on Julian's hands.

"You made it my problem, Zero." Julian glared at him.

Zero clenched his fists. "What did Edwards say?"

"Not a damned thing. I wasn't interested in conversation."

"Jesus Christ, Julian. That was the whole point," Zero growled. "I wanted Edwards to *know* why I had to end him."

Julian let out a short, sharp laugh. "Why? What does it fucking matter? He's dead, Zero. Dead men tell no tales. Dead men don't feel remorse. They're just..." He broke off and scrubbed a hand over his face.

Zero's breath caught as he finally noticed how close Julian was to breaking. *Shit. He's right. I'm an asshole, a shitty lover, and an even worse boyfriend.*

"They're just fucking dead, Zero. That's it." Julian turned his back. "They don't come back to life like in the movies. No one is watching us. There's no giant fucking point to it all. It's just done."

Zero could see the tension thrumming through his lover. "Julian," he whispered, but his voice failed him. He cleared his throat. "Julian."

The younger man turned, eyes red. "What?"

Zero swallowed the guilt and the anger and the disappointment, because none of those things mattered. What mattered was the man standing in front of him, alive and vibrant and so fucking damaged Zero couldn't bear the knowledge that he'd done this to him. He'd set it up so that Julian had no choice except to crack the part of himself that made him a good man into fractured pieces. He hoped he could put the fragments back together somehow. "Come here." He waited a beat. "Please."

"Why? So you can yell at me? So you can tell me that I'm too young to know what the hell I did?" Julian enunciated the words carefully, like every syllable hurt even as he let them go. For all Zero knew, they did. "No. I know precisely what I did, Zero." He made a noise at the back of his throat. "Precisely."

"No. I'm not going to yell," Zero said quietly. "I want you to come here so I can hold you and tell you I'm sorry." Zero could barely get the words out. "I'm so fucking sorry, Julian."

****

Julian stared at Zero as a thousand and one emotions rocketed through him, none of them good. "Do you understand what you're doing, Zero?" He had to ask. He needed to know that Zero was truly on the same page as he was. "You can't just apologize and expect me to be okay."

Zero nodded, and the expression on his face

nearly broke Julian's heart. "You're not a killer, but you killed a man for me."

Julian nodded slowly. "Yes."

"I'm an asshole for not seeing how much you care," Zero said, voice low.

Julian searched his lover's expression. Zero looked like a man who'd been through hell. "Yes. You are." A tiny frisson of hope trickled through him.

"And you're a grown man who makes his own choices." Zero stood there, still hooked up to an IV, fists clenched against nothing but himself.

Julian waited. There was more, and if Zero didn't understand…

"You love me," Zero finally breathed out, looking like he was about to break down crying.

Relief pushed through Julian's anger and frustration. "Yes, you big idiot." He strode over to Zero and dragged him into a tight hug. "I love you. Isn't it totally fucking obvious?"

"I love you, too," Zero said, voice cracking.

Julian held him tighter. "I fucking hope so." He felt Zero shuddering, and eased him back onto the bed.

"I am so sorry," Zero said again.

Julian leaned back. "I don't want your goddamn apologies. I want you to meet me halfway, Zero. I want you to trust that I can carry half the burden."

"I can try." Zero reached for him, and Julian leaned down and kissed him with all of the pent-up misery he'd felt over the past few hours.

"Fuck," he said when he finally came up for air. His cock was so hard it hurt, but he could tell Zero's strength wasn't there. They wouldn't be making love today, and probably not tomorrow, either. *Especially not in this bedroom, with my mother just down the hall from us,* Julian thought. "You need to get better, okay?"

Zero nodded. "I know."

"You're going to stay here, in my childhood room, which is awful, by the way, until I'm sure you're not going to relapse," Julian told him. "You're going to let my mother give you a clean bill of health this time, before you even think about going back to work." He glanced around, shaking his head at the poster still tacked up over his beaten-up dresser. "And I'm going to break my apartment rental contract, and move all my shit into your motorhome."

Zero opened his mouth, but Julian rested a finger on his lips before his lover could speak. "I'm not done." He took a deep breath. "And then we're going to spend the next few months looking for a new place to live. I'm not going to hole up in an underground bunker, either. Got it?" He removed his finger.

Zero nodded. "Yes."

"After that, you're going to ask me to marry you." Julian's heart pounded. They'd only known each other for a week or so, and he knew he was being pretty freaking ballsy, but then Zero smiled, and he knew he hadn't gone too far.

"Yes." Zero grabbed his hands and squeezed. "And right after that, I'm going to make love to you until you forget your name. And I'm not going to share you. No more escorting for you."

Julian grinned. "Hell, no. I have no reason to bother with that anymore. I made a fortune. I paid off my student loans." He lifted a shoulder. "And I've got a business degree."

"You can do the books for me, darling. I have been meaning to expand operations for a while now, but did not have the manpower to accomplish it," Zero said, eyes going distant. "I can hit the Eastern European markets, and possibly move into China with the art business."

Julian laughed. "You just lapsed into your snooty voice."

Zero smiled. "I've used it for so long that it's difficult to let it go."

"I don't want you to let it go, Zeke Graham. I just want you to remember that you don't need to put on any masks with me." Julian kissed him again, softly this time.

Zero threaded his fingers into Julian's hair. "You know all my secrets, Julian Dirk Amon."

Julian pulled back. "Oh my God, my mother told you my middle name. Shit." He shook his head, pretending to be appalled. "No one knows my middle name. I don't want *anyone* to know my middle name. My mother sucks." The quip eased some more of the tension thrumming through him. Oh, he knew he'd have to confront what he'd done to Edwards eventually, probably more than once, but the anger of Zero's response had really thrown him. He needed Zero to be there for him. *And I need Zero to understand that I'm there to support him, too. That's how a relationship works.*

"You don't want anyone to know because you have a porn name for your middle name," Zero pointed out, smiling broadly.

Julian rolled his eyes. "I don't know what the hell my parents were thinking."

"I don't think I *want* to know what they were thinking," Zero said, still smiling.

"You make a good point. Let's not ask my mother." Julian shoved at him until Zero moved over. "This bed is impossible, but I'm exhausted. Move over."

"We are not going to fit," Zero said, but he shifted obligingly, arranging his IV line so it wouldn't tangle.

"We'll fit. You just have to get used to me

invading your space." Julian settled down next to Zero, and closed his eyes. He could feel his lover pressed along his spine as they spooned, and the last of the tension in his body eased. It was only early evening, but he felt like he'd been awake for twenty-four hours. "We can figure the rest out tomorrow," he mumbled.

Zero nodded into the back of his neck. "Yes."

Julian smiled, and then he let himself drift off. Zero wasn't going anywhere, not with that wound and not with the way he'd trapped him against the wall. *And I'm sure as hell not going anywhere. Not today. Not tomorrow. Not ever.*

Epilogue

Three months later

"There. That is much better," Zero said, eyeing the new Harper painting he'd just hung on the wall over the sofa. "That spot was in dire need of some color." He loved the bright colors and modern aesthetic of the painting. It matched the airy loft space he'd finally agreed to buy with Julian. Their building sat along the Hudson River, with amazing views of the New York City skyline. Zero had been resistant to such an exposed location at first, but Julian pointed out that they had the money and the time to make it secure.

"I like it," Julian said, packing the tools he'd used to hang the painting into the toolbox. He set it aside, and joined Zero near the glass coffee table. "It suits the living room." He glanced at the windows. "And aren't you glad I talked you into living somewhere with a view instead of in an underground bunker?"

"This is the great room, not the living room," Zero told him, just to be contrary. "The living room is over there." He pointed.

Julian rolled his eyes. "You're such a snob. Living room, great room ... what does it matter?"

Zero grinned, knowing that would be Julian's reaction. "The living room is the space off the kitchen, and I'm not a barbarian."

"I thought that was the let's-have-sex-in-front-of-the-fireplace room?" Julian quipped.

Zero sighed. "Philistine." He tucked his hand into Julian's elbow and gently pushed him down onto the deep red sofa. "Sit. Do not move."

Julian raised an eyebrow. "I'm not a dog."

"That is entirely evident, given your lack of

obedience," Zero replied, sliding to his knees onto the shining hardwood floor.

Julian sat up, interest sparking in his blue eyes. "This is interesting, though. I like you right there. You look like a man about to start praying." He opened his legs in invitation. "Or about to give me a truly excellent blowjob. You have skills, and I like to take advantage of them whenever possible."

"I have not prayed since I was fifteen." Zero eyed the growing bulge trapped behind Julian's jeans as his own cock twitched in interest. He'd address that later, but right now, he had something else in mind. He reached into his pocket and extracted the small box he'd been carrying around for a week. He'd been waiting for the perfect time, but it seemed that in their life, no time was ever the right time. He had finally figured out this morning that his fear was what was truly holding him back, not a search for perfection. *Because there's no such thing as perfection. Julian is perfect for me, but that's because he's real, not perfect.*

"Oh, God," Julian whispered, attention riveted on the box. "What are you doing?"

"Be quiet, my dear." Zero opened the box, revealing the platinum band with small diamonds embedded into the metal that he'd bought for his lover. "Three months ago, you told me I would ask you to marry me—"

"Yes," Julian said, interrupting him before he could finish.

Zero smiled. "I was not finished, darling."

"I don't care," Julian said, sliding off the sofa onto his knees, too. "You silly man." He kissed Zero, crushing the box between them. "I was joking three months ago."

"You didn't let me ask," Zero protested, voice

rough. His heart felt like he'd just strapped it to a rocket, and it was about to leave the atmosphere. "I don't care if you were joking. I wanted to ask."

Julian hugged him. "I already know what you're going to say, and the answer is yes."

Zero leaned back. "Put it on, then." He smiled, watching Julian reach out and slip it onto his ring finger. It was an excellent fit, of course. He would have nothing but the best for the love of his life.

"When did you buy this?" Julian asked, tilting it so that the stones caught the late afternoon light. "I had no idea."

"The week after we left your mother's house," Zero said. "You had to go deal with your lease, and I went right to the jewelers."

Julian stared at him. "You bought this?"

"Did you think I had stolen it?" Zero wasn't surprised Julian had jumped to that assumption, given his line of work. He snorted. "No. I bought it. This ring has never belonged to anyone else."

"Oh. Wow." Julian kissed him softly. "It's perfect."

"It is not perfect, but it will do," Zero said.

Julian closed his fingers around the ring. "I'm sensing a metaphorical statement in there."

Zero shook his head. "Nothing in life is perfect, but we go on into the world and do what we must anyway. We travel, do our jobs." He paused. "We fall in love." Those last words came out rough. "We choose our way, despite the imperfection of it all."

"You chose me before I even knew what was happening," Julian said, obviously thinking about their time in the motorhome. "You weren't looking for a partner."

"No, I was not." Zero said, and then he sighed. "I

was not looking to get shot, either, but it happened, and I do not regret it. It brought you to me."

"You're so fucking romantic," Julian said, kissing him again.

Zero growled against his lover's mouth. "I'm not romantic."

"Yes, you are." Julian pulled away and took off his shirt. "Also, you owe me a blowjob."

"I just gave you a ring. I don't owe you anything." Zero undid Julian's pants anyway, smiling when his lover's cock sprang out, already hard. "I put a ring on it, and here you are, complaining about who owes who."

Julian gasped. "Good point." He wrestled Zero up onto the sofa. "As it turns out, I have something for you, too." He smiled, slow and heated, and then he drew out a small, extremely sharp knife from his pocket.

"What are you doing?" Zero asked, almost choking as his arousal surged from hot to incendiary. Julian knew his kink, but they'd never seriously incorporated any knife-play into their lovemaking. Too dangerous. Too insane.

"I'm going to show you that there's nothing you need that I won't give you," Julian said, setting the point of the blade against his pectoral muscle. "Watch closely." He pressed in, and the tip of the blade sank into his skin. Blood welled from the tiny cut like a beautiful gem swelling on his body. He drew it down about a half an inch before Zero got control of himself and stopped Julian's movement.

"No." Zero took the knife away. "I would never ask you for this." His eyes kept straying from Julian's face to the cut on his chest. "Jesus." He wanted to press his fingers into the blood and smear it everywhere.

"I know you'd never ask. That's why I'm giving

it to you." Julian undid Zero's shirt, fingers lingering along his scar for a moment. "I'm not actually hurt, you know. It's just a prick."

"Fuck." Zero clenched his fingers around the blade's hilt. "It's too dangerous."

"It is." Julian pushed Zero's shirt off, then started on his pants. "Give me the knife."

Zero shook his head, and with a short, sharp movement, he threw it across the room. The blade lodged in the wall up to the handle. "Leave it. I don't need toys to make love with you." He shoved Julian's pants down and palmed his erection.

Julian's eyes went dark. "Fuck." His hips jerked forward.

"That's the plan," Zero muttered, reveling in the heat of his lover's body. "Down on your knees. Right here." He pushed off his own pants, then waited while Julian kicked his off. "Lean over the sofa."

"We're going to make a mess on it," Julian said.

"It's leather. It'll wipe off," Zero said. He retrieved the lube he'd stashed in the side table, and uncapped the small bottle. "Hard and fast, or slow and steady?"

Julian twisted his head around. "You have to ask?"

Zero smiled tightly as he measured out a generous portion, then slicked himself thoroughly. "Does the cut hurt?"

"Yeah, but only a little. It's just a tiny sting." Julian gasped as Zero ran his slippery fingers across his anus.

"Good." Zero lined up his cock, then slowly pushed in. He groaned as Julian hissed. "Too fast?"

"Too fucking slow," Julian replied, pushing back.

Zero sank inside, resting his forehead on Julian's

back. It was ridiculous how revved up he was, considering the lack of foreplay and how long they'd been together. Shouldn't he have more control after three months? "I will never get used to this," he said, wrapping his arms around Julian's chest.

Julian nodded. "I hope not." He grabbed Zero's right hand and moved it up a bit. "The cut is right here."

Zero shuddered, cock swelling as he felt the warm wet blood on his fingertips. "Fuck."

"Come on, Zero. Do it." Julian squirmed.

Zero exhaled, counting to five. It didn't help. "God help me, Julian," he muttered, and then he surged forward, shoving Julian into the sofa. He could feel just the slightest hint of sticky blood on his right thumb, and the thought that Julian had done that for *him* made him lose whatever smidgen of control he thought he'd had. He fucked inside Julian, hard and fast.

"God, yeah. That's perfect," Julian gasped, hands scrabbling for purchase on the soft leather.

Zero saw the ring he'd given Julian press into the cushions. "You're mine," he growled, hips stuttering as he reached the edge.

"Yeah. Of course I am," Julian replied. The muscles in his arms stood out in sharp relief. "You think I'd carve into my skin for anyone else?"

Zero groaned, and then it was all over. He shuddered as he orgasmed, and then Julian's body clenched around him, drawing another spasm out. "Julian," he gasped.

"God." Julian moaned, hips jerking as he climaxed. "Fuck." He slumped down, head resting on the sofa.

Zero worked on simply breathing, until he could manage it without gasping. He fingered the sticky blood on Julian's chest, and then he pulled out slowly, wincing as his super-sensitive cock twitched.

Julian sighed, turning around. "What the hell was that?" he asked, but his tone told Zero it wasn't really a question. His blue eyes glimmered.

Julian knew the answer to his question, and Zero knew he knew, but he replied anyway. "That was how much I fucking love you." He pulled Julian into his arms and buried his face in his lover's hair.

"I love you, too," Julian whispered, stroking down Zero's back. "I know we don't talk about it." He drew back and touched the small wound on his chest. "But I would fucking die for you, Zero. This is for you."

Zero covered Julian's hand and the small wound with his palm. "You don't have to cut yourself to prove a damn thing to me, Julian. I already know." He leaned in until their foreheads touched. "I know, darling." He closed his eyes and reveled in the sensation of never having to wonder if anyone would care if he lived or died. He knew Julian would grieve him, and maybe it made him a sick bastard, but that knowledge made him *glad*. He'd never been so fucking content in his life.

"I know you do." Julian smiled softly. "'Til death do us part, Zero. And maybe not even then."

The End

www.erinmleaf.com

THE CRIMINALS

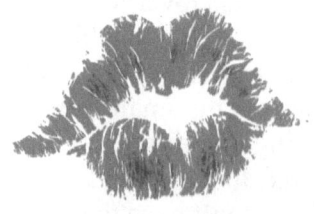

EVERNIGHT PUBLISHING ®

www.evernightpublishing.com